Laura's Way

Laura's Way

Beryl Kingston

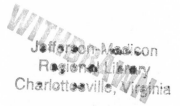

Thorndike Press • Chivers Press
Thorndike, Maine USA Bath, England

This Large Print edition is published by Thorndike Press, USA and by Chivers Press, England.

Published in 1997 in the U.S. by arrangement with Darley Anderson Literary Agency.

Published in 1997 in the U.K. by arrangement with Random House UK Ltd.

U.S.	Hardcover	0-7862-0940-2	(Romance Series Edition)
U.K.	Hardcover	0-7451-5469-7	(Windsor Large Print)
U.K.	Softcover	0-7451-8767-6	(Paragon Large Print)

The text of this Large Print edition is unabridged. Other aspects of the book may vary from the original edition.

Set in 16 pt. Plantin by Juanita Macdonald.

Printed in the United States on permanent paper.

British Library Cataloguing in Publication Data available

Library of Congress Cataloging in Publication Data

Kingston, Beryl.
    Laura's way / Beryl Kingston.
        p.   cm.
    ISBN 0-7862-0940-2 (lg. print : hc)
    1. Large type books. I. Title.
  [PR6061.I494L38 1997]
  823′.914—dc21
                                             96-47455

To campaigners everywhere.

Prologue

July 1946

'Quick! Quick! Come quick!' the little boy gasped. His face was pale with shock, brown eyes bulging. 'Oh please! Please! She's drownded.'

The regulars at the Blue Boar had been sitting out in the sunshine in their triangular village square peacefully enjoying their midday pint and a little light gossip. But when the child came hurtling towards them, they caught his alarm at once. 'Where?' 'Who is?' 'What've you been doing you bad child?' 'What you mean drownded?'

The boy was too far gone in panic to tell them any more. He simply stood before them and wept, his shoulders hunched in distress, his bare feet smeared with river slime, his clothes sagging with water. There wasn't an inch of him that wasn't wet and afraid. Water ran out of his eyes and off the end of his nose, dripped from his hair and his shirt and his short patched trousers, gathered in a black puddle on the gravel of the road. 'Oh please!' he begged. 'We didn't mean for her . . . She went under, mister. We couldn't help it.'

'They been up that dratted culvert, that's what,' the landlady said furiously. 'I knew this

7

would happen. Didn't I say so?' She clattered her tray on to the nearest table and bolted off across the square at once, heading for Water Lane with her clientele running full pelt after her.

Shopkeepers came to their doors still in their aprons to see what the fuss was about. Windows creaked open all round the square. Anxious faces appeared everywhere. The gentle air was raucous with shouts. 'What's going on?' 'What's up?'

'Kiddie drowned,' the runners called.

Within seconds the square was full of hurtling bodies, some on the way to Water Lane, some calling up their neighbours, all in a high state of excitement, there being nothing more thrilling than the prospect of a rescue or a death to enliven a dull day. 'Who is it? Does anyone know?'

The landlady had already reached the river, where half a dozen streaming children stood huddled together on the near bank. There were two big boys standing in mid-stream, buffeted by the current but keeping their balance as well as they could as they poked into the mouth of the culvert with a fallen branch. It had been raining heavily for most of the past week and the river was in full flood, its earth-browned waters rolling and frothing as it poured at speed into the narrow mouth of the tunnel. But there was no sign of a child, alive or dead.

'That's young Pete,' the baker said as the taller of the two looked up. 'Come out a' there you young fools!'

'She was pulled down the tunnel, mister,' the

boy said, his face distraught. 'We couldn't stop her.'

'Who is it?' the landlady called.

'Lorry-Lou.'

'That's Mrs Sheldon's kid,' the landlady said. 'Poor woman. One of you run up to the chemist's and get her. She'll be in the dispensary. Don't say nothing about drowning. Say there's been an accident.'

'She'll be drowned as sure as fate if she's gone down into that lot,' the baker said lugubriously. 'It's a hundred yards at least all the way under the square. She'll never last a hundred yards without air. She's only a slip of a kid.'

But he was wrong. Twenty yards into the tunnel, Laura-Lou Sheldon was very much alive.

Things had happened so quickly there hadn't been time for her to think or even react. One minute she'd been on her feet playing in the rough water — she remembered that — and the next she was being tumbled along in the darkness, struggling to get her mouth above water long enough to breathe, remembering to keep it shut when the flood dashed over her head. Now she'd reached a bend in the culvert and she was stuck, with her feet wedged against the slimy brick of the tunnel wall and her head pushed forward by something hard and heavy.

The river rushed and roared all round her, hurling sticks and stones at her and pummelling her chest so that she could hardly breathe. She was so frightened that nothing existed except ter-

9

ror and the overpowering need to get free. Water filled her mouth until it streamed out of her nose. She'd had to spit to get rid of it — spit, spit, spit, on and on and on — and all the time she was pushing against the onrush, squirming and heaving to turn her body away from that awful slimy, scratchy wall. She might be skinny and undersized for a nine-year-old but she was fighting with all her might. She knew she would drown if she didn't get free and the knowledge spurred her on to superhuman efforts. If she could just catch her breath . . . free one leg . . . turn on her side. Oh please, please, she prayed, let me get out.

There was a sudden surge of water, very weighty and very fast. She was lifted towards the curve of the roof, brick grazing her cheek, and then, in a moment of exquisite relief, she was on the move again, swooshed along in the torrent, kicking her feet and doing her best to swim. She had a momentary glimpse of a round white light blazing a long way ahead of her and then the water pushed her under and it was lost. She broke to the surface spluttering and struggling and saw her pale green arm thrown up in the air as if it didn't belong to her and one of her sandals hurtling ahead of her like a brown ship tossed on the water. Then she was out of the darkness and into the sunshine and it was over.

After the noise in the tunnel everything was very quiet. She could hear a bird singing and people talking somewhere in the distance. But the words made no sense to her. 'Dead!' 'Poor little

10

thing. What a way to go!' She was confused and disoriented and wondered vaguely if somebody had been bombed or shot. She knew they couldn't have been because the war was over and nobody was bombed now. It had been over for a whole year and they were going to let Daddy out of the navy any day, Mum said. At the thought of her mother, it was as if her body was crumbling. She was suddenly cold and she began to shake. 'Mum!' she cried. 'Where are you?' But her voice was a croak.

As she was tumbled onwards, her fingers touched pebbles on the river-bed and she knew that if she could get her balance she could climb out to the bank. She fell forward on to her hands and knees and tried to crawl. But she was so tired she could barely move and her limbs were unwieldy and heavy as if they'd been turned into lead. Mum! Mum! she thought. Oh help me, somebody!

Two men leapt into the water. She could see their legs wading towards her and the wash making a white arch against their trousers. Then they had her by the arms and were lifting her up and carrying her towards the bank. There were crowds of people there, all looking anxious, and one of them was her mother, pushing through the crowd and running towards her, arms outstretched.

'Laura-Lou! Laura-Lou!' she called. 'Oh my darling, what *have* you been doing?' And then, in a rush of warm air, she had her daughter in her arms and was hugging her fiercely, kissing her wet hair and crooning, 'Oh Laura-Laura-Lou, I thought you'd drowned.'

Laura-Lou stood very still with the water running from her clothes, her hands limp and white at her sides. She couldn't speak and she couldn't respond. She knew she was glad to be in her mother's arms because it showed she was safe but her mind was still locked in the terror of that frantic struggle underground.

'Let me look at you,' her mother said, leaning back to examine her. There was a bruise on the child's forehead and grazes bleeding on her cheek and her shins and elbows, but apart from that . . .

The concern on her mother's face moved Laura-Lou to action. She made an enormous effort and put her heavy arms round her mother's neck to comfort her. 'Don't cry Mum,' she croaked. 'I'm all right.'

And at that they both cried, Laura-Lou in great gulping sobs that shook her body, her mother in tears of relief and belated terror at the thought of what might have been.

'I didn't mean to,' Laura-Lou sobbed. 'Oh Mum! It was awful down there. I didn't mean to.'

Mrs Sheldon kissed her wet forehead and rubbed her back, feeling the vertebrae cold and knobbly under her fingers like a string of pebbles. There was nothing to be gained by scolding her now. They would have a good long talk about it when they were both calmer. 'It's all right,' she said, speaking as lightly as she could so as to get them both back to normal. 'You're with me now. It's all over. You weren't meant to drown, I'll say that for you. You must have been saved for a purpose. Come on, I'd better get you home and into some dry clothes. We'll catch the quarter-past bus.'

'I'll never go near the water again, ever, as long as I live,' Laura-Lou promised as she walked away with her mother's arm round her shoulders.

'I'm very glad to hear it,' her mother said, smiling at last. 'You do give me some frights.'

'All's well that ends well,' the landlady said, watching them go.

The baker didn't agree. 'She's a jolly sight too self-willed for my liking,' he complained. 'High time her father came home and took her in hand. Playing in the river at her age! I ask you! She'll come to a bad end. You mark my words.'

At the edge of the crowd, seven-year-old Amy, neat in her green gingham, her spotless white ankle-socks and her nice new Startrite sandals, slipped her hand into her mother's arm and smiled her well-behaved smile.

She and her mother had been shopping when the drama began and she'd watched it from start to finish. She'd enjoyed it very much, admiring the big boys as they stood up to the battering of the flood and imagining what it would be like if *she*'d been the one to fall into the water and they were rescuing *her*.

When the crowd ran to the other end of the

culvert, she'd run with them, holding her mother's hand as they dodged between the lime trees in the square and wondering whether they really were going to see a dead body emerge and what *that* would be like.

Now she watched as the dead body walked away. And she listened to what the baker was saying.

'*I'*m a good girl, aren't I Mummy,' she lisped. 'I don't play in the river. I shan't come to a bad end, shall I?'

Chapter One

September 1990

The storm had been gathering all afternoon, to Laura Pendleton's considerable satisfaction. At half past five, as she drove home from work, it was ominously oppressive, even out in the Sussex countryside, where stubble stood sharp as knives on the waiting earth and the cattle browsing in the water meadows moved reluctantly as though their feet were too heavy for them. The river Rife was grey and sluggish, reeds drooped, trees brooded, hawthorn hedges were dusty for lack of air, and glooming in the distance, the long whale-backs of the Downs grew darker by the minute, shadowed slate grey by gathering clouds, which swelled into the sky, indigo blue and plum purple like some huge cosmic black eye.

By the time she reached the farm track they called Laura's Way and was bouncing her ancient Land-Rover towards her threatened cottage, it was unnaturally dark for a September afternoon and Laura was sticky with sweat. But the oppressive atmosphere felt right to her, despite her discomfort. It so exactly matched her own pent-up, furious mood.

She'd been angry ever since that awful letter

arrived and now she felt as though she was just about ready to explode. How dare they write to her like that! *'It has been decided that Route C is the preferred route for the new by-pass . . . we must warn you that consequently your property is now liable to compulsory purchase.'* The arrogance of it. The sheer unmitigated bloody arrogance. You're in the way, Laura Pendleton. We're going to build a road and that's far more important than you are. So we're going to knock you down and trample all over you. You don't mind do you?

Well yes, as it happens, she thought angrily, arguing in her mind as she often did when she was alone, I do. I mind very much. This is my home you're talking about. The place I've lived in for the last thirty-eight years. It's precious to me *and* beautiful *and* it wasn't built to be knocked down. It was built to last for centuries. The way it's done already. I'm damned if I'm going to let you take it away from me.

She, the car and the cottage were a good match for one another, scruffy but usually good-tempered, untidy but generally comfortable, brindled in colour, often looking as though they could do with a good brush. All three contained a lifetime of odds and ends, they all worked well, even in impossible weather and they were all what Laura called 'a good age'.

Laura had never made a secret of her age. What was the point when she lived in the hamlet where she'd grown up and everybody knew how old she was anyway? At fifty-three she was short and com-

16

fortably rounded — inclining to middle-aged spread if the truth be told — unfashionable and, except for one or two pieces of discreet and beautiful jewellery that had once belonged to her mother, unobtrusive in style. She liked tweedy skirts and warm cardigans, rarely used make-up and had long since allowed her hair to go its own way. Now and then, when she'd finished her day's work at the library, she would stay in Burswood for a trim but, apart from that, she paid little attention to her appearance, telling herself that librarians and grandmothers don't need to be fashion models. So long as she was warm and comfortable that was all that mattered.

And yet there was a style about her. Determination in the way she walked and took up a stand, a touch of hauteur in her straight nose and the way she held up her head when she was annoyed, honesty in that greying hair and the wrinkles she didn't bother to conceal. She looked what she was, dependable, warm hearted, stubborn, independent. A good neighbour. A comforter. The sort of woman who would never willingly harm anyone but would go out of her way to help if she could. The first person her neighbours ran to when they were in trouble — the way they were running to her at that moment, as she turned into the rough drive alongside her kitchen door.

They were led by old Mr Fennimore from the end cottage, his farm boots much in evidence, fleshy nose mottled blue and purple, small eyes dark with rage.

'Bloody council,' he growled. 'Killing's too good for 'em. They want stringin' up and shootin', the whole damn kit and caboodle. Wouldn't be so quick sendin' out bloody letters then.'

For once his misanthropic nature wasn't just acceptable to Laura but enjoyable. She grinned at him as she got out of the car. 'Them's my sentiments tonight, Josh,' she said, half grim, half joking.

The rest of their neighbours followed him into the garden, all talking at once. 'It's a scandal, that's what it is!' 'They can't take our homes away from us.' 'An Englishman's home is his castle!' 'We've got to stop them!'

'They can't really do this can they, Laura?' Molly Fennimore said. Where her husband was grey and grizzled, she was round-faced, tanned and solidly built. Now, flushed with anger and warm from her dash to the cottage, she looked twice his size.

'As the law stands, I'm afraid they can,' Laura said as she gathered up her shopping. 'But it's against all natural justice. We ought to fight them.'

'It's such a pretty place,' Molly said. 'They can't knock it all down. I mean, just look at your cottage for a start.'

It *is* a pretty place, Laura thought, and at its best in autumn, settled on its haunches, snug among the yellowing limes and coppery beeches at the end of the lane, its colours enriched by the

18

stormy lilac of the sky. Eccentric but decidedly easy on the eye. A place worth fighting for.

It was called Holm End, after the two holm oaks that loomed protectively beside it, and was a two-storeyed brick and flint Sussex cottage built in a slight hollow at an angle to the lane to protect it from wind and weather. The years had mellowed its flint stone walls to a brindled tortoise-shell, the brick coins and chimney stacks were pale terracotta and the roof-tiles that she'd pinched and scraped to provide all those years ago were weathered by orange lichen now and looked as old as the rest of the house. True, the windows were a higgledy-piggledy collection, no two the same and some slightly out of alignment, and the disused front door was so completely overgrown by honeysuckle and brambles that most of her neighbours had forgotten it was there, but the overall effect of the place was warm and welcoming. The kitchen door was the natural entrance to the house, being in the side facing the lane. It looked particularly good that after-noon because she'd only recently given it a nice thick coat of green paint to match the rain barrel. The paintwork of Holm End was always green so as to blend with the changing colours of the lane and to act as a foil to the flowers she planted in her wide front garden. They were dahlias and african marigolds at the moment in a blaze of strong colour, pink and purple, gold, scarlet and orange. Oh yes, she thought, a very, very pretty place.

By now, two of her cats had appeared on the kitchen doorstep, avid for their evening meal, big black Ace of the yellow eyes and green-eyed tabby Jack. Queenie the tortoiseshell would be skulking indoors with a storm brewing.

'Come in,' she said to her neighbours. 'I'll just feed the cats and get some coffee on and then we'll see what's to be done.'

As they trooped into the cottage, the storm broke at last with a noise like an explosion. The first clap of thunder was immediately overhead and raindrops began to fall at once, patterning the doorstep with patches the size of pennies. But her neighbours were too angry to pay any attention to the weather. The sight of them made Laura think of an advancing army and she remembered the words of the old hymn — *marching as to war*. It must be a war, she thought. There's nothing else we can possibly do but fight. And we must plan our campaign. She was full of energy now, ready for anything.

Like all citizen armies, they were a motley crowd and very fierce. The Jones boys and their wives were in clean jeans and checked shirts, and so unlike their usual, amiable, farm-labouring selves that Laura had to look twice at them to be sure who they were; John Cooper, the dairyman, was sporting a new jersey and an anxious expression and walked in holding his wife's hand; Fiona Coghlan's three small children were in identical anoraks and on their best behaviour. Only Joan Garston was missing.

20

It was so dark inside the cottage that Laura had to switch on the lights. But her neighbours knew the place so well that they could have found their way in without lights of any kind.

The ground floor of the cottage consisted of one large C-shaped living room built around the inner privacy of the hall and stairs and because it was so spacious and Laura was such an hospitable hostess, it had always been the gathering point for the inhabitants of Laura's Way. It had originally been two rooms, a kitchen and several walk-in cupboards but Laura and her husband had taken down the inner walls when they first moved into the place and had gradually converted it into a single living space with a kitchen at one end and windows to east and west. Now it was long, well-lit and cluttered, full of unexpected nooks and crannies and dominated at the kitchen end by a huge brick fireplace where a log fire was already set and ready to be lit.

She fed the cats, put a match to the fire and filled the percolator while her guests sorted themselves out. It took considerable jostling and joking before everyone found a seat of some kind, either properly on a chair at the dining table, or curled up in one of the window seats, or squashed together on one of the two sofas that were set at right angles to the fire, or crouched among a pile of cushions nursing the cats. But at last they were all settled, the coffee was bubbling and they looked at Laura, ready for business to begin.

But before she could say anything, there was a

disturbance at the kitchen door, a rush of air, two voices raised in argument and Joan Garston and her husband trailed their bad temper into the house.

Laura had expected Joan to join them sooner or later but Ken Garston was a surprise and an unwelcome one. Why couldn't he have stayed at home? she thought. He's always so surly these days and I'm sure he won't have anything sensible to say. But there he was, bulkier than ever in the doorway, sixteen stone if he was an ounce, clutching a Game Boy in his fat hand and staring at its screen, his face empty and concentrated.

'I told him not to come over,' Joan confided in a whisper. 'We got enough on our plates without the noise of that stupid toy all the time. But no . . .' She stood dolefully beside her husband in her rain-spattered work clothes, sleeveless waistcoat over a grubby-looking pink jersey, patched jeans, mud-stained wellington boots. Her long sallow face was drawn and pessimistic.

'I've got as much right to be here as anyone else,' Ken said, without looking up from his toy. 'I might be one of the unwanted four million but it's still my house.' Be-dee, be-dee. 'In case you hadn't noticed.' Diddle-iddle-iddle-iddle-iddle.

'Let me have your coats,' Laura intervened. If there's going to be any temper tonight, she thought, you can direct it against the road, where it'll do some good. I don't want any in-fighting. 'Don't worry, Joan. We shan't hear that thing for the thunder. There's coffee ready on the stove, if you'd like to start pouring. You got here just in time. Look at the rain.'

By now the downpour had set in and a gale was roaring across the fields, bending everything before it, so that trees swished and creaked under its impact. As Laura hung their coats on the hooks beside the kitchen door, the lane was already so dark and wet that she could only just make out the movement of the trees that overhung the duck pond. The drama and speed of the transformation excited her. The weather's on our side, she thought. We can hardly fail on a night like this.

Molly Fennimore couldn't wait to get started. 'So,' she said, as Ken Garston squeezed his bulk into a corner, 'I take it we're all going to fight this damned thing,' waving her copy of the letter. 'We're not going to let them get away with it.'

Their growl of agreement was louder than the thunder. But before Laura could lead them into war, Joan Garston voiced a doubt.

'If there's any way we *can* fight them,' she said. 'We're up against the Department of Transport, don't forget, and the heavy goods lobby and the AA and God knows what else. They'll have the power and the money and the government on their side. And what have we got? We're just a handful of people.'

'There's fifteen of us,' Molly Fennimore pointed out, looking round at her neighbours with some pride.

'Exactly,' Joan said grimly. 'So you see what I mean. It'll be a one-sided fight. Real David and Goliath stuff.'

23

'David won, don't forget,' Laura said firmly, 'and so will we if we set our minds to it.'

'Quite right,' the dairyman agreed from his perch in a window seat. He turned to his wife. 'Didn't I say she'd know what to do?' And back to Laura. 'You got some ideas, in't yer, gel?'

'One or two. Yes.'

'Right then,' he said. 'You tell us what to do, an' we'll do it. First house I've ever owned in me life, this is. When that new feller said it was up for sale I couldn't believe me luck. First house I've ever had that wasn't tied. An' I don't propose to give it up without a struggle. I'll tell you that fer nothin'. You just tell us what to do.'

'I've been on to the Friends of the Earth this afternoon,' Laura reported, looking round at them all, and speaking loudly because the wind was making such a noise. 'They faxed me a list of suggestions. There's a local group in Brighton apparently and an organisation called SCAR — South Coast against the Road. They said they would help us. And a whole list of people we ought to write to. It's my day off tomorrow so I'll key it into my word processor and print off copies for everyone who wants one.'

'That's the style,' Molly approved as rain hit the windows like shot. 'I'll deliver 'em.'

'Who are we supposed to be writing to then?' Annie Jones asked. 'I'm not much of a one for letters but I'll do me best.'

Connie Cooper was reading the list. 'Local MP. Local papers. Well that's easy enough. What

24

about J.G. Turner? You know, the one who keeps writing all those funny letters to the *Gazette*. I like him. I always read his letters, he makes me laugh.'

'He's got ever such a good one in this week,' Molly told her, searching for Laura's copy of the paper. 'About the hospitals being shut down. Here it is.' And she read it aloud.

'Two more teaching hospitals to go. We're told it is in the interests of efficiency, as if we ought to be glad that beds are lying empty and wards are being shut and entire hospitals are closing down. I wonder how long it will be before this Minister discovers that the government could make the biggest profit of all if it were to sell off the NHS to the private sector lock stock and barrel. They've sold off the family silver so they might as well sell the jewel in the crown.'

'That's very good,' Connie said. 'I tell you what Laura, we ought to write to *him*. Get *him* on our side. He'd be marvellous.'

'We can't do that,' Laura said, rather shocked by the idea. 'He's a private citizen. We can't go asking private citizens to act for us.'

'But *we* could write to the paper couldn't we,' Molly said.

'And the telly,' her husband decided.

Plans began to be made as the thunder cracked overhead, the rain drummed against the windows and the Game Boy trilled and gibbered.

'We'll keep records of all the things we're doing and all the people who are doing them,' Laura said. 'I'll pin it on my board.' A very useful article that cork board. 'We'll have more impact if we pool our efforts. I'll tell you something else too. We ought to make a list of all the wild life that'll be affected. They've always made a great scene about *"environmental protection"*. I think we should produce a booklet listing all the habitats they'll destroy if they're allowed to go ahead. Birds, animals, plants. All of it. This is a beautiful part of the country. Let them see how beautiful it is.'

'My badgers,' Mr Cooper said.

'Foxes, herons, warblers, visiting birds, every single thing.'

'With pictures?' Alan Jones asked. He was an enthusiastic photographer. 'I could do that. I got a spotted woodpecker only last week. A real beauty.'

'We did a project on local bird life at school,' Ryan Coghlan offered. He was a sturdy eight-year-old and full of energy. 'I bet we could use that. Miss Smith wouldn't mind.'

'You could watch the bird table too,' his mother suggested. 'Like you done last year. Hannah'll help you, won't you Hannah.'

Hannah was five and rather shy but she nodded seriously.

They were relaxing, warming to the task. It was beginning to feel possible. Animals were remembered, birds listed, wild flowers suggested, the storm and the Game Boy ignored.

'You see,' Laura said happily when they'd been pooling ideas for nearly half an hour. 'We've got

26

a lot of expertise between us. All we've got to do is gather it together and present it as professionally as we can. Good presentation is half the battle.'

But at that point, Ken put down his Game Boy and looked at her with a most unpleasant expression on his face. 'Good presentation!' he snarled. 'Badgers! I ask you. Who cares about badgers? Bloody ridiculous. If they want to build this road they'll build it. That's the reality of life in the nineteen nineties. There were three hundred people worked at Abcocks. Three hundred. And they closed it down in three weeks. Lock, stock and barrel. Couldn't do a thing to stop them. We had the unions in. Perfectly bloody useless. We had the local papers, the people from the telly. You name it, we had it. And what happened? I'll tell you what happened. They closed the firm and threw us all on the scrapheap. And that's what they'll do this time.'

'That was different,' Molly Fennimore said, bristling with annoyance. 'That was business. There was an amalgamation, wasn't there? Well then. This is our homes.'

'Don't you believe it,' Ken said sourly. 'This is business too. Someone's making a packet out of all this road building. An' when someone's making money, ordinary people don't have a leg to stand on. They do you down as soon as look at you. You can make lists and take pretty pictures till the cows come home. It won't make a scrap of difference. If they want to build it, they'll build it.'

Looking round, Laura could see that his scathing tone was undermining their new confidence. No, she thought, as expressions changed around her, I can't have this. Especially when he's been sitting there all evening playing with that damned silly game. 'That's defeatist,' she said, speaking in the stern voice she reserved for borrowers who refused to pay their fines. 'You surely don't expect us to sit back and let them walk all over us.'

He wasn't deterred. 'If you ask me,' he said returning to his Game Boy, 'we should give in to 'em straight off.' Be-dee, be-dee. 'Save ourselves a lot of bother. It's only houses, when all's said and done.' Clunk. 'Take whatever they offer, clear out and buy another one somewhere else.' Diddle-iddle-iddle. 'They'll do us down in the end, you see if I'm not right. Bound to. They always do.'

'Well I don't think you're right,' Laura said passionately. 'And while we're about it, it wouldn't hurt you to put that thing down and listen to us properly. Thank you. That's better. They're talking about pulling down our homes. It isn't just houses we're talking about. It's our lives. Our community. Everything we've built up over the years. We can't just stand by and let them destroy all that. Well I can't, anyway. I can't and I won't. If we really needed this road, if we wanted it, if we were even going to use it, it would be a different matter, but we don't, do we?' She paused briefly to give some of the others the chance to agree, which they did vociferously.

28

'Well there you are then. We've got to stop them. That's all there is to it. We've got to fight. I won't let them ruin our countryside — it's too beautiful — and I won't let them knock down my house. I'm damned if I will. I was born in this cottage, I was christened Laura after Laura's Way and you can't get any closer to a place than that, it belonged to my father before me, I lived here all through the war while he was in the navy, my son was born here, I've lived here thirty-eight years since I was married. That's a lot of living. I shall fight them with everything I've got.'

It surprised her when the rest of her guests burst into spontaneous applause. She'd spoken out of passion, not for approval. But the clapping hands were a good sign. He hadn't demoralised them. 'So we'll fight?' she asked.

'You can do as you please,' Ken Garston said, hauling himself to his feet. 'If you want to make fools of yourselves that's up to you. It'll all be a waste of time. I've told you what I'm going to do. Now I'm going home where I can use my computer in peace. Thanks for the coffee. You coming Joan?'

Joan Garston was looking embarrassed. 'In a minute,' she said. 'You go on.' She watched as the others made way for the lumbering bulk of her husband and grimaced as he took his raincoat and blundered out of the door. 'I'm so sorry,' she said to Laura. 'I knew he shouldn't have come. He's got so negative since he lost his job. I shall have to go after him.'

'Don't worry,' Laura said, putting an arm round her shoulders to reassure her. 'We've done all we can for one night. We've made a good start. And *we*'re all positive, aren't we? We're going on with this.'

'Not half!' the dairyman grinned. 'I shall get a shot of my badgers tonight as ever is. You see if I don't.'

The business of the evening had come to an end. They began to tidy up before leaving, the way they usually did, putting coffee cups in the sink or on the draining board, tucking the chairs neatly under the table, talking happily. The worst of the storm seemed to be over too. Rain was still pattering against the windows but the thunder was a mere rumble in the distance.

'I think we'll cut off now,' Molly said to her husband. 'While there's a lull.' She paused at the door to fish in her raincoat pocket for her torch. 'Mind how you go all of you. It's still as black as pitch out there. I can't see a thing.' Then she opened the door and jumped backwards, shrieking, 'Oh my good God! Ken Garston you did give me a turn! What's the matter with you man?'

The fat man was standing in the doorway, his torch held against his chest and shining upwards so that his underlit face was a hideous grotesque. 'That had yer!' he chortled and laughed in that odd barking way of his, hey-hey-hey. And the thunder crackled behind him like an echo.

'Get away you great fool,' Molly scolded, annoyed to have been frightened and especially by him. 'You're enough to give anyone a heart attack. Thought you was going home.'

'So I was,' he said, switching off the torch and resuming his usual appearance. 'I came back out of the kindness of my heart.'

'What heart?' she mocked. 'That'll be the day, when you've got a heart.'

'Kindness of my heart,' he insisted and called past her to Laura. 'There's some woman knocking at your front door.'

The news made Laura aware of how tired she was. It had been a long day and now she wanted to spend the rest of it with her cats, cook herself a meal and gradually wind down, not attend to an unwanted visitor and especially at this time of night and in the middle of a storm. 'What woman?' she asked and there was annoyance in her voice.

'I don't know,' Ken said cheerfully. 'Never seen her in me life.'

Chapter Two

The arrival of a stranger in Laura's Way was such an unusual event that it stopped them all in their tracks.

'I'd better go and see who it is,' Laura said, looking round for her wellies.

'Borrow my brolly,' Molly Fennimore offered, 'or you'll get soaked. It's still chucking it down.'

'If this is one of his silly tricks,' Laura said, as she ventured out into the rain, 'I shall give him a piece of my mind.'

But there was a woman. Laura could see her quite plainly in the beam from Ken's torch, standing before the front door just as he'd said, her feet encased in long, fashionable boots and with a long, pale-coloured raincoat flicking before her in the wind. There was a travelling bag on the step beside her and her head and shoulders were shielded by a patterned umbrella that she was holding steady with one hand as she leaned back into the wind, looking up at the bedroom windows.

Despite her annoyance, Laura felt a pang of pity for her. A stranger, she thought, or she wouldn't have come to the front door and she'd have known the bell doesn't work. I wonder how long she's been there, poor thing. Perhaps she's lost. It's just the sort of night to go astray.

'Hello!' she called into the rush of the rain. 'Hello! Come round the side. I'm over here.'

'I'll be off then,' Ken said. And crunched off along the path, leaving them in darkness.

The stranger picked her way round the side of the house and arrived at the kitchen door. Now that they were close together and standing in the light from the kitchen window, Laura could see her more clearly. She was extremely stylish, carefully made up, with an expensive silk scarf draped about her neck and an expensive hair style, short, skilfully cut and streaked with gold. When she put up her hand to steady her umbrella, there was a flash of diamonds on her fingers.

'Hi there, Laura,' she said. 'Don't you open your front door these days?'

'No,' Laura said, wondering who she was and how she knew her name. She had an odd accent. That 'Hi there!' sounded foreign — American possibly — but the question was decidedly English. 'I'm sorry. Have you been waiting long? I haven't used that door for ages.'

The fashionable face smiled at her. 'I wish I had a pound for every time *I've* used it,' she said. 'I used to be in and out all the time in the old days.'

Then and suddenly Laura knew who she was. 'My God!' she said. 'Amy! I didn't recognise you.'

Amy laughed at her confusion. 'So I see. Don't I get invited in?'

Laura remembered her manners. 'I'm sorry.

33

Yes. Yes. Of course. Come in.' But she was thinking. Amy Pendleton of all people! Fancy her coming back after all these years. And tonight of all nights. 'How did you get here?' she asked. There was no car in the drive.

'Taxi,' Amy said. 'And it cost the earth.'

The neighbours were still hanging about inside the cottage, intrigued to see who the stranger was.

'Look who's turned up,' Laura said to them. 'It's my sister-in-law, Amy, all the way from Australia. She used to live round here. Married my husband's brother, Joe.'

But their faces were blank. Except for the Fennimores, none of them knew her. Laura hadn't got the energy for explanations so she turned to the one woman there who'd been around when Amy left. 'You remember her, don't you Molly?'

Amy put her bag under the table, took off her raincoat and hung it beside the door, as if she were quite at home. Then she turned to greet her old neighbour.

'Molly Fennimore,' she said, beaming at her. 'Jeez, it's great to see you! You haven't changed a bit. I'd have known you anywhere. Are you still breeding those gorgeous dogs of yours?'

Now Laura could see that her first impression had been right. Her sister-in-law was obviously a wealthy woman. She wore a long cream jacket that certainly hadn't been bought in a chain store, matching trousers and a white silk blouse left unbuttoned at the neck to display an expanse of well-tanned skin hung about with three heavy gold chains, one complete with a medallion made from a gold sovereign. And there were four rings on those brown hands, diamonds and rubies no less, all shrieking money. She's come a long way since she left for Australia, Laura thought. It was a C&A coat then and long brown hair hanging down her back and her blue eyes lined with kohl, like Cleopatra. The things you remember!

'You look very prosperous,' Molly said — and her voice sounded cold which Laura found rather surprising. 'You did all right out in Australia then?'

Amy ran her hands through her hair, flashing her diamonds and her smile. 'It's a good place if you're prepared to work,' she said. Then she caught sight of Josh.

'Why Josh Fennimore, you old rogue,' she teased him. 'Fancy seeing you again! And handsome as ever I see. You don't look a day older than you did when I left. Come and give me a kiss.'

To everyone's surprise, he shuffled forward to kiss her cheek, looking flattered and sheepish, the tip of his long nose grown pink as a rose.

'We'd better be on our way,' Molly said and she began to shepherd her neighbours towards the door. 'Come along Josh. Shift your shanks. Laura don't want us clobbering up her kitchen all night. We've said what we came to say.'

They were all on the move, saying goodbye and leaving quickly. Within seconds Laura and Amy were on their own together with the dirty cups.

And Laura realised that she didn't know what to say to this returning stranger, sister-in-law or not.

They'd never been close, even when they were young, newly married and living in the same village, and although they'd written a Christmas letter to one another every year, their contact had been a matter of duty rather than intelligence. Amy had always been a creature apart, selfish and superior. It had been no surprise to Laura that she and Joe had shot off to Australia like that, hurtful though it was. They'd always been too self-centred to notice how other people felt. It wouldn't have occurred to them that their timing was appalling. And now she's come back at the wrong time too, she thought.

But she made an effort to be hospitable. 'Well this is a surprise,' she said, beginning the washing up. 'When did you arrive?'

'This afternoon. I came straight here.'

She's come to stay the night, Laura thought, as she set a mug to drain. Why didn't she let me know?

'God I'm tired,' Amy said, flinging herself into the nearest sofa. 'You'd never believe the journey I've had.' She retrieved a silver cigarette case from her handbag, and offered it to Laura. 'No? You're a wise woman. I wish I didn't.' She produced a matching lighter, lit up and inhaled with pleasure, her eyes half closed. 'I'll take my things upstairs presently,' she said. 'Where are you going to put me?'

'In Jessica's room I expect. It depends how long

you're going to stay.'

Amy's expression changed. 'Didn't you get my letter?'

'I got the one about Joe and the funeral,' Laura said, still busy at the sink. 'Was there another one?'

'I wrote to you when I got to Hong Kong. Four days ago, it must have been. It's all been a bit of a rush.'

'No. I haven't had a letter from Hong Kong.'

'Then you don't know about this job.'

'What job?'

'Same company,' Amy explained casually. 'They had an opening in Worthing and I was ready to move up so I went for it. I start next Monday. Actually I'd accepted it before Joe had his heart attack. I had to delay it a bit because of the funeral and everything. But that's all done with now and here I am. The wanderer returned.'

Laura turned from the sink to look at her. 'And you want to stay here with me?'

'Just while I'm house-hunting. It shouldn't be for long. You don't mind do you? I've brought a few things. Nothing much. Just a few odds and ends really, to tide me over. Everything else is following on. I sold most of it after the funeral, when I put the house on the market. Furniture, paintings, things like that. I thought I'd make a new start.'

There was sense in the sentiment and Laura had to admit it. Sense and strength. 'I thought it would take you ages to get over Joe dying like that,' she said, returning to the cups. 'When Pete went, it took me years and years to come to terms with it.'

'Ah, but you didn't know where he'd gone, did you,' Amy said shrewdly. 'You never had a body to identify. You came to it by degrees. I remember how you used to write about him, wondering where he was and what had happened to him. It's different when they die in front of you.'

Laura shuddered, her sympathy suddenly and powerfully roused. 'It must have been dreadful,' she said, emptying the washing-up bowl. 'I'm so sorry, Amy.'

Amy looked at her for several seconds as though she wasn't sure what to say. When she spoke again it was with perfect control. 'It was a wrench,' she said. 'Well naturally. You'd expect that. Any death is a wrench. And a heart attack's pretty traumatic. But nothing I couldn't cope with. We'd been going our own way for years. I told you that ages ago, didn't I. We used to meet up at weekends. Sometimes not even then. So it wasn't like losing a lover. Or a husband either. He hadn't been any sort of husband for years and years. Actually I'd taken this job before he had the heart attack. I told you that didn't I? I'd have come here anyway.'

'You were leaving him,' Laura understood, drying her hands.

'We were having a trial separation.'

How matter-of-fact she is about it, Laura thought. And she had to admire that too. 'It sounds as though it was all very civilised,' she said.

Amy was looking at her watch and her expression reminded Laura of her next duty.

'Have you had anything to eat?'

Amy smiled hopefully. 'Not since four o'clock.'

Laura realised that she hadn't eaten either and not since midday. 'I'll rustle up an omelette,' she decided.

Amy didn't offer to help her. 'I knew you'd look after me,' she said. 'You were always the homely one.'

'Well thanks,' Laura grimaced. 'A woman always enjoys being called homely.'

Amy was unabashed. 'You know what I mean.'

Just a tad too well, Laura thought, as she took the tablecloth out of the drawer.

'Isn't this fun,' Amy said, watching as her hostess chopped up mushrooms and onions. 'I'm so glad I came here. I knew it was the right thing to do. This is a gorgeous fire. I love log fires. They're so romantic. We're going to have a great time together, you and I. I can't wait till the morning.'

'I've got a lot of work to do in the morning.'

'Oh don't worry about that. I shan't stop you.'

Laura wondered whether to say something about the road, glanced across at where Amy lay sprawled among the cushions and decided against it. She probably wouldn't be interested. Not yet anyway. What a day this has been, she thought. And what a time she's chosen to come back.

Chapter Three

The thunder was still grumbling when Laura finally got to bed. It growled her to sleep, filling her ears with threatening sound and her mind with memories she would have preferred to avoid. There had been a storm on the night Pete walked out.

No, don't think of that, she urged herself. Find something else. Think of the road. The campaign. David. Jessica and Daniel. But nothing would stay in her mind long enough to be thought about. Despite her efforts, she was remembering how black it had been that night and how the rain came pelting into the hall as he flung open the front door. It had drenched her face and her shoulders, and made a damp patch all down the front of her new blouse. Oh that blouse! Would she ever forget that blouse?

Her young, remembered voice pulled her down into an anguished dream. She stood in the hall, shivering in the cold air, hanging on to his arm, struggling to hold him back, begging him, 'No! No! Why now? Please, Pete! Please don't leave me!'

His face was twisted out of shape by emotions she'd never seen before, emotions she didn't understand. 'For Christ's sake Laura. Let go of me.

You'll wake the boy.'

She held on even tighter, pulling at him, trying to get her arms round his neck. To hold him or throttle him? She didn't know. Didn't care. There was only the enormity of his voice saying those awful, awful words. 'I'm leaving you. I can't stay here. Not now.'

'Please!' she implored, as he shook free of her. 'Please don't go!' Her wet face was crumpled with weeping. 'Tell me what I've done and I'll put it right. I promise. I'll do anything. Anything. Only don't leave me.' Standing in the doorway in the full impact of the rain, the door-mat damp under her slippers, water running down the bridge of her nose and into her mouth. She put up a hand to brush it away and found that strands of her hair were matted together like wet rope. 'What have I done? Please, please tell me. What am I supposed to have done? It's not fair just to walk out. I can't bear it.' Hating the anguish in her voice. Knowing she was making things worse for herself. 'Please! Please!'

'It's not you,' he said and now she recognised that it was desperation she could see on his face. 'It's me. I'm the one. Me and . . .' He frowned and turned his head away from her, staring into the storm, as lightning revealed the emptiness of the lane. 'How can I possibly explain to you?' he said, rough with anger. 'You wouldn't understand. It's all over. That's all there is to it. All over. One of those things.' He was holding his spine so stiffly he looked as though he'd stopped

41

breathing. 'Why can't you accept it?'

'Because I can't,' she said doggedly. 'I love you too much.' Her emotion was plain on her face but although she knew it and knew that, for some hideous reason, it angered him to see it, she couldn't hide what she was feeling. 'If it's something you've done, I don't care what it is. I love you. I shall always love you.' And she reached out her hands for him again, this time to kiss him. If she could kiss him it would be all right. Kiss it better, Mum used to say. Oh, let me kiss it better. Please! A second flash of lightning cast an eerie light over the garden behind him, turning the hedges into white ghosts and edging his averted face with lurid blue.

'I can't take any more of this,' he said as darkness blacked out the world again. 'I'm sorry.' And he pulled away from her, wincing as though her touch were a sting, and ran down the path, disappearing into the slanting curtain of the rain, as if he were being dissolved, first his long, long legs, then his jacket, until there was only a glimpse of his shoulders swinging as he ran into the darkness, then a gleam of wet hair, a mere fold of moving cloth, then nothing.

She put her head against the wet doorpost and wept, aching to run after him and drag him back, but weighed down by responsibilities and unable to move. David was asleep upstairs and even though he was eleven now and very independent, she couldn't leave him on his own in the cottage with a storm going on. She couldn't even dash across to Mrs Fennimore and ask her to keep an eye on him, although she could see their hall light flickering through the trees at the far end of the terrace, so she knew they were in. But it wasn't possible. Not in this weather and not without some sort of explanation. And what sort of explanation could she possibly give?

She was tied hand and foot, bound to the doorpost with harsh wet ropes that bit into her flesh, and she was weeping, 'Don't leave me. Please don't leave me.' If he doesn't come back I'll never walk through this door again, she vowed. Never, ever. Oh Pete, my dear, dear, darling Pete, please come back to me. How can I go on living without you? What shall I do with the rest of my life?

'How about a nice cup of tea?' a voice was saying.

Tea? she thought wildly. What earthly good's tea at a time like this? Can't you see what a state I'm in? And she tried to form the words to tell whoever it was to go away and leave her alone. And was irritated to find that she couldn't do it.

The voice persisted. 'Come on Laura, wake up. Nice cup of tea. Do you a power of good.'

It was sister-in-law Amy in a red velvet housecoat and a pair of Turkish slippers, her face devoid of make-up and her hair set in heated rollers. She was sitting on the edge of the bed with the proffered cup steaming most appetisingly in the air between them. 'You've been having a nightmare,' she said.

'Yes.' Laura admitted, rubbing sleep and bad

dreams from her eyes as she dragged herself back to the world. 'I have. I'm sorry.' She tried to mock her weakness, to make light of it. 'That's not like me. I haven't had a nightmare for ages.' Not since Pete walked out, she thought. I had enough then to last me a lifetime. More than enough. Then she became aware that Amy was yawning. 'Did I wake you up?'

'I was awake anyway. It's half past seven. I thought you could use a cup of tea.'

Laura took the cup and sipped gratefully. She was most surprised to be waited on by Amy Pendleton.

'Joe used to have nightmares,' Amy confided, removing a roller and bouncing the resulting curl with her fingers. 'When we first got out. Used to wake up screaming and shouting. Never saw a man in such a state. And sweating like a pig too most times. I used to make *him* tea.' She put the roller in her pocket and started unwinding the next one, working quickly and skilfully. 'Drink it up while it's hot. It's a lovely day. What time have you got to be at work?'

'I haven't,' Laura said, feeling more herself again. 'It's my day off.'

'Oh well then,' Amy said cheerfully, 'you don't have to rush.'

How kind she's being, Laura thought, gazing at her sister-in-law across the rim of the cup, and how different she looks. There was something rather touching about Amy's unadorned face, something soft and almost vulnerable. Her skin was a great deal too pale — which wasn't a surprise considering what a lot of make-up she wore — her nose and forehead looked greasy and there was a scattering of broken veins across her cheeks, but her mouth was tender and she'd lost the harshness that had jarred so much the night before. Perhaps I've misjudged her all these years and she's a nicer person than I used to think.

'Don't look at me like that, for God's sake!' Amy begged, averting her own gaze and frowning. 'I know I look a right old frump. You don't have to tell me. I always do, first thing in the morning.' She made a grimace and attempted a joke. 'I'll put my face on in a minute and then you'll recognise me.'

'Actually,' Laura said frankly, 'if you don't mind me saying so, I think you look . . .' She was going to say *'better'* but amended it to 'just as good without your make-up. Younger.'

'I look a sight,' Amy corrected, standing up. Half the rollers were removed and the hair she'd released was mounded above her forehead like a Barbie doll's. 'Now then. You're OK now, aren't you? You've got over it. Right. I'll leave you to drink your tea while I get dressed. Then you can have a nice leisurely bath and I'll go down and cook the breakfast. I'm a dab hand with bacon and eggs.'

'My word!' Laura said, even more impressed. 'I *am* being spoilt.' But wasn't that typical of Amy? She'd always spoilt her friends, even when she was a little girl.

'Do you good,' Amy said, gave her a friendly smile and went.

It felt most luxurious to Laura to be wallowing in a bath first thing in the morning, especially as she knew the water wouldn't drain into the cesspit and fill it up now that she'd fixed the pipe. And it was even better to come downstairs to a room full of autumn sunshine and eat a meal she hadn't cooked herself. The cats were sitting on the window sill, wide-eyed and mewing to be fed but, for once, they would have to wait. Amy was right. It was a very good breakfast. Too good not to eat at once.

'That'll set you up for the day,' Amy told her as she scooped the last rasher of bacon from the pan.

'Never mind the day,' Laura laughed, looking at the mound of food on her plate. 'I shall be set up for a week.'

'Good,' Amy said, pushing her own empty plate aside and dipping into her handbag for a cigarette. 'Glad to hear it. Right, I've decided what I'm going to do today.' Now that she was dressed, with her hair arranged and her face made up, she was her old domineering self again, looking the world and Laura boldly in the eye. 'I'm going to Worthing to call in on my new boss and let him know I've arrived and collect my car and then I'm going to start house-hunting and do a spot of window shopping and then I'm going to take in a show, if the theatre's still there. It is! Good oh! So you'll come with me won't you.'

Two days ago, Laura would have accepted such

an invitation like the treat it was. She enjoyed the theatre and seized any opportunity to go there. But now the pattern of her life was changed. There was a campaign to run, a list to prepare, the postman was walking up the path at that very moment with a fistful of envelopes for her attention.

'Get thee behind me Satan,' she laughed as she went into the kitchen to collect them. 'You always were a temptress, Amy. Even at school.'

'That's me,' Amy called after her. 'So what about it?'

'Can't be done,' Laura said, returning with the post. And waved the mail by way of explanation.

'Good God!' Amy said. 'Do you always get as many letters as that?'

'No,' Laura admitted as she sorted through the pile. 'This is a one-off. Here's your letter from Hong Kong, look.'

Amy laughed. 'That's all old hat now. I shouldn't bother with it if I were you, I'd get on with my bacon and eggs.'

Laura took her advice happily. 'I'll look at it later.'

'What are all the others?'

'Things I sent away for,' Laura said. And as Amy was looking a question at her, she told her about the road while she finished her breakfast and opened the letters, skimming them for information. Friends of the Earth (full of stuff), SCAR (even better), the local council and the Department of Transport (very bland and noncommittal), the AA (assuming I want the road. Well they would, wouldn't they.)

Amy enjoyed her cigarette and listened, her eyes narrowed against the smoke. 'So that was what last night's kerfuffle was all about,' she said, flicking ash into her saucer. 'I wondered why you'd got so many people round. Good on yer, as the Aussies say. I hope you win. Pity though, I suppose it puts paid to us going on the razzle, today at any rate.'

' 'Fraid so,' Laura said briskly. It was a surprise to her that Amy was taking a refusal so philosophically. The young Amy would have made a scene.

'Never mind,' the middle-aged Amy said, stubbing out her cigarette. 'There'll be another time. Next week maybe? Hell! Look at the time. My taxi will be here in five minutes. I'd better get my skates on. I'll leave you to it.'

She also left her to the washing up and to various items of dirty clothing scattered over the bathroom floor.

And that's typical of her too, Laura thought wryly. She never offered to do the washing-up in the old days either. If she's going to stay with me for any length of time I shall have to train her into better ways.

She was just dropping the crumpled garments into the dirty clothes basket when a movement in the garden below made her look out of the window and there was Molly Fennimore ambling up the path.

'I been thinking,' that lady said happily as they met in the kitchen. 'When they come to serve this damned order, whatever it is, I could set the dogs on 'em.' Her round, lined face was gleeful at the very idea.

'It'll probably come through the post,' Laura pointed out, laughing at her. 'You could hardly set your dogs on to our postie.' But she was warmed by her old friend's ferocity and glad to see that she was preparing herself for a fight.

'Point taken,' Molly grinned. 'They could bite a few strangers though, couldn't they?'

'Oh, I see!' Laura laughed. 'It's open season on strangers, is it? What about the dangerous dogs act?'

'Gun dogs in't dangerous,' Molly said happily. 'Best tempered dogs in the business. Leastways mine are.' She'd been breeding golden retrievers for over thirty years and what she didn't know about the breed wasn't worth knowing. 'Come on then, where's this old list?'

'I'm a bit behind I'm afraid,' Laura said ruefully. 'I haven't typed it out yet.'

'Give it here then gel, and I'll do it.'

'You sure?'

'Yep. Won't take me a minute.'

In fact it took nearly forty by the time they'd gathered up all the extra information from the morning's mail, printed off twenty copies to make sure there was one for everyone and roughed out the first draft of their first letter to the local paper. The letter was still printing when the phone rang.

'Now what?' Laura said, happily, as she went to pick it up. A phone call in the morning was unusual. Most of hers were in the evening. Not that she had that many.

'I'll be off and deliver these then,' Molly said. She took the leaflets, grinned and went.

It was Amy on the phone, in bubbling good humour. She came straight to the point. 'Now I know you said you didn't want to come to the theatre,' she said, 'or shopping or anything, but this is different. You wait till you hear. I've got someone for you to meet. Right? He's bang in the thick of this protest business. Been in it for years. All sorts of contacts, newspapers, local radio. Well known by all accounts and he's just your style. I've been telling him about your road and he wants to meet you. Isn't that a bit of luck? Anyway I've asked him out for lunch. We're in Fuller's Hotel on the promenade. Do you know it?'

Everybody knew Fuller's. It was the most prestigious hotel in the town. 'Yes. Of course but . . .'

'Great,' Amy interrupted. 'That's all right then. See you here in fifteen minutes.' And rang off.

She hasn't changed a bit, Laura thought. She's still rushing people into things just like she used to. It would be all the same to her if I had something else I wanted to do. But why not go? He could be useful and I ought to grab every chance that offers. I can finish printing the letters some other time. The pace of this unusual day was

50

carrying her along, giving her a sense of impending adventure. Why not go?

It was a very pleasant drive and an easy one. There was so little traffic she even had time to look around her. All trace of the storm was gone and the morning was washed clean, the downs peacefully green, trees and hedgerows rich with autumn colour, the sky summer blue and heaped with rolling cumulus cloud. The scents of autumn filtered through her open window, the warm breath of earth, stubble smelling of baked flour, fruit ripe and sensuous, the first prickle of dying leaves. She passed a shorn field where three pheasants panicked into a long-legged run, and another where a blue tractor bounced and lurched as it curled a long straight furrow behind it. It was trailed by the usual swarm of bickering gulls, which tossed and swirled, dipping to the newly ploughed earth as if they were taking fish from the sea, their plump bodies snow white against the blue of the sky. Laura's heart contracted with affection for it all. This, she thought, is not a landscape to be lost under concrete. I won't let them do it. I'll take help from anyone who offers it. And she hoped this man of Amy's would be useful and wondered what he would be like.

He was a very middling sort of man, middle height, middle class, middle-aged, with a neat beard midway between brown and grey and a shock of brown hair greying round the ears. The only extraordinary things about him were his eyes which were really quite striking, cat-bold, tawny

51

and framed by surprisingly thick eyelashes. But she couldn't help noticing that he was enjoying the fact that Amy was flirting with him.

'This is Jeffrey Turner,' Amy said, making the introductions and giving him the benefit of her big blue eyes. 'Nothing he doesn't know about protest movements. Isn't that right, Jeff?'

Her admiration for him was so open and so charming that he would have been less than human not to respond to it. 'Very far from right,' he laughed, shaking Laura's hand. He had a firm handshake, she noticed, and a warm one. 'It's a complicated business, opposing a government. You learn as you go along.'

They walked into the restaurant. 'Just as well we're not opposing the government then,' Laura said, feeling she should put him right on that score from the outset.

He gave her a look that was both shrewd and mocking. 'Are you not?'

'No we're not,' she told him, bristling a little because his question implied a doubt. 'We're opposing the council. It's a local by-pass we're up against. Didn't Amy tell you?'

'Amy hasn't told me very much,' he said. 'I shall have to tease her to tell me more.'

'I told you it was about a road,' Amy said, flirting with her eyes. 'What more do you want?'

'If it's a road,' he said, still looking at Amy as she sat down at the table, 'it'll be *the* road.'

Laura was beginning to feel superfluous. And dowdy. Like a proper old gooseberry. '*The* road!'

she echoed, mocking him to keep her end up. 'You make it sound as though there's only one.'

'There is,' he said. 'At least there is in this part of the world. I've got the map here somewhere.' He fished in the pocket of his jeans as he explained. 'It's going to be a motorway. But you've probably found that out already, haven't you. It's going to run from Folkestone to Honiton. Yes, here it is. See?' He passed it across the table to Amy as he took his seat.

Amy was more interested in the menu and merely glanced at it. But the gooseberry picked it up and spread it out on the tablecloth.

It was a long narrow map and rather battered but the line of the motorway was clear to be seen even through the creases. Parts had been built and marked already. Seen like that there didn't seem to be any doubt about the intention of it, running from east to west right along the coast, as bold and red as an artery.

Her crestfallen expression stirred Jeff's sympathy. He knew — from personal and bitter experience — what an unpleasant moment it is when you're running a campaign and you realise what sort of power you're up against. 'This is your section,' he said, leaning across the table to trace the line of the proposed bypass with his forefinger. 'It'll link up with this part at Worthing, which is still called the A29 although it might just as well be designated motorway. You've only got to drive on it to see that. And have you been along the new stretch west of

Chichester? Motorway in all but name.'

He was right and Laura knew it but that didn't endear him to her at all, especially after all that flirting. It was simply another annoyance and it changed his feelings about the campaign. Opposing a by-pass was one thing, taking on a motorway was another. 'So you're saying we can't stop it, is that it?'

'Well it won't be easy,' he said.

Amy was still examining the menu while a waiter hovered beside her. Beyond the window, the sea rolled into shore in long white-edged waves. 'I should like a fillet steak,' she said. 'What about you two? Right. Make that three steaks and a selection of veggies. And we'll have a bottle of Beaujolais while you're about it.'

'Not for me,' Laura said. 'I'm driving.'

'Oh for heaven's sake!' Amy mocked. 'So am I. I've got my company car now. That's all propaganda. You don't want to take any notice of that, does she Jeff? You'll have some won't you?'

'Just a glass,' he said. 'To keep you company.' And he made an awkward attempt to be charming. 'I can't let a lovely lady drink alone.' But the words sounded false and shamed him. I never get it right, he thought, and now his smile felt false too, so that he had to look away from both women and gaze out to sea for a few seconds. Flattery's not my style.

The wine was ordered with some mineral water 'for my faint-hearted friend'. And now it was Laura's turn to feel ill at ease and more of a

54

gooseberry than ever. When the waiter had light-footed off on his errands, she closed her face and returned the map to its owner.

The closed face intrigued him. There was more to this quiet one than met the eye. 'So tell me what you've done so far,' he said.

The booklet that had seemed such a good idea the night before was reduced to insignificance by that map. But she told him about it anyway as the wine arrived, adding, 'It's just a first step, you understand. We shall do other things too.'

'It'll appeal to the local press,' he said. 'Especially if you get some good pictures. Send it to Toby Fawcett. He likes that sort of thing. But it won't influence the decision makers.'

'Not at all?'

'Not enough. There aren't any votes in it. You'll only get *them* to re-think if you make them feel they might lose votes.'

'Then we must start a petition and stir up enough voters to worry them.'

Again that shrewd, mocking glance. 'In this constituency? Have you any idea of the size of the majority you'd have to shift?'

'Sixteen thousand,' she said at once, annoyed by his assumption that she was politically naive. 'And a lot of them would vote Liberal Democrat if they thought they had a chance of winning.'

'That's a very sweeping statement,' he said. 'How do you know?'

'I listen.'

'Ah!' he said.

The little word made her feel as if he was putting her down. 'There's a lot going wrong,' she told him fiercely, 'even in this affluent part of the world. You'd be surprised how many firms have gone bust and all sorts of people have been repossessed. There's a lot of poverty. Just because it's hidden, it doesn't mean it doesn't exist.'

Again that shrewd look. 'I know,' he said, 'but you've taken on a fight, just the same.'

'Ah, but then you don't know what a fighter she is,' Amy put in, as her steak was set before her. 'You should have seen her at school. Terror of the playground, weren't you kid?'

'And you were just a shy little thing I suppose,' he said. If he didn't try to flatter, it was easy to talk to her and even easier to tease. She responded so quickly and with such pleasure.

'Right!' Amy smiled at him. She was glowing with well-being, warmed by wine and attention, her tan enriched and her teeth very white. 'I never fight anybody if I can help it.'

'Quite right,' he agreed with her. 'People get injured on demonstrations.'

'Oh come now,' Amy said, helping herself to vegetables and smiling at him in her flirting way, 'that's pitching it a bit strong, don't you think.'

'Injured,' he insisted. 'If you don't believe me, I suggest you go to Twyford Down this Sunday and see for yourself.'

'What's Twyford Down?' Amy asked, posting a large chunk of steak into her red mouth.

'A battlefield,' he told her. 'Where the protesters are fighting the road builders. I wonder you haven't seen it on TV.'

'I've been in Australia. This is all news to me.'

Then *she's* not the one involved in the campaign, Jeff understood. And he glanced at Laura who was listening quietly. 'Ah. Well you should go there on Sunday,' he said to Amy. 'It 'ud be an eye-opener.'

'No thank *you*,' Amy said. 'That sort of thing is strictly for the birds. Tuck in you two. This steak's not bad.'

Jeff laughed out loud at her. He couldn't help it. She sounded so droll.

His laughter irritated Laura. He thinks we're just a pair of nimbys, she thought. 'Is Sunday special?' she asked.

'Rumour has it, they're bringing in some new earth-movers,' he explained. 'There's going to be a punch-up.'

She made up her mind without hesitation. No one was going to call her a coward, even by implication. 'I'll be there,' she said. 'You're right. I ought to see these things for myself. What time will it be?'

'All day,' he told her, his expression changing. 'Could start any time. Depends when they bring in the machinery.'

Was that a touch of respect she could see? Oh she *did* hope so. 'In that case,' she promised, 'I shall set off first thing in the morning.'

'Well now that's agreed,' Amy laughed, 'what

d'you fancy for dessert? Jeff? What can I tempt you to?'

Laura settled to enjoy her food and left them to their flirtation. He was a nice enough man but he wasn't going to be much help to her campaign. She listened vaguely as Amy took the conversation in hand and the rest of the meal passed in light-hearted chatter about life in Australia. After coffee, they parted in a rush because Jeff was in a hurry to get back to work on time. It wasn't until she was halfway home that she realised the full implication of what she'd promised to do and then she went hot to think she'd been so reckless.

It wasn't like her to make a decision without thinking about it. At least it wasn't like her mature self. She'd rushed into plenty of silly situations when she was young, but you expect to be silly when you're young. Now, and a bit late, she realised that, exciting though all this was, it would lead to some inevitable consequences. The senior librarian would have to be told for a start, in case there were cameras there. It would hardly do for him to suddenly see her on TV in the middle of a demonstration. She'd have to prepare him for it. That was only proper. And then there was David, who was so proper and correct she sometimes wondered how she'd ever produced him. She'd have to tell him too and he would *not* be pleased.

Chapter Four

David Pendleton was shocked. Everything about him showed it, from his raised eyebrows and staring eyes to a spine held so tight that he was rigid from neatly-cut hair to well-polished size nines. 'You can't do this, Mother,' he protested, clutching the phone against his ear. 'I never heard such nonsense.'

Laura shifted her tabby cat into a more comfortable position on her lap and gazed around her living room, taking comfort from its familiar muddle, the overloaded bookshelves sagging in every recess, the dresser crammed with crockery. The evidence of the warmth and neighbourliness of her life in this place was all around her, the Sussex chairs cushion-dented where her last guests had left them, used mugs all over the table, the hearth covered in crumbs, the smell of toast still feeding the air. 'I don't think it's nonsense,' she said.

His answer buzzed along the wire, immediate and cross. 'Well of course it's nonsense. People like us don't lead protest movements, for heaven's sake. And they don't go on demonstrations either. It's not proper.' It was the wrong word to use and he knew it the moment it was out of his mouth. She'd never seen the necessity to be proper. The mistake, small though it was, embarrassed him and made him tetchy. 'Oh, come on, Mother, for heaven's sake! You've got a position to think about. What will they say at the library? Have you thought about that?'

'They won't mind,' she hoped. But his annoyance was making her feel less sure of herself than she'd done during the afternoon. She'd taken care to pick a sensible moment to phone him, when she knew he would have finished dinner and when her neighbours had gone and Amy was still out, but the call had been as difficult as she'd feared. He'd been cross enough when he heard that Amy had moved in with her, but when she'd told him about the campaign and the demonstration, he had snorted with annoyance.

'Well I mind,' he said, 'and it's only fair to tell you. I think you're making a big mistake. A very big mistake. You're throwing away your security.'

'This house is my security,' she said. It was all the security she'd had after Pete walked out on them. Surely he could understand *that*.

'This road is going to be built,' he said. 'You'll have to face it sooner or later. There's a need for it. They've done studies. There's serious money involved in it.'

'I don't doubt it.'

'It isn't just Tarmac and firms like that, you know. There are all sorts of companies tied up in road building. Multinationals. PPC even. One of our subsidiaries is Amalgamated Gravels. It's very big business.'

She didn't doubt that either. 'All the more reason to fight them,' she said stubbornly. 'If we don't they'll think they can ride roughshod over anybody.'

David sighed. He could feel this whole affair skidding out of control — the way his life had done when Dad walked out. Couldn't she see how important it was to be in control? 'You're running risks,' he warned. 'And you could lose in the end no matter what you do. You probably will.'

Jack stretched out a lazy paw to touch Laura's chin and spoke to her briefly, in his loving way, 'prrrm'. She ran her free hand along his spine, enjoying the silky texture of his tabby fur. 'Yes,' she said, mildly and rather sadly, 'so you say.'

Her sadness touched his conscience. He changed tone and began to persuade. 'Then think better of it, there's a dear. Change your mind.'

His gentler tone made her feel pressurised. She was proof against being bullied, but persuasion was harder to resist. 'That's not my way, David,' she said. 'If I say I'm going to do a thing, I do it.'

That was so obvious it hardly needed to be said. But he persisted. 'Why does it have to be you? Why can't someone else do it?'

'Because it *is* me, I suppose. And besides, somebody's got to do it. Nothing would ever get done if we all left it to someone else.'

There was a car drawing up outside the back door. 'Here's Amy come home,' she said, relieved that their conversation would have to stop. 'I shall have to go.'

Now he could direct his anger to this distant aunt he couldn't remember. 'And how long does she think she's staying?'

'Till she finds somewhere to live,' Laura said firmly. 'I don't mind putting her up. I'm glad of the company.'

'Well don't let her take advantage of you, that's all. It's very thoughtless of her, bowling in out of the blue like that. You're not a hotel. I suppose we shan't see you on Sunday?'

'No. Not this Sunday. I'll ring you in the week.'

Amy was struggling in through the kitchen door, carrying a box full of groceries and beaming happily. 'Was I right, or was I right?' she said. 'Isn't he super!'

After such a tricky phone call, Laura didn't want to talk to Amy about Jeff Turner or the campaign. So she changed the subject quickly. 'How did you get on with the estate agents?' she asked. 'Any luck?'

'No,' Amy said, grimacing. 'Never met such morons. They're all so young. Still got the cradle marks on their bums. Little boys in cheap suits filling in forms and giving themselves airs. They don't know how to listen, that's their trouble. They just sit there shelling out folders as if they're doing you a favour and when you look at the damn things, they're all full of the sort of houses you've just told them you don't want. It's no way to run a business. Jeez, I'm knackered. Is there any tea?'

Knackered is the right word, Laura thought, as she filled the kettle. One conversation and I'm drained. Why is it always such hard work talking to your children?

It might have surprised her to know that as David put down the phone he was feeling equally exhausted. His mother's unpredictability was always a source of irritation to him but to be told she was going on a demonstration made him feel cross beyond control. It was so totally unsuitable for a woman of her age, so unnecessary, so childish, so self-indulgent. He brushed his hand across the nape of his neck, comforted by the prickle of short hair under his palm — nice, neat, predictable hair — then he walked into the kitchen to offload some of his irritation on to his wife.

He and Maureen and their two teenaged children lived in a detached house on one of the new estates on the outskirts of Burswood. It was a modern house, light and airy, well appointed and very clean, with white walls and immaculate paintwork and a streamlined kitchen equipped with every labour-saving device that any woman could possibly desire. David Pendleton prided himself that he knew how to look after *his* family. Other fathers might walk out on their children without so much as a goodbye but he was a cut above such appalling behaviour. *He* was made of more dependable stuff. *He* surrounded his family with comfort.

His wife and daughter were loading the dishwasher and the kitchen smelled of lemons and disinfectant. Maureen looked up at his approach.

'That was Mother on the blower,' he explained to her, pleased to hear how calm his voice was. 'I think she s gone off her rocker.'

'Has she?' Maureen smiled, fitting in the last saucepan and closing the door. 'What makes you say that?'

'She says she's going to Twyford Down, if you ever heard of anything so stupid.' His handsome face was wrinkled at the very idea. 'The place where all those dreadful hippies are making such a fuss. My mother in with all the hippies! Imagine it!'

'That'll be about the road,' Maureen said, taking a damp cloth to the cooker.

He was surprised by her knowledge and annoyed by her calm. 'You know about it?'

'Jessica saw her in the library yesterday afternoon, didn't you darling.'

'That's right,' his daughter said, tossing her hair out of her eyes as she put the salt and pepper pots back in the cupboard. At seventeen she was a delectably pretty girl, tall and slim with almond-shaped blue eyes and a mane of straight fair hair. 'The council have chosen route C apparently. She was telling me all about it. They'd had the letters that morning. I saw hers. It was horrible. Anyway they're going to fight it. I think it's great.'

David ignored his daughter's opinion for a moment while he rebuked his wife. 'You didn't tell me you knew about it.'

'No, I didn't, did I,' Maureen said, speaking as

though it didn't matter. 'I suppose it got crowded out. I hardly saw you yesterday, what with your conference and my PTA meeting and everything. Still you know now. No harm done.'

'No harm done! What are you talking about, woman? I should have known at once.'

'Why?' Maureen asked mildly, polishing the taps.

He was pursuing his own thoughts. 'It's so undignified,' he complained. 'And it won't do any good. If they want to build the bloody road, they'll build it.'

Jessica suddenly moved into the argument. 'No they won't,' she said. 'Not if they all stand together and fight it. They're going to the papers and the Friends of the Earth and Greenpeace. They might even get on the telly.'

Her opposition made him more sure of himself. 'It won't do them any good,' he said and was annoyed to hear that he sounded pompous.

She stood her ground, tossing her mane at him. 'I don't see why not.'

'You can't stand in the way of progress. That's why not.'

'And a motorway's progress is it?'

How mocking her voice sounded. It was no way for a child to speak to her father. She would have to be put in her place. 'Well obviously.'

She answered him coolly. 'That's not everybody's opinion. We've been examining the use and impact of motorways in Geography and I can tell you . . .'

He was riled by her confidence. Clever women had always made him feel ill at ease, especially when they let everyone see how clever they were. A woman should be reserved about such matters. That had been one of the most attractive things about Maureen back in their college days, she'd always played down her intelligence. 'Allow me to know a bit more than you do, Jessica.'

His daughter gave him one of those awful cocky looks of hers and took breath ready to fight on. But Maureen intervened by walking between them.

'There!' she said. 'That's the kitchen done. Thanks for your help Jess.' She smiled at David as she passed. 'What are we watching tonight?'

There was a pause while Jessica bit her lip and thought hard and David took a deep breath and smoothed his hair. Maureen went on smiling first at one and then at the other.

'I'm off then,' Jessica decided, abruptly. 'See you later, Mum.'

They touched cheeks briefly and the girl was gone, the quarrel avoided.

Thank heavens for that, Maureen thought. Arguing with David was a waste of time, because he *had* to win no matter how good or bad his case might be. She'd given up trying to put her point of view long ago, partly because it upset him so much and partly because she didn't have the energy to fight her corner. Now she didn't have the will either. It was easier to agree with him and to think her own thoughts in private. 'What are we watching?' she asked again, as they walked into the living room.

David was discontented — at his mother's folly and at being denied the argument he'd expected and needed. 'I can't think what's got into my silly mother,' he said. 'Feet off the chair, Daniel.'

Their thirteen-year-old was already comfortably ensconced in the armchair, his evening viewing well under way, but he uncurled his long legs and removed the offending feet from the chintz, giving his mother a quick glance of commiseration and complaint.

Maureen took her own seat at one end of the sofa and smiled her understanding at him. Like his sister he was tall and slim, with long legs and a narrow waist. Buying jeans for him was always difficult because of that narrow waist. But he repaid the effort because he always looked so good in his clothes. A handsome boy, she thought, admiring him. Nice thick fair hair, like mine when I was young. A strong face. His nose might be a bit too big — he was very self-conscious about his nose — and his mouth was a bit too wide — but that was like Laura's mouth and she always thought of Laura's mouth as 'generous'. A good face, all in all. And lovely eyes, as blue as his sister's — or as mine, come to that — gentle, loving eyes. I hope he won't grow up to be too gentle though. Gentle people do get pushed around so.

David was flicking from channel to channel and had begun one of his monosyllabic conversations with the boy, beginning, as always with a command.

'Homework.'

'Done.'

'Properly?'

'Yep.'

'What was it?'

'Maths and French.'

'Show me.'

Danny reached behind the chair for his school bag and found the exercise books his father wanted. Watching him, Maureen was struck by how weary he looked, like an old man carrying too many burdens. There were shadows under those blue eyes and his shoulders drooped with resignation. We put our young under such pressure, she thought. I wish we didn't have to.

'I don't think much of the writing,' David said brusquely. 'You can do better than that.'

'She won't mind,' Danny excused himself. 'She's only worried about the tenses. She said.'

'That's as may be,' David told him. 'I mind. There's such a thing as standards, you know. Where's the Maths?'

'Can I watch in my room?' Danny asked when the inspection was over.

'What's the matter with here?'

'You like different things.'

'We hardly ever see you these days,' David complained. 'I'd have thought you'd have liked to spend a bit of time with your aged parents, now and then.'

The boy was caught between the desire to avoid boredom and the need to please his father. He shot another quick glance at his mother — part plea for help, part question.

'I thought you were going round to see Charles,' she said, rescuing him. 'I promised Connie you'd take my recipe book for her.'

'OK,' he said, seizing his escape but splendidly laconic about it. 'Can if you like. Where is it?'

'You let him out too often,' David complained, when Danny had gone. 'It wouldn't hurt him to spend an evening with us now and then.'

'He's young,' Maureen said.

'And where's Jessica gone?'

'Out with Emma, I think.'

'So she'll be back all hours making a racket.'

Maureen decided to ignore that. Sometimes it was counterproductive to defend her children because it simply increased his irritation. If I let well alone, she thought, ten to one he'll have forgotten all this by the time Jess gets back.

'I sometimes wonder why we bothered to have children,' he said, his face sour.

Yes, Maureen thought sadly, so do I. And not for the first time she wondered what had happened to all the high hopes they'd had when they first got married. Life was difficult with him these days. They all had to be on their guard so much and there was an enervating monotony about the few evenings they spent at home together. Is it any wonder the kids go out all the time? Especially when he gets so cross with them. I do wish he wouldn't.

The television set blared into a volley of whipped-up applause and cackling laughter. 'Damned quiz shows!' David scowled at it. 'There's nothing worth watching. Ah well that's it. I shall go up and finish my orders. Call me for *News at Ten*.' There were times when even routine paperwork was preferable to the sort of rubbish they pumped along the cables. And it would show Cosgrave how keen he was if he came in tomorrow with all his orders up to date.

Left on her own, Maureen took up her library book and began to search for her place. If Laura really was setting up a protest group it might bring some colour to their lives. Good luck to her, she thought, whatever she's going to do. I'll ring her up at break tomorrow, if I get a minute. Then she remembered that she was on duty at break tomorrow and sighed wearily. As a mere 'classroom teacher' there was always too much to do and never enough time to do it in. She ought to be marking books at that very moment, if the truth were told, but she'd had enough chores for the day. What I'd really like, she thought as she found her place, would be a day lounging around in bed with nothing to do and no one to be responsible for and someone to wait on me hand and foot.

Amy Pendleton was still lounging around in bed when Laura set off for work the next morning. It seemed most peculiar to be leaving the house with someone in it, as if it were a weekend or she was on holiday. It took an effort of will to drive in to Burswood and an even greater one to resume work on her rolling stock-take as if nothing had happened during her day off.

Luckily that Wednesday turned out to be one of the days when the library almost seemed to run itself. Meryl Evans manned the desk, Poppy Manning shelved, Nick Ferris loaded the mobile, their regulars came and went, there was the usual subdued buzz that indicated that the place was being well and properly used.

Work had always been a comfort to Laura Pendleton. There was security in it and a sense of worth. As she sat at the computer, keying in the information from her stock-take, she was relaxed and contented again, in charge of her life and in charge of the library, proud of the books ranged so temptingly on show, of the posters brightening the walls, of the children's corner with its low shelves and its encouraging bean-bags. That had been her pet project last year and the results had been even better than she predicted. As she left the office to take her turn on the desk, she was smiling to herself with the pleasure of a job well done.

The smile became a beam when she saw that Jessica and her best friend were waiting at the counter.

'Hello you two,' she said. 'Your Geography books are in. Came this morning.'

71

Jessica smiled too. 'That was quick.'

'We aim to please.'

Jessica put her ticket on the counter. 'I'll get the Geography,' she said to Emma, 'you get the French.'

The books were issued and put away in their school bags but Jessica lingered. 'Look,' she said. 'I've got something to tell you.'

A new boyfriend, Laura thought, looking at her granddaughter's flushed cheeks. I hope it's someone David can approve of.

But it wasn't a boyfriend. The explanation came out with a rush. 'You know you're going to Twyford Down on Sunday. Well I'm coming with you.'

The thought of having Jessica's company on this unpredictable adventure put the crown on Laura's day. 'Are you?' she said and her delight was in her voice.

'If you'd like me to.'

'I'd love you to. You know that.' Oh they both knew that. But they had to be practical. 'Does your father know?'

'No,' Jessica said, frowning a little but looking determined. 'There's no reason why he should. It's nothing to do with him. He's had his say. I heard him on the phone yesterday evening.'

Ah, Laura understood, so that's what it is. You're coming out in sympathy, taking my part. She was touched by the affection and loyalty of it. But there was a queue forming and no time to say any more. 'I'm leaving at six in the morning,' she warned, as she held out her hand to her next borrower.

Jessica grinned. 'I'll be there,' she promised.

'Is it somewhere nice where you're going?' Poppy asked when the queue was gone.

It was an opportune moment so Laura told her. And soon found she was telling Meryl and Nick too. And was being applauded and admired.

'I say!' Meryl said. 'You *are* brave. You won't go getting arrested or anything like that though, will you.'

'I'll try not to.'

'Does Mr Gratwick know?' Poppy asked. Mr Gratwick was the senior librarian and a man to be reckoned with.

'He'll know tomorrow afternoon,' Laura said. 'I'm going to tell him after our weekly meeting.'

'Rather you than me,' Poppy grimaced.

But as it turned out, Mr Gratwick, dour though he seemed, was surprisingly liberal about it. 'What you do in your spare time is entirely your own affair,' he said. 'I know I can trust you not to do anything unbecoming to your position here.'

'No,' she said. 'Of course not.'

He gave her one of his rare smiles. 'We live in interesting times,' he said.

Chapter Five

Dawn had just broken on that Sunday morning when Laura and Jessica set off for Winchester. It was extremely cold but they didn't mind. They were warmly dressed in boots, trousers, thick jerseys and coats and they had a flask of coffee and a picnic hamper to keep them going on the journey.

Since her phone call to David, Laura had been caught up in a mixture of emotions, surprise at the thought that she was actually going on a demonstration — at *her* time of life! — anxiety in case it turned out to be as rough as Jeff Turner predicted, annoyance at herself for making such a silly snap decision — snap decisions were always silly — but determination to go through with it whatever happened because she *had* to show him she wasn't just a nimby. The worst thing was a nagging regret that she'd told David about it and almost provoked a row. It wasn't like her to be so maladroit. Usually the mere thought of quarrelling with him was enough to put a curb on her tongue.

Fortunately Jessica was her usual cheerful self. She'd arrived on her bicycle and bounced into the car as if she were taking possession of it, tuned in the radio until she found the sort of music she liked and produced a packet of Opal Fruits 'in case we get dry'. Now she was eating them steadily, occasionally popping one into Laura's mouth as she drove.

With an irony that wasn't lost on either of them, they made good time as they travelled westward towards Southampton along the new motorway.

'Did you tell your father?' Laura asked as they passed the hill forts above Portsmouth.

Jessica didn't think that was necessary. 'He wasn't up. Mum knows. She cooked me breakfast.'

'She's all right about it, then?' Laura asked.

'Oh yes.'

'So she'll tell him.'

'I don't expect so. And don't make that face. There's all sorts of things she doesn't tell him.'

Laura had suspected as much for a very long time but it was unsettling to hear it said so boldly. She drove on in silence, thinking.

'Oh come on, Gran!' Jessica said. 'I'm seventeen. I can't tell him everything. I've got a right to a bit of privacy now and then. A life of my own. I mean, if I wasn't at school I'd be in a flat somewhere — now wouldn't I? — and he wouldn't know *what* I was doing.'

'True,' Laura admitted.

'He treats me like an infant,' Jessica complained. 'I want to be out with my friends, having fun and meeting people now and then, not stuck in doing homework every day of the week. There's more to life than A levels. But you try telling *him* that. He's breathing down my neck all the time. *"Have you done your homework? Where are you going? When are you coming back?"* It's like the Inquisition.'

'Yes,' Laura smiled. 'I can see it is.'

'Well then. You see what I mean.'

'Oh yes,' Laura sympathised. 'I do see what you mean. The sad thing is he was just like you when he was your age.'

'Pity he's lost his memory, then.'

'It's a human failing, I'm afraid,' Laura said. Poor David. There were times when she felt as though he was older than she was. He married so young, that's his trouble, she thought. It's made him old before his time.

'You remember things,' Jessica said.

'Ah well,' Laura grinned. 'I'm weird. Particularly this morning, going off to a demonstration, for heaven's sake!'

'Then I shall be weird too.'

'You're weird already,' Laura teased.

'I shan't forget how I feel, anyway,' Jessica told her fiercely. 'I'm keeping a diary to make sure I don't. I'm not going to be foul to *my* children.'

Oh the passion of the young, Laura thought, remembering that too. We're so sure of ourselves in our teens and so determined. We think we've got all the answers.

'He'll ask where you've been when you get back though, won't he,' she warned. 'You'll have to tell him then.'

'I shall say I've been doing some work for my

Geography module,' Jessica said. And when Laura grimaced, 'Well so I am, in a way, so you needn't make that face either, you dear old Granny. It's about roads in the south east of England. Value and impact and all that sort of thing.'

'I'll believe you,' the dear old Granny said and made one of her familiar jokes. 'Thousands wouldn't.'

The joke raised a smile. 'It's true,' Jessica said. 'You'd be surprised what sort of things you learn in Geography. It's not just mountains and rivers these days. It's tearing down hillsides to make way for roads too.'

'They're not tearing down the hillside,' Laura corrected, exaggeration disturbing her, as it always did. 'At least I hope they're not.'

'They will if they get their way,' Jessica told her. 'The protestors want them to build a tunnel and leave the hill alone but they want to tear it down and build the road right through the middle. It's been in all the papers.'

They reached the green hill of Twyford Down in comfortable time. It looked much the same as Laura remembered it, except that someone seemed to have removed a chunk of the lower slope so that the underlying chalk was revealed. There were three yellow lorries standing unoccupied among the chalk and several dark figures milling about on the hillside.

'There's your demonstration,' Jessica said, pointing at the figures. 'Up there.'

They parked among a collection of battered coaches and mud-splattered cars. Immediately in front of them was a smart blue Volvo with a young man sitting at the wheel reading a newspaper. He and Jessica sized one another up.

'I'll just find my umbrella and we'll go up,' Laura said, noticing the *oeillades* and feeling she ought to put a stop to them. David would be cross enough to think his errant daughter had gone on this demonstration without his permission, but if she were allowed to pick up some strange youth in a car, he'd be apoplectic. 'Are you coming?'

The answer was carefully cool. 'Wouldn't it be an idea to watch for a little while,' Jessica said, still giving the young man the eye. 'Get the lie of the land, sort of thing.' He was quite a good-looking young man, in a pale gingery sort of way. Much more interesting than the nerds at school. Nice leather jacket. And a G reg. Volvo can't be bad. 'I mean, there's nothing much happening, is there? There's no cameras or anything. They're just drifting about as far as I can see.'

'I'm going up anyway to see what I can find out.' Now that she was here it was the least she could do.

'You go then,' Jessica said amiably. 'It won't take long, will it. I'll stay in the car and keep guard.'

'I think you ought to come with me,' Laura tried as she stuck her feet out of the car.

'It's too cold,' Jessica said, sitting in the passenger seat as if she'd been rooted there. 'I'd

78

much rather stay here, if you don't mind. I've got ever such a lot of reading to do. I could get on with it while you're reconnoitering.'

'I think we ought to stay together,' Laura insisted but the set of that jaw and the vague expression in those pretty blue eyes showed her she was already defeated. Not for the first time, she sighed with the recognition that a teenager's determination is well nigh impossible for a parent to shift. And isn't *this* just typical of the teens too. One minute you're admiring them for taking a stand and the next they're taking a stand against *you* and driving you to irritation. It made her feel a sneaking sympathy for her son. 'Well all right then,' she capitulated, hoping she was doing the right thing. 'I shan't be long. Twenty minutes, that's all. You stay here in the warm.'

Now that she'd won her point, Jessica could be gracious. 'I'll come up and join you straight away if anything starts to happen, I promise,' she said and watched as her grandmother strode off across the rough grass, using her umbrella as a walking stick. The young man was still watching *her* as she could see out of the corner of her eye. She pulled her copy of *Sons and Lovers* from her coat pocket and made a performance of reading, smoothing her long hair out of her eyes.

Presently she became aware that he was standing alongside the Land-Rover. She counted to ten, then looked up and pretended to be surprised, outwardly cool but inwardly warm with the awareness of her power.

'Hi there,' he said, as deliberately casual as she was.

Yes, she thought, allowing herself one glance before returning her attention to D.H. Lawrence. Not bad. Nice and tall. I like the shirt. Thick hair, no gel. She hated men who gelled their hair. The nerds in the sixth form were always gelling their hair. Good skin, not too freckly. Big nose but they said men with big noses had big dicks. 'Hi.'

He smiled briefly, showing strong white teeth, 'Have you come to see the Dongas?'

'The what?'

'The Dongas. The demonstrators.'

She flicked over a page. 'My gran has.'

He gazed across the hill at Laura's disappearing figure. 'Right. You're not from round here though, are you?'

'No.'

'Thought not. I didn't think I'd seen you here before.'

'You're a regular then are you?'

'Every single one, right from the start.'

'A dedicated follower,' she teased, smiling at him — but coolly, of course.

'So where are you from?'

She told him, adding, so that he would see the sort of dedication he was addressing. 'Actually, Gran's starting up a protest group of her own.'

'Is she though?' he asked.

He looked impressed so she told him all about it, as he leant on the roof of the Land-Rover and listened attentively, his pale eyes focused on her face. They were unusual eyes, so pale blue as to be almost grey and set at an odd angle to one another, the right one slanting more than the left, his eyelashes the same pale sandy colour as his hair. Very unusual eyes. She decided he was even more attractive close to than he'd seemed at a distance — and streets ahead of anything in the sixth form. Mature and sophisticated and very courteous. When she paused at the end of her story, he took out a packet of chewing gum and offered her a stick, which she accepted, pushing back her hair and thinking they were just like the couple in the Wrigley's ad.

'You haven't told me your name,' he hinted.

The pressure pleased her because it showed he was interested. 'No. I haven't, have I?'

'Are you going to?'

'If you tell me yours.' It was wonderful to use her power like this, to see how strongly she was attracting him.

'Kevin.'

'Kevin what?'

'Marshall.'

'Right.'

'Actually,' he said, leaning towards her until they were so close she could smell his aftershave. And very nice too. 'I know who you are. You don't have to tell me. You're Jessica Pendleton.'

She was so surprised she let him see it. 'How did you know that?'

The pale eyes flickered a smile. 'It's on your book.'

'Only on the inside.'

'You had it open when I walked over.'

Sharp, she thought, impressed by his ingenuity. And his interest. But it had probably revealed that she was still at school. 'It's one of my A level texts,' she explained.

Another half-smile showed that her status impressed him. He slid his tongue over his lower lip so as to show her his teeth and went on smiling at her. 'That's what I thought. I did English too.'

'So what do you do now, Kevin Marshall?'

He drew himself up. 'I'm a contractor's PA.'

'Hence the car.'

His pride was touched. He couldn't allow her to think he only drove a company car. 'No, that's mine,' he lied. 'Actually.'

She had recovered enough to be deliberately unimpressed. 'So what's brought you here today?'

'The demo. I told you.'

'So why aren't you up there with the rest of them?'

The truth was that he had instructions to stay near his car phone, but there was no need to tell her that. He admired her for a good second — and it *was* a good second — before he answered. 'There's a better view down here.'

She was flattered, answering him glance for glance. Oh yes, this could be the start of something.

He put one arm casually across the roof of the Land-Rover and moved on to the next stage. 'So what's it like where you live?'

She gave him the standard answer and the standard bored expression. 'Pretty grotty.'

Out on the hillside, Laura was so caught up in the extraordinary atmosphere that, for the first time in her life, she had actually forgotten her family responsibilities and was paying no attention to her granddaughter at all. It was such a cold, windswept place and there was such a sense of impending danger there that it made her feel insignificant and vulnerable. The protesters were really awful-looking people, wild and ragged, with long unkempt hair and dirty faces. They prowled about or stood in small groups waiting and watching, sharp eyed and alert, and their stress was obvious and contagious. It made her realise how far from civilisation she was and how close to harm. There's no cover out here, she thought, shivering. Anything could happen and I couldn't prevent it. I don't belong here. I should never have come.

But that wasn't the way to let her thoughts run and she knew it. She was here now. She took herself in hand and gave herself a silent talking to. Stop all this silly nonsense, Laura Pendleton. Find someone to talk to. Someone sensible who'll tell you what's going on. And she looked around for a suitable candidate.

There was a middle-aged woman standing a few paces away who seemed to be on her own. She was a stolid-looking individual, bulky in a sheepskin coat and a green bobble hat and she

83

was more than happy to talk. Her cheeks were reddened by the cold and her eyes watered in the wind but she was informative and blessedly cheerful. She said her name was Freda and that she lived in Winchester.

'We've trashed their schedule this week,' she said. 'That's why they're bringing in these JCBs. It's been a triumph. Must have set them back weeks.'

Talk of trashing a schedule made Laura feel uncomfortable. 'But you won't stop them, will you,' she said, looking at the hole in the hillside. 'I mean they've started now, haven't they.'

'All the more reason to fight on,' Freda allowed. 'We're going to make life bloody difficult for them and keep this place in the news. The battle isn't over, not by any manner of means. You wait till you see what's going to happen today.'

That brought Laura renewed alarm despite her decision to be sensible. 'What *is* going to happen?' she asked and was annoyed to realise that her voice sounded sharp and that her chest was tightening with a rising and unexpected sensation. I'm afraid, she thought, as she wiped sweaty palms on the sides of her trousers. And yet she felt full of daring too. Even coming to a place like this showed how seriously she was opposing this destruction.

One of the demonstrators stopped beside them to light a cigarette, cupping the match in her mittened hands to shield the flame from the wind.

She blew smoke through her nostrils like a dragon and picked a piece of tobacco from her underlip with dirty fingers. 'ITV's here,' she said to Freda.

She was a slatternly looking girl with a grimed face and long, tatty, straw-coloured hair, like unravelled wool, and she wore the same hideous gear as the others, a patched overcoat, a huge pair of Doc Martens, a silver ring in her nose and five or six assorted rings in one ear. She looked so outlandish that Laura recoiled from her in horror.

'This is Kapok,' Freda said. 'She's a traveller. This is Laura, Kapok. She's come up from Sussex.'

Kapok grinned at her introduction. 'This your first time here?' she asked. And when Laura nodded, 'It's all image these days you know. Not what you do but what you're seen to be doing. We push to get things out in the open and the politicians grovel about to keep 'em covered up. An' we're winning, ain't we Freda. That's why they hate us so much. Stick around and you'll see. Hey-up! Here we go!'

A cry had gone up on the far side of the site, the words echoing across the empty spaces. 'They're coming! They're coming!'

Now Laura was in no doubt about her feelings. She was very, very frightened, her heart beating uncomfortably and her throat taut. She wanted to yell or run away but there wasn't time to do either because the crowd was on the move and she was running with it, panting from the unaccustomed exertion, trembling with excitement, tumbling across the grass with Freda beside her and Kapok streaking ahead. She caught a glimpse of two large yellow machines trundling towards the work site and realised that the crowd were streaming towards it. Ahead of her, protestors had gathered into a dark, threatening mass from which arms waved like tentacles. Angry voices punctured the air. Soon she was close enough to the action to hear what was being said.

'You're bloody trespassing!' a man's voice yelled.

He was answered by a woman, speaking in a middle-class accent and very politely. 'No. I don't think you'll find we are.'

'You're bloody trespassing! And you're holding up the work.'

A third voice joined in. 'Clear off out of it or we'll have you arrested.'

'You can't do that,' the woman's voice said. 'We have a right to walk on this hillside.'

How cool she is, Laura thought, admiring her, and how brave to stand up to him like that. I wonder who she is and where *she's* come from.

The man's voice was rough and furious. 'Oh can't I? Watch me.'

There was a chorus of growls and somebody set up a chant. 'No more roads! No more roads!' A skinny young man with a tom-tom was leaping about at the edge of the group beating time, totally absorbed in what he was doing.

The driver of the nearest JCB had stopped arguing and seemed to be talking into his collar.

'He's got a walkie-talkie,' Freda explained. 'He'll either be calling the police or the security guards.'

There was a swirl of movement behind them as more demonstrators moved in to support their friends. Laura found she was standing next to a young man with dreadlocks who wore a long leather coat down to his ankles and was carrying a walkie-talkie of his own. He spoke into the machine quietly and with authority. 'Right. Right. Got you. That's what we'll do. Right.' Then he walked into the crowd and began to deploy his troops.

'ITV are filming,' he told them as he walked. 'We go in. Right.'

The words reminded Laura of the war. 'What does he mean "go in"?' she wanted to know. But the demonstrators were already taking up positions and she was swept along with them whether she would or no, closer to the JCB and the argument. Some of the younger ones began to climb on to the machine, swarming like monkeys, chanting as they climbed. This is awful, she thought. If the police arrive now it could turn nasty. But she realised she was excited by the prospect as well as anxious.

It wasn't police who arrived. It was a posse of security guards in dark blue boiler suits and bright blue helmets, clutching ribbed truncheons and red-faced for trouble. They ran full tilt at the earth-movers and began to pull the climbers down, grabbing them by the legs and arms, seizing their jackets or any handful of cloth that came to hand. Some were dragged along the ground with their jerseys pulled over their heads as if they were sacks of coal. It was brutally done and there was a lot of swearing.

'Someone'll get hurt,' Laura said, as a young girl with vermilion hair was hauled to the ground and shoved out of the way. 'He can't treat her like that. He'll do her an injury.' She called out to the security guard above the yells and thumps of the struggle. 'Stop that! You'll hurt her.'

The guard took no notice. He was setting about another, even younger girl, a respectable-looking girl with long blonde hair. This time, because she clung to the front wheel on her way down, he hit out with his truncheon. The sight of it put Laura into a fury. To hit a young girl like that! She couldn't be much older than Jess. He would have to be stopped.

'Oh no,' she said. 'I'm not having this!' And without thinking any further, she waded into the melee and whacked the aggressor across the shoulders with her umbrella.

Then several things happened all at once and very quickly. The blonde scrambled out of his grasp and climbed to the top of the digger, shouting 'Bastard! You bastard!', the crowd surged towards them from right and left, answering her cry, the guard turned in a temper and coshed his assailant across the head and shoulders.

For a split second Laura was too stunned to understand what had happened. Then her legs gave way under her and she fell backwards on to the rough chalk, rolled on to her side and lay where she'd fallen with her eyes shut. There was an odd singing in her ears and when she opened her eyes again, she couldn't see more than an inch in front of her, she was so closely hemmed in by jeans and boots. I must get up, she thought, and tell them I'm all right. But she couldn't summon up the energy to do it.

There was a lot of pushing and shoving going on and she sensed that the guard was being man-handled by the crowd. She struggled into a sitting position. 'Don't!' she begged, hanging on to the rough cloth of the nearest pair of jeans for support. 'I'm all right.' Then she realised that there was blood dripping on to the sleeve of her coat and, in a total and unnatural calm, gradually understood that it was her blood and it was coming from the back of her head.

I must stand up, she told herself. I must stand up and get out of this crowd. If I faint I shall be trodden underfoot.

Somebody was kneeling beside her. She had a vague impression that it was a man and that he was removing her woolly hat. The air struck unpleasantly chill on her exposed head and she put up a hand to prevent him. 'I'm all right,' she said, annoyed to hear how weak her voice sounded.

'You are now,' the person answered.

And she looked into his face and it was Jeffrey Turner. 'Good God!' she said. 'What are you doing here?'

'The same as you only with less injury,' he said. 'We'll get you moved out of this scrum and then I can see how bad you are.'

'I don't want you to see how bad I am,' she protested. 'I'm not bad. I told you. I'm all right. Just a bit stunned, that's all.' But he and another man were easing her to her feet and leading her to the side of the crowd.

She sat with her back against a chalk boulder and put her head in her hands and knew she wanted to cry.

'That's a nasty gash,' Jeff said from somewhere above her head. 'It'll need stitches. Stay there and don't move and I'll get a pad.'

She didn't have the energy to argue. Even when she looked up and saw her two new friends striding towards her all anxiety and anger, she hardly had the energy to reassure them.

Jessica had been following the proceedings with growing alarm. She'd seen the two JCBs arrive and watched as the demonstrators formed a line to oppose them, linking hands as the two machines rolled up the chalk towards them. They looked very small and dark against the size of the JCBs and the white dazzle of the earthworks.

'What are they doing?' she asked her new friend.

'Blocking,' he said, casually. 'It's what they always do when new machines arrive.'

'They're not going to just stand there,' Jessica said, suddenly fearful for the little dark figures as the great machines picked up speed. What if Gran were among them? 'They'll get run over.'

He wasn't concerned in the slightest. 'No they won't,' he said. 'The drivers always stop in time. It's a sort of game.'

But it didn't look much like a game to Jessica when the demonstrators clambered on to the machines and the security guards charged in to pull them down. She began to wish she'd gone with her grandmother. She ought to have done, especially as she'd come here to look after her. There was no sign of her in the mass of bodies encircling the two earth-diggers. She could be anywhere. 'I can't see my gran,' she said, leaning forward to peer through the windscreen. 'I didn't realise there were so many of them. I ought to go and find her.'

'I've got a pair of binoculars in the car,' Kevin offered. 'You can borrow them if you like. They're army binoculars. Very powerful.'

It seemed a sensible idea, so she got out of the car and they walked across to the Volvo together. The binoculars were found and handed over. And there was Laura right in the middle of the crowd, as clear as if she were an arm breadth away, with blood running down her neck on to her anorak and her face as pale as the chalk.

'Oh my God!' Jessica said, her heart leaping with alarm. 'She's been hurt. There's blood all over her. Oh Christ! I should have been with her. I must go.' She thrust the binoculars into Kevin's hands. 'Thanks,' she said. And ran.

He was thrown into confusion by the speed of her reaction. 'Don't go,' he begged. She was the best-looking girl he'd met for a very long time. She couldn't just run off and leave him. Not when they'd just got started.

She'd already put a distance between them but she looked back over her shoulder as she ran. 'Must.'

He called after her. 'Shall I see you again?'

She stopped for a second, poised to run again, hesitated, made a quick decision. 'Ring me,' she called. 'Burswood 284737.' Then she ran on and didn't look back. Poor Gran! she was thinking. Oh God, I should have gone with her. All that blood! Don't let it be bad, please God.

It was a relief that she found her with comparative ease and an even greater one when Laura looked up and smiled in her old wide-mouthed way. 'Don't fuss. I'm all right. It's only a cut.' But it was a limited relief. She was still in a panic of guilt and concern.

She sat on the chalk beside her grandmother and put an arm round her blood-damp shoulder to cuddle her fiercely. 'Who did it?' she said.

The group gathered protectively around them told the tale with varying degrees of accuracy and embellishment. Laura closed her eyes and let them get on with it even though they were making a drama out of it and exaggerating terribly. Her head was beginning to throb and she could feel that the cut was still bleeding. The hair on the nape of her neck was quite sticky with blood.

Perhaps she *would* have to have stitches. But how on earth would she get to the hospital? She was too shaky to drive and Jessica hadn't learnt yet. And then there was the long drive home. She'd never manage *that* in her present state. Not all along that motorway. I should never have come, she thought. I knew it was wrong.

The little crowd parted to make way for Jeffrey's return. He'd brought a box with him, grey metal with a red cross on the lid. Where had he got *that* from? 'This is Jessica,' she explained to him. 'My granddaughter.'

He acknowledged the introduction with a nod. 'If you'd just move to one side for a little while,' he said to the girl. 'I'll get your grandmother tidied up.'

Jessica bristled at him, furious at being given orders and especially by a stranger. 'Shouldn't she see a nurse or something?' she said, giving him a disparaging look.

He took a dressing out of the box. 'I am a nurse.'

That was a surprise to them both. 'Are you?' Laura said.

'Yes. Just turn your head a bit. This way. That's fine. Good. Good. Now if you could hold the pad, Jessica, while I bandage it in position.' He worked deftly, smiling at his patient whenever she looked at him. 'I'm the company nurse at your sister-in-law's firm. Didn't she tell you? That's how she met me. She had a headache and came down to the surgery for an aspirin. There, that's fixed. Now if you can just walk to where the cars are parked, I'll take you to hospital.'

Laura stood up, annoyed to be feeling so shaky that she had to cling to Jessica for support.

'Can you manage?' he asked.

Now she was annoyed to have her competence questioned. 'Yes, of course. I'm fine.'

He didn't argue with her, but took her other arm so that she was supported on both sides. 'Take your time,' he said. 'There's no rush.'

They stumbled over the chalk together, walking very slowly. The demonstration was still going noisily on with two cameras in close attendance and the security guards in furious action round the two JCBs.

'Your coat's in a dreadful mess,' Laura said to Jessica.

Now that Laura was being taken care of, Jessica was feeling a little less guilty. 'It'll wash out,' she said. 'I'll put salt on it or something. Anyway so is yours. We're a proper pair.'

Laura looked at the stains on her own coat. 'Your father would say we were a most *improper* pair. Oh Jess! He'll be so cross.'

'Now don't you go worrying about him, you dear old Granny. I'll handle him.'

Below them, a man in a camel coat had gathered a crowd and was making a speech. Scraps of it blew towards them on the wind '. . . we don't want this road. We don't want it and we don't need it . . . don't want the deaths it will bring, nor the injuries, nor the pollution . . . lead in our children's lungs . . . asthma . . . this year alone the increase . . . We are told we need these roads because of the economy . . . absolutely the reverse. Why do we have to transport food for thousands of miles when we can buy the same produce, locally grown, cheaper, fresher and easy to come by, in our own market towns? . . . it's a nonsense . . .'

I should be down there listening, Laura thought, as she stumbled on. This is the sort of thing I ought to know about. But she couldn't get her brain into focus.

They reached the coaches and cars. She noticed that the blue Volvo was gone, its space taken by a motorbike and side-car. Jeffrey Turner's vehicle turned out to be a dilapidated red Escort, which was the sort of car she expected. Dilapidated or not she was relieved to have reached it and glad to ease herself into the passenger seat, out of the wind and with no need to walk any further.

Jeffrey was busy organising. 'Let's have your car locked, then I'll just wrap this blanket round you and we'll be off.'

She let him look after her, glad that she wouldn't have to drive. She was suddenly very, very tired.

Chapter Six

When Laura arrived on that Sunday afternoon, the Accident and Emergency Department of the Royal Hampshire Hospital was full of weekend casualties, sportsmen still in full kit with blankets over their shoulders, subdued children sitting anxiously beside their mothers while their healthy siblings made havoc in the nursery area. There was a young girl in one corner nursing a blood-stained hand, a young man in the other ashen-faced with distress and between them two old men sitting side by side, wheezing and raggedly patient.

Above their heads a long scrolling screen presented a series of messages in neon red, round and round and round, with computer monotony:

Welcome to Accident and Emergency. Please report to the nurse on arrival. There are two doctors on duty. The waiting time to be seen is approx 40 minutes. Please do not use your mobile phone in the waiting area. Mobile phones affect vital life support systems. Welcome to Accident and Emergency . . .

Jessica had been biting her nails with guilt all though the journey there. Now she exploded into irritability. 'Oh for heaven's sake!' she said, surveying the crowd. 'Look at them all. Two doctors for all this lot! It's ridiculous. We shall be here for ever.'

'That's the way things are in the NHS nowadays,' Jeff told her and he turned to Laura with a wry smile. 'I don't suppose you've got private health cover have you?'

'No,' Laura said, her mouth turned down in a grimace that was part regret and part self-deprecation.

'That's what I thought,' he said. 'Stay here and I'll find the staff nurse and check you in.'

Staff was a cheerful young woman. She examined her patient briefly, told her that she'd need a few stitches, checked that movement in her shoulder wasn't impeded and agreed that she would probably have quite a long wait.

'You chose a bad time to get hurt,' she said as she wrote up her notes. 'It's always like this at the weekends, what with sport and that demonstration. How did it happen?'

There was no way Laura was going to tell her story and confess to hitting a security guard. She stood, hoping that the examination was over — and Staff smiled at her to agree.

They trailed back to the chairs, found three that weren't occupied and settled down to their wait, making desultory conversation as the minutes slummocked by. After the speed and drama of the demonstration and their rapid drive to Winchester, Laura felt devitalised, as if time had been switched off and all her energy had been drained away. She sat very still, enduring a pulsing headache and gazing emptily at the pale green walls, the brightness of that rolling screen, the dull brown sisal of the carpet.

Jessica was still fierce. 'This is all my fault,' she said, her blue eyes strained. 'I should've been with you.'

Jeff tried to comfort her by dismissing the idea. 'It wouldn't have made any difference.'

'How do you know?' she said, rounding on him angrily. 'You've only known her five minutes. You don't know anything about her. I could have stopped her whacking out at that guard and then none of this would have happened.'

Laura gathered what little energy she had, ready to placate her. But Jeff wasn't thrown by her anger at all.

'You're right,' he allowed easily. 'I haven't known your grandmother very long. That's true. But I can tell you one thing about her. If she's made up her mind to do something, no one in the world could stop her. You don't have to know her live minutes to find that out.'

It was a compliment, as Laura realised, and she was warmed by it, even though Jessica was still scowling. 'Actually, I don't know what got into me,' she apologised. 'I'm not normally a violent person. Am I, Jess?'

'No,' Jessica said loyally. 'You're not. You're very gentle.' And she gave Jeff a bold look as if to say, *'Now disagree with that.'*

'It's crowd psychology,' he said succinctly. 'Comes of being a herding animal, so they say.

Individuality gets taken over by the mentality of the herd. It catches us all the first time. You'll get used to it.'

'I'm not going to make a habit of it,' Laura said, her pleasure in his compliment melted away by annoyance at being misjudged. 'If I've learned one thing this afternoon, it's that *that* isn't the way to oppose a road building scheme.'

He was giving her his mocking look. 'And what is?'

'Anything legal,' she said. 'Petitions, public meetings, things that are serious. Respectable things. All that prancing about and shouting just infuriates people.'

For a second he looked as though he was going to argue with her. But then he changed his expression and stood up. 'I don't know about you two,' he said. 'But I could do with a sandwich and a cup of coffee. What could you fancy?'

Jessica was scathing. 'Where will you get it? They won't have a canteen in *this* place. 'Specially on a Sunday.'

'There's a whole big city just down the hill,' he teased her. 'Called Winchester. I'll find something. So, what'll it be?'

Waiting for him to return used up another ponderous half hour, eating his impromptu picnic took another twenty minutes. The bloodstained girl was called and escorted through the swing doors. But their long wait went on.

'We've been here *hours!*' Jessica said, sighing dramatically. 'Why don't they get another doctor or something? I think we ought to complain.'

Jeff tried to reassure. 'It won't be long now.'

'Long? It's endless! She could be bleeding to death for all they care.'

'But she isn't, is she.'

Being talked about in the third person made Laura feel ignored and cross. '*She*'s sitting in front of you,' she rebuked. 'She's me, if you don't mind. And I haven't lost the power of speech or my wits. Or my marbles, come to that. I'm quite capable of speaking up for myself.'

It was a relief to all of them that a nurse was walking towards them, businesslike in her blue and white striped uniform, her waist cinched by a neat red belt. 'Mrs Pendleton? If you'll come this way.'

'And not before time,' Jessica said. But Laura was already through the swing doors.

The doctor was as tired as she was but he examined her carefully, accepted her vague story about a ladder falling on her, gave her an anti-tetanus jab, stitched her up and pronounced her fit apart from the wound to the back of her head.

'No sign of concussion,' he said. 'Your shoulder bore the brunt of it. No bones broken. But I'd take things easy for the next twenty-four hours, if I were you. It's just possible it might be delayed — the concussion, I mean. I don't think so, or I'd keep you in, but take it easy anyway, just to be on the safe side.'

'Home for you,' Jeff said, when she emerged

into the waiting room again, stitched and bandaged but smiling with relief.

'If you could just drive me back to my car . . .' she suggested.

He wouldn't hear of it. 'I'm taking you home,' he said. And did.

It was late afternoon before he finally drove them into Laura's Way and by then the rain had set in so heavily and the light was so poor that he was using his headlights. But he could see what a pretty house it was, even in those conditions.

'So this is what you're fighting for,' he said, as he edged into the driveway and crunched towards the kitchen door.

Laura looked at the cottage too. 'This is what I'm fighting for,' she agreed. 'And I shall go on fighting for it. Nobody's taking my home away from me.' She was looking for Amy's car, but it wasn't on either drive so, with luck, perhaps she was out. I do hope so, she thought. I'm in no fit state to cope with Amy. Not after all this. 'I feel as if I've been away for a week,' she said. 'Just look at this rain!'

'Use your umbrella,' Jeff suggested.

'It's a bit bent,' Laura said, examining it. 'I don't suppose it'll open.'

But it did and although it was lopsided and decidedly tatty it kept both women more or less dry as they scuttled out of the car and into the kitchen. To Laura's relief, there was no sign of Amy in the cottage either, apart from a lipsticked coffee cup on the draining board, a dog-eared

101

paperback on one of the sofas and a mound of ash and dog-ends under the busy lizzie.

'Is your sister-in-law not here?' Jeff asked.

His voice was so deliberately casual that Laura was alerted. Ah! she thought, so that's the way the wind blows. 'Sorry to disappoint you. No. She's not.'

He grew huffy so quickly she knew she'd hit a nerve. 'You're not disappointing me,' he said. 'I only wondered. I thought she'd be company for you. When are you expecting her home?'

'I've no idea. She's a law unto herself.'

Jessica had been hanging up her coat. Now she took the umbrella from her grandmother and did her best to furl it. 'Your hands are like ice,' she said.

'Well it's cold.'

'But you shouldn't be as cold as that. Should she Jeff?'

He became his professional self again, touching her hands, briefly and thoughtfully. 'No. She shouldn't. Is that a coal fire?'

'Logs,' Laura told him.

'Make her a pot of tea,' he said to Jessica, 'while I light that fire. Have you got a blanket or a rug anywhere Laura?'

Within ten minutes, the tea was made, the fire lit and Laura was tucked up on one of the sofas with a rug round her knees, declaring she felt very silly to be fussed over so.

He paid no attention to that at all. 'Now you need feeding,' he said. 'What's in the fridge?'

There was a chicken she'd intended to cook for herself and Amy.

'You're not cooking for *Amy*,' Jessica rebuked. 'Dad 'ud be *furious*.'

'I've got a much better idea,' Jeff said. 'We'll cook it for *you*, won't we Jessica?'

'*I'll* cook it for her,' Jessica said.

'Many hands make light work,' he argued.

Laura wasn't sure. 'That's carrying nursing care a bit far, don't you think.'

'It's to settle my guilty conscience,' he told her.

She couldn't read the expression on his face which surprised her a little because she prided herself on her skill with body cues and expressions. Was it mocking? Deprecating? Sly, even? 'What guilty conscience?'

He explained — patiently but with the same expression on his face. 'If I hadn't told you about Twyford Down, you wouldn't have gone there, and if you hadn't gone there you wouldn't have been injured.'

'Quite right,' Jessica said, glad to offload some of her own guilt.

Laura dismissed it out of hand. 'I'd have gone to a protest sooner or later, to see what it was like. Your influence was minimal.'

That provoked a grin. 'Then you must let me cook for you because I like cooking.'

'So do I.'

He turned to Jessica for help. 'Is she always so stubborn?'

Jessica had been enjoying the argument, delighted to watch her grandmother getting the best of him. 'Worse sometimes,' she said. 'OK then Gran. We'll all cook it together. How about that? I could make a blackberry and apple pie, if there are any blackberries.'

'Masses,' Laura told her. 'It's been a good year.'

'That's agreed then?' he asked.

'On one condition.'

'Which is?'

'That you stay here and share it with us. Unless you've got other plans, that is.' Now let's see what you've got to say to that.

He checked his watch. 'I ought to be home by nine o'clock,' he said. 'Until then my time's my own. So it's a bargain. Right Jessica, off we go.'

It was a very good meal. Even Laura had to admit that, although the chicken wasn't as crisply cooked as she would have liked and the bread sauce was rather lumpy. But the vegetables were steamed and Jessica's pie was very nearly perfection.

'I haven't been as spoilt as this for a long time,' Laura told them, as Jessica brought in the coffee. 'I can see I shall have to get my head split open more often.'

They were all in a very mellow mood now. Jeff grinned at her, his beard bristling. 'You're on your own if there's a repeat performance.'

It was almost time for the news. 'D'you want it on?' Jessica asked eagerly. 'We might be on it.'

'We?' Laura laughed.

'You know what I mean. The demonstration.'

It was the lead story, to Jessica's delight and Laura's perturbation. She watched as the camera panned over jostling bodies, lingering over tangled hair and a forest of punching fists, recognized the young man with dreadlocks whispering into his walkie-talkie and winced as the cameraman suddenly zoomed in on the dark cavern of a bellowing mouth. 'They make it look so ugly.'

And then suddenly there she was herself, sitting with her head in her hands and blood running down her fingers. And there was Jess, kneeling beside her, shouting at someone off screen, her face distorted with fury.

'Oh my goodness,' Laura said. 'How did they do that? I didn't know there were cameras *there*.' She felt aggrieved to have been caught in such an undignified state. It wasn't the way she saw herself at all. Then another thought struck her. 'Oh Jess! What will your father say?'

But there wasn't time to consider the implications because there was a sudden roar of approaching cars, a swirl of gravel outside the windows, then a cacophony of door-slamming, feet running and loud voices shouting and guffawing. And Amy burst in through the kitchen door with so many people tumbling in after her that in less than a second they had erupted out of the little space of the kitchen and were filling the living room.

They were all young and loud, the men in jeans and T-shirts, the women in party gear of every description, and they all seemed to be carrying things. One had a ghetto-blaster the size of a suitcase, some carried crates of beer, others had wine bottles. One girl, wearing six-inch heels, was making a great to-do of staggering in with six packets of crisps.

'Well hi!' Amy cried, making a bee-line for Jeff and kissing him on both cheeks. 'You got my message then. Great!'

'Where d'you want the lager?' a dark haired youth demanded. From the look of him a great deal of it was already inside him.

'Anywhere'll do,' Amy said expansively. 'Use the table.'

Laura struggled off the sofa to pre-empt him. Her head was aching again and there was so much happening she felt she couldn't cope with it all but she was noticing things as if she were on automatic pilot. Jessica looked stunned, Jeff slightly shamefaced, Amy was flushed. With drink? Or excitement? The teetering girl was taking the best glasses out of the cabinet and banging them down on the table. There was another girl giggling out of the kitchen with a bowl full of ice cubes, slopping them about as she staggered back into the room. It was like being invaded.

It took considerable effort to speak up under such an assault but it had to be done. 'Just a minute,' Laura said, holding out a preventing hand to the dark-haired youth. 'Not on my best cloth, if you don't mind.'

'Well where then?' he said, frowning at her.

'Now look,' Laura said to Amy. 'What *is* all this?'

'It's my starting-work party, darling,' Amy said.

'You never said anything about it to me.'

'You're invited too, darling. Naturally. Hurry up with that lager Nigel, there's a sweetie.'

The ghetto-blaster had been plugged in and was thudding like a sledgehammer. 'Turn that thing off,' Laura said.

'Oh come on Laur,' Amy protested. 'We can't have a party without music. Can we kids?'

'You haven't understood me, have you,' Laura said. 'You can't have a party at all. At least not here. This is my house, in case you hadn't noticed and I need it to be quiet.'

'It can be quiet tomorrow.'

'I need it quiet now.'

'What on earth for?'

Laura walked across the room until she and Amy were standing toe to toe and she was sure she could be heard. 'I've been in hospital all afternoon, having my head stitched up. See? I'm supposed to be resting. A party's the last thing I want.'

She was appalled when Amy took no notice of what she'd just been told. Then she realised that her sister-in-law was bright with drink. 'It'll cheer you up,' she said smiling vacantly. 'Bring a bit of life to the old place, eh Jeff?'

Jeff was caught between his interest in one woman and his professional concern for the other. But before he could say anything Laura turned away from them both and pushed her way into the group to talk to Jessica.

'I think you ought to go home, my darling,' she said, putting her face close to Jessica's so as to be heard. 'We've got a lot of drunks here.'

Jessica grinned at that. 'I can handle drunks.'

'I'm sure you can,' Laura agreed, and moved on to her second and more pressing reason. 'But you ought to go home just the same. If they've seen the news they'll be worrying. We don't want your poor mother worrying, do we.'

That *was* a good reason and Jessica could see it. 'Well . . .'

'You will go, then,' Laura urged.

'If you think you'll be all right.'

'I shall be fine. I'm much better now.'

'Well if you're sure . . .'

The party-goers were opening bottles and dancing and shouting and dropping crisps on the carpet. Jessica and Laura kissed one another goodbye, and Laura felt she was losing her only ally.

'Mind how you go,' she said. 'I hope he's not too cross.'

'I'll ring,' Jessica promised and she slid through the mass of bodies into the kitchen and was gone.

'Now then,' Laura said, metaphorically rolling up her sleeves. 'This has got to stop. You'll have to go somewhere else.'

Amy had reached the scowling stage of drunkenness. 'You're such a kill-joy!' she said. 'It's no wonder Pete got sick of you.'

The criticism stung. Cruelly. 'We're not talking about Pete, we're talking about this . . .'

'A kill-joy,' Amy insisted. 'I can quite *see* why he wanted to leave you if that's the way you went on all the time. Quite see.'

'He didn't want to leave me,' Laura said hotly. 'And in any case, that isn't the point.' But she was thinking, *How did you know?*

'What's up?' one of the girls asked.

Laura knew that her cheeks were hot with embarrassment and distress but she persisted. 'You can't have your party here,' she told the girl. 'You'll have to find somewhere else.'

The girl was as bold as Amy. 'Why not? It's plenty big enough. Just the right place I should have said.'

'I'm not well,' Laura said and was annoyed with herself for sounding feeble. Like some awful old woman wittering away about her ailments. 'I've had . . . an accident. Look.' She turned her head so that the girl could see the stitches, hoping that the sight of them would persuade her of the need for quiet. But it provoked quite the wrong sort of attention and a great deal more of it than she bargained for.

'Here, come an' look at this, Charles!' the girl said, her voice thrilled. 'She's got all stitches in her head. Tracey, Carole, come an' look at this. All down there look. What was it? A car crash?'

'What car crash?' another voice said. 'Let's have a look.'

There were bodies charging towards her from

every side and that awful ghetto-blaster was pounding a hole in her skull. 'Please!' she begged. 'Please go away!' But her voice was lost in the din. 'Please!'

Somebody had turned off the ghetto-blaster. Thank God for that. Somebody was shouting above the din. 'Hold on. Just a minute.' The noise was diminishing. She looked up, feeling grateful to the speaker, whoever it was, and saw that Jeff was standing on a kitchen chair, holding up his hands for quiet.

'You can come to my place if you like,' he said when most of them were listening to him. 'I've got a flat on the sea front. You're welcome there if you like.'

They yelled agreement. 'Yeh! yeh!' Gathered up their things. Wedged into the kitchen laughing and giggling. Two of them were taking Laura's best glasses with them but she was too down to stop them. She didn't care what they did so long as they went away.

For five more battering minutes, they charged in and out of the kitchen door, pulsing cold air and raucous noise back into the house. Then car doors banged, engines were revved up, last minute instructions shrieked and the convoy racketed away.

The silence in the house was the most blissful thing Laura had ever experienced. She removed the rest of her glasses from the table, put two more logs on the fire, found her library book, wrapped herself in her rug and settled down on the sofa to recover.

Presently she could hear one of the cats scratching at the door that separated the inner hall from the living room. So she got up to let it in and found that all three of her pets were in the hall, Jack, the tabby, beside the door, Queenie and Ace waiting patiently on the stairs.

'They've all gone,' she told them. 'You can come down now. We've got our house back again.'

They stalked into the room one behind the other and took possession of it, in the lordly way of all felines, Ace on the hearthrug, languidly washing his face, Jack and Queenie on the sofas, sprawled out and smug with satisfaction.

You know where you are with cats, Laura thought, admiring them. They never disappoint you, which is more than you can say for human beings. They're independent and hoity-toity and charming and totally uncompromising. They'll give you their affection when they feel like it and if they don't feel like it you must learn to live without it. Even their unpredictability is predictable.

Queenie crept on to Laura's lap where she curled into a comfortable position and began to purr. 'Yes,' Laura said stroking her long fur. 'You're the best. You're all the best.'

And yet, she thought, he *had* been very kind to her, especially at the start just after she'd been hurt. And driving her to the hospital like that and all the way back here was well above the call of

111

duty. She remembered his voice calming her and his hands parting her hair, warm, gentle hands although they were obviously strong too. You only had to look at them to see that. The kind of hands to make you feel confident and cared for. 'In good hands', as they say. He's a good nurse, that's what it is, she thought. A good nurse but a fool over women. The way he looked at Amy when she arrived was enough to make anyone sick. Well, she thought, stroking Queenie, he'll live to regret it, poor fool. She might look attractive, but none of her love affairs has ever lasted. He'll soon find out how selfish she is.

Ace had finished his ablutions. Now he jumped neatly on to her sofa and flung himself down beside her knees. The logs shifted position, hissing and crackling, the clock on the wall ticked like a quiet heart, all three cats were purring rhythmically. The cottage hunkered down into its customary peacefulness.

But I've been selfish too, Laura thought. I took Jessica with me, when I knew it could be dangerous. That was selfish and silly. Whatever else I mustn't involve my family in all this. And I must see to it that my group always acts lawfully.

Chapter Seven

Jessica took her time to cycle home that evening. It was dark and wet and there was quite a lot of traffic on the roads so she had good cause to be careful but the real reason for her lack of speed was her reluctance to face her father.

Perhaps he'll be out, she hoped, as she swung into the lawned close of Canterbury Gardens. But no such luck. Even before she reached the drive she could see the blue flicker of the television screen through a gap in the curtains and the unmistakable shadow of his profile as he sat on the black settee watching in his serious way. There was no avoiding him. He had the front door open before she'd put her bike in the garage and his face was furious.

'What sort of time do you call this?' he demanded.

She tried flippancy, making a great play of looking at her wrist. 'Wart past mole?'

That made him worse. 'Get inside!' he ordered, pointing her into the house. 'And try not to be so bloody stupid.'

She took her time putting her bike away, answering him coolly. 'I'm not a baby, Dad! You've got no right to boss me about.'

'You live under *my* roof,' he told her. 'And

while you live under my roof I've got every right.'
He stood aside and waved her peremptorily into
the house, scowling at her horribly.

Maureen and Daniel were in the hall, walking
towards her and both speaking at once.

Maureen was saying, 'We've just seen it on the
news. Oh Jess, why didn't you phone and warn
us?'

And Daniel, his eyes round with the excitement
of it, 'You're covered in blood. Look at you.
You're covered all over in blood.'

'It's not mine,' Jessica said with studied insouciance. 'It's Gran's.' And turning to her father,
'Your mother's, in case you're interested.'

David had been taut with anxiety ever since he
saw the news. Now he couldn't contain his feelings. 'Rude little thing,' he roared at her. 'How
dare you talk to me like that!' He was so angry
his ears were bright red.

His anger frightened her so much that she
sneered at him. 'The truth hurts, doesn't it.'

'Oh Jess! Shush!' her mother tried.

But too much damage was done. 'Go to your
room this instant,' he roared. 'I can't bear the
sight of you.'

Jessica was very near tears but she fought back
valiantly. 'The feeling's mutual,' she said and she
climbed the stairs — slowly, her head held high
and her expression under rigid control so as not
to give him the satisfaction of seeing her weep. I
could have been hurt too, she thought. He doesn't
care.

Upstairs in her white bedroom, she switched on her bedside lamp, sat on the white bed and took off her coat to examine it. Poor old Gran, she thought, rubbing her thumb over the stains. She *did* bleed. I suppose I ought to try and wash some of this out. But she felt too exhausted to start washing clothes, and too upset. So she dropped it on the carpet instead and flung herself backwards on the duvet to rest, glancing sideways at her wardrobe mirror to see how upset she looked.

She was surprised by how brown her face was and what red cheeks she had. She'd half hoped to look pale and interesting. I must have got tanned by the wind, she thought. It was cold enough out there to tan an elephant. God, what a day it's been! I shall have something to tell Emma and the others tomorrow. I wonder if that Kevin will ring me. She wasn't quite sure whether she wanted him to or not. It had all been a bit too quick for her to be certain what she felt about him. But it was nice to speculate and nice to recall how much she'd been admired — especially when her father had just been so foul. She remembered the young man's voice saying *'It's a better view down here'* and the look on his face as he said it. And quite right too, she thought. I'm pretty so why shouldn't men admire me?

She fluttered her fingers for effect and was charmed to see that her nails were shell pink in the light from her bedside lamp. Then she arranged her hair so that it tumbled over her shoul-

115

ders in a long blonde swathe and thought how romantic it looked. It would serve Dad right if I just walked out of here one morning and got married, she told her reflection. He shouldn't treat me like this. It's not fair. It wasn't my fault that foul man attacked poor old Gran. He ought to show some sympathy for her. It wouldn't kill him. If he'd been attacked we'd never have heard the end of it. You'd have thought at the very least he'd have asked how she was instead of taking a pop at me.

Someone was coming upstairs. Mum, she could tell from the soft footsteps. The door was opened — tentatively — and her mother's face peered round the edge.

'Are you all right?'

Jessica didn't move from her position on the bed and she managed to make her answer criticism, endurance and dismissal all at once. 'I'm fine. What d'you expect?'

'Have you had anything to eat?'

Jessica was warmed by her mother's concern but she didn't show it and she didn't say anything about the meal she'd eaten at Laura's Way either. 'Eat?' she said. 'After the way he went on at me? I'd choke.'

'Yes but you must have something. You can't go without food.'

'Tell *him* that. He's well out of line. He doesn't care about anybody.'

'Oh darling he does. He's downstairs phoning your grandmother now. He only shouted at you

116

because he was so worried.'

Now her mother's kindness provoked tears. 'Oh Mum!' she wailed. 'It's so unfair.'

Maureen was into the room and had her weeping daughter in her arms in a second. The tale was told — with certain omissions — sympathy given, tears dried.

'He doesn't mean it, you know,' Maureen said. 'His bark's worse than his bite.'

Jessica sniffed back her tears. 'Well I wish he wouldn't bark, that's all. Other men don't. That Jeff was ever so nice. You should have seen the way he looked after Gran. He stayed with her all afternoon.' *And I'll bet Kevin wouldn't bark either.*

'Better now?' Maureen hoped. 'That's good. You just stay up here quietly. You've got your television. I'll sneak you up a tray later on.'

It was lonely in the bedroom alter she'd gone and there wasn't anything on the box worth watching, until the film. Jessica washed her face and brushed her hair, listening to the sounds of life below her. Then she took out her diary and settled down to write up her adventures.

'Thanks to my father, I am imprisoned in my room, suffering a surfeit of silence.'

The phrase pleased her. 'A surfeit of silence.' It was very good. *When I'm a Booker Prize winner,* she dreamed, *won't he just have to eat his words then.*

In his flat on the sea front at Rustington, Jeff

Turner was suffering a surfeit of noise.

When he'd made his offer to give the party house room, he hadn't stopped to consider what a squash it would be nor to assess how many of his guests had reached the irresponsible stage of drunkenness. He'd acted on impulse, partly to help Laura and partly to grab the chance to spend time with the glamorous Amy. Now he was learning the hard way. In his tiny living room the noise of the ghetto-blaster was ear-shattering, there were people eating and drinking in all three rooms, two half-dressed couples were sprawled across his bed, well away, and the young man with black hair was being sick in the sink.

Amy wasn't paying attention to any of it. She was riotously happy, dancing with two young men at once and flirting with them both. She'd sent one of her new friends out to replenish the drink supplies but, apart from that, her guests could look after themselves.

'Now this is what I call a party,' she beamed at Jeff, as he squeezed past her to rescue a couple of discarded glasses that were in danger of being trampled into the carpet.

'Glad to be of service,' he called back. And then felt foolish because he wasn't trying 'to be of service', he was on the pull and he knew it and was feeling ashamed of it.

The young man with black hair staggered out of the kitchen and collapsed into Jeff's easy chair, his face the colour of cream cheese. 'Oh God!' he said. 'I do feel bad.'

'Cheer up!' one of the girls said as she danced past. 'We've sent for reinforcements.'

Not more people, Jeff thought. I've got quite enough with this lot. But he could hardly turn them away, could he? Perhaps she's joking.

It was a vain hope. The drinks brigade returned mob-handed with six new guests and more six-packs than he could count.

'Smashing party!' a young man with glasses said, opening a can with a flourish that sprayed the contents across the piano keys. 'Reggie said to come. He's gone off home. Can't think why. Is there any grub?'

'You'd better ask Amy,' Jeff told him, closing the piano. 'The one in red.' He was beginning to have second thoughts about the glamorous Amy.

Two of the girls were chortling out of the kitchen bearing plates of sandwiches and sausages on sticks. The party guests descended upon them, hands outstretched.

Jeff realised with some relief that he was standing next to somebody nearer his own age and that it was somebody he knew, Toby Fawcett from the *Burswood Gazette*, fair hair tied back in its familiar ponytail, round glasses on the end of his nose.

'Hello Jeff,' he said.

'Where's Kate?' Jeff asked, looking round for Toby's partner.

'At one of her women's meetings. You know Kate. I didn't realise this was your party.'

'Neither did I,' Jeff told him. 'Actually it's hers.'

Nodding towards Amy who was still gyrating in the middle of the living room.

Toby Fawcett wasn't impressed by Amy Pendleton although he could see how attractive she was. 'Not my type,' he said. 'Where d'you find her?'

'Work. She's the new senior sales manager at Beautibelles.'

'That figures,' Toby grinned as he took a can of Fosters from the girl who was standing next to him. 'Ta, sweetie. So she talked you into it, is that it?'

There was no way Jeff could let that pass. It made him sound like a wimp. 'No, no. Nothing like that,' he corrected. 'I volunteered.'

Toby was drinking thirstily. 'Then you're either a noble soul,' he said, wiping his lips on the back of his hand. 'Or a prat.'

Jeff's male pride was piqued again. 'It's a long story,' he explained. 'I was up at Twyford Down this morning and someone got walloped by a security guard. I had to take her home and there was this party and I thought she could do without that on top of everything else.'

'Now that sounds like a story for me,' the reporter said. 'Local is she?'

'Amy's sister-in-law, actually. Lives in Laura's Way.'

'Ah! Is she a dazzler too?'

Jeff had a sudden and vivid recollection of Laura Pendleton's speckled eyes and the tangle of that uncompromising hair. 'No,' he said.

'You'd like her. There's something really nice about her. She's the genuine article.'

'So tell me,' Toby said.

The party thumped raucously on. At a quarter past twelve one of the neighbours arrived in his dressing gown to complain about the noise. At a little after two the owner of the ghetto-blaster finally took his music home and several of the noisier elements departed with him. By now the dancers had collapsed in exhausted heaps all over the living room and the remaining pair of lovers were fast asleep on the bed.

'I shall have to be making a move,' Toby said, pushing his glasses up his nose. 'Kate'll be wondering where I am.'

'We all will,' Amy agreed, smiling up from the male bosom she was using as a pillow.

It seemed a possible moment for Jeff to make his play. 'How will you get home?' he asked her. If she said she didn't know he would offer to put her up for the night.

She turned her head and addressed the owner of the bosom. 'Walk, won't we Conrad?'

'Yep!' Conrad said happily. 'It isn't far.'

Despite being schooled in such reverses it was a disappointment. I don't know why I try, Jeff thought, gazing at the wreckage of his room. All this mess and she's going to swan off with somebody else.

'Two of your friends are asleep on my bed,' he said, disguising his disappointment by being de-

121

liberately laconic. 'Wake them up before you go, will you.'

Toby was standing by the window looking out. 'Rain's stopped,' he told them. 'It's a beautiful night.'

Not to me it isn't, Jeff thought. And then felt ashamed at himself for being so sour and ashamed of himself for trying to pull a woman who wasn't interested in him and ashamed of himself for letting her friends wreck his house. 'We shall have thick heads in the morning,' he warned.

'Speak for yourself,' Toby said, admiring the moon. It was full and silvery white and hung like a paper lantern over the black expanse of the sea. Now that the wind had stopped, the sea was calm and the waves rippling in to shore were as white as cream. 'I shall have the clearest head in the business. I'm going to interview your patient.'

Chapter Eight

The first thing Laura did as soon as she was dressed the next morning was to phone Jessica. Niggling pain from her stitches had woken her several times during the night and wakefulness had given her time to wonder and worry about her. David hadn't said anything about her the night before and she hadn't rung as she'd promised either.

As if to make amends for the rain and strain of the previous evening, it was a beautiful, tranquil morning, the sky summer blue and full of fleecy cloud, the trees glossy with sunshine, the living room flooded with mellow light. As she dialled the number, a robin was singing its shrill sweet song in the branches of the may tree just outside the window.

'I'm sorry,' Maureen's voice answered. 'She isn't here. She went before we were up.'

Despite the gentleness of voice and morning, that sounded disturbing. 'Is she all right?'

'Oh yes,' Maureen reassured, 'she's fine.' And speaking quietly and confidentially, 'She's just avoiding her father, that's all.'

I knew it, Laura thought. Poor Jess. 'They had a row.'

'Well you know David,' Maureen smoothed.

'It's all right. She's gone to Emma's. She left me a note. I shall see her in school. That's the one good thing about working in the same place.'

'Give her my love,' Laura said. 'And thank David for phoning me yesterday. I was a bit short with him.'

'He understood that,' Maureen said. 'Any other message?'

'Tell him I'm a lot better.'

'How will you manage without your car?'

'I'll get a taxi.'

'I'll come over after school tonight and take you to collect it, if you like.'

The offer was a surprise and a very pleasant one. 'That's very good of you.'

'I'll be a bit late,' Maureen warned. 'It's staff meetings on Mondays. But I'll be there, I promise. See you then.'

'Isn't that kind,' Laura said to the cats who were sitting in their customary places on the window sills waiting to be fed. 'Yes, yes, all right, you poor starving things, I'll feed you first.'

But she'd barely had a chance to open the tins before Mr Fennimore was bustling in through the door with a brown paper bag in his hand.

He was sharp-nosed with excitement. 'How's your head?' he said, looking at it. 'Gaw, dearie me! They made a right old mess of you, didn't they. Rotten buggers. We seen it on the telly. They want stringing up, the lot of 'em. That's what I think.'

Laura wasn't sure she wanted to discuss it. 'It

was all a bit silly really.'

But Mr Fennimore was staring at her stitches, deeply impressed. 'All them stitches!' he said. 'You're a heroine. You ought to tell the papers. Be all over the front page, I'll bet.'

Laura had no desire to be all over the front page and certainly not for being coshed by a security guard. 'Are those the snaps?' she asked, looking at the paper bag.

He took a pile of photographs out of the bag and spread them over the table, full of importance. 'Look at that badger. D'you ever see such a good shot? An' we got a flock of greenfinches, an a robin an' a thrush singing. That sort a' thing should do it, don't you think. They'll think twice about that old road with snaps like this, eh?'

His enthusiasm was so touching, Laura didn't have it in her heart to put him wise, but she felt as if she'd travelled a thousand miles since she saw him last.

'Is someone taking pictures of Laura's Way?' she asked, filling the three cat bowls.

'Alan's done that. Molly's bringing 'em up. They're beauties. She thought you'd like to see 'em all before you went to work.' And at that point, Molly herself arrived, breathless and full of concerned curiosity.

'We seen it on the news,' she said, taking a surreptitious glance at the stitches. 'It looked awful. You won't get fired or anything will you?'

'I shall have to wait and see,' Laura said, pouring tea for them both. It was her day at Tillbury

125

village and the library there was under the firm control of Miss Finch, who was polite and thorough and didn't approve of 'goings-on'.

Molly spread out Alan's snaps alongside the teacups.

'Well, anyway, we've started now,' she said. 'There's no going back is there? I think that one's ever so good.' Then a thought struck her. 'Here. Where's your lodger? She made enough row last night, didn't she.'

Laura had forgotten all about her. 'Is her car there?'

'No.'

'Then she's still out on the tiles.'

'Typical. What was she up to last night then?'

'It was a party. They thought they were going to stay here.'

'Good job they didn't,' Molly said, 'or I should have had something to say. You should have locked her out. Worse'n a flea in a fleece, that sort.'

'I couldn't do that,' Laura said as she poured herself a second cup of tea. 'She's my sister-in-law.'

'I would,' Molly said trenchantly. 'But then I wouldn't have given her house room in the first place. Not after the way she went on with . . .'

But at that she caught her breath so sharply that Laura looked up from the teapot thinking something must have happened. She was just in time to catch the last flicker of a warning glare that was being passed between Mr Fennimore and his wife. 'On with whom?' she asked, intrigued.

'Some feller,' Molly said, looking shifty.

For the second time in as many days Laura had the strong feeling that there was something going on that she didn't know about. Or that something had been going on in the past that she hadn't known about and should have done. It was rather disquieting. But at that point the phone rang so she lost the chance to pursue it.

'My name's Toby Fawcett,' the voice said. 'I'm a reporter.'

'Yes?' Laura said guardedly.

'A friend of yours said I should phone you. Jeff Turner. I'd like to write a piece on your experiences at Twyford Down. Would you be agreeable?'

Laura fingered her stitches gingerly. 'Possibly,' she said. 'Providing you tell people why I'm doing this.'

'Which is?'

'It's to oppose the new road and all the damage it's going to do.'

'Yes. Jeff did say something of the sort. Your house is under threat I believe.'

She admitted it even though she was afraid the admission would make her sound like a nimby.

'I suppose you haven't got any pictures of it, have you?'

'Yes,' she said, looking up at the snapshots spread all over her table. 'I've got lots of pictures. They've just come this morning. Wonderful ones.

We're making up a booklet, you see, featuring *all* the places that are going to be destroyed by this road — it isn't just mine, you see — and the animals and birds that are going to be endangered. It's a local beauty spot that's under threat. Did you know that? We thought we ought to record it.'

'Lots of pictures you say?'

The interest in his voice encouraged her. 'Dozens.' Now if she could get him to tell *this* story it would be worth being interviewed.

He thought about it for several seconds. 'When can we meet?'

'This evening?'

'Seven thirty?'

Laura made rapid calculations. 'Make it eight.' That would give her time to get back with the car. 'There you are,' she said to the others as she put the receiver down. 'We've got ourselves some publicity.'

'Told yer,' Mr Fennimore said, smacking his chops with satisfaction.

The robin was singing again. This, Laura thought, is the way to start a new day.

In the party-wrecked chaos of his flat, Jeff Turner started his day with a groan. The sunshine had woken him like a knife blade and now his head was throbbing, his fingers were like thumbs and he was frantically searching for a paracetamol and a clean cup so that he could fix himself some coffee.

Why did I ever invite her? he asked himself as he groped about the kitchen. How could I have been such a fool? There were dirty cups and glasses everywhere and the floor tiles were multicoloured with trodden food. The idea of cooking breakfast in such a mess made him heave.

He groaned into the bathroom, thinking that a shower would make him feel better, only to find that someone had been sick in the shower cubicle. The smell in that enclosed space was too nauseous to be borne even when he'd opened the window. He washed in the basin as quickly as he could, cursing himself for allowing such vandals into his home. He knew he ought to set to and start cleaning up but he couldn't face it. Not first thing in the morning. No, there was only one thing to be done and that was to leave the place as quickly as he could. He opened all the windows, found clean clothes, dressed and set out for work and his nice, clean, sweet-smelling, antiseptic surgery. It was really only a first-aid room in a prefabricated hut in the middle of a factory site but he looked upon it as his surgery and at least he'd be comfortable there. He could pick up a couple of croissants at the bakery and breakfast in peace and quiet before the workers arrived.

He didn't notice what a fine day it was until he was out on the open road and heading for the factories. Then the demoralisation of the early morning was lifted by the pleasures of autumn scents and unexpected sunshine. It was as if his mind had suddenly shifted gear. It's a lovely day, he thought, as the haze evaporated from the fields. So what if I made a pig's ear of everything yesterday. People are always silly at parties. She'll see things differently this morning, on a day like this. We all see things differently in the morning.

He arrived so early that, except for the cleaners, the site was still deserted. But that pleased him. It gave him a chance to eat his breakfast in peace and to organise his first-aid room before the rush began. It was important to him to have the place in order because he never knew how many casualties he would have to deal with at any one time. There were three factories on this section of the site and he was responsible for all the minor accidents, so his day was always unpredictable. That was one of the things he enjoyed about it. That and being employed at all which was little short of a miracle after being blacked at the hospital. But there was no point in thinking about *that*. It was past and done with, like so many other things in his life.

He ate his croissants hungrily and was finishing his mug of coffee when the first cars began to turn in at the gate. He wondered idly whether Amy would be an early arrival or one of the ones who scrambled in at the last minute, and was impressed when her new Peugeot purred in just behind the managing director's white Mercedes.

He stood at the window and watched as the two cars were parked, hoping she would notice him and enjoying the sight of her. She might have been a disappointment at the party but she certainly knew how to dress. And how to get out of a car. Her long legs stretched elegantly before her, high heels gleaming in the sunshine and then, with a dip and sway, she was standing, locking the car with a flick of the wrist. She looked cool and contained and classy, like a model, dressed in a pale linen suit with a greeny-blue scarf at her neck. How had she got hold of that so early in the morning? Had she driven home to get it? Or did she carry a change of clothes about with her? It was impressive however it had been done. Fancy being able to look like that the morning after a party.

She was walking out of the car park, turning towards the entrance of Beautibelles. And just as he had decided to go back to his desk, she suddenly caught sight of him, waved and blew him a kiss.

Sunshine warmed his forehead and cast stripy patterns on the white paint of the medicine cabinet beside him. I shall phone her this evening he decided. I can find the number in the book. I ought to check how Laura is anyway as she's my patient.

The sunshine continued all morning, warming the sixth form at Burswood Community College as they ate their packed lunches *al fresco* in the school grounds. Watching them from the window of the staff room, Maureen was relieved to see that Jessica was gossiping and laughing with her friends and looked as though she hadn't a care in

131

the world. But the longer she watched the less she was reassured. Both her children were a bit too good at keeping up appearances and both were expert at hiding their hurt. Like me, she thought ruefully. I've taught them a bit too well and now it's catching us all out. And not for the first time, she wished they didn't live such separate lives.

In Tillbury library, Laura and Miss Finch took their usual 'lunch on a tray' and were careful to talk shop. Miss Finch had drawn up a list of the new books she would like ordered so they spent the entire lunch hour discussing it and remembering old favourites. Laura was glad of her companion's discretion. It reassured her that her working life had not been affected by the weekend's extraordinary events — or at least, it hadn't been affected yet. It also gave her a chance to gather her strength for her first interview with the press.

Although she read the local paper every week — since it was delivered free to every house in the area — she'd never had anything to do with either of its reporters. She knew them by name and was usually entertained by what they wrote, but that was all. Her image of reporters depended almost entirely on what she'd gleaned from television, packs of paparazzi hounding a celebrity, or celebrities themselves complaining about how badly they'd been mishandled or misrepresented. Consequently she was awaiting this coming interview with a certain amount of trepidation, feeling that she would have to take care to make her meaning very plain so as not to be misquoted and that she might even have something of a fight on her hands.

So when Maureen arrived at Holm End that evening to ferry her to Twyford Down, she gathered up all the pamphlets and booklets she'd been sent and took them with her to study on the way.

'Doing your homework?' Maureen said.

'Be prepared,' she smiled. 'That's me. I was always a good girl guide.'

'How's the head?'

'On the mend.'

'I thought it would look a lot worse,' Maureen confessed, overtaking a lorry. 'What a bit of luck there was a nurse there. Jess said he was very good.'

'Yes,' Laura agreed, turning a page. 'He was.'

'I know David's being a bit silly about all this,' Maureen said, keeping her eyes on the road, 'but I'm all for it. I thought you'd like to know.'

She spoke so casually that Laura almost missed the importance of what was being said. She set her leaflet aside and turned in her seat to read Maureen's expression. 'You don't mind an old rebel as a mother-in-law then?' she checked.

'I think it's marvellous,' Maureen confirmed and this time she allowed herself a second to turn her head and smile. A warm smile and very open. 'You're like the suffragettes, in a way. They were my heroines when I was young, you know. I used to think how wonderful they were, standing up for their beliefs. No, I told you, I'm all for it. In fact, if you ever want any help . . .'

'Seriously?'

'Seriously. You'd only have to give me a ring.'

'I might take you up on it,' Laura warned. But then she thought better of the suggestion. I must be careful here, she told herself, or I shall come between husband and wife.

Maureen saw nothing wrong in it. 'Do,' she said. 'It'll get me out of the house.' She smiled at Laura again. 'Between you and me, I've often thought I could do with a cause. To bring a bit of spice into my life. Housework's so boring, day after day all the time.'

'Isn't it just,' Laura agreed.

'Actually,' Maureen said, 'I'm thinking of taking on a new job at school.'

'Yes?' Laura prompted.

'It's only temporary,' Maureen explained. 'The Deputy in our department is leaving. They'd like me to take over until they can appoint a new one.'

'Why not?' Laura encouraged.

'Because I'm not sure how David would take it,' Maureen confessed. 'I'm very fond of your son. I'm not thinking of leaving him or anything. It's just . . . Well, between you and me, he's a bit . . . well . . . too much in control, I suppose. It makes me want to escape. Not that I ever would. I mean it's not as bad as all that. He's a good provider — a very good provider. I must speak fair. A good husband. A good father in his

way. I know he goes on at them but th￹   ￹
way of caring. He's a good father in eve
that counts. That's half his trouble — ho
he is. I suppose what I'm saying is you can have
too much of a good thing. He'd be more fun if
he ran risks now and then.'

Laura was saddened to hear her son being criticised — especially as the criticism was so accurate. But she didn't comment. 'So you're going
to run the risks instead, is that it?' she said, keeping her tone light.

'Leave the kitchen and join the world,'
Maureen joked.

Which is exactly what *I'm* doing, Laura
thought. 'You and me both,' she said.

'It's *The Rector's Wife*,' Maureen said. 'I haven't
been quite the same since I read it. It set me
thinking.'

Now they were on much safer territory, Laura
thought, relaxing. 'That would please Joanna
Trollope.'

'I was so pleased when Anna decided to walk
out on that awful rector,' Maureen said. 'I sat
and cheered. All on my own in the living room
cheering. Silly isn't it. But it made me think. It
rang so true.'

'She took a stand against conformity,' Laura
agreed. 'I think that's what we all admired.'

'Against everything she'd been brought up to
believe in. That was the wonderful thing about
it. She was speaking for all of us, all the women
brought up to think they have to give way to their

usbands, live where he wants to live, run the house the way he wants it run, think the way he wants to think. I've been doing it for such a long time, it's second nature to me. I don't know how to stop.'

Laura was intrigued. 'Do you want to stop?'

'Well not in everything,' Maureen temporised. 'But in some things. Yes, if I'm honest, I do. I've often envied you your independence, you know. Living your own life, going your own way. Oh I know it must have been dreadful being widowed so young — I don't envy you that — but at least you've had a life of your own. You don't have to pretend things or hide things. You can be yourself.'

'We all hide things,' Laura said, thinking of the secrets in her life. But she could see that Maureen didn't believe her so she didn't press the point. It didn't matter. What mattered was that after more than eighteen years of being careful and distant with each other, they were suddenly talking like friends. And *that* wasn't a consequence she'd foreseen when she took up the cudgels. How extraordinary life is.

It seemed odd to be back at Twyford Down in the calm of twilight and without the demonstrators. And seeing her old Land-Rover standing on the rough grass all alone was even odder, when she remembered the crush of cars and protesters there had been the last time she was there. But it was pleasant to be behind the wheel again and in control. Kind though Maureen had been to drive her back, she'd felt distinctly uncomfortable in the passenger seat. She hadn't realised how much she disliked being driven. When Jeff had chauffeured her home she'd felt too woozy to notice, but now there was no denying the fact.

She tuned in to Classic FM, found herself some chewing gum, waved to Maureen and set off towards the motorway. Now that she was on her own, she could use the homeward journey to plan what she wanted to say to the reporter. I'll condense it into three main points, she decided, the way I do when I chair the monthly divisional meeting. She felt she could cope with anything. Even a reporter, no matter how tricky he might be.

She was agreeably surprised when Toby Fawcett arrived at Holm End and turned out to be a mild and patient man. It threw her a little when he put a tape recorder on the coffee table between them but even so it was easy to talk to him.

He let her establish her first two points at once, that the road wasn't necessary and that communities shouldn't be destroyed to make way for it. Then he asked about her injury.

'I fell,' she said, dismissing it. 'There's no story in it. I mean, it really isn't important. A little accident. What's important is what's happening to people's lives.'

'Which is?'

It was the opening she needed and she took it at once. He listened attentively to what she had to say, asking the occasional question to nudge her into the next phase of her story.

'You must have seen a lot of changes,' he suggested, when she told him she'd been born in the cottage and spent her early childhood there.

She had a sudden vision of the cottage as it had been when she was a child, the uneven stone flags on the floor, the old butler sink in the scullery, the little dark rooms lit by yellow gaslight, the cupboard doors that never closed properly, the rickety stairs that creaked as you climbed, candle in hand, to the bare boards of the bedrooms under the eaves.

'It was primitive,' she said. 'We got our water from a well in the garden. I remember there was a frog in the bucket the first time Pete pulled it up. A great brown frog, swimming about in the bucket. One of our neighbours came over to see how we were settling in and she said we ought to throw it back because they keep down the insects.'

He laughed at that. 'What about sanitation?'

'Oh, no sanitation. A bucket and chuck it. But I loved it even then. It had been our holiday home for more than ten years when Pete and I moved in. You should have seen the garden in those days. The nettles were thigh high and there was an enormous elderberry bush in the corner and a buddleia thick with butterflies and the wisteria was growing in through the bedroom windows. It was like something out of a fairy tale.'

'It must have taken a long time to get it like this.'

'Years. And a lot of hard work.'

'I can see why you're up in arms,' he said.

'It's not just that,' she said. 'Oh, the house is important but it's more than that. If this road is built it will change a whole way of life, you see. And it's a good way of life, quiet, peaceful, complicated but — well — good. It's worked for centuries. We've found a harmony in the Way. We're good neighbours. There's room for wildlife and birds as well as humans. It's an entire eco-structure and once they bring the bulldozers in it will all go. There'll be no harmony then.'

'And that's important to you?'

'Very,' she said earnestly. 'We need to live in harmony. Don't you think so? Humans with humans. Humans with animals. We should never allow one group of people to ride roughshod over everybody else.'

He was checking the tape recorder so she paused and waited, hoping she hadn't gone over the top in her enthusiasm. And the phone rang.

'I'm sorry,' she said, moving out a hand for it. 'I'll be as quick as I can.' Now that she was into her stride she didn't want to be interrupted.

He pushed his glasses up the bridge of his nose and smiled at her. 'No problem.'

'Yes?' she said into the phone.

'It's only me,' Jeff said, disquieted by the sharp edge to her voice. 'I wondered how you were.'

'I'm fine,' she told him briefly. 'Look, I can't talk. I've got your friend Toby here.'

Her brusque tone disappointed him. 'No. All

right. I just wanted to know how you were. And to see whether Amy . . .'

Oh no, she thought, I'm not going to waste time talking about Amy. Not in the middle of all this. 'Call me tomorrow,' she said. 'I'll have more time then.' And she put the phone down.

Toby was looking at the photographs which she'd laid out on the table for him. 'How many of these could we have?'

'As many as you like.'

He chose half a dozen and put them neatly into his briefcase. 'Well that's fine,' he said, putting away the tape recorder too.

She felt suddenly deflated. 'Is that it?' she asked. Oh surely not. There was so much more she ought to say. And she'd have said it all if Jeff hadn't interrupted her.

He'd taken a small camera out of the bag. 'That's it,' he said. 'Nearly done. Just one picture of you — if you don't mind.'

She wanted to delay him, to expand on the points she'd made, to be sure he'd understood. She'd spent too much time talking about her childhood and nowhere near enough explaining about the campaign. But there was no opportunity now. She posed for her picture, said goodbye, waved as he drove into the lane, but despite her smile, she was feeling confused and more than a little guilty.

I haven't handled this at all well, she rebuked herself. It didn't seem proper to have told him so much about her private life. And it certainly

140

hadn't been necessary.

Yet, she comforted herself, she hadn't revealed any of her secrets, the things she'd always concealed and always would conceal, the things she'd remembered on the way to Twyford Down. She'd told Mr Fawcett the truth but it hadn't been the whole truth and nothing but the truth. Thank God. She'd had more sense than that.

She looked up at the sky to where the Great Bear pointed towards the Pole Star. And she remembered.

Chapter Nine

The Great Bear had been bold in the night sky all through that first April. That first, magical, love-dizzied, rapturous April.

'Let's go down to the cottage,' her mother had said on the last day of the spring term. 'We've got enough petrol coupons, haven't we Tom? We could have Easter in the country. It would do us all good. Nice fresh air in our lungs. Country food. Put some colour in your cheeks Laura-Lou. Set you up for your O levels.'

Laura didn't want to think about the exams, even though she was fairly confident of passing. Too much turned on them, whether she would stay on in the sixth form, whether she would go to college, which college she could aim at, how much she would please her parents — and she *did* so want to please her parents. But an Easter holiday in the country was a wonderful idea.

'Oh yes,' she said. 'Let's. I'd love it.'

So there they were, bumping along the earth path between the trees in Dad's rackety old car, as she hung out of the window, straining her eyes for the first sight of the cottage. 'There it is Mum! There it is Dad! Look!' Creaking open the front door, rushing into the hall with its odd unused smell of ancient dust and mildew, running upstairs to throw open the bedroom windows and let in the air, while Dad unpacked and Mum went out to the well to draw water for their first pot of country tea. Country tea and country bread, fresh from the baker's in the village, strong-tasting and warm and wondrously crusty. And eaten on a cloth damp from the drawer and smelling as musty as everything else in the place — just as if they were adventurers out in the wilds.

The daffodils were massed in the front garden, bobbing and swaying and bright as butter against the green paint of the kitchen door, the hawthorn hedge was in tiny grass-green leaf, the cherry tree veiled by pink blossom. There was a blackbird in the holm oak singing its beautiful fluid song. And on that first night the sky was full of bright, white stars.

She leaned out of her bedroom window enjoying the chill of the night air on her bare arms and savouring the remembered smell of the countryside, that heady combination of rotting leaves and fresh buds, of living earth and stagnant waters, of cess-pit and seedling, compost and creation. She knew then that something wonderful was going to happen. I'm like Juliet on the balcony, she thought, realising in that moment how well she understood the character. Except that there's no Romeo in the garden.

There was a rustle in the undergrowth behind the boundary hedge. A badger? she wondered. That would be nice — to see a badger on her first night. But then she thought she saw a shadow leaping the ditch and she realised that their visitor was human.

'Who's that?' she called, her voice ringing in the clear air.

There was a long still pause. Then a voice answered, 'Only me.'

'Who's me?'

The shadow stepped out of the hedge, solidified and became a young man. 'Pete. Pete Pendleton. You're Laura Sheldon, aren't you. I remember you. We used to call you Lorry-Lou. We were in the juniors together.'

He strode through the tangle of weeds until he was standing on the path immediately under her window. Lit by the yellow glimmer of her candle and the distant glimmer of the stars, he was darkly handsome, brown skinned and lithe with thick dark hair and large dark eyes. He had a jacket of some kind slung over his shoulder and wore a white shirt open at the neck, as if it were summer.

She couldn't remember being at school with him. As far as she was aware — and she was very, very aware — she'd never seen him before. Romeo, she thought, *Wherefore art thou, Romeo?* 'Were we?' she said and her voice was full of disbelief.

He grinned up at her, his eyes glinting in the candlelight. 'Matter of fact, I nearly saved your life once. When you fell in the culvert and nearly drowned. I bet you remember that. I was a hero for days after.'

The memory swelled in her mind like a nightmare, dark waters pummelling her along that awful tunnel as she turned and twisted, struggling for breath. Oh yes, she remembered *that*. But she had no recollection of being rescued. 'You're making it up,' she said.

He grew more candid, grinning at her again. 'Well no — tell the truth — I didn't actually pull you out or anything like that. I got a stick and poked it about in the mouth of the culvert, that's all really. I thought you were stuck.'

'I was,' she said. It made her shudder to think of it, even after all these years.

'There you are then. I was right. I'd've pulled you out if I could.'

This was beginning to be a bewitching conversation. 'Would you?'

'Yes. Course. 'Specially if I'd known we were going to meet like this.'

The sibilance of the words reminded her of Romeo and Juliet again. *How silver sweet sound lovers' tongues by night.* And she thought how romantic this meeting was. 'What are you doing in our garden?'

His answer was disappointingly prosaic. 'Short cut,' he explained. 'I've been up the Long Dragon with some of my mates. Carl. D'you remember him? Used to have a dog followed him to school all the time. And Martin Hacker. You must remember Martin. I'm not trespassing or anything. I mean, we always cut through the backs.'

'Do you?' she said in some surprise. 'I've never seen you out there before.'

145

'Well not when you're down, naturally. Only when it's all shut up.'

'Didn't you see the light?' *But soft, what light through yonder window breaks? It is the east and Juliet is the sun.*

'Not till you called out. You don't mind do you?'

No she didn't mind. She was enchanted.

'Stay there,' she said, 'and I'll come down and open the gate for you and then you can cut through the lane.'

Oh the thrill of it, sneaking down the stairs on tiptoe and out of the front door — taking care to open it without letting it squeak — running round the side of the house and into the garden, standing beside him in the moonlight, talking and talking — and quite forgetting about the gate.

They talked for over an hour, drinking in the sight of one another, shivering in an exquisite combination of cold air and heated excitement. He told her he'd been a sailor since he left school and she told him that her father had been in the navy during the war. It was wonderful to think they had something in common.

'I'm in the merchant navy though,' he said. 'Not quite the same as your dad.'

But the glamour was the same. He was so handsome and so tall, as he stood beside her with his sailor's jacket slung over his shoulder, smelling of salt and spice and tobacco and the exotic otherness of the seafarer.

They strolled about among the trees at the end

of the garden, talking and talking. At one point he bent to move a bough out of her way. He lifted it so easily it was as if there were no weight to it at all. How strong he is, she admired, and how considerate, stepping aside so that I can walk through first and taking care to hold the branches so that they don't spring back on me. The courtesy of it made her feel like royalty.

Even now, standing at the kitchen door thirty-nine years later, she remembered everything she'd felt that night. He'd asked her — very casually — if she'd like to go to the Saturday dance with him. Just the thought of it had taken her breath away and she'd accepted at once, proud to think she was going to be his partner. And when they'd finally said goodnight, she'd crept back to her room, breathless with the wonder of what had happened. She'd made her first date. She was going to her first real dance. And with the most handsome man she'd ever seen in her life.

The Saturday dance was in the Memorial Hall and there was a band playing jive. They'd all jumped about like idiots. She could remember the sweat running down the small of her back and her hair sticking to her forehead — and feeling so happy she wanted the dance to go on for ever and ever.

Then they'd lowered the lights and the band had played something slow and smoochy and he'd put his arms right round her and held her close as if he was going to kiss her. They hadn't danced, just swayed from foot to foot, in a trance of rising desire, too overwhelmed by sensation to speak. She lifted her head dreamily so that they were cheek to cheek and she thought, *So this is love. This is what the poets are always on about. Love at first sight.* And she wondered if he'd fallen in love with her and hoped he had but didn't dare to ask. It was enough to be in his arms, smelling the salty scent of his skin, touching the rough hair at the nape of his neck, breathing his breath.

Afterwards, they'd strolled home through the moonlit fields with their arms about each other and he'd stopped at the edge of the copse to kiss her. Oh how well she remembered that, the lovely salty, sea-going smell of him, the strength of his arms around her, the gentleness of that soft, soft mouth.

'Sweet sixteen and never been kissed,' he teased.

'Yes, I have,' she lied.

'Not by me though.'

They went to the Long Dragon the next evening and met up with Carl and Martin Hacker and so many other mates of his that she couldn't count them. Even though she didn't want to share him, she was impressed by how popular he was and how easily he made friends. But what she was waiting for all evening long — and it *was* a long evening — was the moment when he would walk her home through the moonlight and stop to put his arms round her and kiss her again.

Oh the pleasure and terror of those kisses, her heart pounding under her old white blouse, her breasts rising, rising, aching to be touched, her hands round his neck pulling him closer and closer. 'Kiss me! Kiss me! Kiss me!'

Her eagerness was pure delight to him. 'Greedy guts!' he crowed. But his eyes were tender and full of love.

It was a springtime of kisses, a short, endless, springtime fortnight spent aching the day away until it was night and she could be in his arms again. He had to go to Plymouth to join his ship on the day before she was due to return to London and the summer term. The thought of parting tore her apart.

'I'll be back,' he promised on their last evening. 'I'll see you in the summer.'

'Write to me,' she begged.

He laughed at that. 'When I can,' he said. 'It'll be a bit few and far between, sort a' thing. We don't have postmen on a merchant ship. You have to write to the port we're heading for. Tell you what though, I'll send you a message along the stars.'

She laughed too. 'You are daft! How can you do that?'

'See that group of stars up there,' he said, pointing to them. 'Shaped like a plough. See. There's the handle and there's the plough-share. Well that's the Great Bear. Never sets. We use it to find the Pole Star. See. Follow the far edge of the plough straight along and that bright star all on its own is Polaris, the Pole Star. We use that to steer by.'

She'd never noticed any shapes in the stars before but now she saw them clearly. 'There's a W up there.'

'That's Cassiopeia.'

It was so quiet out in the fields that she could hear the silence — a sort of gentle hissing in the vastness of sky above them. She thought of him out on the ocean, far, far away from her, steering by the stars, and she sighed with the misery of loss.

'Don't do that,' he begged. 'I can't bear it.'

But she was too young to disguise her feelings and her anguish was clear on her face.

'Please don't,' he said, stroking her cheeks with his thumbs. 'I can't bear you to be unhappy. I love you.' He hadn't been quite sure about it until that moment but now that the words were spoken, there was no doubt.

'I love you too,' she said. And tears welled out of her eyes.

He kissed her most tenderly. 'I'll soon be back,' he promised, 'It's only three months. It'll soon pass. Really. You look up and find the Great Bear and think of me and I'll look up and see it and think of you. It'll be our special message.'

She'd looked up every night all through the long summer term, telling him things in her heart — about the Queen being crowned and how she'd seen it on television and how moving she thought it was — about the exams and what a relief it was that they were over — about how very very much she wanted to see him again. She wrote to him too, long letters that took two or three days to complete. Always saying the same thing. *'I love you. I can't wait to see you again.'*

It was weeks before she got an answer but when it came it was so exactly what she wanted that she put it away and vowed she would keep it for ever.

'My own dearest darling Laura,' he wrote. *'Your letter was waiting for me. I shall treasure it for ever. You know I said the time would pass. Well I was wrong. Every day is like a week. I think of you all the time. I reckon I've got you under my skin, like in the song. I keep think of the way you walk and your laugh and the way your hair grows up from your forehead in those two peaks and the way you kiss me. I shall never love anyone the way I love you. If I close my eyes I can see you. If I could part the sea I would make a path way and walk straight back to you. I can't wait to see you again. I love you. I love you. I love you. Yours till the sea run dry, Pete XXXX'*

The months *did* pass, although very very slowly. She and her mother went down to the cottage by train as soon as the exams were over, leaving her father to toil on in the bank on his own. By then there was the usual tangle of weeds in the back garden and the two of them had found their fag-hooks in the shed and set to on that very first afternoon to make a clearance.

Laura stood in the midst of their abundant growth, trailing her fingers over the rough white flowers of the cow parsley, watching the butter-flies as they fluttered around the buddleia bush

151

or settled to feed, their brown wings spread. Summer sunlight dappled the overgrown lawn with patches of pale green and the wisteria that covered the back of the cottage was hung with blossom like miniature bunches of grapes. She was so happy she flung her sunhat up into the air, yelling and laughing, for the pure joy of being where she wanted to be and knowing she would soon see him again.

What happened that summer was as inevitable as sunshine. How could she have denied him when she loved him so much, when she'd waited three whole months to see him again, when she couldn't think of anything by day or by night except being in his arms? It simply wasn't possible.

Yet how terribly she regretted it in the autumn, when her mother wept so bitterly and her father took himself off for a long walk, grey faced and anxious, 'to think what can be done'.

'Firstly,' he said when he returned, 'you can't go back to school. I shall write and tell them we've changed our mind about you staying on. Secondly, you must write and tell him what's happened — or have you done that already? No. Then you must write tonight. Thirdly, when he gets back he must arrange to marry you, up here and very quietly. Fourthly, you must go down to the cottage as soon as you can. What a blessing we've got the cottage. You and Mother can pack a few things and I'll drive you down this weekend. I've just about got enough petrol. You can stay there for a few days to get people used to the idea that you're married and that you're going to come back and live there when your young man comes home. I'll buy you a wedding ring tomorrow so that you can let them see it. You must tell everyone you married him in the summer. Your mother will see his family and tell them what to say. He's got a brother, you said. Who else is there?'

'Only his mother,' she'd whispered not daring to look him in the eye. She felt so ashamed. So deeply, deeply sorry. 'His dad died in the war.'

He'd put his hand on her bowed head and ruffled her hair. 'It's all right, Laura-Lou,' he said gruffly. 'You're over the worst now. We'll handle it. You and Pete can live in the cottage, nice and quiet, right away from everyone. It'll be like a little fortress. He can pay me a peppercorn rent and you can do it up between you the way you want it. Make it comfortable. At least you had the good sense to tell us in good time. By the time the — erm — baby's born they'll all be so used to you being a married woman and living in the Way, no one down there will think twice about it. Don't worry. And no one here need know anything about it at all.'

'They'll find out,' she said dully. 'They'll know I wasn't married in the summer.'

'Only if you tell them,' he said firmly. 'And you won't do that, will you.'

No, she shuddered, she wouldn't do that. But she was trembling at the thought of what Pete

153

would say when she told him. It would alter everything.

But it didn't. Two days after she got back from her visit to the cottage he sent her a telegram. *'Coming home. Don't worry.'*

And as soon as his ship put in he caught the first train to London. There was no doubt in him at all. He took her into his arms as soon as she opened the door, there and then, in front of her mother. He'd brought her an engagement ring from Malta and was full of plans for their wedding.

'I'm sorry about this, sir,' he said when her father came home. 'I love her you see.'

'Obviously,' her father said drily.

'We'll soon have things ship-shape,' Pete promised. 'We'll call the banns this Sunday.'

Her father had warmed to him already, despite their bad start. 'Very wise,' he said.

Once they were on their own together Laura wept. But he'd dried her eyes and told her there was nothing to cry about.

'I'll look after you,' he said. 'You'll see. We'd have married and had children anyway, wouldn't we. Course we would. Sooner or later. This one is just coming a bit sooner.'

'You do still love me?' she asked tremulously.

'Course,' he said, hugging her hard. 'More than ever now. You're going to be my wife.'

And so, three weeks later, quietly and in the local registry office, she was.

They went down to the cottage immediately

afterwards and she began her new life as a house-wife. She'd never told anybody her secret, not even when Molly Fennimore came across the road to welcome her and made some rather pointed remarks.

'You are a funny little thing,' she'd said, with the most knowing expression on her plump face. 'Fancy going off and getting married on the quiet like that. I always thought you'd have a big white wedding with a choir and a veil and everything. I was looking forward to it.'

I told my first lie on that day, Laura thought, remembering it. And I've been living the lie ever since. I've ploughed it in and watered it down until it's become so much a part of my life that it's grown into my bones. It was all right while I was tucked away in my little backwater, minding my own business, but now I'm out in the open stream and there's no protection there. The waters of nightmare rolled into her mind, heavy and rough and powerful, tossing her away from the good green light into the muddy darkness of the earth, downwards and onwards. And she knew she was afraid of her impetuous nature, and alarmed by the course she'd undertaken.

I shall go to church on Sunday, she decided, and pray for good sense. She knew she ought to pray to be forgiven for the lie, but she'd given up on that years ago. It was good common sense she needed now and the strength to use it.

Chapter Ten

Toby Fawcett's article in the *Burswood Gazette* turned out to be better than Laura expected. Her neighbours were thrilled with it. Molly and Joan Garston rushed their copies straight to Holm End as soon as they'd been delivered that Thursday morning.

'Have you read this?' Molly said, beaming as if it were a personal triumph. 'Look at all the pictures. And all in colour too. He's done us proud.'

Joan liked the headline. *Laura's Way with Unwanted Roads.* 'That's clever.'

Laura wasn't too sure about *'local librarian, injured at Twyford Down, vows to continue the fight'.* Injured was well over the top and talk of a fight made her sound belligerent. But she was delighted that he'd finished the article by quoting her words and read them with pride, pleased by their rhythm and their good sense. ' *"We need to live in harmony. Humans with humans and humans with animals. We should never allow one group of people to ride roughshod over everybody else."* He's got that right at least.' Then she was embarrassed because she felt she was being conceited and ducked her head and her vanity to read some of the other things on the page.

Only Amy seemed equivocal. She'd been

checking her makeup in the wall mirror when the two women burst in. Now she turned, lipstick in hand to drawl her comment, 'My sister-in-law the celebrity.' There was such an odd tone to her voice that Laura wasn't sure whether it was praise or criticism.

'You've got your friend Jeff Turner to thank for it,' she said. 'He told the journalist.'

'He would!' Amy said, fluffing up her hair. 'He's a professional campaigner. I told you that at the start. Jeff the do-gooder.'

'I thought you rather liked him,' Laura teased.

'Oh he's nice enough,' Amy said, admiring her reflection in the mirror. 'But he's hardly *my* type. I like a bit more class. Have you seen the car he drives?'

'I was driven home in it,' Laura pointed out, 'and very glad of the chance, I can tell you.'

Molly Fennimore was scowling at the back of Amy's head. 'You off to work then are you?' she enquired tartly. 'I'd look sharp if I was you.'

Amy applied another layer of lipstick, concentrating on her image.

'How's the house-hunting going?' Molly needled.

Amy ignored that too. 'You'll have to treat yourself to some new clothes,' she said to Laura, 'if you're going to make a habit of being in the papers.' Then she scooped up her handbag and stalked out

'Hoity-toity!' Molly said. 'She don't change I see.'

Laura had gone back to reading the rest of the paper. 'There's a map here,' she said. 'Have you seen it? It shows the whole route right the way along. It's going to be very close to the primary school.'

'Which one?' Joan asked.

'Glendale. They're going to build it just north of the estate. See? I wonder whether anybody's doing anything about it. I shall be in Burswood library all day today. I'll ask if anyone knows.'

Neither of her friends thought much of the idea and their expressions showed it. 'Haven't you got enough on your plate?' Molly asked.

'Possibly,' Laura conceded to placate them. 'But if we want to start a petition, the more people we can get involved the better, and you think how many we could get in touch with through a school. Has our MP answered any more letters?'

'The Coopers had theirs yesterday,' Molly said.

'And?'

'Exactly the same as all the others. *"I note your concern and will bear in mind what you have told me."* You ask me, I don't think he even bothers to read 'em.'

'Let's get our booklet done first,' Joan urged. 'Fiona's kids have been bird-watching like crazy.'

'We'll make a start after supper,' Laura promised. 'See you then. Right? Now I'd better be off or I shall be late.'

Of the three libraries that Laura worked in, Burswood was well and away her favourite, partly because it was the oldest and had the most charm,

158

partly because the staff there were all old friends but mostly because it had originally been the village school and she had once been one of the infants.

Set at the top of one of Burswood's surrounding hills and facing the church of St Margaret, it had been founded in 1682 as a charity school for the sixty children of the village and it still looked the part. It was a single-storey flint building, like so many village schools, and wonderfully eccentric, decorated with stripes and lozenges of red brick as though it had been designed by the children themselves, with lancet windows to match the windows in the church, a tall brick chimney at one end to cope with its two enormous open fires and an even taller bell tower at the other, turreted and capped and still containing its old school bell.

Every time she walked through the doors she was glad she'd made her start in such a romantic place and no matter how busy she became, she was buoyed up by happy memories of the dangers and delights of those far-off infant days.

Inside under a vaulted roof there had once been three classrooms, one for the infants and two for the juniors. How well she remembered them — with their rows of little double desks each with its own inkwell and a ridge to hold your pen and pencil — and voices chanting tables, on and on and on. Now it was a single open space, roomy under its high black beams. She particularly liked the beams because they were still supported by

159

the noble plaster faces she remembered from her school days, a king dreamy under his white crown, a bishop stern under his mitre, an androgynous youth celestial under flowing hair, their colourless faces pure with ineffable authority and total lack of expression.

She was enjoying them again that morning when she became aware that there was a young man waiting for her at the counter. He was a scruffy-looking character in torn jeans and a camouflage jacket, his long face sunken-cheeked and grimy, his stubby nails bitten to the quick, but his expression was so anxious and earnest that she warmed to him at once and went across to attend to him.

'You *are* the one in the paper, aren'tcher?' he asked as she took the book he wanted to borrow. *'Laura's Way with Roads.'*

Laura stamped the book, *Vegetable Gardening for Beginners*, checked the name on his card — A. Todd — and agreed that she was, half knowing what was coming next.

'I know we shouldn't ask,' the young man said, 'but this road's going right past our kiddies' school, you know what I mean. They sent us papers explaining it an' everything, how there'd be minimum inconvenience an' that. An' how they're gonna plant a hedge to keep out the noise but I'm not so sure. I don't think they're tellin' us the truth. Well not all of it anyway. I mean, it'll be a bit late to start asking questions when they've built it.'

'Quite right, Mr Todd,' Laura encouraged him. 'How can I help you?'

'Well it's like this,' the young man said. 'We got a sort of meeting arranged for next Wednesday.' He produced a homemade leaflet from his breast pocket and smoothed it out on the counter for her to read. 'We was wondering if you'd be our speaker, if you got the time I mean. Tell us how you got going in Laura's Way. There's no one much to organise things down our way — well not at the minute — you know what I mean — only me an' Sharon. But we got to do something.'

Sharon appeared from behind the shelves and ambled to the counter to join him. She was as underfed as he was, her long dark hair thin and straggly and the fingers of her left hand stained by nicotine. 'Our kiddies go to the school,' she explained. 'They keep tellin' us it'll be all right only it looks too close to me. If you could see your way to just coming along it 'ud be ever such a help.'

'I'm not a public speaker,' Laura felt she ought to warn. 'I mean, I've never given a speech to anyone in my life. I could answer questions and tell you what I've found out if that would be any help.'

'That 'ud be great,' he said. 'Just what we want.'

'They shouldn't build a by-pass so close to the kiddies, should they?' Sharon asked. 'I mean, I said to Toddy here, it's only a by-pass. It could go anywhere really.'

161

For a second Laura was tempted to tell them what she knew about the road there and then, but she stopped herself in time, remembering where and who she was. Then she remembered Jeff and how she'd bristled when he explained it to *her* and realised that in less than a fortnight she'd come right round to his point of view. I ought to ring him, she thought. He means well and I *did* cut him off short.

'What was all that about?' Meryl asked when the couple had gone. And when Laura told her, she beamed. 'You'll be in politics next,' she predicted. 'Riding round town in an open-topped bus with a rosette in your hat.'

'I don't wear a hat.'

'On your bosom then.'

'No,' Laura said. 'I'm not a politician. Never have been, never will be. This is a one-issue affair, that's all.' But, even so, she couldn't help feeling proud of herself. And her pride increased as other borrowers arrived during the day to tell her that they'd seen the article and approved of what she was doing.

The last pair arrived just as she was closing and talked for nearly twenty minutes so she was late shutting up, late getting home and so late preparing dinner that there was no time for phone calls. In fact the potatoes still weren't cooked when a car pulled up outside. Not Amy's Peugeot as she could tell from the sound of it but before she had time to wonder whose it was, Amy breezed in through the door.

'That damned car!' she said. 'Flat battery, if you ever heard of such a thing. Quality car and it lets me down just when I need it most.'

'So how did you . . . ?' Laura was beginning to ask, when the answer walked in through the still open door. Jeff Turner, in another shapeless jersey, following her hopefully and looking rather embarrassed when he saw Laura standing by the sink.

'Well what a surprise!' she said to Amy, her voice catty. 'So you managed to get into his car after all.'

Jeff looked puzzled at that but Amy ignored it. 'Isn't he a sweetie,' she said. 'A real Good Samaritan. I don't know how I'd have got home without him. Jeez! Is that the time. I must shower.' And she was out of the room and on her way to the stairs at once, her scarf gauzing behind her.

'Dinner in twenty minutes,' Laura called after her.

'I've got a dinner date,' Amy's voice called back. 'That's why I'm in a rush. Didn't I tell you?'

Jeff was so annoyed he shouted at her before Laura could open her mouth to answer. 'No you did *not!*' he called up the stairs. 'If you've got a date, why the hell didn't he drive you home?'

'Couldn't be done,' Amy called back. 'You didn't mind though, did you?'

'It 'ud be all the same if I did,' Jeff said, looking at Laura. 'Apparently I'm just the chauffeur.'

She understood the bitterness of his tone.

'You're too kind,' she said. 'That's your trouble.' And she thought, you let her take advantage of you and it's a weakness. But then so do I and it's a weakness in me too. We're a pair of fools together. 'She didn't tell me about this dinner date either,' she said. 'I've cooked a meal for her and now all my good food will go to waste.'

He sniffed appreciatively. 'It smells marvellous.'

The solution occurred to them both at the same time. 'I suppose you wouldn't like to . . .' she offered.

'I'd love to,' he said, licking his lips. 'I thought you'd never ask.'

They set the table together and, on impulse, she found a bottle of red wine to add to the feast. By the time Amy came tripping down the stairs in a little black dress, very high heels and an enormous string of pearls, they were dishing up and had almost forgotten her.

'How do I look?' she said, addressing the question to Jeff as if Laura wasn't there.

He glanced at her briefly and without expression. 'You'll do,' he said.

There was a car sounding its horn in the Way. 'There he is!' she said, checking her image in the wall mirror. 'I'm off! Don't wait up!'

'Who is it?' Laura asked, when she was gone.

Jeff walked to the window and peered out. 'It's too dark to see,' he said. 'One of the salesmen probably. Could be anybody. She's very popular so my patients tell me.'

'She's a charmer,' Laura said, looking at him shrewdly. 'Look how she charmed you into giving her a lift.'

'I'm a sucker for a sob story,' he said, answering her unspoken question. 'Lady in distress. That sort of thing. Gets me every time.'

Laura opened the oven door and changed the subject. 'Food,' she said. 'Pull up a chair.'

It was a leisurely meal because they talked all the way through it, about her work in the library and his at the first-aid post, about Sharon and Toddy and how she was going to speak at their meeting.

'If they think a hedge is going to make any difference to the noise,' he said, 'they ought to go to Chichester and listen to the traffic there.'

'I've half a mind to go there myself and record it for them,' Laura said. 'Only I don't think my little tape recorder would be adequate to the task.'

'You could borrow mine, if you'd like.'

She smiled at him. 'That's very kind.'

'Or better still I could come with you and we could record it together.'

She hesitated. It wasn't what she'd expected but it was a tempting offer. 'When?'

'Tomorrow? After work. We could go for a meal afterwards. My treat. That's only fair. You keep on feeding *me*.'

'Twice isn't keeping on.'

'It is in my book,' he said earnestly. 'I like to pay my way.'

His high principles impressed her. 'All right

then,' she agreed. 'But only to appease your conscience.'

He enjoyed that, laughing at her, his beard bristling. 'And now you'll let me wash up for you,' he offered.

'I thought you'd never ask,' she teased.

So he stayed to wash the dishes and when her working party began to arrive — first the Fennimores and Joan Garston and then the Coopers with Fiona Coghlan — he stayed to lend a hand with that too, fitting into the group as easily as if he'd always been a part of it. The eight of them sat round the table with their lists and photographs before them and scissors and paste on the tea trolley beside them and set to work at once.

By midnight they'd produced a mock-up of the first ten pages of their booklet and at his urging had decided to make two copies, one for the enquiry and the other for the record.

'It's too valuable to be a one-off,' he said. 'Evidence like this should be preserved.'

They decided other things too — to take a lot more photographs — and to draw up more lists. They'd already got quite a long list of the rarer birds that could be seen in the area. Fiona Coghlan read it out with great satisfaction — yellowhammer, heron, fieldfare, bunting, nightingale, partridge, chiffchaff, siskin, meadow pipit, goldcrest, wheatear and woodpeckers. And the lists of wild flowers and animals were well on their way.

'I think we ought to list the trees too,' Molly

166

said. 'They'll root up trees by the million an' we got some beauties round here. It's not just oak an' ash an' hawthorn. There's silver birch and wild cherry and sycamores.'

'An' Scots pine,' her husband said. 'An' hazel and crab apple.'

'I tell you something else we ought to do,' Joan Garston put in. 'We ought to make a note of all the animals we've found run over. There was a rabbit only yesterday and that poor cat last week an' you think of how many there'd be if we had a great superhighway here.'

'And the pond,' Connie Cooper said. 'You think of all the creatures that live there and they'll dig that up as sure as fate.'

'Seems to me,' John Cooper said, sagely, 'the more we do the more there is to do. It leads you on, this sort a' thing.'

'How long have we got?' his wife asked.

But nobody could answer that. 'It all depends on when the council decide to hold the enquiry,' Jeff told them. '*If* they decide to hold it at all.'

'We'll set ourselves a target,' Laura said. 'Say the middle of October. How would that be? We'll do as much as we can and see how far we've got by then. I've got a feeling this could all happen faster than we think.'

'And a working party every week?' Joan Garston hoped.

It was half past twelve and Fiona was yawning. 'It's been a long day,' she apologised.

'I suppose me lady's out on the tiles again,'

Molly said as they all left. 'You should give her the push.'

'Yes,' Laura agreed, smiling ruefully. 'I probably should.' But for the moment she was too preoccupied with the campaign.

'She's bad news, that one,' Molly warned and she seemed to be directing her warning as much at Jeff as she was to Laura.

'Don't worry, Molly,' he said. 'I don't drive a good enough car to suit your Amy! I've got her measure.'

'I'm very glad to hear it,' Molly said. 'She's done enough damage for one lifetime.'

'Right then,' he said to Laura as Molly opened the door. 'See you tomorrow. I'll come and pick you up.'

'I'm at Furrow's Edge library all day,' Laura told him, aware of Molly's interest. 'Do you know it?'

'No,' he said, 'but I'll find it.'

'It's well signposted,' she said. 'And you can park out the back.'

Somebody else came to park behind the library that Friday. Just before midday, when Laura was taking stock in Fiction M — N, a strange woman joined her beside the shelves. She was beautifully dressed in a long wool coat with a mock fur collar and a mock fur hat, black suede gloves and high-heeled boots, and she smiled at Laura as if they were old friends.

'I hope I'm not disturbing you,' she said.

'Not at all,' Laura said, turning to her politely.

'How can I help you?'

'I'm Freda,' the woman said. 'We met at Twyford Down. I was in the area, visiting friends, and I saw your piece in the paper. So I thought I'd call in to see how you are. They told me at the main library that you'd be here.'

'That's very kind of you,' Laura said, looking at her with renewed interest. Could this really be the same person she'd met out there on the Down? That expensive coat was a far cry from a sheepskin and a green bobble hat.

'You weren't badly hurt then?' she said.

'Stitches, that's all,' Laura told her. 'I'm having them out in a day or two.'

'I'm so glad,' Freda smiled. 'We were quite worried about you, you know. You took a nasty blow. Those security guards are such pigs! Well I mustn't keep you. I can see you're busy. I'll give you my card and then I'll be off.' And she took a small card from her handbag and handed it across. 'It's the address of our local group,' she explained, 'in case you should need reinforcements at any time. Or information. We help one another whenever we can. But you know all about that, I'm sure.'

'Actually,' Laura said, smiling at her, 'I'm just beginning to learn.'

'That's my phone number in the corner,' Freda told her. 'I work during the day, except for Fridays, but I'm there most evenings.'

Laura smiled at her again. The sense of being befriended and supported was touching. Of

169

course, there was no likelihood that she and her friends would ever need to ask for this particular sort of help. Or that they would ever want to. They knew what they were doing and none of them had any intention of breaking the law. Waving placards and fighting with security guards wasn't really their style. Their methods were democratic and respectable and would succeed on that account. But the offer was kindly meant. There was no doubt about that. She put the card in her pocket with a happy sense of its value.

'Thank you,' she said. 'I appreciate it.'

Chapter Eleven

The events of that Thursday evening had brought Jeff Turner face to face with an unwelcome truth about himself. He'd been avoiding it ever since his wife walked out on him. Now it was inescapable.

When he'd explained to Laura that he'd given Amy a lift home because he was a sucker for a sob story he'd only been telling her half the truth. Of course it *had* been a sob story, but the fact that the glamorous Amy had turned to him when she was in difficulties had encouraged him so much that he'd agreed to help her at once, hopeful that this time she would agree to a date. The awful moment when he'd realised she was simply making a convenience of him had been a turning point. It wasn't just anger at her that he'd felt. It was rage at himself.

Ever since Eve had left him he'd been looking for a woman to replace her — if only temporarily and despite spectacular failures. He hadn't been consciously aware of what was motivating him in his search, but now he knew. He'd been chasing an image, deliberately seeking out the most stunning women he could find — because Eve had been a beauty. She still was. Just to walk down the road beside her had given him such a good feeling he could remember the glow of it even now. What he'd been doing was trying to recapture that feeling. But he'd been using his eyes, as if his other senses had deserted him. Just his eyes, choosing an appearance instead of a person. What a fool he'd been.

The surprising thing about all this was that it hadn't upset him. He would have expected such sudden self-knowledge to be painful but instead of that he was comforted by it, released and encouraged, as if scales really *had* fallen from his eyes.

That Saturday he treated himself to a new shirt and spent a long time before his bathroom mirror, trimming his beard. As he drove to Furrow's Edge library at the end of the day, he felt easier than he'd done for years.

'You look smart,' Laura said. 'I like that shirt. It shows up the colours in your beard.'

'Bought in your honour,' he told her happily. 'I've booked a table at the theatre restaurant. Is that all right?'

'Oh dear,' she said, making a face. 'Had I better go home and change?'

'No,' he told her. 'You're fine as you are.' She was wearing a tweedy suit with little green flecks in it. 'I like that suit,' he said, and following her example. 'It shows up the colour of your eyes.'

'Touché!' she joked, putting on the jacket.

They joked a great deal that evening, and especially while they made their recording, for the noise of the road they'd chosen was so appalling that they either had to joke or cry. Even when they were recording behind one of the hedging 'screens' the racket was so loud they had to shout at one another to be heard. But when they played back the tape they were well pleased with the result.

'If that doesn't persuade them I don't know what will,' Jeff said. 'It's enough to split your eardrums.'

Laura was checking her watch. 'It's taken us nearly an hour,' she said. 'Do you realise that?'

'How time flies when you're having fun!' he grinned. And when she grimaced, 'Never mind. The city's pedestrianised.'

'Then let's go and be pedestrians.'

After such a good start the rest of the evening was easy and pleasurable. They enjoyed their meal, discussed her campaign, saw a film at the Minerva and finally drove back to the library to pick up her car a great deal later than either of them had intended and in very good humour.

The Land-Rover was standing all by itself in the deserted car park. He drew up beside it and they both got out, shivering a little in the night air.

She rummaged in her bag for her keys. 'It's been a lovely evening,' she said as she unlocked the car.

He hadn't analysed the evening until that moment but she was right. 'Them's my sentiments,' he said. 'I haven't enjoyed myself so much for ages.' And added impulsively, 'I suppose you wouldn't care to repeat it, would you? I mean if there are any more roads you'd like recorded.'

She considered the offer, turning to look at him quizzically before she answered. 'No more roads,' she said. 'I've had enough of *that* to last me for a long time, but I think I'd like to repeat the rest of the evening.'

It was suddenly important for him to agree a time. 'Sunday?' He couldn't ask her for a Saturday date but Sunday might do.

'No,' she said. 'Not Sunday. I have a standing date on Sundays.' And as he seemed rather crestfallen, she explained, 'I go to tea with my son and my grandchildren. I couldn't miss that.'

'Ah!' he understood. 'Then Monday?'

'Monday I work late, Tuesday's the working party, Wednesday's the meeting. Oh dear, I'm beginning to sound like a teenager. I shall be saying I've got to wash my hair next.'

'I'll come to the meeting,' he decided. 'Bit of moral support. We can sort something out then.'

'Thanks,' she said. 'I'll be glad of the company.'

There was something about the tone of her voice that made him feel protective. 'You're not nervous about it are you?'

'Petrified,' she admitted. 'Even with this recording to help me. But don't tell anybody.'

He was touched to think she would tell *him*. 'Your secret is safe with me,' he joked. And for a brief and rather silly moment he wondered whether he could kiss her goodnight.

She was opening the car door. 'Well goodnight

then,' she said as she climbed in. 'Thanks for all your help. See you Wednesday.'

He watched her drive out of the park and along the empty street until her tail lights disappeared round the corner. She's a good woman, he thought. And Wednesday suddenly seemed a long way away.

In Canterbury Gardens, David Pendleton was thinking about Laura too. He'd had a bad day at work and having spent two hours willing himself to sleep without any success at all, he'd succumbed to wakefulness, got up quietly and taken himself off to his study. There he poured himself a double malt and settled down to do battle with his accounts. As he was so infuriatingly wide awake he might as well make use of his time.

The study was the only room in the house that he could truly call his own, the place where he could retreat to be himself, where he kept his malt and his silver cigarette case, where he could allow himself the occasional luxury of dreams. It was decorated in the same stark black and white as the rest of the house, the walls painted his ubiquitous magnolia, the office chair upholstered black, the desk sombre in black wood with brass trimmings, the filing cabinet pristine as a refrigerator. But, either as a concession to his individuality or because he'd bought them one day in a fit of defiant and uncharacteristic exuberance, the box files were all pillar box red.

'My life blood,' he would explain to friends and

colleagues who visited him there, 'Drained away by the company!'

'Mega symbolic,' they agreed, enjoying his malt. Despite his puritanical obsession with work and his aggravatingly accurate timekeeping, he was an open-handed host.

The sight of his box files always cheered him although he didn't know why. Even now, in the small hours of the morning. Even now, when he was feeling guilty about his mother. Damn it, how could he concentrate on the accounts with so many other things going on in his head?

He got up and walked over to the window, glass in hand. His study had been built as a single bedroom overlooking the front garden and the kidney-shaped lawn at the centre of the close, and one of the reasons he'd chosen it was because the view pleased him so much. Now he pulled back the curtains and looked out.

There wasn't a sign of life anywhere in the close and no light either except for a little orange courtesy light glowing like a jewel beside the porch of the house directly opposite. It's a nice quiet close, he thought. A respectable close with respectable houses. Well-kept detached houses. You get a better class of people altogether in detached houses. They use their garages to keep their cars in at night, instead of filling them with junk the way they'd done in the last place he'd lived in. Well-kept trees — even if they *were* all bent over sideways by the prevailing wind. Well-kept lawns. He took a great pride in his own lawn, mowing it every week in the summer. Well-kept families. No motor bikes in this part of the village, thank God. And no teenage parties.

If it hadn't been so dark he would have been able to see the Downs from his window and the road they were making such a fuss about. The sooner they got that by-pass built the better to his way of thinking. It was childish for people to make a fuss about it when they knew it would have to be built eventually. But he prided himself that he could see both sides of the question. He could even understand why his mother wanted to go on living in that ramshackle old cottage of hers but he was sure she would feel quite differently about it once she had to move. He kept pointing out the conveniences. Proper drainage for a start. How she could go on coping with a cess-pit being emptied every three months was quite beyond him. But then she'd often been beyond him. If only she wasn't such a difficult woman.

But a good woman, he thought, arguing against himself, a loving woman. And he wished he hadn't been treating her so badly. It was nearly a week since that awful demonstration and he hadn't been to visit her once. He ought to have done. He knew that only too well. He should have taken her flowers or a box of chocolates, shown a bit of concern and sympathy, been there to see what she had to say instead of skulking behind the telephone. But he hadn't done any of those things. The thought of her being ill had filled him with irritable terror. She *couldn't* be ill. She was

177

never ill. In all the years they'd lived on their own since Dad walked out on them, she'd never been ill once. It was unthinkable and he wouldn't think it.

But he *had* thought it, of course, and with increasing irritation because it was all her own fault. He'd *told* her not to go on that stupid demonstration, exasperating woman. And she *would* go.

Well, he thought, returning to the desk to pour himself a second malt, let's hope she's got all this nonsense out of her system now and we shan't hear any more about it. We'll lay on a special tea to make amends. Flowers on the table. That sort of thing. Mo can make one of her fudge cakes.

He wrote himself a note to that effect. 'Special tea for Mother. Discuss Mo A.M.'

Then he went back to the accounts.

Laura went to church that Sunday morning as she'd promised herself. She wasn't a regular church-goer — the church was too far away and there was usually too much housework to be done for that — but she enjoyed the occasional visit and invariably came home refreshed by it. She liked the familiar welcome of the place, the sense of being among friends and of being supported. She relished the bouquet of scents that greeted her — incense, burning candles, wax polish, fresh flowers, ancient stone — and was soothed by the comfortable rhythm of the hymns and the timeless reassurance of prayer.

If anyone had asked her, she would have admitted that she didn't share all the beliefs of the congregation and probably wouldn't see eye to eye with the rector on a good many points of doctrine either. She certainly didn't see God as a patriarch who would reward and punish His followers nor as a benign entity who would interfere in human affairs. To her He was a power of a different order, something outer and ultra that couldn't be understood. The nearest she'd ever got to a definition was to say He was a source of cosmic strength and even that didn't sound right. When she prayed it was never for heavenly favour, rarely for forgiveness, but usually for grace of some kind — to understand a situation that was baffling her, to cope with something or someone in the least hurtful way, to endure what had to be endured, to find the strength to do what had to be done.

That morning her prayers were very particular — for courage to face the meeting on Wednesday and for tact and common sense to see her through that afternoon's tea party. I mustn't upset my poor David, she explained to her maker. I need to find some way to tell him about this meeting that won't alarm him or make him feel threatened.

The bond between them had always been unnaturally tight. That was part of the trouble and she knew it now — when it was too late to do anything about it. While he'd been a little boy their closeness had felt like strength but once he was in his teens and pulling away from her into a life of his own, she'd grown to realise that there was weakness in it too. By the time he'd married, she'd had to face the fact that their evolving relationship was too delicate to withstand more than the mildest disagreement and that it would have to be maintained with extreme care and self-control. To her credit, that was how she'd managed it ever since — until the council's awful letter arrived. But now it was going to be put to the test. Tact, she prayed, that's what I need. Tact and good timing. Grant me that, Lord, and I think I can manage.

The litany was coming to an end.

'Almighty God, who has given us grace at this time with one accord to make our common supplications unto thee . . . Fulfil now, O Lord, the desires and petitions of thy servants, as may be most expedient for them; granting us in this world knowledge of Thy truth, and in the world to come life everlasting.'

'Amen,' Laura said and meant it.

Back at Holm End, Amy was lounging on the sofa enjoying the fire and a cigarette.

'Where have you been?' she said, when Laura walked in.

'To church,' Laura said, noticing the dirty dishes on the table and the Sunday papers strewn across the carpet.

Amy raised her elegant eyebrows, 'Good God!'

'Exactly.'

Amy yawned as her hostess picked up the papers but apart from shifting her legs out of the

180

way she made no effort to help her.

'Now,' Laura said, rather tartly, 'I'm going to make myself some lunch. And you're going to clear the table and do the washing-up.'

'Must I?' Amy pouted, flicking ash into the hearth. 'I'm waiting for Conrad to pick me up. We're going motor racing.'

Laura was remorseless. 'Then you'd better look sharp, hadn't you. There's the washing-up bowl.'

Rather to her surprise, Amy stubbed out her cigarette and began to clear the table. 'OK, OK,' she said. 'I can't stand you *and* Jeff.'

'What's Jeff got to do with it?' Laura asked, busily chopping an onion.

'He's been giving me lectures about pulling my weight,' Amy told her. 'Well *a* lecture anyway. I went down to the surgery on Friday to get an aspirin and he bent my ear something rotten. He's turning out to be a proper old woman.'

But he's right about this, Laura thought. 'Don't forget the teapot,' she said. 'That needs washing too.'

Amy picked up the teapot and stood with it between her hands. 'Look,' she began. 'I should have said this before. I'm sorry about the party — the way we all went on.'

Laura acknowledged the apology with a wry smile. 'So you should be.'

'I was a bit drunk.'

'I *had* noticed.'

Amy put the teapot on the draining board and

started to wash the dishes. 'I couldn't help it,' she said. 'It's the only way I can get through the first day in a new job. It's all very well for you. You've only had the one job in all these years. But I've been a rolling stone.'

'I had a child to bring up,' Laura reminded her. 'You can't go flitting from job to job when you've got responsibilities.'

'OK. OK. Point taken. All I'm saying is it's been dreadful for me. I can't even *remember* half the jobs I've had. And if I didn't get drunk the night before my first day, I couldn't face it. I'm not excusing myself. It's an explanation, that's all. I thought I ought to tell you.'

There are other things you ought to tell me too, Laura thought. 'What about your house-hunting?' she asked. 'While we're talking. Or aren't you serious about it?'

'Oh I'm serious,' Amy said, rinsing out the teapot. 'If they'd send me something halfway suitable I'd be after it like a shot. But they don't. You never saw such a load of rubbish.' Then her voice and expression suddenly changed, becoming light and girlish and animated. 'There he is!' she cried. 'I'm off!'

Laura hadn't heard a car but when she glanced out of the window, there it was, sure enough, cruising up the drive with a dark-haired man stiff as a tailor's dummy behind the wheel. She watched as Amy leapt from the cottage, ran gaily across to greet him with a kiss and then smoothed herself into the passenger seat beside him.

Molly's right, she thought, she's not making any effort to find a house. I haven't seen any details lying around and there haven't been any letters from the estate agents either. I don't think she's trying at all. When I've got this afternoon's tea party behind me — and the meeting — I shall have to take her to task about it. Still at least I've got her to help with the housework. And that's something.

In Canterbury Gardens that afternoon, Maureen came out on to the drive to greet her mother-in-law as she arrived. And to forewarn her.

'I think David's got a bit of a guilty conscience,' she said. 'He's been in a mood all day.'

Laura was surprised. 'Whatever for?'

'Not visiting you, I think.'

'I didn't expect to be visited,' Laura said truthfully, searching in the glove compartment for her scarf. 'We've all got too much to do.' She climbed out of the Land-Rover and tucked the scarf into the neck of her cardigan so as to hide her stitches. 'Did you get the blood out of Jessica's coat?'

They walked towards the house. 'Not all of it, no,' Maureen admitted. 'You know what blood's like.'

'I'll treat her to a new one.'

'No. It's all right,' Maureen said as they reached the hall. 'I mean, there's no need . . .'

'There's every need,' Laura said firmly. '*I* took her there. Hello David.'

David bent to kiss his mother's cheek and winced before he could control himself. Despite her efforts with the scarf some of her stitches were still visible. He could see two of the awful things, sticking out of her hair like barbed wire. The sight of them made him feel anguished. 'How are you, Mother?' he said stiffly.

She felt so sorry for him, for his awkward concern and his fraught expression. You're so like your father to look at, she thought. If only you could have inherited his easy nature too.

'I'm fine,' she said, adjusting the scarf. 'You know me. I heal quickly.'

He couldn't think what to say to her next, but at that moment Jessica came tripping down the stairs, wafting the scent of shampoo from her long blonde mane and dressed in the full glory of her Saturday purchases, a pair of purple leggings and a chunky sweater in a bold pattern of red, purple, royal blue and gold on a black background.

'How's the dear old Granny?' she said. 'I saw your article in the paper. Everyone's talking about it.'

The words resonated like bombs in the white space of the hall. Both her parents coloured, Maureen with embarrassment, David with annoyance. 'I hope not,' he said.

'Tea,' Maureen suggested diplomatically. 'The kettle's on the boil.'

'I'll make it,' Jessica offered, hair swinging as she headed for the kitchen.

But before they could move out of the hall,

someone rang the doorbell.

'Now who's that?' David said, frowning as he went to answer it.

It was a young man in a blue Pringle jersey and an expensive pair of jeans, a tall fair young man with rather odd eyes.

'I'm sorry to disturb you,' he said. 'But does Jessica Pendleton live here? I've got a message for her.'

The boy with the blue Volvo, Laura thought, recognising him. That's torn it.

But Jessica had everything coolly in hand. 'Oh it's you, Kevin,' she said, joining her father at the door. 'Don't tell me! I know why you've come. You've brought back my book, haven't you? *The one I lent to your cousin.*'

He responded so smoothly that Laura was the only one to notice it. 'Well actually,' he said, 'no, I haven't. She wants to keep it for another week. She sent me to ask if you'd mind.'

Well there's a transparent excuse if ever I heard one, Maureen said to herself and she flashed a quick eye signal to Laura, who flashed back, Yes, you're right.

Kevin was still talking, this time addressing his remarks to David — with elaborate politeness. 'I hope I'm not being a nuisance, Mr Pendleton, calling on a Sunday. It's just I was in the neighbourhood and my cousin's rather a stickler for returning things.'

David was impressed. What an excellent young man, he thought, to run errands for his cousin.

And so polite. 'No, no, not at all. Come in,' he said, standing back to encourage him into the house. 'We were just going to have tea. Would you like to join us?'

More eye messages. This time from mother to daughter, Maureen questioning whether that was what Jessica wanted, Jessica signing by a shrug that it was no big deal.

Well, well, well, Laura thought watching her granddaughter as she led the way into the dining room, now how will she handle this? There was something about the young man's eyes that she found distinctly disquieting, something shifty and dishonest. She tried to be fair to him, arguing with herself that it could have been because they were so very pale and set at such an odd angle to one another, but she found them disturbing just the same.

Jessica was effecting introductions as she went so as to preempt any further misunderstandings. 'This is my kid brother Danny. This is my Gran. *You haven't met her have you?*'

'You're the local heroine I believe,' he said as he took his seat at the table. 'I recognise you from your picture in the paper.'

Oh do you? Laura thought. Well you're slick enough, I'll give you that. She decided to tease him. 'Did you read the article?'

He temporised. 'Bits of it. Badgers aren't my thing, if you'll forgive me for saying so. Don't get me wrong. I'm sure they're lovely animals and well worth preserving and all that sort of thing.

186

It's just they're not my scene.'

'But you don't mind other people sticking up for them?'

'Good Lord no. Free speech and everything. Part of the great British tradition.'

'I'm going in for a bit more free speech on Wednesday,' Laura said and told them quickly while they were in a good mood.

David looked annoyed but, mindful of the stranger in their midst, he didn't comment, Maureen gave her mother-in-law half a smile as she went off to make the tea, Kevin looked guarded. It was only Danny who reacted.

'Smashing,' he said, grinning at her. 'Will you be in the paper again?'

'Of course not,' David told him firmly. 'It's only a little local meeting. There's nothing news-worthy in that.'

Laura took pity on him and changed the sub-ject. 'Not quite such a big slice, Jess. Half would do.'

Jessica put the intended slice on her grand-mother's plate. 'Eat it up,' she ordered gaily. 'Or you'll never grow a big strong girl.'

'Who won't?' Maureen asked, carrying the tea-pot into the room.

'Gran. If she's going to be a public speaker —' darting a daring glance at her father — 'she'll need all her strength.'

This time it was David who changed the sub-ject. 'So tell me,' he said to Kevin. 'What line of business are you in?'

'I know,' Danny guessed. 'You're a financial advisor.'

'I wish I was,' Kevin sighed. 'No, I'm a PA for my sins. I work for a building contractor. Very boring stuff.'

'But it brings home the bacon,' David said.

Kevin contrived to look modest. 'The odd rasher now and then. I'm not in your league, of course sir, but a job's a job these days.'

'I'm in pharmaceuticals,' David told him with some pride. 'PPC. Been with them for eighteen months. I was with Sterling Health before that.'

'A good firm.'

Laura sat beside Daniel and enjoyed her slice of fudge cake and noticed things. She realised she was watching as though she were at a play and that, despite her misgivings about him, she couldn't help admiring the act this young man was putting on. She was dismayed by the ease with which he was hoodwinking David but at least his arrival had taken the edge off their family awkwardness. He dominated the occasion, but politely and easily, as if it were the natural thing to do. And he was certainly giving David something else to concentrate on.

They talked about football, and deplored the hooligan element, about soap operas and how ridiculously facile they were, about cars and how they both wished they could afford a Mercedes.

By the time the meal was over and the young man asked for permission to take Jessica out to a 'local concert' it was given as if he were an old and trusted friend.

'First-rate chap,' David approved as the young couple left the house. 'Straight as a die. You don't get many like that these days.'

Chapter Twelve

Once the Volvo had purred out of the close, Jessica shook out her hair and sank back into the passenger seat with relief. 'Nice one!' she said. 'That was brilliant.'

Kevin was well aware of the importance of what he'd done and knew how skilful he'd been, so he was nonchalant about it. 'Any time,' he said. 'I gather they don't know you were at Twyford Down.'

'Oh they knew about *that*,' she said lightly. 'I didn't tell them about *you*, that's all.'

He was a bit put down. 'Oh great!'

She was pleased to see how easily she'd got an advantage over him, then realised that she was being perverse and explained so as to put things right. 'I'm not supposed to talk to strangers.'

That reassured him. 'Well they know about me now.'

'Yes,' she agreed cheerfully. 'They do. You were brilliant.'

'That's me,' he said.

'And modest with it,' she laughed. 'How did you get my address?'

'Easy,' he said. 'I phoned you last night. Got your dad on the answer phone. *"David Pendleton speaking."* Looked you up in the book.'

She was impressed. And thrilled. It was really cool to be driving away with someone who'd just outwitted her father. Especially when her father had given her permission to do it.

They were driving north out of the village, heading towards the disputed road. 'Where are we going?' she said. 'It's not really a concert is it?'

He looked pleased with himself. 'It's a rave,' he said. 'How does that grab you?'

'Round here?'

'Do they have such things in this part of the world?'

She had to admit they didn't. 'Where then?'

'Where would you like it to be?'

'I don't know.' Why did he have to tease so much before he would answer a question?

'London,' he said with a flourish. 'The big bad city.'

She smiled. 'Brilliant!' Especially when they'd fooled Dad that she was safe and sedate at a concert. 'Are we going on the motorway?'

'I thought you didn't believe in motorways?'

'They're all right in principle,' she said loftily. 'It's knocking down houses I'm against.'

'Like your gran's.'

'Right.'

'She's a feisty old girl, your gran.'

She scowled against the hint of criticism in the words. 'She's lovely.'

'I never said she wasn't. She's a fighter. That's what I meant. Are you going with her when she makes her speech?'

'I might. I don't know. I haven't made my mind up.'

'You should.'

She scowled again. 'Why should I?'

'Moral support,' he said. 'And then you can tell me all about it next time.'

'What makes you think there'll be a next time?'

He gave her a devilish grin, pale eyes flickering. 'Hope,' he said. 'Fasten your seat-belt. I drive fast.'

He did too. It was thrilling. She'd only been driven to London once before and that was years ago in a grotty old coach on some awful school trip to some awful boring play. Shakespeare probably. She couldn't remember. This was totally different. Belting towards the city at 90 m.p.h., overtaking everything in sight, while the round white eyes of oncoming traffic owled out of the darkness towards them, all driving in predictable order and obeying the rules. She felt like a queen.

Once or twice, as he swooped from lane to lane and she was thrown violently about, she realised she was afraid of his driving as well as excited by it. Alarm swelled in her throat and she wanted to close her eyes until the danger was past. She didn't of course, and she didn't say anything either. Not that it would have mattered if she had because he was too busy swearing at his fellow drivers to notice. 'Get out the way you morons!'

By the time they reached the suburbs, she was

dizzy with excitement. They drove along streets stabbed with artificial light, blazing white and psychedelic orange, past lines of parked cars — most of them seedy — past clubs and pubs where drums thumped towards them as they approached, past hordes and hordes of people — all of them young — milling about or standing around at street corners. She felt as free as a bird just to be part of it. The big, bad city. Wicked!

'Not far now,' he said.

'Where are we going?'

'You'll see.'

It was a huge hangar lurking bulkily in one corner of an empty industrial site. Teenagers were streaming into it from all directions and it was pulsing with light and sound like a spacecraft ready for take-off.

'You won't need your jersey,' he said, explaining rather needlessly, 'it gets hot in there. Leave it in the car.'

If the outside of the place was extraordinary, the inside was mind-blowing. The noise was so intense that Jessica could feel the beat throbbing through the soles of her feet, rising through her body, expanding as it went. Above her the darkness exploded into synchronised flashes of colour, as though they were all suspended in the sky in the middle of some gigantic firework display. And all around her there were people dancing, the heat of their bodies palpable even in that huge arena, the stamp of their feet an echo of the drums, their raised arms undulating in the intermittent light like pale weed under the sea. Dad would have kittens if he could see me now, she thought. What a place!

Kevin put his mouth close to her ear. 'Come on,' he said. And pulled her into the writhing mass.

He's no dancer, she thought, as she watched him shuffling from foot to foot. He's off the beat for a start. But it didn't matter. *She* was a very good dancer and she knew she would be noticed and admired — and not just by him. She liked being noticed. If you've got it, she thought, flaunt it.

They danced until the sweat was running down their backs so she was glad when he suggested a pause for some bottled water. Down by the drinks counter they found a group of his friends, all very well dressed and very cool and led by a dark-haired man who was wearing sunglasses. They asked her what she thought of it and when she said it 'wasn't bad', one of the girls said *she* thought it could do with 'livening up' and produced a handful of pills which she offered round as though they were sweets.

Jessica hesitated. She'd heard about drugs being sold at raves. They'd had at least three gross lectures about it at school. And until that moment she'd told all her friends she'd never be such a fool as to get hooked on to *that* sort of thing. But it was quite a different matter to be in the middle of a crowd of people who were all popping pills into their mouths as if it were the most natural

194

thing in the world and to actually have a pill dropped enticingly into her palm.

Kevin had taken out his wallet and was talking to the man in sunglasses. A twenty-pound note and a fiver changed hands. Then he turned to Jessica. 'Try it! Go on!' he urged. 'It's great!'

'What is it?'

'Experience,' he said, grinning at his friends.

She didn't know what to do. There was so much noise and pressure that it was almost impossible to think. She knew she was being foolish even to consider it but the faces all around her were urging her on so strongly. 'Go on! Try it! It won't hurt you!' The sense of being in danger was an almost irresistible temptation. She couldn't be the only one to refuse when everybody else was taking them. She'd look like a nerd. Maybe one wouldn't make much difference. It was only a pill. And yet she wasn't certain.

'Well . . .' she dithered.

'Trust me!' Kevin said. And he lifted her palm towards her mouth, pill and all.

So she took it, washing it down with a mouthful of water and splendid bravado. And they cheered her. Then they all bought bottles of water as if they were off on a safari, tucked them into belts or back pockets and trooped back to the dance.

Jessica's heart was juddering with alarm at the risk she was running but once she began to dance it calmed down and she felt perfectly normal again. All that fuss in school, she thought, and it doesn't have any effect on you at all. What a sell!

But whatever Kevin had taken had certainly had an effect on *him*. His dancing was transformed. Now he was moving marvellously and very, very fast, real dirty dancing stuff, using his entire body, writhing to the rhythm and so close to her that she was suddenly and powerfully excited by him.

I'm in love, she thought wildly. This is it. She was charged with energy, expanding with it, lifted up and up and up. If I wanted to, she thought, I could fly off into the stratosphere.

Hours passed as though they were minutes. They danced as if they were never going to stop, drinking water to quench their heat and thirst as they danced. The music exploded into gigantic bubbles of sound. There was no roof to hold them down, only an infinite, timeless sky where stars throbbed and flashed. There were no walls to hem them in, only the excitement and terror of a magical forest where wolves sang and bears danced and pinegreen birds swooped and called, their golden beaks as bright as sovereigns in the immeasurable darkness. And she knew that she was singing too, in an effortless, wordless way. Let it go on for ever.

As one disc was bellowed into the next, Kevin put his mouth close to her ear. 'Got to make a phone call,' he said. 'Shan't be long. Stick with Pauline.'

She felt lost and miserable without him in that heaving throng, as if the lights had all been switched off. She went on dancing — what else

196

could she do? — but she danced mechanically, thinking dejected thoughts. He'll never find me. He's probably walked out on me — gone for good. How would I know? If he's gone for good, I shall have to find my own way home. He'll never find me.

And then suddenly somebody put an arm round her waist and she was being scooped towards his body. Relief and desire sprang up in her together.

'Oh!' she shouted. 'I thought you'd lost me.'

'I never lose anybody,' he shouted back. 'That's my job. Did you miss me?'

She was near tears. 'Yes. I did.'

It seemed the most natural thing in the world that he should bend his head and kiss her long and hard.

Much dancing and many kisses later, she remembered that she had something she wanted to ask him. 'Where were you when you went away?'

'Told you. Had to make a phone call.'

That was puzzling. 'Who to?'

'Your dad. It's past midnight.'

'Is it?' She didn't care what time it was nor what her father thought.

'I told him my car's been vandalised. Windscreen's smashed. Gonna take hours to get it mended. He said he'd come and pick you up. Imagine that. Anyway I told him you were staying with a friend of mine. Nice married couple with a single bed. So you've got an excuse. Right? To stay out as long as you like.'

'Brilliant,' she admired. She hadn't understood half the things he'd been telling her but it sounded wonderful. He was *so* clever.

'That's me,' he said, scooping her against his body to kiss her again.

It was past four o'clock before the rave finally racketed to an end. The DJ was packing up when Kevin and his friends drifted out into the emptying road of the factory site and the softness of moonlight.

'Where to now?' Jessica asked. 'Are we going home?'

He had his arm tightly round her, his fingers caressing her thighs. 'Not if you don't want to. Do you want to?'

She knew that his question wasn't simply about whether or not she wanted to go straight home. It was also about whether or not she wanted to have sex with him. If she said yes, she would be committed. She hesitated, torn between desire and apprehension.

He kissed her open-mouthed to encourage her. 'You do want to, don't you?' It was a claim not a question.

'Yes,' she said, still breathless from his kiss. 'Yes, I do.' And she did really. It was about time. All the other girls had done it years ago. Or months anyway. Even Emma. It was stupid to be a virgin at seventeen.

'We're all going back to Ralph's place,' he said. 'Come on.' And led her to his car.

She was disturbed that he was so matter of fact

about it, that all the arrangements for the rest of their night together had been so carefully made. It made her feel that he'd had it all planned, especially when they were in the car and on their own together and instead of kissing her again, he asked her whether she was on the pill.

'No,' she said, her alarm showing on her face. 'I'm not.'

'No problem,' he said. 'Leave it to me.'

But it was decidedly thrilling to be accepted as a pair by the man in the sunglasses and told they could have the double bedroom.

'Cheers,' Kevin said to his host and led her straight up the stairs.

And after all that, it was a disappointment, over so quickly she hardly felt a thing. And an even greater one was that instead of talking to her and cuddling her afterwards, which was what she expected, he rolled away from her and fell instantly asleep.

She lay beside him on the tumbled bed and thought. About the rave and what an experience it had been, about deceiving her father and how she wished she didn't have to, about sex and what a sell it was, about taking pills. Now that she was calmer she assumed it was ecstasy she'd taken. All that dreadful thirst was a sign of ecstasy. She knew that from the lectures at school. She was thirsty now but she daren't go downstairs for more water because there were people still up. She could hear the hi-fi. This is a grotty room, she thought, gazing round her, and she wondered who it belonged to and what sort of life they led. And while she was wondering, she drifted into an uncomfortable sleep.

And was woken almost immediately by a loud bell clanging. 'What is it?' she said, sitting up at once.

Kevin reached across her to switch off the alarm clock that was making all the row. 'Six o'clock,' he said. 'Time to go.'

'What?'

He was putting on his clothes. 'If you're going to be home in time for school. I promised your old man you'd be in time for school.'

She didn't want to get up. She was tired to her bones. She wanted to stay in bed all day. Even in this smelly bed. 'I can't be bothered.'

'Come on,' he said, hauling on his trousers.

'What about breakfast?'

'No time,' he said and stooping, gathered up her tumbled clothes and dropped them on the bed beside her. 'Get dressed.'

It was a miserable awakening, in a frowsy bed in a cold room with a man who just gave her orders instead of telling her he loved her, the way he ought to have done. She rubbed the sleep from her eyes and dressed slowly, found her bag, retrieved her brush, tried to remove the tangles from her hair.

'We'll get some tea at the nearest service station,' he said. 'Right?'

She agreed meekly. She didn't have the energy to argue or even talk. Even when they were in the car and heading back to Sussex along virtually empty roads, she didn't say anything. She was numb with fatigue and disappointment. A pot of tea and a roll and butter improved things, but only marginally. She needed a bath and clean clothes and a bowl of cocoa pops. It was horrible to be sitting there in the same clothes she'd worn the night before. There was no adventure in *that*. It was just sordid, the way their sex had been.

'Cheer up,' he said as they walked back to the car. The first pale light of dawn was staining the sky. 'It's not that bad.'

She stopped in mid-stride to look at him in the garish light from the service station. She wanted to ask him how he felt about her, to find out if she'd just been a one-night-stand, but she couldn't do it.

He looked back at her but went on walking. 'You're all right, aren't you?' he asked.

She decided to tell him one home truth. 'You haven't said anything to me since last night.' Now see what he makes of that.

He denied it. 'Yes I have. Plenty of things.'

'Nothing important.'

'Like what?' he said, getting into the car. 'I've arranged to get you home on time, haven't I?'

'That's not important.'

'It is if we're going out again.'

A faint hope stirred. 'Are we?'

'Course. You want to don't you?'

He seemed sure of himself but he wasn't saying the right things. She got into the passenger seat, thinking hard. 'I didn't know if *you*'d want to,' she said.

He gave her a long look. 'I thought I'd — like — proved that last night.'

'You never *said* anything.'

'That's not the time for saying things.'

'People usually say things.' There wasn't a film or a magazine that wasn't full of examples. They called it pillow talk.

'Like what?'

'Like . . . like . . .' But she couldn't put words into his mouth. That would be humiliating. If he couldn't work it out for himself it showed he didn't love her. Last night was just sex. She didn't mean anything to him.

'I don't say things,' he told her. 'That's not the way I am. I mean — like — actions speak louder than words.'

She shrugged her shoulders. 'I'm not bothered.'

He turned in the seat and put an arm round her shoulders, pulling her towards him so that he could kiss her. 'The thing is,' he said afterwards, his cheek against hers. 'Like — we wouldn't be here if I didn't — like — love you.'

His unshaven cheek was rough as emery paper against her skin but she didn't care. He *did* love her, after all. He was the first and he loved her. 'Yes,' she said, stroking his hair with her finger tips.

He held her gently for a little while and kissed her again. 'We'd better get going,' he said. 'I mean, I could stay here for hours but we can't put your old man in a lather. 'Specially if I'm going to take you out tomorrow.'

She was bold enough now to ask, 'Not tonight?'

'Tonight I'm working,' he said. And put the car into gear.

It surprised her that her father took her first night out with such calm. He and Danny were sitting at the kitchen table when she got home and Mum was cooking his usual bacon and egg breakfast. It smelled divine.

'Bad luck,' he said to Kevin, folding his newspaper. 'You got it fixed though, I see.' He had a good view of the Volvo through the kitchen window.

Kevin stood just inside the kitchen door and smiled apologetically. 'Eventually,' he said, making a face. 'Took for ever.'

'That's Sunday night for you,' David sympathised.

'Yes,' Kevin agreed.

'Did they steal your radio?' Danny wanted to know.

'Don't they always?' Kevin said. And went on, speaking to David, very politely. 'Look, I know this isn't the right time to ask, but is it all right if I take Jessica out again? Tuesday maybe. Or Wednesday?'

'I've got a sales conference at the end of the week so I shan't be here,' David told him. 'It's up to the others. What do you think Maureen?

203

Have you got anything planned for Tuesday or Wednesday?'

'We were thinking of going over to see Laura on Wednesday, weren't we Jess? Danny'll be at Michael's sleep-over.'

Eye messages from mother to daughter, which Danny picked up. Eye messages from Jessica to Kevin, which made Maureen wonder.

'Tuesday then?' Kevin said, keeping a politely straight face.

David decided to tease him. 'If you can guarantee to keep your car in one piece and get her home at a reasonable time.'

'Course.'

'OK then.'

'Cheers,' the young man said, smiling as if he were relieved by the decision. 'See you tomorrow then Jessica. Must rush.'

Now that it was settled, Jessica sank into the nearest chair and closed her eyes. She was so tired she couldn't think how she would manage a day at school. It was a relief that he'd left them with so little fuss. Oh for a bath, she thought.

'A nice lad,' her father approved. (If only you knew!)

'I hope you didn't sit up all night,' her mother said. (Trust you to come homing in on that.) 'You're all eyes.'

Jessica managed to make her voice sound wearily cool. 'No, Mum. I didn't sit up all night.'

'So where did you sleep?'

I could do without this, Jessica thought. It's an

invasion of privacy. But she answered in the same cool way. 'One of his friends put us up.'

Maureen sniffed. 'Not that it did you much good from the looks of you.'

'I need a bath, that's all.'

'Have you had any breakfast?'

'Cup of tea.'

'You won't survive long on a cup of tea. Go and get ready for school and I'll fix you something. What do you fancy?'

A long lie-in, Jessica thought. A bit of peace and quiet to think things over and sort out what I feel. But as that wasn't a possibility, she opted for eggs and bacon and resigned herself to a difficult day.

It was even worse than she feared. She couldn't concentrate on anything, was late to every lesson, left her books behind after English, almost fell asleep in Geography. By the end of the afternoon she was so tired she could have cried. It was a relief that her mother had driven her to school so she didn't have to cycle home. Never again, she thought, as she sat in the back of the car with her eyes closed. If he wants to take me to another rave it had better be on a Saturday.

'Tea,' her mother said as she stopped the car on the drive. 'I don't know about you but I'm ready to drop.'

There was a card balanced against the garage door. Interflora had tried to deliver. *Flowers are in garage.*

They were a dozen roses, blood-red under their cellophane wrapper, tied with red ribbon with a message attached. *'Say it with flowers. Kevin.'*

She could feel a blush rising into her cheeks and had to swing her hair across her face to hide it. Red roses! she thought, thrilled by the sight of them. No one had ever given her red roses before. It was really romantic.

'Good heavens!' Maureen said.

'I'll put them in the living room,' Jessica said, trying to be cool about it. 'On the window sill. Put a bit of colour in the place.'

Maureen was concerned about what David would think. In her opinion, red roses after a first date was a bit much. It gave her the feeling that Jessica was being rushed, the fear that history was repeating itself. And who better to understand that than David who had rushed *her* off her feet all those years ago.

She needn't have worried. David seemed to have forgotten their experience. He was delighted by the flowers. 'Guilty conscience,' he approved. 'Which is no bad thing. Shows he realises he shouldn't have kept you out all night, eh Jess?'

Jessica laughed at him and agreed that he was probably right. 'He *did* phone you,' she pointed out.

'Oh yes,' her father said easily. 'He did the best he could in the circumstances.'

But Maureen was wondering what else might have happened and hoping that it hadn't. Jessica wouldn't confide in her — teenagers never did —

and the signs were ambiguous. That blush could have been pleasure or surprise. Her fatigue could be simply due to lack of sleep. If only his excuse hadn't been quite so plausible and if only David hadn't accepted it so readily. Of course, she could be wronging him and it could all turn out to be perfectly true, but the fact remained that this young man had kept Jess out all night and left her totally exhausted all next day.

The phone rang into her thoughts.

'I'll get it!' Jessica said, springing to her feet as though she wasn't tired after all. She actually ran into the hall. 'Yes,' she said into the receiver. 'They have. They're lovely. You shouldn't have.'

As she watched her daughter listening to the answer she couldn't hear herself, Maureen's heart contracted with pity for her. They're so vulnerable, she thought, and it's even worse for them than it was for us. They might avoid getting pregnant — I must see if I can talk to her about *that* at least — and VD is curable but there's AIDS now. She yearned to protect this newly adult child of hers and knew she couldn't do it. We all make the same mistakes, she thought, generation after generation, that's what's so awful. And in our family the mistake is marrying young and not realising what a weight of responsibility you're taking on.

There were always so many things to worry about. She'd accepted her temporary job, was enjoying it and doing it well, but she still hadn't plucked up the courage to tell David about it.

And now they were asking her to take on another responsibility and she ought to tell him about that too. But she knew she couldn't do it.

Chapter Thirteen

The Memorial Hall on the Glendale estate was packed to the walls that Wednesday evening. Every single plastic chair was taken and people were standing hip to hip at the back of the hall, talking angrily. There were even half a dozen crouched on the floor in front of the stage and another three perched uncomfortably on the sill of the bay window. It dried Laura's mouth just to look at them — even though she knew that a packed house was just what the campaign needed.

She sat on the stage behind a rickety trestle table, too far away from the blue curtains to be shielded by either of them, and smiled nervously at her audience, struggling to appear calm. Inwardly she was quailing. So much depended on this meeting. If it went well, it could be the start of a mass campaign and that was what they needed. She knew that now beyond any doubt. But *would* it go well? Could she make it go well? She was afraid of her lack of experience, afraid that she wouldn't be heard, or even worse, that they wouldn't listen, afraid that she might do more harm than good. It was one thing to chair a meeting of fellow librarians, quite another to address a public meeting.

She'd thought out what she was going to say

and provided herself with carefully printed notes — well spaced so that she could read them when she was standing — but they all hinged on the evidence of that tape and like a fool she'd let Jeff Turner go off with the recorder, tape and all. Now it was nearly time for the meeting to begin and there was no sign of him and despite all her attempts to keep calm she was beginning to panic. She would have to rethink the entire speech if he didn't turn up. I should have taken that recording home with me the night it was made, she thought. Or phoned him to remind him to be here on time. When push comes to shove it's no good depending on other people.

Sharon and the young man called Toddy were greeting new arrivals at the door. From time to time they smiled across at her but that was no encouragement. She glanced at her watch and saw with rising panic that it was 7.28. It was like waiting for the dentist. Please God, she prayed, help me to do this well, tape or no tape, help me to be calm.

And, as if in immediate answer to her prayer, there was a sudden movement at the entrance and there were Maureen and Jessica, smiling and waving at her and behind them Jeff, hung about with a camera and the much-desired tape and carrying a huge black portfolio under his arm.

'What's kept you?' she said as he struggled on to the platform. 'I thought you weren't coming.' It was ungracious to be cross with him but he deserved it, cutting things so fine.

He was too busy to notice or to answer her, giving instructions for a screen to be found and set up in front of the curtains. Toddy and Sharon ran to do his bidding and for several seconds there was a confusion of noise and movement. Then he put the tape recorder on the table.

'There you are,' he said. 'We'll just test it for sound.' And switched it on.

The noise it made was so sudden and so loud that it silenced the audience at once. Heads swivelled in their direction, jaws fell open, the remaining talkers were shushed. Laura put out her hand to switch it off, but Jeff shook his head. 'Run it,' he mouthed through the racket. And walked into the wings.

The meeting had begun, whether she would or not. After thirty crashing seconds she switched off the tape and stood up. 'That,' she said, 'is the sound of the super-highway recorded from behind a screening hedge at the exact distance it will be from Glendale School.'

Gasps and whistles of disbelief and horror.

'Yes,' she said. 'It shook me when I heard it. But that is what your children will endure every single day of their lives if this scheme goes ahead. To say nothing of the pollution it will cause.' She was into her prepared speech now and she didn't even have to look at her notes. 'There is a considerable body of evidence to suggest that lead in the atmosphere is responsible for an increase in childhood asthma. Children's lungs are closer to car exhausts than ours, you see, so they're more vulnerable. I expect most of you will have seen the map in the local paper, so you'll know how close this road is going to be.'

There was a movement in the wings and she turned her head to see what it was. Jeff and Toddy were carrying a large screen on to the stage. Pinned to it and facing the audience was a blown-up photograph of Glendale School with the open fields green behind it and painted across the green, in eye-catching red, the proposed new road. It looked so big and so close to the school that it caused the second gasp of the evening.

'Yes,' Laura agreed. 'It isn't until you see it that you realise what an impact it's going to have. And of course that usually happens after they've built the thing and when it's too late to do anything about it.'

'That's monstrous!' one man shouted. 'They didn't tell us it was going to be like that.'

Other voices yelled in agreement and outrage. 'It's right on top of the school. They can't *do* that.'

'They said there would be the minimum inconvenience,' a woman said.

'Perhaps this is what they mean by minimum inconvenience,' Laura told her. 'Perhaps that's bureaucrat-speak for turning our lives upside-down.'

The outcry continued for several minutes but when it finally stopped and Laura continued with her speech, there was an attentive silence. She told them what she'd learned from Greenpeace, the Friends of the Earth and SCAR. She told them how many acres of good agricultural land would be lost by the Laura's Way section alone. 'We've worked out that this scheme, as it stands, which is to say, the new stretch of road plus a junction, would destroy approximately two hundred and seventy acres of West Sussex countryside.' And how many animals and birds were killed every week on the existing road.

Finally, she described how brutally the demonstrators had been handled at Twyford Down. 'It's a real fight,' she warned. 'Make no mistake about that. There are people who want to build this road and will oppose us with all the power they can command. If we start a fight here that is what we must be prepared for.'

'Who's pushing for this motorway then, or whatever it's going to be called?' one man wanted to know. 'It can't just be the council can it? Who are we really fighting?'

She knew the answer to that now. 'The Ministry of Transport,' she said. 'But they're too cute to take the first step and they don't always come out into the open about it. That would make their intentions just a bit too obvious. They wait until there's been a road accident in the area they're interested in. That gets in the papers — which is quite right and proper — so it should — and then people start asking for a by-pass to take the traffic away from the road where it happened. The Ministry simply encourage the demand. Sometimes they don't even have to do that. Either way they can say it's "sprung up locally" and that they're just responding to it. It's very clever.'

'It's diabolical,' another man said. 'But what can you expect with this lot in power?'

'I think,' Toddy said, standing up to make his point. 'I think we ought to start up a petition for a public enquiry into whether this road should be built or not.'

The vote for it was unanimous and, even when he asked for volunteers to gather signatures, hands went up, gingerly at first, but then steadily all over the hall. It wasn't long before he had a queue of helpers waiting to sign up.

I've done it, Laura thought. It's beginning and now it will spread and spread. We're not going to be pushed around. We're going to stop them. For a moment, she felt so exhilarated it was as if her body had doubled in size and strength, as if she stood giant-tall on the platform, a larger-than-life general mustering her troops. Then she saw that there were people rushing to congratulate her, among them Maureen and Jessica and Jeff Turner, who was grinning all over his face, and she came down to size again.

'Success!' Jeff yelled. 'You were marvellous!'

'Yes,' she agreed. 'And no small thanks to you. That photograph was an inspiration.'

'The whole thing was an inspiration,' he said. 'It was bloody magnificent. How about a drink? I'll bet you could use one.'

She'd recovered enough to be sensible. She could but not if she was going to drive home.

'I'll take you back,' he volunteered. 'You too

Jessica. And your mother.'

'We can walk,' Maureen said. 'It's no distance. We walked here. But thanks, yes, a drink would be great.'

'The Blue Boar?' Jeff suggested.

It was the obvious place, right in the centre of the village. Soon they were all settled round the great open fireplace there, plying Laura with red wine and telling one another how marvelously everything had gone. The crowd around them grew larger and louder as more people arrived from the meeting to congratulate and plot. Toddy and Sharon joined them 'for a quickie' saying they couldn't stay long because their babysitter was waiting. And Toby Fawcett strolled across from the bar, glass in hand, to tell them to watch the *Gazette* on Thursday week.

'Tomorrow's edition has already gone to press or I'd have got it in there for you,' he said to Laura. 'But it's a great story. Just the sort of thing to get a debate going.'

'With luck . . .' Laura hoped. She was so full of confidence she felt that anything was possible now.

'What we want,' Jessica said, 'is a letter from that man who's always writing. You know, Mum, the one who makes you laugh. J.G. something-or-other.'

'Turner,' Jeff said, grinning at them.

There was so much wickedness in the grin that Laura was alerted. 'You're not related, are you?' she asked.

215

'Better than that,' he told her, grinning more wickedly than ever. 'Or worse, depending on your point of view.'

'Good heavens!' Maureen laughed at him. 'The man himself!' And she turned to Laura to tease. 'Why didn't you tell me you knew a celebrity?'

'Because I didn't know I did,' Laura said. What an extraordinary thing to keep a thing like that under his hat. She'd never have imagined he'd be so modest. Anyone else would have bragged about it.

'Well if I'm a celebrity,' Jeff laughed, 'I suppose I'd better buy another round.'

It was well past official closing time when they finally said goodnight and went their separate ways. And by then they were warm with drink and success.

'Pleased with yourself?' Jeff asked as he drove into the darkness of the country lanes.

'I am rather. I'm surprised at you though.'

'Are you?'

'You never told me you were J.G. Turner.'

Again that wicked grin. 'You never asked me.'

'I always read your letters. The last one was superb.'

'Written for you,' he joked.

'I should have guessed. But why didn't you tell me?'

'A man likes a little mystery.'

She laughed at that and snuggled down into the seat.

'Tired?' he asked.

'A bit drunk,' she admitted. 'But no, I'm not tired. I ought to be but I'm not.' It was true. Although she was relaxed she was full of energy, as if she'd just got up in the morning. 'In fact I was wondering if you'd like to come in for a drink. Nothing alcoholic because of you driving home. But coffee maybe. I need some to sober me up.'

'I thought you'd never ask,' he joked.

They were enjoying their conversation so much and it had been such an easy drive, that neither of them were prepared for what happened next.

Jeff was signalling that he intended to turn right into the minor road that led to Laura's Way. He'd driven into position and was waiting for a gap, when a white Mercedes appeared beside them and suddenly turned right across the oncoming traffic without signal or hesitation. Two cars were almost upon them, a Fiesta and a Metro. Both took avoiding action, sounding their horns, but for an horrific second Laura fully expected the driver of the Metro to crash into her passenger seat. Terror rose in her chest and filled her throat. She was aware that Jeff was swearing and crashing the car into reverse gear. There was a squeal of brakes, a swirl of light, a strong smell of rubber and then it was all over. Both cars had come to a halt. The Mercedes was out of sight.

Laura took a deep breath to regain control of herself. She needed a second or two to digest what had happened before she could react to it. But Jeff was already taking action. He drove the car across the empty road, parked it in the side road and was out of the driving seat and away, pausing only to check that she'd be all right and to tell her to 'Wait there'. She turned in her seat to watch him, feeling she ought to go with him, but she was still too stunned to get out of the car. He was running towards the main road, his first-aid kit under his arm.

He was back quickly too, running easily, bending down to put his head in the car.

'Sorry about this,' he said, 'but we'll have to make a detour. The chap in the Fiesta's gone on, but the Metro driver's in a bit of a state. And his wife's worse. He says he's OK to drive but he isn't really. I've told him we'll follow him just to be on the safe side. It's not far.'

'Was he hurt?'

'No,' he said, putting the car into gear. 'Just shocked. But that can be worse. He was still shaking when I got there. Just as well I was around.'

'You're so quick,' she admired as he turned into the main road again. 'Are you always so quick?'

'That's my trade,' he said and flashed his lights at the Fiesta. 'Go ahead. The road's clear.'

They drove for a mile or so, very carefully, at an easy stopping distance behind the Fiesta.

'We'll take the top road back,' Jeff said. 'It's not a lot out of our way.'

She recognised that he was apologising to her and was touched by his concern. 'Don't worry,' she told him. 'I don't mind a detour. You couldn't have left him to struggle home on his own. It's not in your nature.'

'Thanks,' he said, smiling at her briefly.

There was so much relief in the smile she was intrigued. 'Did you think I'd object?'

'No. Actually I didn't.'

She was pleased that he'd understood that much about her at least. 'I'm glad to hear it.'

'My wife would have done,' he said, feeling he had to explain. 'She said my "impetuosity" would be the death of me. Fact, it was one of the reasons she gave for divorcing me. She said I neglected her, always rushing off to help other people. So now tend to be a bit careful about it.'

Laura was surprised to be given such a confidence. Discovering that he was the famed letter-writer had shifted her perception of him and now she wasn't quite sure how she should respond. Did he want sympathy? she wondered. It didn't seem likely or in character. He didn't look as though he was pitying himself. Did he simply want her to know he'd been married? And if so, why?

'I don't think you're impetuous,' she told him. 'You act quickly but that's not impetuosity. You're in control. You know what you're doing. Impetuosity is acting without thought, like I did when I hit the security guard. And you usually get paid out for it. Like I did.'

'Would you say you were impetuous then?'

'No,' she said at once. 'Not basically. I like to have everything thought out before I act. Now

219

and then I get carried away and do something silly. But basically I'd say I was pretty sensible.'

He was grinning again. 'Basically I'd say you were too. I wish my wife could have said the same about me.' And he made a rueful face.

'Did you never rush off to help *her?*' Laura asked. 'Was that the problem?'

'She was jealous, you mean.'

'Some women do envy their husbands, don't they, especially when their jobs are demanding. Not that it's any of my business.'

Eve's remembered voice filled Jeff's mind as it had done so often in the last fraught years of their marriage, sharp with pain and jealousy. And it had been jealousy. Laura was right. *'It's always the same with you, dashing off after other people. You never think about me and the girls. We don't count, do we. It's always other people. Other bloody people and causes. Causes. You make me sick.'* 'I suppose it could have been possible,' he admitted, but he was beginning to wish he hadn't started this line of talk. It was getting a bit too intimate for comfort. 'It was all a long time ago.'

And you don't want to talk about it any more, Laura understood, noticing the knitted brow. She allowed a silence between them before she spoke again. 'The man in the Mercedes should be done for dangerous driving,' she said.

He was relieved to have the conversation turned so neatly. 'You'd have to catch him first. He didn't exactly hang around.'

'True. Did you see his number plate?'

220

'No. I was too busy.'

'That's how they get away with it. Would you know him if you saw him again?'

He grinned. 'I doubt it. When you've seen one white Mercedes you've seen them all. Anyway I don't suppose we'll ever see that one again. He'll be miles away by now.'

But he was wrong. As they drove into Laura's Way at the end of their lengthy detour, what should be driving towards them but a white Mercedes. They were both arrested by the same thought. Was it the same car? Or another? But before they could say anything it was upon them and they could see the two occupants, staring at them, shining faced through the windscreen — a grey-haired man with glasses and Amy Pendleton, waving gaily.

'Good God!' Jeff said as he brought his own car to a halt in front of the kitchen door. 'Do you know who that was?'

Someone it shouldn't have been, Laura guessed. 'No.'

'The managing director. Mr Brooke Curtis. The managing director of Beautibelles.'

'Surprise me,' Laura said, getting out of the car. 'So what's he doing with our Amy?'

The answer was pinned to the chalk board among all the other messages. *Gone to sales conference. Back Tuesday. A. P.*

'I wonder whether he's taking his wife too,' Jeff said.

'Oh, there's a wife is there?'

'Yes, there is and she's formidable.'

Laura was carrying their coffee to the table and spoke without looking at him. 'Good,' she said. 'I'm glad to hear it.'

'You don't like Amy do you?' he said, taking his cup.

'No,' she told him, surprised by how honest she was being. 'To tell you the truth, I don't. I never have.'

'Why not?'

'I think it's because she's such a queen bee. She has to be the centre of attention all the time. Nobody else gets a look-in when she's around. She can be really kind when she likes — usually when you least expect it — but for most of the time she's insufferable. She treats this house like a hotel. I mean, look at the state of this room.' There were dirty cups all over the floor and papers scattered on both sofas.

'Tell her you're not going to put up with it.'

'I do. Frequently. But she forgets.'

'I'm surprised you let her stay here. Why don't you chuck her out?'

'I can't. Well not yet, anyway. She's only just arrived. She's supposed to be looking for somewhere — so she says.'

'Then tell her to get on with it. She earns good money.'

Laura was looking round the room, her face alert and suspicious. 'Where are the cats?' she said. Then she got up and strode towards the inner door to the hall. 'Oh for heaven's sake, she's locked them in again. She will keep doing that and I have asked her not to . . . Come on then my darlings. Yes. She's lousy to you, keeps locking you in all the time. You tell me.'

All three cats emerged into the room, and rubbed around her legs, meowing at her, as if they were having a conversation.

Jeff was amused. 'Do you always talk to your cats?' he asked.

'They're my companions,' she said. 'My familiars.'

There was someone knocking at the kitchen door. Molly Fennimore, all dark-faced curiosity. 'How'd it go?' she said.

'You smelled the coffee,' Laura laughed at her. 'Come on in and I'll tell you. Get yourself a cup.'

'I'll get one for Joan too, shall I. She's on the way.'

And you're *in* the way, Jeff thought. He drank the last of his coffee, aware of how much he'd been enjoying their conversation, how much he resented this intrusion. 'I'd better be off,' he said. He hesitated for a second wondering whether he had the nerve to ask her out in front of Mrs Gossip. And decided he had. 'How about a meal on Saturday evening?'

She smiled at him. 'Yes. I'd love it.'

'I'll pick you up here at seven.'

'Splendid,' she said but she was already turning her attention to her neighbour.

Jeff looked back at her briefly before he left the house. She makes no concession to beauty, he thought — greying hair, creased skirt, rough hands, awful shoes. Even in her best suit, she looked untidy and crumpled, like a well-used sofa. But the more he got to know her, the more he liked her. There was something absolutely dependable about her. Despite her talk of being impetuous, he knew she would never do anything to hurt her friends and she would never let them down. Yet there was a dangerous edge to her too. She could be reckless and daring — lashing out at that guard, for example and starting this campaign. She'd been fearless at the meeting, she was very intelligent, she could be outspoken. Look at the way she'd talked to him in the car. A woman with depths, he decided. Roll on Saturday.

'Saturday afternoon,' Laura was saying to Molly. 'I shall be at the library all morning but I'll come down to the square the minute I've finished. We'll take a trestle table and set up a stall. Our precious MP might be ignoring our letters but he'll have a job to ignore this.'

'My eye gel,' Molly said happily. 'You have started something an' no mistake.'

Chapter Fourteen

'We seem to have a fight on our hands,' the County Surveyor said, looking up from the map that he'd spread across the board-room table. 'This librarian person — whoever-she-is — is making rather a nuisance of herself.'

'I suppose you've seen the article in the *Gazette*?' a councillor asked, his tone scathing. 'They're taking it up in a big way. Making an issue of it. *"Thriving community under threat."* All that sort of thing. Chocolate-box pictures. Absolutely throwing publicity at them.'

'That dreadful man Turner's written another one of his dreadful letters,' Councillor Mrs Smith said, pursing her lips with distaste. 'According to him we're all vandals.'

'Ignore him,' the leader of the council advised. He was a portly man with an overweening sense of his own importance and a habit of barking at subordinates. He certainly wasn't going to allow himself to be put out by some bolshevik letter-writer. 'He's just a commie with a chip on his shoulder. Got into trouble with the authorities, some years back, I believe. Nobody takes him seriously.'

'That's as may be,' Councillor Mrs Smith frowned. She read the letters every time they appeared and took them very seriously indeed, nasty mocking things. 'But we can't ignore the *Gazette*. Now that it's a freebie, it has an enormous readership. If they run a campaign against this development it could prove tricky.'

'It wouldn't do us much good,' the leader admitted. 'I'll grant you that. But it won't help the protestors in the long run either. They'll have to come to terms with progress in the end.' He turned to the map. 'Where *is* this Laura's Way?'

It looked very small and insignificant under the surveyor's broad thumb.

'Is there no possible compromise we could offer?' Mr Cranbourne asked. As the first Liberal Democrat to be elected to the council he felt it incumbent upon him to ask the difficult questions. 'It seems hard to me that we have to hurt people.'

'Somebody has to be hurt,' the leader barked. 'That's inescapable. You can't build a road in this part of the country without upsetting somebody or other and this one's got to be built somewhere.'

'Unless it isn't built at all,' Mr Cranbourne wondered.

'That is not an option, Mr Cranbourne,' the leader said, giving him the flicker of disapproval that was usually all that was needed to keep a subordinate in line. 'There is enormous pressure for it.'

Mr Cranbourne persisted. 'I was thinking of public opinion,' he said.

'Public opinion is in favour of it,' the leader

told him. 'This is nimby opinion. That's all. They're all shrieking Not In My Back Yard. Fortunately there are very few homes in Laura's Way. Which is why we plumped for Route C in the first place.'

'We may have to face the conservationists,' one of the women councillors pointed out.

'For half an acre of scrubby woodland?' the leader said. 'I doubt it. In any case, there isn't an acre of land between here and Horsham that isn't precious to someone or other.'

'You don't think we might run into trouble over the school?' Mr Cranbourne persisted. 'There's been rather a lot about the school in the local press. And they do seem to be gathering rather a lot of support. Two thousand signatures already, according to the *Gazette*.'

The leader wasn't quite so sanguine about the school. 'The petition could be a nuisance,' he conceded. 'We sent out the usual disclaimers. Promise of a hedging screen. That sort of thing. So there shouldn't have been a problem. It's only a council estate when all's said and done. No, it's these people in Laura's Way who are causing all the trouble. They're the subversives.'

'Two thousands signatures by last weekend according to the *Gazette*,' Mr Cranbourne insisted. 'I'm only playing devil's advocate you understand, but I feel we should consider what they are saying.'

'If there proves to be the demand for it — I'm not saying that *will* be the case, mind, but if it is

227

— we will set up a public enquiry,' the leader conceded. 'It will be a nuisance, and we might have to face a little delay, but it will make no material difference to our overall plan.'

'So we stand by our decision?' the County Surveyor wanted to know, rolling up his map.

'Unquestionably,' the leader told him. 'With certain — shall we say — precautions taken just in case. It's mostly hot air, you know, this sort of thing. People getting worked up. I'll make a few contacts on the quiet. See what can be done to — shall we say — ameliorate the situation. I shall mention it to Amalgamated Gravels for a start.'

Pull strings, Mr Cranbourne thought sadly. As a newcomer to the political scene and still something of an idealist, he was dismayed by how underhand things could be. He'll mention it at his next Masonic meeting, he thought, and get the rolled-trouser-leg brigade into action. And he felt a twinge of pity for the inhabitants of that narrow road on the map. The poor things don't stand a chance.

In Burswood, the petition grew by the day. By the end of the fourth week it was nearing five thousand signatures. Laura spent every Saturday afternoon standing in the square beside her makeshift stall with one or other of her neighbours, spreading rebellion. Sharon and Toddy gathered support in the school playground morning and afternoon. And both copies of their evidence were nearly finished too.

'If they call a public enquiry now,' Laura said to her neighbours as they sat round her table binding the first booklet together, 'we're ready for them.'

'I'm quite looking forward to it,' Molly Fennimore told them. 'I like a fight. My dogs are raring to go. Give 'em hell, eh Fiona?'

But Fiona took such a long time to answer that Molly looked up at her with a query. 'What's up gel?'

Fiona ducked her head, looking distressed. 'I probably shan't be here,' she said.

'Why not?' Laura asked, gently. Whatever the reason it obviously wasn't a good one. As a welfare family Fiona and her children had little enough security as it was.

'They're not going to renew my lease,' Fiona explained. 'I heard this morning. We've got to go.'

Her two companions were most upset. 'I call that a real shame,' Molly said. 'After all the work you've done.'

'When have you got to move?' Laura asked.

'Soon as I can find somewhere else,' Fiona said. 'We've got three weeks.'

'Three weeks!' Laura exclaimed. 'But that's monstrous. You can't find somewhere else in three weeks.'

'I did last time,' Fiona said and, seeing how cross Laura looked, 'It's all right. It's always like this. We been lucky to stay here so long. First place we had we was only there a month.'

'We'll give you a send-off party,' Molly promised. 'Guy Fawkes night. Your kiddies'll love that.'

Laura was feeling saddened at the loss of one of her fighters. 'We shall miss you,' she said.

'I shall miss you an' all,' Fiona said. 'You been ever so good to me.'

The news dampened Laura's spirits. It seemed to have been such an arbitrary decision.

'She doesn't have the slightest idea why they've decided to move her on,' she said to Jeff on their now-customary Saturday evening out. 'If she'd been a bad tenant, it would have made some sense, but she hasn't. She keeps that little house like a palace and she's scrupulous about paying her share of the rent.'

Jeff was mopping up his gravy with a chunk of bread-roll. 'Who's the landlord?' he asked, without looking up.

'Colonel FitzHenry, I expect,' Laura told him. 'He owns most of the land round here.'

'Oh well then! There's your answer. He stands to make a good profit on the land he's selling to the Ministry.'

'Now that's cynical,' Laura objected. The idea had crossed her own mind but she'd dismissed it.

'It's the reality of a situation like this.'

Laura sighed. 'I wish politics wasn't so sordid.'

'We live in the sleaze age,' he reminded her.

'Well I wish we didn't. I'd like you to be proved wrong.'

'You may not believe it,' he said, 'but so would I.'

His earnest expression was so touching she couldn't doubt him. You're a good man, she thought. I wish there were more like you. Especially in government. 'I hope you're coming to our party,' she said.

He smiled at her. 'I thought you'd never ask.'

She was pleased to think he would be with them but her pleasure didn't last. 'There's no doubt power *does* corrupt,' she said sadly. 'It's dreadful feeling you can't trust anybody. But the longer I go on with this, the more I feel it.'

'If it's any comfort to you, that's the general experience when you're running a campaign.'

'Takes one to know one?' she asked. He was so knowledgeable she was sure he'd been involved in something or other. And Amy had hinted at it right at the start.

'That's about the size of it,' he admitted. 'I'll tell you about it some time.' But not now when you've got all this to contend with. 'Have you had any answers to your letters?'

'Not much. No. Format replies mostly. We get most of our information from the protest groups. They *are* helpful.'

'Would you like to see my latest offering for the *Gazette*?' he asked, pulling it out of his pocket. 'Now you've blown my cover you might as well have a preview. See if there's anything you'd like me to add.'

She held out her hand for the letter, aware that

he was proud of it and appreciating that he was trying to cheer her.

'*What are the parents of Burswood thinking of? It isn't as if they don't know how they ought to behave. We've been told, over and over again, that it is our duty as parents to see that our children get the best possible education in the best possible environment. And now here's our wonderful Ministry of Transport going out of it's way to please them and all they can think about is signing petitions and complaining. Some people have no gratitude. You really would think that having a lovely new superhighway built within a few yards of their children's school would fill them with joy and thankfulness. All that lovely exciting traffic for their infants to enjoy, to say nothing of the pleasant sound it will make (such a nice change from all that monotonous country quiet) and the health-giving fumes it will give off (especially beneficial to asthmatics and children with a tendency to bronchitis so I believe). They should be down on their knees fasting, not thronging the school playground morning and afternoon to add their signatures to the petition.*'

'It's good,' she said, handing it back to him. 'Just what we need if we're going to get this petition sent off by the end of the month.'

'Is that what you're planning?'

'The end of the month or six thousand signatures,' she said, 'whichever comes first. I do hope you're wrong about Colonel FitzHenry.'

'Amen to that,' he answered, smiling at her sadly because he knew what a vain hope it was.

And he was proved right. At the end of the week, when the petition had reached five and a half thousand signatures, the two Jones boys called in at Holm End on their way home from work. They were still in their farm clothes and their boots were encrusted with mud so they said they wouldn't come in, if Laura didn't mind. 'Onny we got something to tell you.'

The mixture of guilt and excitement on their faces revealed their news before they spoke. The Colonel had offered them a better job on another farm.

'All four of us this time,' Alan said. 'We're to be foremen and there's places for the gels in the farm shop. He says he can't give us cottages side by side but we'll be near enough.'

'An' the rent's the same,' Graham put in. 'Two old fellers moving out apparently. Retiring or some such. He said he thought of us the minute the vacancies came up. Good eh?'

'The onny thing is,' Alan said, looking anxious, 'we shan't be here to help you with the enquiry. That's the onny thing.'

And that's the real reason for the offer, Laura thought. Jeff was right. We *are* being stitched up. But she kept her thoughts to herself. There was nothing to be gained by telling the brothers now. She simply congratulated them on their good fortune and asked them when they'd got to move.

'Second week in November,' Alan told her. 'Lot a' work apparently.'

'It'll be a real farewell on Guy Fawkes night

233

then,' Laura said. 'Three families instead of one. I'd better lay in some more fireworks.'

'Quite right,' Molly Fennimore agreed when she and Joan Garston arrived to make plans for the party later that evening. 'Give 'em a rousing send-off. No good getting downhearted.'

Joan Garston's heart was in the depths. 'D'you realise the terrace'll be half empty when they've all gone,' she said gloomily. 'There'll only be the three of us left, you an' me an' the Coopers.'

'Won't be for long,' Molly comforted. 'Not with housing the way it is. There'll be three lots a' newcomers all raring to go. Look at it that way.'

Or will there? Laura wondered. Seen from Jeff's viewpoint, it didn't seem likely. I started this for the best reasons, she thought, and it's cost Fiona her house and sent the Jones boys to the other end of the county. If only human affairs weren't so unpredictable. But Molly was right. It was no good getting downhearted. 'We'll make this the best party there's ever been in Laura's Way,' she said. 'And on Monday we'll take our petition to the Town Hall. It'll be plenty big enough by then. They needn't think they can push *us* around. There is such a thing as a democratic process and they'd better remember it.'

She was full of furious energy, sitting up into the small hours to paint a huge banner to hang over their stall the next morning. *'Last chance to make your protest.'* And the next day she was indefatigable, manning the stall long after the light had gone, even using a megaphone to drum up support, as if she were a huckster at a fair. They passed their target at a little over one o'clock but they worked on until the shops were shut and by then the sheaf of papers filled a box.

'Very impressive,' she approved, beaming round at her helpers. 'Now for the Town Hall. One o'clock sharp. Best bibs and tuckers. I've arranged for Mr Fawcett to be there with a photographer.'

Mr Fawcett wasn't the only one. As they emerged from the car park, carrying their precious, weighty boxes, they saw the camera with its nice, bold, friendly sign. *Meridian* had come to film them.

They stood on the Town Hall steps, holding the boxes before them, and were filmed from every angle while a reporter did a voice-over on the other side of the road. A crowd gathered to watch what was going on and a policeman appeared to direct the traffic. Laura had never felt so proud in her life. This is what democracy is all about, she thought. Ordinary people making a stand, letting their voices be heard, out here in the streets where everyone can see. As the director called to them to 'Turn this way please!' she felt like a star.

'We've really done it now,' she said triumphantly to Molly. 'They won't be able to ignore us after this.'

They were a little disappointed that after all that filming the item only ran for thirty seconds in the early evening news, but it was on television and that was what mattered.

'We can have our statutory fifteen minutes of fame some other time,' she told her neighbours. 'Now we've got a party to get going.'

Over the next few days, she threw herself into the preparations as wholeheartedly as she'd gathered the signatures, and her enthusiasm was catching. Soon everyone in the Way was involved. The Coghlan children made a guy and Joan rooted out an old chair for it to sit in, the Jones boys laid in crates of beer, the bonfire mounded until it was over six foot high, the feast was planned down to the last paper plate.

Maureen promised to drive over as soon as school finished on Guy Fawkes afternoon and put the potatoes to cook while Laura was still at work.

'It'll be fun,' she said. 'It's a bit staid in Canterbury Gardens. The most we ever run to these days is a packet of sparklers. Something on the grand scale will do us all good.'

'All?' Laura wondered.

'Well not David,' Maureen admitted. 'He'll be working late and he doesn't approve of open-air parties — unless he's in charge of them. But the kids'll be there. They wouldn't miss it. Is Jeff coming?'

'Of course,' Laura said. 'After all the help he's given us. He's part of the gang.'

Even Amy offered her assistance. 'I'll do you sausages on sticks,' she said, 'and a couple of dips. You don't mind if I bring a few friends do you. The more the merrier.'

'How many?' Laura asked. 'I'm not feeding the multitude.'

'One or two,' Amy said, vaguely. 'It won't be like that ghastly party. I promise.'

So Laura accepted the offer and agreed to the friends. At least they won't be in the house this time, she thought, and I shan't have stitches in my head.

'I think I shall treat myself to a new outfit,' Amy said. 'I've seen just the coat. Sea green with a fur-lined hood. Do they sell jodhpurs round here? They must do, mustn't they. Jodhpurs and boots. What are you going to wear?'

Laura hadn't thought about clothes. 'I don't know,' she admitted.

'You ought to dress up, Laur'. It's part of the fun.'

'I had rather a nice shawl once. That might do, if I can find it.'

'No time like the present,' Amy said. 'Where's it likely to be?'

It was nearly eleven o'clock at night and Laura had had a long day but what the hell! It would be fun to dress up. And she knew more or less where the shawl would be. In Pete's old sea-chest at the back of the cupboard in the eaves.

It was cold in the bedroom away from the heat of the fire and the sea-chest had been pushed so far back into the cupboard that it was quite a struggle to manoeuvre it out into the room. It was more battered than Laura remembered and covered in dust. She had to go downstairs for a damp cloth to clean it before she could open it up and by then the cold in the room was making her nose run.

'Jeez!' Amy said, as the lid sprang open. 'Just look at all these clothes. They're museum pieces. You've even got *flares* for Christ's sake.'

I'd forgotten all these things, Laura thought, as she rummaged about in the mass of cloth. What memories they brought back. There was the little leather camel from Egypt still wearing its embroidered saddle, and that awful Chinese back-scratcher with its ivory hand. I'll bet those long beads are here somewhere. I didn't realise I'd kept so many treasures hidden away. David's baby clothes neatly packed in cellophane wrappers, Pete's whites and his spare cap, that stupid hat she'd worn at their wedding, old gloves — why had she kept them — a school tie, that dreadful nylon blouse she'd bought to save money. Nasty sweaty stuff nylon. It stuck to your skin and made you feel hot and breathless.

'I remember that,' Amy said, pulling it out. 'You bought it for some party and Pete didn't like it.'

'It was his birthday party,' Laura told her. 'I bought it cheap because I wanted to spend my money on a present for him. He'd just got promotion and he needed a new sextant. It cost the earth.'

Amy rounded her eyes. 'I never knew that.'

'Why should you?' Laura said, thinking, it was nothing to do with you, it was my secret.

Amy had found the shawl. 'Here it is!' she said. 'Oh Laura! It's a beauty.'

It was a lovely thick Paisley with a fringe six inches long, all in subtle shades of soft brown, sand, sage green, bottle green, ochre and smoke blue. A gorgeous thing, Laura thought, and I've hidden it away all these years.

'Have you ever worn it?'

'No. I didn't think it would suit me.' And after Pete walked out I didn't think I deserved it. I didn't think I deserved anything pretty or pleasant in those awful days. How silly I was.

'It'll look stunning with your camel coat,' Amy said, throwing the shawl over her own shoulders and turning to admire herself in the dressing table mirror. 'What sort of hat will you wear? You ought to go the whole hog and treat yourself to something new.'

'I've got a green hat in the wardrobe somewhere.'

Amy didn't think much of that. 'What sort of hat?'

'Knitted,' Laura said, searching for it. 'Here it is.'

'You can't wear a knitted hat with a shawl like that,' Amy disparaged.

But to her surprise it was a remarkable match. 'OK then,' she conceded. 'It might do if you fluff your hair out round the edges. Where's your coat? Put it all on and we'll see.'

The image they assembled before the wardrobe mirror was so extraordinary that Laura was quite stunned by it. It makes me look younger, she thought. Younger and really quite pretty — if it's not too vain to think it. She adjusted the hat a little and turned up the collar of the coat to frame her face. She was playing dressing-up just like she'd done when she was a child, stepping away from the workaday world into a land of make believe where there were no road schemes, no political machinations, no rivalries, no worries, no winter, where no friends were spiteful, no sons difficult and no husbands ever disappeared — and success was just around the corner.

'What d'you think?' Amy asked.

'I think it's going to be a great party,' Laura said. 'A night to remember.'

Chapter Fifteen

Laura found it hard to get to sleep that night. Retrieving the shawl had released too many memories. Now they buzzed about her like wasps from a broken nest, brightly coloured, swarming, uncontrollable, full of life — and with the latent power to sting.

She closed her eyes and Pete's ardent face loomed before her, offering kisses, his red mouth parted. Pete home from the sea with a present in his hands. Pete saying, 'Sweets to the sweet.' Oh how she remembered.

There had been so many presents, one for every trip and all of them exotic, unpredictable, given with love. Her most vivid memory of those early years was Pete standing on the doorstep, tanned and handsome in his whites with a kitbag over his shoulder and a brown paper parcel in his hands.

'Present for you,' he would say, his eyes warming at the sight of her. But the present, however rich and rare, was nothing to the joy of seeing him again. He was home and that was all that really mattered to her. She would leap into his arms to kiss him and hold him, her greeting always the same. 'Pete! Pete! My darling Pete!'

They were such marvellous home-comings, like

honeymoons, full of love and talk and laughter and a happiness so acute it was almost like pain. She would remember them for ever.

But now she remembered how lonely she'd been while he was away, living from day to day, doing the housework, tending the garden, looking after David all by herself. She went back to London at regular intervals to see her parents and she made friends in the neighbourhood, naturally, but, even so, she felt lost out there in the countryside, especially in the winter when the three-mile walk to the village seemed a very long way. But once Pete came home everything was different.

It was bliss to have someone to talk to whenever she wanted to, bliss to hand over the baby for half an hour while she got on with the cooking, bliss to walk to the village arm in arm while David slept in his pram. Was it imagination or did he sleep better when his father was home? Perhaps it was because she slept so well herself, warm and safe in Pete's arms, enriched by their lovemaking, knowing he would be there beside her when she woke. They'd been the best and happiest moments of her life.

She lay on her back as the moonlight shone through her window and looked at the dark shadow of the shawl where it lay draped over the coat she'd hung against the wardrobe door. And the memories vibrated in her mind. How hard they'd worked when he was home! And what a worker he'd been! Bit by bit, leave by leave, they'd changed the cottage. The first thing they'd done was to enlarge their living space, knocking down the inner walls and taking out ramshackle cupboards until they'd created the one C-shaped living room she'd enjoyed so much ever since.

At the start of it, she hadn't been at all sure about knocking down walls, but he'd discussed it with her father and was so confident she'd agreed to it in the end.

'Are you sure the ceiling won't fall down?' she'd asked.

'Trust me,' he told her. 'I know what I'm doing. Just wait till you see how light it'll be.' And hadn't he been right? She remembered how staggered she'd been when the walls were finally down. With five windows to let the sunlight into their new large room, the entire ground floor of the cottage was transformed.

'I'll re-plaster the walls next time,' he promised. 'You can think what colour you'd like them to be while I'm away. Give you something to occupy your mind.'

But she'd had more than enough to occupy her mind that trip. He'd barely been gone a week before her mother was taken ill and within days they knew it was cancer. Such a little time to turn their family existence upside down. She was stunned by it because her mother had always been so healthy. She remembered thinking that it couldn't be true, that they must have made some mistake. But there was no mistake. The speed and horror of the disease were remorseless. Pete was still away at sea when she died.

Everybody said what a mercy it was because her mother had been suffering terribly — oh those well-meaning voices mouthing platitudes — but Laura and her father were cut to pieces. It made her ache to remember it even now, at all this distance. She'd done what she could to comfort her father and kept her own sorrow hidden, writing it out to Pete, page after page, on and on and on, weeping as she wrote.

Now, looking back on it, with the shawl a softening shadow in the moonlight, she could see what a burden she'd put on him. It was the first time a letter of his had been a disappointment. To his credit, he'd written straight back and he'd said all the right things — that he'd soon be home and that she was to try not to get too upset — but the tone of his letter was so flat it could have come from a stranger. She'd needed his company and his arms round her to comfort her and six months had seemed an appalling time to wait for them.

That was the summer he bought me the shawl, she thought, gazing at it. No wonder I hid it away. The summer when Amy married Joe and those awful dinner parties began, when Dad was gradually fading and it was always raining, when David had the measles. When things began to change.

It had been the wrong time for presents. Even the thought of receiving them jarred her. It had almost been the wrong time for Pete to come home. The night before he arrived she'd been up until four in the morning, sponging David down with lukewarm water because he was running such a high temperature he was delirious. When she went to answer his knock on the door that morning she was tired to her bones.

He was standing on the doorstep wearing his cap at a jaunty angle and thrusting a large brown paper parcel towards her. 'Present for you,' he said, as if nothing had changed. 'Sweets to the sweet.'

It was the first time she hadn't leapt into his arms. She simply took the parcel and stood holding it, aware that her shoulders were aching and that it all seemed unreal.

'Well?' he asked hopefully. There was so much energy in him. So much life. He was like a huge dog wagging its tail waiting to be praised. It exhausted her to look at him.

'Thanks,' she said dully.

He stepped into the hall, resolutely cheerful. 'Aren't you going to open it?'

She pulled away the brown paper obediently but the shawl meant nothing to her, gorgeous though it was. She couldn't even raise a smile. 'Thanks,' she said in the same flat tone. 'It's lovely.'

Her lack of response had annoyed him and she'd seen that and understood it even though she didn't have the energy to explain it. He'd obviously spent a lot of money on this present because he wanted to cheer her up and to show her how much he loved her. And now it was all going wrong.

'I brought it halfway round the world for you,' he told her. 'The least you can do is try it on.'

She pushed her hair out of her eyes, wearily, and made excuses. 'My blouse is dirty. I shall spoil it.'

That had hurt him terribly. She'd seen the disappointment on his face and regretted it even though she couldn't respond to it. She'd told him she'd try it on later, said she did like it really. But the damage was done. He'd flung his kitbag down in the hall and turned away from her. 'Suit yourself,' he'd said. 'I'm off up the Dragon.'

Had that been the start of it, she wondered, whatever it was that had dragged them apart? At the time she'd been too numb with distress to know. It was such a petty, silly quarrel. They both said so afterwards. And they'd made it up almost at once. He'd come back from the pub, cheerful with beer and full of affection, and had instantly done what he could to make amends.

He was horrified when he heard how ill David had been and said he was a brute to walk out on them. And after that he'd sat up all night keeping watch over the child's broken sleep. But there was a distance between them just the same, something edgy and not quite right about the entire leave, and when he went back to sea he signed on to go tramping. That had upset her, because taking on casual cargoes wasn't the same thing at all as working an established run. It was unpredictable for a start and she knew that it would keep him away for at least a year. And besides that, it was a step in the wrong direction. A step down.

'I need the experience,' he told her, 'if I want my second mate's ticket.' She could see the truth of it but, in an instinctive and more reasonable part of her mind, she knew there was more to his decision than that.

In the long, lonely months while he was away, working one unpredictable cargo after another or kicking his heels in ports while the master tried to drum up their next trade, she turned things over and over in her mind, wondering whether that silly quarrel had driven him to this long trip. She didn't want to believe it, nor that he was deliberately staying away from her but the thoughts were in her head and couldn't be quietened.

She wrote to him when she had an address but for most of the time he had no idea where he would be heading next. The months passed and became a year. He sent her a card from Sumatra and that hideous back-scratcher from Hong Kong. She'd disliked it at the time. Such a useless, ugly thing, with its little claw-like hand. 'Ivory,' he'd written, but that had made her feel worse about it, thinking of the elephant that had been sacrificed to produce it. But there were other gifts too and other letters that were full of affection and yearning home-sickness. And although she was sad to see how painfully he missed them she was glad of it too, for it showed her that her suspicions were wrong.

Then, when he'd been away more than eighteen months, she had to write him a sad letter of her own to tell him that her father had died quietly in his sleep. This time he wrote back at once and at length saying how much he'd admired her father and remembering how good he'd been to them. But there was no news about when he was coming home.

The cottage was now legally hers. She and David celebrated his tenth birthday with a party for all his school friends. It was much too big and much too expensive but she felt compelled to throw it, to make amends for his father's long absence. Poor David. Two years is a lifetime when you're only ten.

He loved Pete so much and Pete doted on him. They spent hours of every leave together, off fishing or playing football in the garden. In the evenings Pete would entertain them with traveller's tales and David would sit at his feet and listen, believing every word, his brown eyes shining.

His eyes had shone when the leather camel arrived. *'All the way from Egypt,'* Pete had written to him. *'By the time you get this I shall be through the Med and on the way home.'*

It was the best leave they'd ever had. They were like children, playing games together and so, so happy. But then he was gone again and she'd found the tickets. Two cinema tickets for a film she certainly hadn't seen with him and on an afternoon when he'd claimed to be in Brighton with his mates. I should have taxed him with it there and then, she thought, remembering. I should have written to him and told him what I thought. But she hadn't. She'd hidden the tickets in her jewel box, under the long beads he'd brought back from Ceylon, and tried to put it out of her mind. What a coward! And how silly because it didn't work. She'd thought of it every time she used the box, every time she passed the cinema, every time she saw a film advertised in the local paper.

But when he came home she forgot all about it. They'd all been so happy together. He'd signed up with Esso after that and taken some very long leaves. She remembered every one of them most vividly. At the start of the last one, he'd got his second mate's ticket and she'd planned his birthday party as a special celebration and bought the sextant as a special birthday surprise. It should have been a wonderful occasion. Even now she couldn't understand how it had gone so disastrously wrong. There hadn't been any sense or logic to it at the time and she couldn't see any now.

He'd been a bit cross at the party because that nylon blouse was so ugly but it was nothing that couldn't be put right with a few kisses, which was how they'd put it right. In the most loving way. She remembered thinking, Never mind! Just wait till he sees the sextant.

And at the very moment when she handed him the parcel everything had collapsed into incomprehensible misery.

He'd turned his face away from her when he

249

opened his gift almost as if she'd struck him.

'Oh Lorry-Lou,' he said and his voice was anguished as if she'd done something wrong. 'You shouldn't have.'

'I love you,' she told him, thinking he was afraid of the expense. 'You're worth the best. I saved up for it.'

But he went on looking grieved. 'Now of all days!' he said.

The tone of his voice made her prickle with alarm. 'What's wrong with today?'

He'd walked away from her and stood looking out of the window for a very long time. 'I'm going back to sea,' he said.

'But you've only just got home,' she protested.

'All right, all right,' he said and now he sounded angry. 'I know. It can't be helped. I've got to do it.'

She didn't argue with him. What could she say? When things went wrong it was better to leave him to explain about them in his own time. She didn't even ask him when he was going. Not until the night of the storm when he suddenly came downstairs with his kitbag. And then it was too late.

'I'm off,' he said, speaking roughly and scowling at her as if she'd annoyed him.

'Not tonight!' She couldn't believe it. Why hadn't he given her more warning?

'Yes. Tonight. Now.'

It was so abrupt, so careless. She couldn't believe he was treating her so badly. He couldn't just walk out like this.

'But what about David?' she said, aghast. 'You can't leave him without saying goodbye.'

'I'll write to him when I get there.'

'Where? Where are you going?'

He picked up the kitbag and walked out of the room into the hall, his face averted. 'Don't keep asking me questions.'

She followed him, her thoughts in a turmoil of alarm and distress. He means it, she thought miserably. Oh God! He means it. But why? Why? 'I must know where you're going,' she said, trying to be reasonable.

'All right then,' he said angrily. 'Devonport. Does that satisfy you?'

She walked over to stand beside him, put her hand on his arm, willing him to look at her. 'What's the matter Pete?' she asked. 'What's wrong?'

He shook her hand away, thrust the sextant into the kitbag, put his hand on the door. 'I'm leaving you,' he said.

I must stop this, Laura thought, and she got out of bed so as to turn the memory away. It's foolish to go over it again like this. I've thought it out so many times and I've never understood it.

She stood by the bedroom window, with the shawl wrapped round her shoulders for warmth and gazed out into the garden. It was very peaceful out there and silvered by moonlight.

You've got a party to plan, she told herself, so be positive and plan it. If he left you for someone else, he left you for someone else. It's over and done with. The world's moved on and you've moved with it.

Chapter Sixteen

The Guy Fawkes party began with a bang — or, to be more accurate, with six bangs in rapid succession, for John Cooper, having set up an elaborate pyramid of rockets at the far end of the lawn, accidentally touched them all off at the same time so that the air was full of screams and cordite and the sky a riot of tumbling stars. The guests were delighted by such drama and screamed as loudly as the rockets. And Laura, who was standing on the path to the vegetable garden between Molly Fennimore and Fiona Coghlan, greeting her guests, looked up at the torrent of lights above her and was released into a sudden and total sense of well-being.

'My eye, John!' Molly admired as the dairyman came loping back across the lawn towards them. 'How d'you manage that?'

John Cooper had recovered from the shock he'd given himself and was now modestly taking credit. 'Skill!' he said, beaming up at the display.

'Three cheers for Mr Cooper!' Fiona urged her children and their friends.

Jeff Turner, struggling through the garden with the two boxes of cream cakes he'd promised and a flagon of cider as an extra, made his appearance to their chirruping applause and the fading stars of the display.

'Where's Laura?' he asked Molly.

She bellowed with laughter. 'You great lummox!' she said. 'She's standing right next to you, look. Where's yer glasses?'

And she was. Good God! He'd walked right past her and hadn't recognised her. How embarrassing! But then, as he looked back at her in the flickering light, he realised why. She was transformed, wearing a great paisley shawl over her shoulders like a cape, her face framed in the upturned collar of her coat, her tousled head crowned by a green hat trimmed with gold tinsel and set off by a huge cockade of evergreen leaves. How was he supposed to recognise her got up like that? It was as if she'd been re-made in a different shape and entirely different materials. In the light from the lanterns, her hair curled round the edges of her hat like tawny fur, her eyes gleamed, dark, dark brown, so that he thought of water by moonlight and, most disconcerting of all, her skin was gilded as though she were a golden statue come to life. He was suddenly aware of the power of the bones beneath that skin, of the hauteur of that straight nose, the strength of her forehead, the determination of her jaw. There was something awesome about her, something mythical, pagan, powerful.

'You look like the Queen of the Wood,' he said, speaking without thinking because he was admiring her so much.

She accepted his admiration and his greeting

254

as though they were natural — as they were on an occasion as wild as this one. 'Yes,' she said. 'It *is* pagan. That's the whole point of it.'

'Earth, air, fire and water,' he said, remembering the four elements. 'You ought to have a pond here to complete the picture. Your lights would look wonderful reflected in water.' There were coloured lights everywhere, from lanterns in the trees to fountains in the sky, and John Cooper was busy setting a line of Catherine wheels to spin against the garage wall.

To his surprise the idea made her shudder. 'No thanks,' she said. 'I've no desire for a pond. I can't be doing with water.' Then she changed the subject so abruptly he knew he wasn't to pursue it. 'Come and help us light the bonfire.'

He handed the flagon to Alan Jones who had a table for drinks beside the vegetable garden, left the cakes with Maureen who was supervising the barbecue under one of the holm oaks and went where he was bidden. The last few bonfire nights he'd attended had been soggy occasions, mostly remembered for squelching through mud, eating half-cooked food and waiting endlessly for the fireworks to be lit. But this was plainly going to be an event and he was going to share it with a woman who looked like a goddess.

The bonfire blazed at her touch. Within minutes it was a burning bush spitting orange sparks high into the sky and the guy was a dark grotesque slouching sideways on a throne turned tipsy by flame while his audience gathered around him to watch and eat.

The air in the garden was spiked by rich scents — wood smoke aromatic, roast beef succulent, cordite harsh and tinny — and there were so many people crammed on to its sloping lawns that it looked like a fair ground, men with beer and burgers, women with sausages and cider, eyes gleaming and faces warmed by fire, children bundled like eskimos either biting toffee apples or clutching baked potatoes in their mittened hands.

Behind the lights and movement in the garden the cottage was diminished to an unlit shadow. She's transformed the place as well as herself, Jeff thought, the Way full of cars, the garden full of people, fire and shadows everywhere, the house barely visible. She's cast a spell on us.

'I've locked the cats in and shut it up,' she explained prosaically when she saw he was looking back at the cottage.

'And kept Amy's friends out,' he understood.

'Right!' she agreed. 'I had quite enough of them last time.'

'However many people have you invited?' he asked, surveying the crowd.

'No idea,' she said cheerfully. 'I gave up counting ages ago, didn't I Joan?'

Joan Garston had wandered over to join them, paper cup in hand. 'The only person who hasn't come is my old man,' she said, grimacing. 'There's a surprise! Not that he's any loss.'

Laura laughed. 'Did you expect him to come?'

'Not really,' Joan said, finishing her drink. 'Specially now he's got that damn computer.'

That was news to Laura. 'What damn computer?'

'They delivered it this afternoon,' Joan said. 'He's been locked upstairs playing with the damned thing ever since. Wouldn't come down for his tea or anything. I had to take it up to him. Reckons he's going on the Internet or some such. God knows how he's going to pay for the thing. Instalments he reckons, if you ever heard of anything so daft. Can you imagine paying instalments when you're unemployed. He wants his head examined.'

'Well at least it'll keep him off the streets,' Jeff joked, trying to cheer her.

'It'll drive me round the bend,' Joan said lugubriously. 'And he needn't think I'm going to pay for it. I've got enough on my plate without that, what with the housekeeping and the mortgage and everything.' And she wandered away to join another group.

'Oh dear!' Jeff said when she was out of earshot.

'Yes,' Laura said. 'It is "oh dear". I wanted her to enjoy this party. I thought it would do her good.'

'She can't leave him behind. That's the trouble.'

'I feel sorry for her sometimes,' Laura said. 'He's terribly difficult. Forever complaining about something or other and so disagreeable.'

'All the more reason to leave him behind. I wonder she stays with him.'

257

'So do I,' Laura said. 'None so queer as folk, I expect. We none of us really know what goes on behind closed doors, do we. But I've got a lot of time for Joan. She's been such a help in this campaign, out in all weathers gathering signatures.' And she looked round the garden to see where her friend had gone, her face full of sympathy.

There was a tall woman striding towards them across the lawn. She wore a black velvet cloak, a highwayman's hat and black knee-length boots and she was moving at speed. Even in the darkness, they could sense something threatening about her.

'That's torn it!' Jeff said. 'It's Mrs Brooke Curtis, the managing director's wife.'

Laura wasn't surprised. The woman radiated trouble. She walked straight up to them and spoke to Laura without preamble or introduction.

'Are you Mrs Laura Pendleton?'

Laura acknowledged that she was.

'Then where is Amy Pendleton?'

'On the far side of the bonfire with her friends,' Laura told her and when the newcomer turned to look at the dark figures milling about the blaze, 'She's the one in the sea-green jacket with a hood.'

'Thanks,' the woman said shortly and strode off towards the fire.

'She's on the warpath,' Jeff said.

'Yes,' Laura said cheerfully. 'That's what I thought. And she's after old Lead-'em-on-let-

'em-down. And about time too.' It pleased her to think that Amy was heading for a comeuppance — and that he was going to witness it.

The row had started already. Black arms were waving behind the orange flames, temper and fire crackling together.

'Come on,' Laura said, seizing his hand. 'This I must see.'

Her guests made way for them as they ran round the blaze.

'. . . and if you think I'm going to sit back and let it happen you're very much mistaken,' the woman was shouting. 'Nobody takes my husband away from me. Nobody. Do you understand? I own that bloody company. I built it up from nothing to where it is today. I'm the major shareholder. The major shareholder. So just you think on that. He wouldn't amount to a row of beans if it weren't for me. I own the company and I own him and nobody's going to take him away from me. Nobody.'

'Nobody's trying to,' Amy said, stepping back from her rage but speaking coolly. 'I don't know what you're raving about.'

'Oh yes you do! You know perfectly well.'

'No. I don't. You come in here bellowing and shouting. I don't know you from Adam. Never seen you before in my life.'

'But you know my husband, don't you,' the woman shouted. 'Oh yes! Brooke Curtis. You're not going to tell me you don't know him.'

Amy was still cool. 'Well of course I know

him. He's my boss.'

'Oh yes!' the woman mocked. 'Your boss! Well let me remind you of something else. He's the man you were with on Saturday night. That's who he is. The man you've been leading up the garden path. You were seen. Well now I'm warning you. Hands off! He's not for sale.'

"Who's buying?' Amy sneered. 'I'm sure it isn't me.'

The sneer enraged her opponent to a white-hot fury. 'How dare you speak to me like that!' she spat. 'You want to watch your mouth, speaking like that. I could have you fired.'

Amy met fury with fury. 'You do and I'll take you to court for wrongful dismissal.'

'Bloody effrontery! You run off with my husband . . .'

'I do not!'

'You were seen.'

'Oh yes! Who by?'

'Never you mind who by. You were seen.'

'And when was all this supposed to be?'

'Saturday night. I told you. You were seen going into the Hilton . . .'

'Now you listen,' Amy said, moving into the attack, 'and you listen good. I don't know who's been feeding you all this garbage but it must have been someone with bloody poor eyesight. *Bloody* poor eyesight. I was with this gentleman on Saturday. All evening. He can vouch for me, can't you Jeff?'

Laura was so surprised she could feel her eyes

stretching. How could she say such a thing? The audacity of it! When she knew it wasn't true and that Jeff was bound to deny it. Go on, Jeff, she urged him, put her in her place. It's high time someone did.

But Jeff was thinking fast, assessing the situation. It needed taking in hand and quickly or there would be a brawl. There was only one thing to do and he did it at once.

'Yes,' he lied, addressing the boss's wife. 'That's right, Mrs Curtis. She was with me.' He could hear Laura sucking in her breath with disbelief, was aware that Amy was looking sly and triumphant, that her adversary was frowning, but it was done now, it was said, the immediate danger was over.

'All evening?' Mrs Curtis asked.

'Until half past twelve,' Amy said. 'We went for a meal. What did I tell you? Someone's been making mischief. You ought to go and sort them out. This could have been nasty.'

Mrs Curtis was still looking at Jeff, her eyes hard. 'Are you sure about this?'

'Quite sure. We went for a meal.'

That's our meal he's talking about, Laura thought, anger at his dishonesty rising in her chest. He was with me on Saturday. And I thought he was such an honourable man.

'Satisfied?' Amy asked.

'For the moment,' Mrs Curtis said icily. 'Just so long as you know the score.' She was pulling her cloak and her control about her, casting round in her mind for a dignified way to end the scene. 'I'm sorry about this,' she said to Laura, 'but I thought the sooner I dealt with it the better. These things go down deep if they're not dealt with and then they fester. You do understand, don't you.'

'Yes,' Laura agreed, anger festering in her as she spoke. 'I understand perfectly. You'll be able to find your own way to your car, I daresay.'

The watchers parted to let the lady pass and watched her out of the garden with a mixture of curiosity and sympathy. From the corner of her eye Laura saw Amy swooping towards Jeff, was aware that she had seized his face in her hands and was kissing him. Two smacking kisses that she could hear above the crackle of the fire. And her voice was clear too. 'You're an old sweetie!' she said. 'Thanks. I owe you one.'

Dear God! Laura thought. The indelicacy of it, the opportunism, the dishonesty. How could he have been such a bloody fool? *I owe you one.* Seething with anger and disappointment, she turned on her heel and swept away from them, moving so quickly that her shawl flowed behind her like a sail. Bad enough to have seen him being manipulated, heard him being dishonest. She certainly wasn't going to stay to see Amy make capital out of it. Whatever he was saying now, she didn't want to hear it. She strode through the crowd, heading for the patio, to Maureen and the kids and the safety of family.

"What was all that?' Maureen asked, turning a

line of hamburgers.

Laura swallowed her anger and made as light of it as she could. 'Amy, I'm afraid, being warned off by an irate wife.'

Maureen made a face. 'Oh!'

'Are we surprised?' Laura said in a joking way and then changed the subject. 'Where's Jess? I thought she was coming with you.'

'She's waiting for her boyfriend,' Danny said. He was wearing a large cook's apron and was importantly busy cooking sausages.

'He'll bring her along later,' Maureen said, poised above the barbecue.

'If he turns up,' Danny said. 'He doesn't always. I don't know why she bothers with him.' He was looking at the bonfire. 'The guy's alight,' he said. 'Are we going to sing?'

'Sing?'

'You know. Gunpowder treason and plot. Please to remember the fifth of November. We did at Charles' party last year.'

Laura looked towards the bonfire too. The irate wife had vanished and so had Jeff and there was no sign of Amy either. She hadn't gone into the house which was still completely dark, so perhaps she'd taken off with her friends. 'Yes,' she said. 'Why not? We ought to have a sing-song.' And she began to lead the way back to the blaze, gathering her guests as she went. 'Come on everybody. *Please to remember the fifth of November.* Grab hands!'

Dark figures tumbled out of the shadows to

leap about the fire. Fiona and her three in their bright red anoraks, the Jones brothers and their wives, hand in hand and trailing scarves, even Molly and Josh. The ritual chant went on and on until they were all caught up in the circle. *'Please to remember . . . please to remember.'*

'And we will remember,' Laura said when they'd danced to a halt and were waiting to see what would happen next. 'We're saying goodbye to eight of our neighbours tonight but we shan't forget you. And when you come back to Laura's Way to visit us, I promise you *we shall still be here.'*

'We never had any doubt about it,' Alan Jones called out to her. And at that somebody set up a cheer.

It was warming to be trusted, Laura thought, looking round the circle as they all cheered, dark mouths opened wide in golden laces. Then she realised that someone was singing and turned, as they all did, to see who it was.

It was Molly Fennimore, standing a little apart, holding a sparkler in her hand like a conductor's baton and singing in a high quavery voice. *'We shall overco-o-ome. We shall overco-o-ome. We shall overcome some da-a-a-a-ay.'* Out there in the dark and cold, in the stink of cordite and the crackle of fire, it was suddenly and almost unbearably moving. One by one they joined in and the hymn swelled and deepened until it had become a chorus, full of hope and affirmation. *'Deep in my heart, I do believe. We shall overcome some day.'*

At the end of it there was nothing more to be

said or done but to kiss their departing neighbours goodbye and wish them well. The guy was
burnt to ashes, the fireworks spent, the bonfire
dying down.

'I'll come back tomorrow for the barbecue
things,' Maureen said. 'After school. When I can
see what I'm doing. I've got something I'd like
to talk to you about.'

'Phone me,' Laura said.

'I will.'

There was a muddle of leave-taking, the Way
was full of cars revving up and, above the general
noise, Laura sensed that a slight wind had begun
to blow. There'll be ash everywhere, she thought.
I ought to clear some of it up. But she was more
tired than she expected and besides, it would take
too long. It would have to wait until her next
afternoon off, whenever it was. She was so tired
she couldn't even work *that* out.

She walked slowly back to her shadowy house
and unlocked the door with some difficulty because the lock was stiff with so little use and she
couldn't see what she was doing. Then she
switched on the light and called to the cats, who
emerged from behind chairs and sofas and stalked
towards her to be stroked and greeted.

'Whisky,' she said to their three hopeful faces.
'Whisky for me and warm milk for you. How will
that be?'

She felt better settled on the sofa with a rug
round her legs and Ace on her lap and the tumbler
in her hand. But she'd hardly taken two mouth-

fuls before the phone rang. That'll be Maureen, she thought, and prepared herself to give a sympathetic ear.

It was Amy. 'Sorry I had to rush off,' she said, 'but I knew you'd understand. I'm with Barbara. Thought I'd better tell you. She's asked me to stay till we go to the conference.'

Who's Barbara? Laura wondered. But she asked a different question as it seemed more pressing. 'What conference?'

'Didn't I tell you? Another sales conference. It's at York this time, which is a bit of a bind. All next week. I'm sure I told you.' There was a voice talking to her in the background. Rather a deep voice for someone called Barbara. 'OK. OK,' she said to it. 'Keep your wig on. I shan't be a minute. See you later then Laur'.' And hung up.

Laura didn't know whether to be annoyed at being kept in the dark about the conference or relieved because she didn't have to endure Amy's company for a week or so. She readjusted the rug round her ankles and picked up her glass again. And there was a knock at the door.

'It's open!' she called, expecting one of her neighbours and looking round to see which one it was. 'Come in!'

It was Jeff Turner, looking sheepish and hesitating on the doormat, as if he wasn't sure whether he'd be welcomed further into the room.

She wasn't pleased to see him and made no pretence about it. 'What are you doing here?' she said, frowning at him.

'I'm sorry about all that,' he said. 'The — um — by the bonfire I mean.'

She sniffed. What was the good of saying sorry? The damage was done. 'Amy's not here.'

That made him wince. 'I know,' he said. 'She's staying with a friend. She told me.'

'Oh well she would, wouldn't she.'

'Look,' he said, walking into the room at last. 'I can see you're cross about it but I didn't have much option. I could hardly have . . .'

She turned away from him to drink her whisky and stroke the cat. 'I'm not cross,' she said as coolly as she could. 'It's nothing to do with me. If you want to make a fool of yourself that's your look-out. Only don't expect me to praise you for it. I think it was disgraceful and that's putting it mildly.'

He sat on the other sofa opposite her, willing her to look at him. 'For Christ's sake!' he said. 'I did it on your behalf.'

'On my behalf!' she mocked, giving him the briefest of glances. 'Oh that's rich. You did it to save her skin. That's what you did it for.'

'I did it to avoid unpleasantness,' he said, struggling to be reasonable. 'I did it on *your* behalf to avoid a row in *your* garden.'

'You did it because you were too weak not to,' she told him, glaring at him. 'That's why you did it. All this is just self-justification.'

He tried to deflect her attack by mockery. 'Thank you Mrs Freud.'

It didn't work. 'I was appalled,' she said. 'To

267

hear you lying like that . . .'

He was glaring too. 'Oh fine! I suppose you'd have liked a row. Is that it?'

'Yes,' she said fiercely. 'I would. At least that would have been honest.'

'Oh come on! A public brawl. In your garden. In front of all your friends.'

'Yes, yes, yes,' she said, hot with anger. 'A public brawl. It's what she deserved. I'd have enjoyed it. She's had it coming to her for years. But oh no! You couldn't have that. You had to protect her. You told a public lie to protect her. She twists you round her little finger. I thought you were made of sterner stuff.'

'What bloody rubbish!'

'It's not bloody rubbish. It's the truth.'

He stood up, paced towards the door. 'You're vindictive,' he said. 'That's your trouble. You're bloody vindictive.'

'With justification,' she said, swigging the last of her whisky. 'You don't know the half of it with that one. She treats men like dirt.'

He was back on the doormat again. 'So it's OK for you to justify yourself then?' he said, turning towards her. 'I mustn't do it but it's OK for you. Is that it?'

She was so angry with him she wanted to shout. But she spoke coldly instead. 'Have you said what you came to say?'

'You know your trouble,' he said. 'You're jealous.'

'I am not.'

'Riddled with it.'

That was too much. 'Go away!' she yelled. 'It's none of your business!'

'If it had been anyone else but Amy you'd have understood . . .'

'Go away! Go away!'

How did we get to this? he thought. An hour ago she was like a goddess, the Queen of the Wood, with half the garden in her hat and that shawl flowing behind her. Now she's a shrew in a cardigan, her face hard and challenging. He was disappointed in her, disappointed in himself, wrong-footed, ashamed of his lies, shaken with fury and he couldn't fight her any longer. 'You don't bloody listen,' he said. And went.

Left on her own in the empty room, Laura wanted to cry. I've lost my ally, she thought, blinking back tears. My strongest ally. How could he have been so stupid? How could *I* have been so stupid? It's all Amy's fault. She's been nothing but trouble all through my life. Putting on her good-little-girl act at school — with that stupid lisp and those awful curls — and getting us the stick; hunting poor old Joe until he gave in and proposed to her and then putting him down every time they came to dinner — I hated those dinners; always having to be the best, the one all the men were after, the one who had the most expensive holidays, wore the most expensive clothes, ate the most expensive food. She could make me feel shabby just by walking into the room. Why oh why did she have to come back to England? I was

269

all right until she turned up. My life was in order. I never lost my temper. And now this . . .

'I shall have another whisky,' she said to Queenie, who was sitting on the hearthrug hoping for a fire.

But even two more whiskies didn't cheer her. 'We'll go to bed,' she said to the cats, 'that's what we'll do. We'll go to bed and sleep on it.' The choice of words struck her as funny and she began to giggle drunkenly, gathering her glass and her rug ready for the climb upstairs.

She was halfway up when the phone rang. That's more like it, she thought. He's had time to consider how silly this is and now he's phoning to make amends. And she went downstairs as quickly as her now rather shaky legs would take her.

To her crushing disappointment the voice on the other end of the line belonged to Maureen. 'Have you got a moment?' she asked. 'Can we talk?'

Laura was too drunk to hear the urgency in her daughter-in-law's voice and too down to respond to it if she had. 'No,' she said, 'I'm sorry, Maureen. It'll have to keep. I'm all in. I was just on my way up to bed.'

'Oh!' Maureen said flatly. 'Oh well then, I'll call you some other time. Only you did say to ring you.' But as she put the phone down she felt snubbed. And very disappointed.

Halfway up the stairs and too late, memory struggled through the fog of whisky and Laura realised that she'd asked Maureen to phone and felt ashamed of herself for not making the effort to listen. That's two bad mistakes in a row, she rebuked herself, first I shout at Jeff — and he didn't deserve to be shouted at — why was I shouting at him? — and then I hang up on Maureen. The sooner I get to bed and put this evening behind me the better. Oh, why is life so complicated?

'Please don' get unner my feet, cat,' she said to Ace, who was preceding her up the stairs. 'Or I shall tread on you.' Her head was swimming with whisky. I shall have a hangover in the morning, she thought, and it'll just serve me right. And she thought of Jeff again, this time with anger. It's all very well for him. He can just swan off and forget it.

But she was wrong. Jeff Turner's state was every bit as parlous as hers. At that very moment he was striding along the empty promenade in Worthing in the drizzling darkness, pounding his anger into the pavement but feeling more and more at fault with every step.

This, he told himself miserably, is what comes of taking on other people's problems. I do something because I think it's the right thing to do and I louse everything up. I did it at the hospital and wrecked everything with Eve and now I've done it again with Laura. He was stone-cold sober and resolutely reasonable so he knew that this mistake was on a smaller scale and of a different order,

271

but he'd made it himself and he couldn't avoid the consequences.

It was very cold and the rain, slight though it was, had soaked his hair and his beard and was stinging his face. The sea and sky were impenetrably black. I never get it right, he thought, striding onwards. I should have stood back and let them get on with it. It was their quarrel, not mine. Why do I always interfere? It only complicates my life.

Chapter Seventeen

The drizzling rain continued over the weekend and into the next week, dampening clothes and spirits, turning footpaths into quagmires and roads into a treachery of grease. Laura started a head cold and was so down that she did the unthinkable and phoned Maureen to say she wasn't well enough to come to Sunday tea. Then she felt ashamed of herself for making excuses and miserable because she wasn't going to see Jessica and Danny and spent the afternoon huddled by the fire in a fug of vapour rub and self-pity. Jeff didn't phone, there was still no response to the petition — after all that effort — the garden was full of debris from the fireworks — and she hadn't the energy to clear it — and on Monday she got the stock into a muddle at Burswood library, for the first time that anyone could remember. The one and only good thing in her life — or, to be more accurate, out of it — was Amy's absence from Holm End.

On Monday evening, Fiona Coghlan brought her children across to say goodbye. All three of them had chesty coughs and were pale and unhappy.

'It's always the same when we move,' Fiona said. 'They always go down with something.'

'Look after yourselves,' Laura advised as she kissed them all.

'You too,' Fiona said earnestly. 'I hope you win.'

'So do I,' Laura told her, 'after all this.'

'I'll write to you,' Fiona promised. 'We all will, won't we kids.'

She moved the next day in a muddle of cardboard boxes and tatty furniture and with all three of her children in tears. She'd hired 'a man and a van' to help her and Molly and Joan lent a hand whenever they could sneak away — Molly from her dogs and Joan from the farm shop — but it was a demoralising business. The man was hardworking and cheerful but the van was little more than a wreck, rusty, much-dented and splattered with mud.

'It'll do,' Fiona said when she caught Molly looking askance at it. 'We ain't got much. Well you can see that, can'tcher.'

Molly was fierce with pity. 'You make sure you keep in touch,' she ordered. 'I think it's a scandal you having to move out like this.'

The next day, the Jones families went, sharing a pantechnicon and with a great deal of noise and laughter. Once the great van had turned the corner and lumbered into the darkness of the November afternoon, the Way felt forlorn.

'I hope they move some new people in soon,' Molly said, when she came over to Holm End to report to Laura that evening. 'I don't like an empty house next door. It don't feel natural.'

274

'They never stay empty long,' Laura said, as much to comfort herself as her friends, for she still remembered Jeff's cynical view of the subject. 'Fiona moved in on the same day the Fredericks moved out, remember. We shall hear something by the end of the week. I'll lay money on it.'

They did but it wasn't quite what they expected. The landlord had arranged to have his cess-pools cleared on Friday. Did they wish to avail themselves of the service at the same time?

Joan and Molly and Connie Cooper came straight across to Laura, letters in hand, to ask her opinion before she went to work.

'I suppose we'd better,' Joan said. 'Get it over an' done before Christmas. Yours must be pretty full Laura, the number of guests you've had.'

'You mean Amy,' Laura said, putting the breakfast things in the sink to soak. 'Yes. She *has* made a difference.'

'Wasteful, you ask me,' Joan said. 'She has that washing machine of yours going all hours. No one's going to tell me you need all *that* amount of washing.'

There speaks the countrywoman as opposed to the townie, Laura thought. 'I'll order it for all of us, shall I?' she asked. She would have to swap her day off, which might be tricky, but Joan was right, it was better to have it done, no matter what the weather. And there was something symbolic about doing it now, clearing out the mess, freshening the air, making a clean start.

The tanker arrived early in the morning, preceded by its stink and with its yellow buckets hanging on the back rattling. The driver climbed out of his cab and made straight for Holm End, as he usually did.

'Do you first missus?' he asked Laura, standing by the kitchen door, elbow-length gloves making his arms look like balloons.

The smell was as bad as she'd ever known it and it took a hideously long time. She tried to be reasonable about it, pointing out to herself that she had a full tank and that it takes a long time to clear four and a half thousand gallons. But it was another misery in a miserable week. And in the middle of it all, just when she least wanted her, Amy drove her Peugeot into the drive.

' 'Lo Laur',' she said brightly, as she walked into the kitchen. 'Is there any tea? I'm gasping. You wouldn't believe the week I've had. Sales conferences are the absolute end.' Then she wrinkled her nose in disgust. 'Jeez! What *is* going on?'

'This is part of the price you pay for living an idyllic life in the countryside,' Laura told her. 'We're having the cess-pools emptied.'

'Jeez! What a stench! Is it always like this?'

'It has been for the last sixteen years,' Laura said, steadily clearing the worktop beside the sink. 'Before that we had a bucket and threw it out in the garden. A bucket and chuck it, we used to say.'

The look of horror on Amy's face was a delight and quite the most cheering thing Laura had seen in days. 'I never knew that,' she said. 'I mean, we used to come here for dinner. Often. It was all perfectly normal. I mean, you had a loo in the garden but it didn't seem . . .'

'Well we didn't ask our guests to empty the bucket, naturally,' Laura said enjoying herself. 'But that's how life was.'

Molly put her head round the half-open door. 'How's it going?'

'Nearly done,' Laura told her. 'He'll be across to you in about half an hour. I'm just getting the kitchen cleared.'

'You're back I see,' Molly said to Amy.

But Amy was looking out of the living room window. 'Where's everybody gone?' she said. 'There's three houses empty.'

'Moved out,' Molly said, adding firmly, 'You'll be next.' It was a command rather than an observation but Amy took it as a joke.

'Not with the sort of garbage they send me,' she laughed. 'Why is it so damned cold in here? Why haven't you got a fire?'

The answer clanked in through the kitchen door at that moment, carrying one of his yellow buckets which he filled at the sink. The smell in the room was overpowering.

'I've just got to flush it all down,' he said, sloshing the water with a gloved hand. 'You ready to come and see?'

Amy's thoughts were so plain on her face they could have been written there. To have a cesspool at all was bad enough, to have it emptied was worse — especially if you were supposed to

277

go down the garden and look at it — but to have a great stinking bucket put right down in the sink where you prepared food and washed up was too disgusting to be borne. 'I've got to get back to the office,' she said, gagging. And went before she was sick.

Molly and Laura stood on the path, where the air was marginally sweeter, and watched her drive away before they laughed.

'Do her good,' Molly said happily. 'Bring her down to earth a bit. Just what she needed.'

Perhaps it'll persuade her to start house-hunting, Laura thought, and she was just about to walk down the path to check the cess-pool when a small van turned the bend. 'There you are,' she said to Molly. 'Here's our new neighbours come.'

But it wasn't a furniture van. It was neat and green and had the words *FitzHenry Estates* printed on the side. The two women watched with growing concern as it pulled up outside Fiona's old house and two men got out, opened the back, and pulled out several thick sheets of rough wood, which they propped against the wall. But the shock of what happened next was like a blow to the stomach. They produced hammers and nails and began to board up the windows.

'Oh my God!' Laura said. 'We can't have this.' And was off across the road to stop it as fast as she could run.

The workmen were cheerful but implacable. 'Orders,' the older one said. 'Nothink to do with us, ma'am. We just do as we're told. Job a' work

278

you might say. An' lucky to get it.'

'But you can't *do* this,' Laura protested. 'It's vandalism. These are good houses. They ought to be used.'

'Orders,' the man insisted. 'If you want to stop it you'll have ter give the office a bell. I told yer, s'nothink ter do with us.'

By this time Joan and Connie had come out on their doorsteps to see what was going on. 'Come on,' Laura said to them. 'We'll see about this.'

It took six attempts and considerable temper before she could get through to the estate office and by then she'd inspected the cess-pool — because that had to be done no matter what else was happening — and all three houses had been boarded up and the workmen had driven away.

But at last, when it was nearly two o'clock and she was beginning to wonder whether they'd packed up and gone home for the day, a polite voice answered. 'FitzHenry Estates. How can I help you?'

She plunged into the attack straight away, her voice angry. 'This is Mrs Laura Pendleton of Laura's Way.'

The voice continued polite. 'Yes, madam. You are one of our tenants?'

'No, no. I live in the Way. A private house. You've sent the bailiffs in.'

'To you madam?' He was still polite but his voice was sharpened by disbelief.

'You've boarded up three houses in St Mary's terrace.'

279

Papers were rustled. 'Yes. That is correct. The properties in question are empty and due for demolition, I believe.'

It was so cool and complacent, it took her breath away. 'Due for demolition!' she repeated, scandalised.

'A road scheme,' the voice explained.

'Now look here!' Laura said. 'That scheme is still under consideration. There's going to be a public enquiry.'

'That is for the authority to decide. We have had no news of it. As far as we are aware the scheme is going through.'

'You can't do this,' Laura said, trying to keep calm and failing. 'These are good sound houses. If you leave them boarded up they'll go to wrack and ruin. And don't tell me you haven't got plenty of tenants who'd jump at the chance to live here. It's a lovely place and you're wrecking it. It's vandalism, that's what it is.'

This time the voice was chilling. 'I don't know who you are, madam, or what authority you have, or presume to have, but I can tell you you have no right whatever to take such a tone with this office. The houses you are talking about are the property of Colonel FitzHenry and if he chooses to have them boarded up I hardly need point out to you that it is his affair and nobody else's.' And the phone was crashed down.

It was a defeat and it felt like one. The four women swore and complained and prowled about in the lane bewailing the damage and trying to

280

think of some way to get the offending boards removed. Molly was all for pulling them down there and then, which alarmed Connie who thought they ought to write to the council. Joan said she thought they ought to phone the telly and get them to come down and film it and 'see what people made of *that*'. And Laura thought of Jeff and wished she could talk it all over with him. But what was the use of that when he was still sulking in his tent?

'They've only done it because they think this damned road's going to be built,' she said. 'That's all it is. It'll be a different story when we've won. They'll be down here the next day, then, opening them all up again. You see if I'm not right.'

But their grievance was too extreme to be stilled by good sense and they went on swearing until there was another cess-pool finished and they had to go and inspect the empty pit. And after that the laborious business of scrubbing up their kitchens took them away from the eyesore in their midst. But it was still a defeat and, for all her encouraging words, Laura was angry about it all afternoon.

Just after five o'clock when she was wondering what to cook for supper and whether Amy would deign to come home to eat it, she had a phone call from the lady herself, apologising quite fulsomely for 'rushing off like that' and offering to bring in a take-away. 'You're bound to be tired,' she said. 'I'll bet you've been cleaning all afternoon. What d'you fancy?'

Isn't that just typical, Laura thought, as she put the phone down. Just when you're furious with her she does something kind and spikes your guns.

It was a tasty meal and a decided relief not to have to cook anything for once. Afterwards, when the plates were cleared and the coffee made, they sat by the fire to discuss the day. Amy hadn't noticed the boarded-up houses when she drove in because it had been too dark but she said she wasn't particularly surprised to hear about them.

'Just the sort of thing they would do,' she said, lighting her second cigarette. 'Pity you can't talk to Jeff about it. It's just up his street.'

Being reminded that she couldn't talk to him made Laura feel cross. 'I might give him a ring later,' she said — just to show how easy it would be.

Amy's smile was rather unpleasant, superior and mocking. 'You'll have a job,' she said.

Laura wasn't going to be riled by snide remarks or superior smiles. 'Oh I don't think so,' she said. 'It's only a matter of dialling his number.'

'Ah!' Amy said, still with that mocking smile on her face. 'You do know he's gone, don't you?'

It was such an unexpected and unwelcome piece of news that Laura was winded by it. 'Gone?' she echoed. What's she talking about, *gone?* He can't be gone. Gone where?

'Well he's not in the surgery, let's put it that way,' Amy said smugly. 'Hasn't been there for a week, so they say in Beautibelles. I only know

282

because I nipped in on my way across the compound. I felt so sick after that awful bucket so I thought I'd get an aspirin. And there was some horrible woman there instead of him. Nasty bit of work she was. Most unfeeling. Wouldn't give me anything at all. Said aspirin would "increase my nausea" if you ever heard such cobblers. So I had to go on feeling absolutely dreadful all afternoon. Anyway, apparently Jeff's gone and she's his replacement. I thought you'd have known. Didn't he tell you?'

Laura was too shocked to say anything. It was the second blow of the day and much the worse of the two. She felt as though she'd been abandoned, judged and found wanting, and at just the moment when she wanted him most. He couldn't have left without saying goodbye. It was too cruel. OK, they'd had a row but it hadn't been that bad. They could have patched things up. He couldn't just have upped sticks and gone. She was so agitated she had to get up and walk about.

'My cup's empty,' Amy said, waving it at her. 'Fill it up for me, while you're on your feet.'

Laura was still grappling with rejection and barely heard her. 'What?'

'Get me another cup of coffee, will ya. There's a sweetie.'

Sweetie! Laura thought, stung by the word. Sweetie, for Christ's sake! It was what she'd called Jeff to reward him for telling lies. 'What disease did your last servant die of?' she said crossly.

Amy was enjoying her cigarette and wasn't in

the least abashed. 'Now you're up,' she wheedled. 'I've had a hideous day.'

Laura didn't take the hint or the cup. 'And I haven't!' she said. 'No, I'm sorry, Amy. I won't wait on you. You're just as capable of pouring coffee as I am.' And she sat down again.

Amy rose from the sofa with a martyred sigh. 'What's got into you?' she drawled.

'Nothing's got into me. It's you. You're so lazy it isn't true. I don't think I've ever met anyone as lazy as you.'

Being criticised didn't bother Amy at all. 'So what's new?' she yawned as she filled her cup. 'I've always been lazy. You knew that when you asked me to stay so I can't see why we're having all this now.' She was looking around for something. 'Didn't you get a paper this morning?'

Now that she'd started to criticise her unwanted guest, Laura couldn't stop. Her resentment had been brewing a long time and now she was hot with it. She comes in here, she thought, telling me things I don't want to know, treating me like a servant, causing trouble. It was all her fault we had that row in the first place and she doesn't even realise it. 'You're lazy,' she said, delivering the word like a sting. 'You're greedy. You're arrogant. You tell lies.'

'No I don't,' Amy said mildly, still looking for the paper. 'I might tell the odd white lie now and then — everybody does — but I never lie outright.'

'Don't give me that. You lie through your teeth.

Look at the way you went on when that woman gatecrashed my party.'

'Oh *I* see,' Amy drawled, looking straight at her. 'This is about Jeff Turner, isn't it. You've had a row. That's why he's gone. I thought it was something like that.'

It was a biting truth and, as such, rejected immediately and violently. 'No,' Laura said hotly. 'It's nothing to do with Jeff Turner. It's to do with you and the way you behave — the way you treat this house. My house, in case you've forgotten.'

Amy gave up hope of the paper. 'I treat this house the way I treat any house,' she said, flicking ash at the grate on her way back to her seat.

Laura looked at the ash and the coffee cup and hardened her face and her tone. 'Molly's right,' she said, sitting down on the sofa again, 'It's high time you found a place of your own. This has gone on long enough.'

'Oh come on!' Amy said. 'Be fair. I'm doing my best.'

'Are you?'

'You know I am.'

'I don't see any letters coming from the estate agents.'

'They're sent to the office.'

'And you don't bring them home?' Laura mocked. 'Don't give me that. I wasn't born yesterday. This is transparent. You're not house-hunting at all.'

'Are you calling me a liar?'

'Yes. I'm calling you a liar. You're not making any effort to find yourself a house and it's high time you were.'

Amy was fighting back strongly. 'I thought you liked having someone to share with. I thought I was company for you.'

Laura sighed. 'You don't have the least idea do you. Well all right then, let me make it clear to you. I *don't* like having someone to share with. I don't want to share my house, period. Not with you. Not with anyone. It's mine and I like it the way it is, not ankle deep under someone else's dirty clothes or smothered in someone else's dirty dishes. If I'd wanted a lodger I'd have had one years ago. But I didn't. I didn't want one then and I don't want one now. Especially you.'

At that, Amy jumped to her feet in a rage. 'You're just vile!' she yelled. 'I go out of my way to be good to you and all you do is call me names. I've had the most appalling time in York with that Curtis woman. You wouldn't believe how vile she was to me. On my back the whole time — *"That's not very good. You haven't made much of a hand of that. You could improve there."* — and I came home thinking at least you'd be kind to me, my own sister-in-law, and now this. You haven't got an ounce of love in your whole body.'

'Now look,' Laura said, leaning forward on the sofa and speaking sternly. 'Yelling abuse won't get you anywhere. It just proves my point. You've got to find somewhere else to live.'

'Oh I see!' Amy yelled. 'I've got to take any old

rubbish that comes along. Is that it? Some stinking hole in a corner and then you'll be satisfied.'

There was someone shouting out in the Way. Someone shouting and banging. 'Oh for God's sake, now what?' Laura said, turning her head towards the sound. 'Listen.'

Amy went on shouting. 'All these years,' she cried. 'You don't know what it's been like . . .'

'There's something going on,' Laura said, on her feet and thoroughly alerted. 'Someone's breaking things.' She strode across to the window, opened it wide and leant out.

The sudden rush of cold air turned Amy's wrath to complaint. 'What are you *doing?*' she protested. 'You're letting in the cold. We shall freeze.'

Laura didn't have time or desire to explain. The noise was coining from the Garstons' house and now that she could hear it properly, it sounded alarming. Through the latticework of the bare branches she could see that there were lights coming on all along the terrace and as she watched, the Coopers opened their front door and came out on to the step, silhouetted by their hall light.

'What's up?' she called across to them.

Before they could answer, Joan Garston ran out of her house and hurtled across the Way, looking wildly to right and left, as if she didn't know who to appeal to. 'He's gone round the bend,' she cried.

'I'll be right out,' Laura told her.

Joan reached the gatepost and clung to it, weeping. She was in her dressing gown and slippers and looked totally distraught. 'He's gone round the bend. Gone round the bend. Round the bend.'

'Come on in,' Laura said, taking her neighbor's arm and leading her into the cottage. 'Make a pot of strong tea,' she said to Amy. This was no time for tantrums. 'With lots of sugar. Then stoke up the fire. She needs keeping warm. I'll be back as soon as I know what's what.'

'Ken . . .' Joan worried, standing behind the sofa.

'Don't worry. I'll see to him. You sit down by the fire and let Amy look after you.'

'It's been coming on for months,' Joan wept. 'I've seen it coming. I can't say I haven't.' But she allowed herself to be eased on to the sofa and Amy went off obediently to make tea, so it was safe for Laura to leave them. She ran across the road, putting her coat on as she went.

By now all her remaining neighbours were either leaning out of their windows or standing about in the road. The Coopers were hesitating on Joan's doorstep and she noticed that John was carrying a sledgehammer.

'She all right?' he asked. And when Laura nodded, 'We thought he was doing her in. Did you hear it?'

'Come on,' Laura said. 'I told her we'd sort it out. The door's open.'

They went in cautiously. Unlike the rest of the houses which consisted of two simple rooms upstairs and down with an outhouse for the kitchen and bathroom at the back, the Garstons end-of-terrace was larger by two rooms — a long narrow 'best parlour' to the left of the hall with an equally narrow attic above it. There was no one in the parlour, which was mustily unused like all best rooms, nor in the living room, where the television was playing to itself, nor in the kitchen, although the chairs had been thrown on their sides and all the crockery swept from the table, which was smeared with spilt cocoa. But there was someone crashing about upstairs so that's where they went, moving quietly and holding themselves alert and ready for anything.

'Ken? What are you doing?' Laura called up the stairs.

There was no sign of him but they could hear his voice and the sound of heavy furniture being dragged about. 'Bugger off! It's all your fault, Laura Pendleton. I'm moving out. I told her. We should've gone right at the start. That's when we should've gone, when we had the chance. But would she go? Bloody fool. No, she wouldn't. Always got to know best — that's her trouble. We should've gone. And now look where we are.'

'Why don't you come downstairs,' John Cooper tried to coax. 'We can't make out what you're saying.'

The top half of Ken's torso emerged aggressively through the door to the attic rooms. It looked massive in the narrow confines of the landing, like a buffalo head on a wall too small for it.

'Bugger off!' it said. 'I've told you. And you can put that thing down for a start —' glaring at the sledgehammer — 'unless you want it wrapped round yer head.'

John propped the offending article against the banisters. 'We thought you might ha' got stuck in somewhere,' he said mildly.

'I am getting stuck in,' Ken growled, squeezing out of the door and blundering across the landing into his bedroom. 'Stuck right in. We shall never sell out now. Not with all the windows boarded up. All right then. I'm getting stuck in. I'm going on the Internet, me. Should ha' done it months ago. What do I want with the rest of you? Bloody fools the lot of you. You should ha' sold out. I *told* you. Out of my way!'

Old Mr Fennimore had been listening from the foot of the stairs. There was no point in climbing up if no one had been hurt. 'He's only playing silly buggers,' he said. 'I'm off home. You coming Molly?'

But Molly stayed where she was. 'I want to see what's he doing.'

He was dragging his mattress across the landing, bending it in half and trying to squash it through the attic door.

'It won't go through there, mate,' John Cooper advised.

And got sworn at for his pains. 'Yes it bloody will.' He was heaving at it with his shoulders, his face dark with effort. 'If I say it'll go in, it'll bloody go in.'

'You'll only have to drag it all out again,' Connie said. 'Later I mean.'

Ken paused in his efforts and wiped his forehead with the sleeve of his jersey. 'Who asked you to put your oar in?' he panted. 'Haven't you got anything into your thick skulls any of you? I'm not coming out again. Ever. I'm going to live here. Where it's safe. The rest of you can go hang as far as I'm concerned. I'm going.' And he gave the mattress such a violent kick that it shifted at last and with an enormous heave he managed to push it through into the attic, tumbling in on top of it in a thresh of elephantine legs and swinging boots.

His neighbours gathered about the emptied doorway and peered in, their four faces clustered about the jambs. The narrow room was full of furniture, a bedstead and duvet, a chest of drawers spilling shirts, a pile of huge coats and jackets, most of them filthy, a computer, a printer, a pile of heavy manuals, cricket bats and fishing rods and even a battered keep-net.

It looks as if he's preparing for a siege, Laura thought. But none of them said anything for fear of aggravating him and as he rolled himself into a sitting position and swivelled his head round to glare at them, they turned with one accord and left him.

Joan was sitting by the log fire drinking her tea and confiding in Amy who seemed to have made a complete recovery and was her usual well-groomed self again, renewed mascara and all.

'Well?' she asked, when the four trooped in.

Laura spoke for them. 'He says he's going to live in the attic.'

'He means it,' Joan said. 'He's dismantled the bed. I don't know where he thinks I'm going to sleep.'

There was nothing for it but to put her up for the night. 'You can have Danny's room,' Laura offered. 'It's all mutant turtles but it's better than the floor.'

But it was hours before they'd talked everything out, longer still before they stumbled to bed and well into the early hours before Laura finally got to sleep.

What a day! she thought, gazing through her window to where the reassuring pattern of the Great Bear studded the black sky. I feel as if I've been riding a roller-coaster. A day like this makes you wonder what on earth can happen next. And for a few silly seconds before sleep washed her away, she thought she would phone Jeff in the morning and tell him all about it. Then she re-membered that he was gone and felt bleak with loss. I thought I knew him, she mused, but I was wrong. I thought I was growing fond of him but I suppose I was wrong about that too. One thing was unarguable. She would certainly miss him.

Chapter Eighteen

'Having a relationship is great for your skin,' Jessica Pendleton told her diary. *'It's not bad for your hair either.'* She paused to tap her teeth with her pen and consider what she'd just written.

In the last few weeks she'd learned more about life than she'd done in the preceding seventeen years. She and Kevin were an item now, accepted by both sets of their friends, with a style and language of their own — and they'd managed it without letting her parents know what was really going on, which was pretty fantastic. They'd got off to an iffy sort of start but that was because she hadn't known enough. It made her blush to think how she'd whined at him on that first night. What a nerd! Now she knew better. She understood that all that lovey-dovey sort of thing was just girlie magazine stuff. She read *Cosmopolitan* now. Avidly. She'd learnt a lot — about his sexuality and about hers. All that girlie stuff about 'love' was old-fashioned. You know you're loved by how horny you both are and how good the sex is. Their sex was terrific.

'It is the most brilliant experience of my life. I have never felt this way before, ever, about anyone. He phones me every single day on his mobile and we talk for hours.' It had actually been a mere three min-

utes the last time but she hadn't yet reached the stage where she was prepared to tell the unvarnished truth to her diary. And anyway he'd explained that he was on his way to work so it didn't count. He often had to work at odd hours which was rather a disappointment to her because it cut into the time they could spend together. They'd missed Gran's Guy Fawkes party because of some job he'd suddenly had to do. But she accepted it, hard though it was, because the time they actually did spend together was so good. *We have sex every time we meet. He can't wait for it. And he sends me flowers the next day. Sweet. I think of him all the time. It is screwing up my A levels but I don't care. Having a relationship is more important than exams.*

It was seven o'clock on Saturday evening and she was upstairs in her white bedroom supposedly finishing her homework, during the last twenty minutes before she was due to go out. She'd arranged her English books all over her desk and switched on the angle-poise lamp so that she could look busy should her father put his head round the door to check on her. He was *always* doing that and it *did* annoy her. Now she was lying on the bed with her newly washed hair turbaned in a towel, amusing herself by confiding in her diary — and she had something really special to confide that night.

'Tonight we're going to Southampton and we're going to stay there for the weekend. I don't know where. It's a surprise but it's all arranged. He's

thought of all the angles. I've told Mum I'm sleeping over at Emma's. I've got to be back for Sunday tea but apart from that my life's my own.'

Writing the words made her aware that she was uncomfortable to be deceiving her parents. But it couldn't be helped. It was the price she had to pay for freedom and independence. Well worth paying when she considered how much Kevin loved her.

She glanced at the clock. Time to go. A quick brush through her damp hair — that'll annoy Dad — then she grabbed up her coat and her bag and was off, leaping down the stairs two at a time.

Her mother came out into the hall to kiss her goodbye. 'Oh Jess!' she reproved. 'Your hair's soaking. You can't go out with it like that. You'll catch cold. Let me dry it for you.'

Jessica shook the offending hair but didn't stop in her stride towards the door. 'Don't fuss, Mum.'

Maureen followed her. 'Have you got everything you need?'

That was dismissed too, 'Yeh, yeh.' The door was opened and she was off down the path, walking so fast she was almost running.

'Aren't you going on your bike?' Maureen called after her.

She was at the gate. 'I fancy a walk.'

'What if it rains?' Maureen called. 'Take an umbrella.' But her daughter was already out of the close.

'She does worry me,' she said to David as she walked back into the living room, 'rushing off like that with her hair all wet. And on foot too. I can't see why she didn't ride her bike round. They'd have kept it in their garage for her. She'll take cold, you see if I'm not right.'

David was absorbed in a documentary about the drug industry. 'She'll be all right,' he said without much interest. 'It's not far to Emma's.'

'It's bitter out,' Maureen complained. 'I don't like to think of her walking in this weather. What's the point of spending all that money on a mountain bike if she doesn't use it? Danny rides *his* everywhere.'

'He's a boy,' David said, as though that explained everything.

And she's a worry, Maureen thought, picking up her library book. It was a sign that she wasn't going to annoy him by talking to him any further and she knew he'd received it even though his eyes hadn't left the screen. I wish teenage daughters weren't so tricky, she thought. If I make scenes I could make everything worse. On the other hand it would be dreadful to find out later that she was trailing her coat and wanted me to take a stand. Still at least she'll be safe and warm with Emma.

She was very warm indeed, in an overheated car, being kissed by an overheated young man.

'You're fucking gorgeous,' he told her, fingers busy.

It thrilled her the way they swore when they were having sex. It was so mature. 'You're not so fucking bad yourself.'

296

'Let's,' he suggested happily.

Jessica didn't really enjoy sex in the car, at least not always. It was difficult to come when she was all cramped up and she was aware that someone could walk by and find them. She usually had to fake it so as not to disappoint him. She didn't say anything about how she really felt, naturally, because that would have made him feel inadequate, but the truth was she preferred it in a bed or on a sofa or some place where they were more private and she could move as much as she wanted.

'Oh go on then,' she said.

He paused long enough to say, 'Only if you want to.'

'Yes, yes,' she assured him, encouraging them both. 'Course I want to.'

He'd parked the car in a lay-by on the country road that led down to the new superhighway. It was a good place — one of the best — as he knew because he'd sussed them all out right at the start of this relationship.

'Brilliant!' he said when they were rearranging their clothing again. 'Now for Southampton. Fasten your seat-belt, gorgeous! Let's see what sort of speed we can make.'

This was the part of their journey that Jessica enjoyed the most now that she'd got used to belting down a motorway at his sort of speed. It was good to sit beside him with the engine purring and lights patterning the darkness and the road signs bearing down upon them as if they were flying. He always drove so fast after sex. So much for the idea that it calms you down. They were passing the hill forts in no time, with the lights of Portsmouth massed below them and the long line of the motorway stretching before them into distant Southampton.

'Where is it?' she asked. 'Am I allowed to know?'

'Not till we get there. I told you. It's a surprise.' He liked the power of a mystery.

'Is it a house or a flat?' she teased.

'Wait! You'll see.'

It was the top flat in a small terraced house in one of the narrow side streets that run down to the harbour. Not a very prepossessing place, Jessica thought, after the space and luxury of Canterbury Gardens. It was poorly lit, there were no front gardens and the nearest parking space they could find was yards away. But she kept her opinion to herself as Kevin was perky with enthusiasm.

'Wait till you see inside,' he said, lifting their cases out of the car.

She took her own and followed him along the road. It might be better inside.

It was a revelation, all newly furnished and decorated in such beautiful colours she was lifted just by the sight of them. The kitchen was all golden pine units with bronze-handled saucepans and china patterned in emerald green and sapphire, the living room was in shades of green and gold, even the bookcase and the table and chairs were green, a lovely muted sage as if it had grown that way. But the bedroom was the best of all, with scarlet walls and a duvet and curtains in scarlet and two shades of blue.

'Well?' he asked, pale eyes beaming.

'It's gorgeous!' she said, stroking the duvet.

'Told you.'

'Is it yours?'

The temptation to lie was very strong but he resisted it. Some lies lead to such appalling complications they're not worth it. 'Wish it was,' he said and pulled a rueful face. 'It belongs to a friend of mine. It's his holiday home. But we can come here whenever we like — except over Christmas or if he wants it for something special.'

'Brilliant!' she said. A place of their own. They really were an item now.

After such a start, and with a bed like that at their disposal, the weekend was a great success. They did the round of pubs and clubs that night, discovering friends and acquaintances of his in every one, returned home in the small hours to late-night music and some very satisfying sex and slept in so late on Sunday that they decided on a pub brunch instead of breakfast.

On the way back to the flat, he bought the Sunday papers. And was very surprised by what he read in them.

'Have you seen this?' he said to Jessica. 'Your gran's in the Sundies.'

Jessica was cool about it. 'Well of course she is.'

He read the article with great interest. 'I

thought it was preserving badgers she was on about,' he said, 'but it says here she's one of the leaders of the anti-road campaign. Feisty old girl!'

Jessica was pleased to hear the admiration in her voice. 'She's been running the campaign for months,' she said. 'You should have seen the size of the petition she got up.'

'Big?'

'Mega. Nearly seven thousand signatures.'

'Um,' he said thoughtfully, looking at the article. 'Then she's an important lady.' He pulled Jessica towards him and she put her head on his shoulder while they went on reading the papers. 'What time have you got to be back for tea?' he asked.

She smiled lazily. 'Who cares?'

'No, seriously.'

'About four o'clock, if you must know. Hours yet. Don't let's think about it.'

'Is that when your gran gets there?'

'Usually. She's coming early today to help with the cakes.'

'Great! How early?'

'About three. Why?'

To her surprise, he threw the papers down and rushed into the bedroom.

She was annoyed and couldn't help showing it. 'What are you doing?' she said following him.

He'd already flung the duvet over the rumpled bed and was busy packing.

'We're not going back now, are we?' she asked, her disappointment plain.

'That's right,' he said. 'Or we shall lose the light.'

'What light? What are you on about?'

'I'm going to film your gran's cottage.'

'What for?'

He caught the edge in her voice and stopped packing to look up and smile at her. 'A Christmas surprise,' he said. 'You can pick the best shot and we'll have it made up for a Christmas card.'

She was overwhelmed by his thoughtfulness. 'Oh Kev!' she said. 'That's sweet!'

'That's me,' he agreed. 'Come on!'

He drove back at even greater speed than he'd driven out but, even so, the light was fading by the time they reached Laura's Way. There was nobody about, the lane was rutted and streaked by muddy puddles, what little of the sky they could see through the bare black branches was ominously grey and below it the three boarded-up houses looked shoddy, like something out of an inner-city slum. Holm End was the only house with any colour in it, and even that was subdued, the green paint darker than usual, the mottled tiles more brown than orange.

'Right!' Kevin said. 'Let's get cracking.' And took an expensive camcorder from the boot.

Jessica was most impressed by it but there wasn't time to admire or even comment, because he was already filming, first from one end of the Way and then from the other. He looked very professional and seemed to know exactly what he was doing.

'Is that water I can see through the trees over

301

there?' he asked.

'It's a pond,' she told him. 'Been there years.'

'Let's take a look.'

She led him through the wood, picking her way along the edges of the footpath where fallen leaves had mopped up the worst of the mud, deeper and deeper into the trees until the darkness folded in upon them, the sky was gone and the mottled trunks of the silver birches gleamed on either side of them like slender ghosts. In that primitive half light, the pond was so dark green that it looked almost black, dark and deep and mysterious and silent in the midst of forest sounds, the hiss of fallen leaves disturbed and the susurration of evergreens.

'What a place!' Kevin said. 'You can see why people were afraid of woods in the old days. I suppose they'll dig all this up when — if they build this road.'

Jessica didn't know. 'They're not going to build the road,' she said. 'They're going to have an enquiry.'

He was gazing at the water, his face intense. Out there, standing so still beside that mysterious water, the colour drained from his clothes and his eyes as pale as his skin, he looked like a statue. 'This is spooky!' he said and he spoke without moving anything at all except his lips.

'What is?'

'This pond.'

'That's what Gran thinks. She won't come near it.'

'What never?'

'Never. It's water, you see. She keeps away from water.'

He looked a question at her so she explained. 'She was nearly drowned once, when she was little. She doesn't like water.'

'A phobia?'

'Something like that. Look, *are* you going to film this? I'm getting cold.'

'No,' he decided and turned away from the water, becoming himself again, 'the light's not good enough. Come on, I'll take you back. Mustn't have you late for tea or they won't let you stay over with Emma again.'

The tea party had begun without her but they were all in such good mood she hardly got rebuked at all for being late. Only by Mum and only mildly. Dad didn't seem to have noticed.

There were all the usual cakes and sandwiches on the table. Really boring. But Gran was on good form, in the middle of a tale that was making them all laugh.

'Now I suppose I shall have to begin at the beginning again,' she said, smiling at Jessica. After all the difficulties of that dreadful Friday she was determined to make light of everything now.

'The fat man's locked himself in his attic and won't come out,' Danny explained. 'He says he's going to live there. Try the fairy cake. I made them.'

'Ugh!' Jessica said, taking a sandwich instead. 'What fat man?'

They explained, taking it in turns to embroider the tale for her benefit. 'Ridiculous!' she said, laughing with them.

'He'll come out eventually, surely,' Maureen said. 'I mean you can't *live* in an attic. What about baths and things like that?'

'What about going to the loo?' Danny dared. 'Or will he do it out the window?'

David opened his mouth to rebuke but Laura was already laughing at the idea. 'He'll have a job. It's a skylight.'

Danny pushed the joke a bit further. 'Perhaps he'll stand on a ladder.'

'Daniel!' David protested. But the others were all laughing.

'I can just imagine it,' Laura said. 'I wouldn't put it past him either. He can be very peculiar.'

'What about his dole money?' Maureen asked. 'He'll have to come out to collect that won't he.'

'What made him do it?' David asked. 'That's what I want to know.'

Laura hadn't intended to tell them about the bailiffs. But with such a direct question, she had to.

Instant sympathy all round the table. 'But that's awful,' Maureen said. 'Oh Laura I *am* sorry.'

Laura had decided how to cope with *that* before she set out that afternoon. 'They'll only have to take it all down again after the enquiry,' she said. 'They've just made work for themselves. More fools they. Can I have another slice of fudge cake?'

'Any news on that front?' David asked.

'No. Not yet.'

'What front?' Danny asked.

'Never you mind,' his father said in the heavily jocular style he assumed when he was feeling pleased with his children and wanted to demonstrate his control over them. 'Eat your cake and don't make crumbs.'

Beyond the drawn white curtains it was raining again, the swoosh of the wind and the tinny patter against the windows a foreign foil to the cheerful voices in the room.

This is what family life should be, David thought, looking at the well-fed faces around the white cloth on his black table. Three generations laughing together, plenty of good food, courteous behaviour — a certain amount of daring but within limits — troubles shut out, complete security within. That's the basis of it. Security.

He's an old fart, Danny grumbled to himself. He didn't have to put me down like that. *Don't make crumbs!* I never make crumbs. And I know what they're talking about anyway. It's that petition. I'm not a moron.

Here's another week gone, Maureen mused sadly, smiling at David as she poured him another cup of tea, and I still haven't had a chance to work out what I'm going to do about this job. But there you are, that's typical. Once you've got a family you don't get any time to yourself from one week to the next, I wonder what my life would have been like if I hadn't got married.

I hope to God they decide about the petition soon, Laura thought grimly. It's been three weeks now and that's quite long enough. It's worse than waiting for the dentist. There were altogether too many uncertainties in her life at the moment, which was why she was making a joke of everything. Amy had taken off after breakfast on Saturday morning and she hadn't seen or heard from her since so *that* wasn't resolved, and Joan had gone home soon afterwards, saying she was going to make up a bed for herself in the spare room, but there was no knowing what would happen next in that quarter either. After they'd both gone, she'd taken a chance and phoned Jeff. She really didn't expect an answer, which was just as well as she didn't get one, so he *had* gone, demoralising though it was to have to face it. I wonder where he is, she thought, stirring her tea, and what he's doing. I wish he'd write.

They never change, Jessica told herself. They always cook the same old cakes and sit in the same old places and crack the same old jokes. But she knew she was fond of them, boring though they were. And smiled at Gran to prove it to them both.

Chapter Nineteen

The southern regional office of PPC Pharmaceuticals is housed in an imposing building on the outskirts of Crawley. It looks what it is, the headquarters of a company that has status, immense wealth and the power to brook no nonsense from anybody. Its vast underground laboratories are rumoured but rarely seen and although its seven storeys of tinted glass may admit light they are designed to exclude all public interest and scrutiny. Their function is not to serve as a window but to protect an image and a very powerful, modern image it is — the huge calm of the Sussex sky, the tower blocks of its competitive neighbours, the incessant movement of multi-coloured traffic on the motorway below. Although he would never have admitted it to anybody, it made David Pendleton's heart sink every time he approached it.

Of course it was pleasant to have a car-park attendant to keep an eye on his precious BMW and a secretary to take his calls and attend to his correspondence and serve him coffee but neither of these things could make amends for the undercutting sense of insecurity that subdued his days and plagued his nights with unsettling dreams. It is just a little too easy to lose your job in the unemployed nineties and he was acutely aware that, with a mere eighteen months' service under his belt, he had very few rights and that the new system of hiring staff under contract put everybody at risk, including him.

The monthly sales conference was a torment to him. Even when he'd reached his sales quota — even when he'd surpassed it — he felt under threat, as if at any moment the Senior Sales Manager would summon him to his office with the dreaded query, *'Have you got a moment?'* It sounded so soothing and friendly and yet nine times out of ten it was the prelude to dismissal. He'd heard it so many times in the last six months and said goodbye to so many colleagues that it was demoralising to think about it.

However on that particular Monday morning he felt, if not exactly confident, then at least that he'd done everything that could reasonably be expected of him. So when the dreadful words were spoken he didn't look up to see who was being addressed but went on stacking his papers.

The question was repeated with marginally more insistence. 'Have you got a moment, Mr Pendleton?'

The shock of being summoned by name in front of the entire sales team made David's heart judder. Oh God! he thought. What haven't I done? Where have I slipped up? But he didn't say anything and he didn't look at his colleagues. He crammed his papers into his briefcase and followed the SSM into the torture chamber.

Mr Cosgrave, the SSM, was rotund, smooth and falsely friendly. He urged David to sit down and make himself comfortable. He smiled.

'Excellent sales figures,' he said.

David agreed that they were.

'And for the third consecutive month, as I recall.'

'The fourth actually.' There was nothing to lose by pointing it out. It might even help.

'The fourth eh? Well as I said, excellent. Keep it up.'

So it's not sales, David thought. So far, so good. But if it's not sales what else could it be?

'This is a delicate matter,' Mr Cosgrave said smiling vaguely. 'The AMD has asked me to have a quiet word.'

David waited to be enlightened. The initial shock had almost subsided now. He felt he could face this out, somehow or other, whatever it was.

Mr Cosgrave fitted his finger tips together so that they made a white steeple just below his nose. That's very mottled, David thought, looking at the nose. I wonder why I never noticed it before. And how ugly it looks when he sucks in his breath like that.

'Very delicate,' Mr Cosgrave said. 'And personal, of course, very personal.'

For a fleeting second David wondered whether he'd developed BO without noticing it but Mr Cosgrave was rambling on.

'. . . your mother. Something of an eccentric I believe. No harm in that, of course. A little eccentricity here and there. No harm at all. It's the juxtaposition that gives cause for concern, if you take my meaning, the juxtaposition.'

At that point, David understood what was going on. 'My mother is a very good woman,' he said coldly.

'Of course she is, old chap,' Mr Cosgrave hastened to assure him. 'A very good woman. A librarian. It's just that her current activities are just a little too — how shall I put it? — a little too political. Adverse publicity can have such an impact on sales, as you know. I'm sure you take my point.'

'Yes.' Anger was boiling in his belly. You leave my mother alone, you rotten bastards!

'Quite. Well that being so, perhaps you would feel it appropriate to have a discreet word with her. I'm sure she wouldn't want to do anything that would have an adverse effect on your career.'

'Warn her off you mean?'

Mr Cosgrave winced at such crudity. 'Oh no, no, no. Nothing like that. Discuss the matter with her. I'm sure you can distinguish between activities that are perfectly proper and those that might be — shall we say — inappropriate.'

'Is there any urgency?' David asked, speaking as coolly as he could. He knew he was running risks by asking questions but he was too angry to stay silent. 'When would you like me to have this discussion?'

'There's no rush,' Mr Cosgrave said, lowering his fingers. 'Before the enquiry, naturally, because that is — shall we say — public.'

There was a discreet knock at the door, a waft of perfume, blonde hair swinging towards Mr Cosgrave as his secretary delivered her message. 'That will be all, Mr Pendleton, I mustn't keep you. Thanks for your co-operation.'

He walked stiffly back to where his colleagues were waiting to hear bad news. They looked up as he opened the door, questioning with eyes and eyebrows. Barry Brough drew an imaginary knife across his throat.

'No,' David said. 'Sorry to disappoint you fellers. You've still got to put up with me. It was personal.'

'Thank God for that,' Barry said, as they walked down the corridor. 'Who's the lucky girl?'

'My mother,' David told him. 'I've got to tell her to call off her campaign against that bloody by-pass.'

'Ah!' Barry understood. 'Personal as in blackmail. That'll be Amalgamated Gravels putting on the pressure. They don't like opposition to their road. What will you do?'

'Go and talk to her,' David said. 'See what she says.'

Laura had spent a pleasant morning in the Tillbury library working with Miss Finch. There was still no news of the enquiry and none of Jeff, which was a continuing disappointment, but Amy hadn't come back and there was no phone call from her either, which had to be a relief. Ken

Garston was still ensconced in his attic but he seemed to be living there quietly enough and they were all getting used to the boarded-up houses. She'd come to work that morning feeling that her life was almost back on an even keel again.

The library was crowded all morning so she and Miss Finch were kept too busy to talk but at one o'clock Miss Finch closed the doors and came cheerfully across to the counter to tell her that she'd got 'a surprise'.

'I've made a quiche and a little tossed salad for our lunch,' she said. There was a bottle of Mateus Rosé too and two pink wine glasses she'd brought from home, all neatly laid out on the side table in the inner office.

'How very nice,' Laura said, taking her place at the table. 'Are we celebrating?'

'No, no,' Miss Finch smiled. 'I thought we deserved a treat, that's all.' It had actually been planned to cheer Laura up because she seemed to have been rather down since Guy Fawkes night. But it would have spoiled the whole purpose of the exercise if she'd explained *that*.

'Is there any news of the enquiry?' she asked as she served.

Laura made a grimace to show that there wasn't.

'It all takes time I suppose.' Could that be the reason for the sadness in her? 'But they'll have to agree to it won't they. After your petition. Six thousand signatures, I mean! They can hardly ignore *that*. Mr Gratwick was talking about it only last week.'

'With approval I hope.'

'Absolute approval,' Miss Finch said, dabbing her pale mouth with her napkin. 'Between you and me, he's quite a revolutionary.'

'You surprise me.'

'We quiet ones are the worst, you know,' Miss Finch said confidentially. 'Nobody can tell what we're really capable of. My father used to call me the family firebrand.' She looked across the table with such a devilish gleam in her blue eyes that Laura could well believe it. 'Are you ready for this enquiry?'

'As ready as we'll ever be,' Laura told her. 'Our evidence is ready anyway. We all know what we're going to say. I don't think there's anything we've overlooked.'

The telephone was ringing in the outer office. 'Shall I get it?' Miss Finch offered.

'No,' Laura said. 'I'll go.' As the senior librarian on the premises it was her responsibility. It was bound to be library business.

But it wasn't. It was Amy and she sounded out of breath, as though she'd been running.

'Hi!' she said. 'I've caught you.'

That seemed rather an odd thing to say, as if she'd been travelling around looking for her. 'Where are you?'

'Well I'm at home actually. Packing. I've — um — I've got to go to our Birmingham office. I've been — well — sort of posted, I guess you'd say.'

Mrs Brooke Curtis has manoeuvred her out of

313

the way, Laura thought. How clever! And how splendid! She didn't escape scot free after all. 'A new job?' she asked, hope rising.

Again the drawling admission. 'Well not exactly. Area sales. I'm sort of standing in. Only temporary. To do them a favour really. Two or three months. No more. The trouble is they want me there yesterday. You know how it is.'

Laura felt she understood exactly how it was. 'When have you got to go?' she asked, trying not to sound too pleased.

'This afternoon. I'm not too keen on Birmingham, to tell you the truth, but there it is.' She was still rankling under the indignation of being pushed around. Brooke had been really unkind, talking to her as though she were no better than a typist. And after all she'd done for him. God-awful man! 'I thought I'd better let you know,' she said.

'Thanks,' Laura said. 'That's good of you.'

Encouraged by her kinder tone, Amy began to confide. 'It's a bloody nuisance,' she complained. 'I hate being rushed into things. And being sent to Birmingham is . . .'

'Better than being sent to Coventry,' Laura said, enjoying the joke.

Being laughed at cast Amy down again. 'See yer!' she said. And hung up.

'Top up the glasses,' Laura told Miss Finch. 'This *is* a celebration after all. I've just got rid of my lodger.'

'Good for you!' Miss Finch smiled. So that's

what it was. And she filled both glasses to the brim.

Laura was still full of happy energy when she got home that evening. She took out the Hoover, found dusters and polish and set to work to remove all traces of her untidy guest. The room was restored and she was on her knees coaxing the fire alight when she heard David's car turning in at the gate.

'Well how nice,' she said, as he came in. 'I've had a lovely day and now here you are to put the icing on the cake. Miss Finch made a quiche for us at lunchtime, imagine that. We had a picnic in the inner office. Very civilised. And guess what else has happened. Your aunt's moved out.' Then she looked up and saw his face and knew that something was wrong. 'What is it?' she said, her tone changing. 'Tell me quickly.'

Now that they were face to face, David didn't know what to say. He'd been struggling to find a suitable formula all the way from Crawley but now he couldn't lay his tongue to any words at all. He smoothed his hair, cleared his throat, fidgeted from foot to foot.

The sight of him was alarming. Whatever this is, Laura thought, it's serious, and it will need eliciting. She left the hearth and went into the kitchen to make tea and hide her anxiety. If he saw how worried she was, he would get worse. 'Is it the children?' she called, keeping her voice calm.

He tossed his head as though he were flicking her query aside. 'No. They're fine.'

She waited to give him a chance to begin but he still didn't explain. 'Maureen?'

'No.'

'You then?'

'No,' he said irritably. 'I'm fine too. Healthwise anyway.'

Then it's his job, she thought, and probed there as she set the cups on the tray. 'Is everything all right at work?'

At that, his anguish broke into anger. 'No it's not. It's a bloody disaster, if you really want to know.'

Oh my poor boy, Laura thought. What a dreadful thing to happen — and just before Christmas too. 'You've lost your job.'

'Not yet,' he said and now his distress was obvious. 'But it's on the cards.' He sat on the sofa, heavily as if he were collapsing, and put his head in his hands. 'Oh Christ, Mother, this is all your fault. Why did you have to get involved with that stupid road? I did warn you.'

She was chill with foreboding, knowing by instinct that somebody had been pulling strings, that the situation had become political and cruel. She left the kettle to boil, came back into the room and sat on the other sofa facing him, making sure that all her movements were calm and slow so as to keep herself under total control. 'You'd better tell me all about it,' she said.

'Mr Cosgrave asked to see me this morning,'

316

he said and, gradually and painfully and without looking at her — he'd never been able to meet her eyes when he was in trouble, not even as a very little boy — he told her all the things that had been said at his interview.

'So there it is,' he said, when the story was finally over. He too was holding on to his control and finding it very difficult. The flames of the fire were so strong they were hurting his eyes.

'But that's ridiculous,' she said. 'They can't tell *me* how to behave. Who do they think they are?'

'They're the parent company of Amalgamated Gravels,' he explained. 'That's what this is about. If the road isn't built Amalgamated will lose their contract. It's serious money. They'd pull any strings to keep their hands on it.'

'That's a disgrace.'

'That's business,' he said. 'Well there you are. You know about it now. They've put me in an impossible position.'

The kettle was whistling so she left him, briefly, made the tea and returned with the tea tray which she set on the table between their opposing sofas, her heart juddering painfully. 'They've put us both in an impossible position,' she said. 'What you're saying is that you don't want me to give evidence at the enquiry, is that it?'

'No,' he said, speaking slowly. 'That's what *they* want.'

'We're talking about you. What do you want?'

'*I* never wanted you to get involved in the first place,' he said angrily. 'I told you that. I knew it was a mistake but you would go on with it. People like us don't *do* things like that.' Then he looked at her — for the first time — and tried to be reasonable, to show her that he could see her point of view. 'But you *are* involved so I can't just bowl in and tell you to stop, can I?'

But that's exactly what you *are* doing, she thought. 'They won't really sack you, will they,' she hoped.

'Yes,' he said angrily. 'They will. It's a multi-national company, for Christ's sake. That's how they go on. They'll say my presence in the company will affect their profits. If they think anything's going to cut into their profits, they're ruthless. It's *the* most important thing, profits. Increased sales. Increased profits. Make your mind up to it, if you go ahead with this, they'll sack me.'

'Well then,' she said, 'suppose for the sake of argument they do. Would that be such a very bad thing?' But as soon as the words were out of her mouth, she could see that it would be a very bad thing indeed. She changed her tone and tried to comfort. 'You'll get another job.'

That didn't work either. 'I'm too old,' he said.

'Oh come on!' she reproved. It was ridiculous to say a thing like that.

'I'm thirty-six.'

'That's no age at all.'

'Nowadays you're old at any age,' he said stiffly. 'I've got to take this seriously.'

'OK then, we'll both take it seriously. What

318

you're saying is you don't want me to go on with this campaign.'

'If you do,' he said, spelling it out to her, 'they'll have me out of a job.'

'If I don't,' she said, spelling it out to him, 'they'll have me out of this house and knock it down. If I stand back and let them do it, they'll have all sorts of other people out of their houses too. It's a matter of principle. I can't let them do it, David. It means too much to me.'

His answer was bitter. 'More than me apparently.'

She tried to be patient. 'No, not more than you. Don't be melodramatic.'

'Oh that's nice,' he exploded, leaping to his feet and striding about the room. 'It's only my job we're talking about. My living. If I'm out of work, how do you think we'll run *our* house with no money coming in? You tell me that. Who'll pay the bills? Have you any idea the sort of bills we get? They're bloody astronomical. And how much those kids cost? Who'll look after them and pay for their clothes and their shoes and their bloody school uniforms? We even have to buy books for them these days. Did you know that? The school can't afford books any more. They have to pay managers so they can't afford books. And another thing. Who'll pay the mortgage? Have you thought of that? It won't pay itself. We shall be repossessed. And don't say it couldn't happen. It's happening every bloody day of the week. But that's being melodramatic, I suppose.'

He hadn't spoken to her at such length and with such passion for years. It was as if she'd pierced an emotional dam and now his feelings were all pouring out and he couldn't stop them.

This is getting out of hand, she thought, and she made another effort to reassure him. 'That's looking on the very worst side. That's assuming you won't get another job. But there *are* other jobs. You're young. Well relatively young. A good worker. Even if they *were* to sack you I'm sure you'd find something else.'

'No,' he said frantically. 'I won't. I've told you. I know I won't.'

'But you might.'

'So that makes it all right does it?' he said in a fury. 'I might get another job so you can go ahead and do what you want.'

'There are other jobs,' she said, made stubborn by his anger. 'There's only one house. I can't pull out now. You must see that. I've spent months on this campaign.'

'I can see . . .' he spluttered. He was shaking with rage, his face white. 'Don't you worry. I can see all right. Don't you imagine I can't. I can see just what sort of a woman you are. Too bloody self-centred to help your own son. *Your* house. *Your* campaign. And I can go hang. I can see and I'll tell you what I can see. I can see why my father ran out on you.'

The shock of hearing him say such an awful thing filled her throat. She got up, fled to the kitchen, looked about her frantically for some chore to mop up the pain. 'This has got nothing to do with your father,' she cried, re-filling the kettle so clumsily that she splashed water up her arm. 'You leave him out of it.'

'I can see why he left you.'

She had to argue against such a charge. 'He didn't leave me. He went missing. We don't know what happened to him.'

He stood in the middle of the room, glaring at her, as she mopped the sleeve of her cardigan with a wodge of kitchen towel. 'He left you. He didn't write, did he? No. You know he didn't. He walked out and never came back. He left you. And I had to grow up all these years without a father. You think of that.'

She put down the wet towel and walked back towards him. 'This has got to stop,' she pleaded, spreading out her hands as if she were warding off evil spirits. 'You don't know anything about it.'

But nothing she said or did could stop him now. 'You're unyielding,' he shouted at her. 'Stiff-necked. Full of yourself. Your house. Your campaign. I can go hang. I can go bloody hang. You don't care. Just so long as your bloody house isn't pulled down. It's only bricks and mortar for Christ's sake. I'm your son!'

She was shouting too. Following him about and shouting at the top of her voice in the most awful vulgar way, like a fishwife. She couldn't help it. 'Stop it! Stop it! Do you hear.'

'I hear all right,' he said turning on his heel so

that they were face to face. '*I* hear and *you* don't listen.'

She put her hand on his arm. Such a rigid arm. So full of anger. 'Go away,' she begged. 'Stop it now, please. Stop it and go home. I can't take any more. Can't you see that?'

He took his coat and hat from the peg, put them on, stood at the door. He was panting as if he'd been running. 'What about my job?' he insisted.

'I'll sleep on it,' she said, dragging the answer from a throat clogged with unshed tears. 'I can't give you an answer now. Not after all this. We've said too much . . . It's all been too . . . Just go away and give me a bit of peace and I'll think about it.'

He left without another word, too full of anger, shame and pity to trust himself to speak, and she let him go without looking at him. It was only when the sound of his engine had faded away that she began to cry. How can I make a decision like this? she wept, aching with the anguish of it. After all these years of putting him first and doing the best for him, to be caught in a situation like this. It's cruel. Impossible. Even if I sleep on it, it will still be impossible. I can't make the right decision because there isn't one. Either way, whatever I do is bound to be wrong. It's Catch 22.

David was thinking much the same thing only in a more muddled way. He had driven to the nearest lay-by and pulled in to give himself a chance to recover a bit before he had to drive home and tell Maureen. He'd never wept in front of anybody in the whole of his life — at least not since his father left — and he had no intention of making a public exhibition of himself now. Bad enough that he'd let himself down so badly in front of his mother. He wept with frustration at the system, because they were both caught in a situation they couldn't control, with fury at PPC for their impossible demands, with anger at himself because he'd behaved so badly, with despair at his mother because she was so stubborn. It was over an hour before he was in a fit state to drive on and even then his face was splotchy.

He'd call in at the nearest pub and have one drink to keep him going. Then he'd have to go home and tell Maureen.

Maureen was on her own in the living room when he finally got home two hours and far too many drinks later. She was curled up on the sofa marking papers. 'You're late,' she said mildly. 'Was it a meeting?'

He felt as if his face was frozen. 'I've just had a row with Mother,' he said.

And been in the pub, she understood, looking at his flushed cheeks. But she gave him the sympathy he needed and instantly. 'Oh David! You haven't! What about?'

'Where are the kids?' He couldn't begin to tell her if they were up and about. What if one of them were to come in?

'In bed,' she reassured him. 'At least Danny is. Jess is sleeping over with Emma again.'

So he told her, his eyes bolting and his words slurred by drink and emotion.

She was admirably calm about it. 'Then there's going to be an enquiry,' she said when he'd finished.

'Yes,' he said. 'I suppose there is.'

'And they know about it.'

'Yes.' He wasn't really concerned about the enquiry now. 'Oh Maur, I said the most dreadful things to her. We were like lunatics. What *am* I going to do now? All these years arid I've undone all my good work. I've never ever spoken to her like that. Never in the whole of my life. It was dreadful. What am I going to do?'

She put her arms round him and drew his head down on to her shoulder as if he were one of her children. 'Wait till the morning,' she advised. 'Nothing ever seems quite so bad in the morning. Then you can phone her up and apologise and put things right.'

He'd reached the pessimistic stage of drunkenness. 'I don't think I shall ever be able to put things right, ever again,' he mourned.

'Yes you will,' she comforted.

He was too miserable to agree. 'You didn't hear us.'

Maureen decided to try a slightly different tack. 'What did she say when you left her?'

'Nothing. I don't know. I told you what she said.'

'What was the *last* thing she said? How did you leave it? Think.'

He thought. 'She said she'd sleep on it.'

'Well there you are then.'

The cliché infuriated him. 'Oh God, Maur!' he said. 'There are times when I just don't believe you. What a perfectly bloody silly, fatuous thing to say! *There you are then. Diddums a poor boy! Kiss it better!* This is my *job* we're talking about. You can't kiss *that* better.'

She was searching for something in the cupboard above the bread bin — a small brown medicine bottle. 'It's no good crossing bridges till you come to them,' she advised. 'Two of these. You need to sleep on it too.'

'Sleep?' he agonised. 'You must be joking! At a time like this?'

She was still calm although she didn't feel it. 'Three then,' she said, counting them into her palm. 'Just to be on the safe side. We both need our sleep. We've got lives to live.'

He took the pills begrudgingly. 'They won't work,' he warned.

But to her considerable relief they did. And to his relief, they gave him a sleep without dreams. Which was more than was granted to his mother.

Chapter Twenty

'He seems to have disappeared off the face of the earth,' the union official joked, his bald head looming towards her.

I'm dreaming this, Laura thought. She knew she was dreaming because her mind was like cotton wool. It couldn't be happening. She pushed her handbag firmly down on to her knees, as though pressure would help her to think. That awful nylon blouse was sticking to the small of her back, making her feel clammy and uncomfortable. Why was she wearing it? To punish herself for failure? Was that it? To remind herself of the price she'd paid for that sextant? All useless. All totally, utterly useless. Nightmare tumbled random images round and round in her mind, close and disconnected like clothes in a spin drier — the sextant in its mahogany box, each bright brass section snugged down into purple velvet, the cheap blouse sticking to her back, rain staining the wallpaper in the hall, cow parsley shoulder high in the garden, the pulse and heat of the Saturday dance, Pete's eyes enormous as he kissed her, a brown frog swimming in the bucket, the Great Bear a bold ploughshare in the night sky.

'I must find him,' she said, struggling to concentrate. 'Haven't you any record of him at all?'

'Not this trip, Mrs Pendleton. Are you sure he went to Devonport?'

Sure? she thought wildly. How can I be sure of anything? 'That's where he said he was going.'

'And he's a Second Mate you say?' checking his books.

'Yes.'

'Well he's paid his dues,' the official said, bald head gleaming in the electric light, 'but that's all I can tell you. I'd try the shipping lines if I were you.'

Shipping lines, Laura thought and pushed her cotton-wool brain to list them. Elder-Dempster Holdings. BP. Shell. Esso. Exon. The company that traded out of Liverpool to West Africa. What was that called? There are so many. It'll take me for ever to get through them. Who'll look after David while I'm doing it? If Pete doesn't send me some money soon, how will I pay the rent? If he's gone tramping, he could be away years and God knows where he'll end up.

There was a paper under her fingers. Another list. 1, Mercantile Maritime office in Southampton, London or Liverpool. 2, Shipping pool. 3, Board of Trade. 4, Union. Ebbisham Road, Epsom. The printed words swelled and bubbled and slid off the edge of the paper.

'He took his sextant,' she said, but the paper was receding into blackness as nightmare dragged her down into a kaleidoscopic tumble of images, half seen and less than a quarter understood. 'I

327

promised I'd sleep on it.'

She was four years old and she had to find her father. He was going away to the war and if she didn't find him she would never see him again. People died in the war, Mummy said. She was frightened and excited and she knew she didn't want him to go but she wasn't allowed to say so, because she had to be a good brave girl so as not to upset him. A pair of strong arms lifted her up. She could smell tar and seaweed. And tobacco. And sweat. Summer time sweat. His beard was tickling her. 'Kiss your daddy goodbye.'

'Pete!' she begged. 'Please don't go.' The tears were running down her face and she couldn't leave the house because David was asleep upstairs.

'Look up at the sky,' Pete said lovingly. 'Send me a message. Find the Great Bear and send me a message and I'll know.'

She was sixteen and it was so quiet out in the fields that she could hear the silence. 'Oh Jeff!' she said. 'I shall love you for ever.' But that wasn't right. It wasn't Jeff. It was Pete and he'd gone away and she didn't know where he was. But Jeff had gone away too and she didn't know where *he* was.

Doors opened into her line of vision. Mouths spoke. 'No record of him.' 'Not with our company. Not this time.'

'He might be with the Royal Fleet Auxiliary again,' she said, her heart pounding with anxiety. 'He went all over the place last time, replenishing ships. You remember, don't you. Hong Kong, the Persian Gulf, East Africa, Indonesia, the Red Sea. He signed on for two years.'

'Not this time.'

'Singapore,' she said. 'He likes Singapore. They spend three hours on a meal out there and think nothing of it and the waiters see to it that your glass is always full. He told me so.'

'Sorry. No. Not this time.'

She was walking down a corridor, a nasty dark place with olive green walls and dark brown doors. She had a vague feeling that there was something hurtful behind the last door and she wanted to stop and turn back because she knew she couldn't bear it but her feet kept on going as if they didn't belong to her.

'Poor cow,' a man's voice said. 'He's run off and left her. That's the size of it. Run off and left her and she can't face it.'

'No, no, no,' she cried. 'He hasn't. It's not true. I love him. He wouldn't do such a thing.' And she woke with tears running down her cheeks to find that she was slumped on the sofa with Ace pushing his nose into her chin and Jack and Queenie sleeping among the cushions beside her. The fire was dead and the room cold but the lights were still blazing. It was half past three in the morning.

But he did leave me, she thought, automatically stroking Ace's sleek head. He shouted at me — out there in the hall — shouted at me and left me. And now Jeff's done exactly the same thing.

Both of them. Exactly the same. History repeating itself. There must be something seriously wrong with the way I treated them. Something hurtful or harmful that I didn't notice at the time. But that wasn't what she was supposed to be thinking about. There was something else. Something much worse. And with a sudden tightening of the chest she remembered what it was.

She sat up and dried her eyes and did her best to recover. 'This is me saying I'd sleep on it,' she explained to Ace who was sitting beside her giving her his narrow-eyed loving look. She realised that she was very cold, that her neck ached and her back was stiff and she was no nearer a solution. 'Bed,' she said, switching off the standard lamp.

Bed was more comfortable, even though all three cats decided to share it with her, but it brought no answer to her problem. How could it when it was so hideously clear-cut? If she went ahead and gave her evidence, David would lose his job, if she pulled out and kept her mouth shut, she would lose her house. How could anyone find a solution to a problem like that? She lay on her back with Ace purring beside her and turned it over in her mind, prodding at it endlessly and uselessly, like a tongue at a sore tooth. If I say nothing they'll pull down this house: if I speak out they'll give David the sack. She thought of the years of effort, pinching and scraping to give him a good education, of how proud she'd been when he got his degree, of what a success he was. But the house had taken years of effort too. She remembered what a mess it had been when she and Pete moved in and thought of all the work they'd done, of the hours that she and her neighbours had spent gathering signatures and preparing their evidence. Was she to step down and say nothing now, as if she didn't care?

Sleep was sucking her down into darkness, swirling her into dream again. She was talking to her neighbours, here in this house, urging them to fight, her voice full of energy.

'It isn't just houses we're talking about. It's our lives. Our community. Everything we've built up over the years. I can't stand by and let them destroy all this. I've got to fight. I won't let them ruin the countryside either — it's too beautiful — and I'm damned if I'll let them knock down my house. I was born in this cottage, it belonged to my father before me, I've lived here thirty-eight years since I was married, my son was born here. I shall fight them with everything I've got.'

They were applauding her, Molly and Josh, Joan Garston in her pink jersey, the Jones boys and their wives, John and Connie Cooper sitting by the table, Fiona and her three kids, Pete, standing up to applaud her, looking straight at her, his eyes full of affection.

'You do understand, don't you Pete?' she begged. 'I've got to keep this house.'

He had his arms round her and the baby was kicking her ribs. 'This is where we're going to bring up our son,' he said. 'In this house, safe and sound.'

331

'Your little fortress,' her father said, ruffling her hair. 'Safe and sound.'

The baby was kicking her ribs and there was something against her back too, pushing her down into the water. *Water!* she thought, as the black weight of it swirled around her. *Oh dear God, I'm under the water, I'm going to drown.* Her legs were like lead as she struggled to right herself pushing her hands against the slimy bricks of the culvert, struggling to get her mouth up into the air. I'm drowning, she screamed. Help me! Help me!

Her mother's hands were smoothing the water out of her eyes and rubbing the small of her back. 'Oh Laura-Lou. You do give me some frights. I'll say this for you, you weren't meant to drown. You must have been saved for a purpose.'

Saved for a purpose, Laura thought, pleased by the sound of the words. Saved for a purpose. The school bell was ringing. She could hear it quite plainly, on and on and on. I must run, she thought. If I can get there before it stops ringing I shan't be late. But it didn't stop ringing. It went on more shrilly than ever — and became the telephone giving its double shriek on the table beside the bed.

'Yes?' she said wearily into the mouthpiece. Is it morning? It was still dark so she couldn't tell. What time is it? I must have missed the alarm.

'Switch your wireless on,' Molly Fennimore's voice instructed happily. 'We've got our enquiry. It's on the news.'

The relief was so strong it brought tears to her eyes. 'Thank God!' she said. 'When?'

'Two weeks before Christmas,' Molly told her. 'How's that for timing? They think it'll put us off. Saucy buggers. Being all women I expect. They think we'll all be making Christmas puddings. Humph! Well that's all they know!'

Chapter Twenty-One

On Tuesday evening the enquiry was given a five-minute slot on the local television news. Laura caught the tail end of it when she got in from work. If only that awful decision hadn't been pressing down on her all the time, it would have been a moment of total vindication. They'd used the democratic process and done things properly; now they were being justified. But even though she enjoyed a moment's pride as she watched the presenter talking to camera in front of Glendale School, she had to face the fact that her problem would be compounded by this publicity — and by her neighbours' excited expectations. How could she tell them she was going to desert them — if that *was* what she was going to do — at the very moment when their petition had been granted? But if it came to that, how could she tell David she was going to put his job at risk, with all that that entailed?

Her thoughts were interrupted by Connie Cooper tapping at the door as she walked into the kitchen.

'I had to just toddle over and tell you,' she explained, her face creased with smiles. 'We're on the telly. Oh, you've got it on. Isn't it grand! Did you see the school? Clear as clear. Now everything'll be all right, won't it my dear.'

Laura said she certainly hoped so but it took an effort to sound enthusiastic.

More faces at the door, Joan and Molly, giggling with triumph. 'We shall all be on the telly now, 'fore we know where we are,' Molly declared. 'Didn't you say this would happen, you clever old thing. My Josh says you're a giddy marvel.'

But a troubled giddy marvel, Laura thought, welcoming them in. The sight of their beaming faces made her remember David's face last evening, pale with such anguish that he couldn't look her in the eye. I wonder how he is, she thought. I ought to phone him. We shouldn't let it drift or it'll get worse. But what on earth can I say after a quarrel like that? How would I begin? It's all so bloody silly. We've been so careful with one another all these years and then we undo all our good work in a few stupid minutes and end up in a position where neither of us can win. I must phone him and put it right somehow or other.

The trouble was that her neighbours were much too excited for a fleeting visit. It took a considerable time before they'd said all they wanted to say and were prepared to go back to their own homes. But at last she and the cats had the cottage to themselves again. She walked straight across the room to the phone while her determination was strong. And just as she stretched out her hand to pick up the receiver, it rang of its own accord, so suddenly and sharply that it made her jump.

It was David, gruff with embarrassment. 'How are you? I mean are you all right?' She could hear a buzz of voices and a machine clacking in the background so he must be calling from his office which was something he only did when he wanted to avoid being overheard at home.

'I'm all right,' she said guardedly. 'How are you?' For a fleeting second she was glad he was in the office because that meant he wouldn't have seen the broadcast. Then she rebuked herself for being a coward. He would hear about it sooner or later. It wasn't something that could be hidden.

He cleared his throat. Paused. Cleared his throat again. He'd been in a terrible state since their row, tense and short-tempered and irritable with anxiety. But he couldn't tell her that. He had to apologise to her, quickly, while he could do it, before his anger stormed up again and got in the way. 'I'm sorry I went on at you,' he said, speaking quietly and glancing round to make sure that nobody in the office could hear. 'I shouldn't have said all those awful things. I wish I could take them back.'

That could be answered and truthfully. 'I'm sorry I went on at *you*,' she admitted. 'I said some pretty awful things too.'

'Yes.'

'We were in a state,' she explained, as much to herself as to him. 'It really wasn't like us at all.'

'I can't talk much,' he warned, in case she

started to discuss the row. An apology he could cope with but not another quarrel. 'I'm at work.'

'I know. I can hear.'

'It's just I thought you ought to know,' he said, his voice easier. 'I had no right to say things about Dad. It was out of turn. I shouldn't have done it. I wanted you to know.'

'Forgive and forget, eh?' she suggested. It was the phrase she'd used when he was a child and had done something wrong or silly. Forgive and forget, she'd said, and then she'd given him a hug. Was *this* apology really going to be as easy as that?

There was another pause and for a horrid moment she thought he was going to ask her if she'd made up her mind about the enquiry. But he didn't. 'Yes, I suppose so,' he said. 'If we can do it. I don't deserve it though.'

'Nor me,' she told him quickly. 'If we all got what we deserved we'd be in a pretty bad way.'

'Yes, we would.'

There was another pause. 'I *am* glad you rang,' she said. 'I was just on my way to the phone to ring you.'

He was pleased at that. 'Great minds think alike.'

'Yes, don't we. We used to think alike when you were a little boy. Do you remember the blanc-manges?'

'And the tortoise.'

'Oh my God, that tortoise!'

It was much easier for both of them now. 'It's

dreadful to quarrel,' he said.

Which is why we try not to do it, she thought. But we've come through. The childhood ritual of apology and forgiveness had lifted them into loving kindness again. She knew now that neither of them would mention the enquiry. At least, not yet. *That* wound was too raw to be probed and had to be left to scar. But they'd made a start. They were on the mend.

'Shall we see you Sunday?' he checked.

'Of course,' she told him, feeling almost happy again. 'I'm going to make an orange layer cake.'

But for once food was only a marginal comfort to her however many dainty dishes she cooked. The problem remained and couldn't be resolved. For the first time since Pete's disappearance, she knew she needed another adult to confide in. Someone to advise her and put things in perspective. If Jeff hadn't walked out on her, she could have talked to him about it. Whatever else, he had a lot of sense. I've grown a bit too accustomed to him, she thought, realising how much she missed him. It was ridiculous for him to have packed up and gone like that. He should have phoned and put things right, the way I've just done with David. If *we* can make up, after a quarrel like *that,* I could have patched things up with *him* in no time at all. It wasn't as if it was a particularly bad quarrel. It couldn't have been, because she couldn't remember what it had been about. He'd just over-reacted. If only he'd write.

On Wednesday morning she had two letters, but neither of them was from Jeff. One was from Alan Jones and the other from Fiona, both saying the same thing. 'Isn't it wonderful. Now you'll be able to show them our evidence and they'll have to change their plans.'

On Wednesday evening Maureen phoned to say that they'd all seen the broadcast and that David was being iffy about it, but she and the kids thought it was wonderful. She seemed cheerful and didn't say anything about the threat to David's job, which was a relief and very sensible of her because she must have known about it. She's a good woman, Laura thought. I haven't treated her particularly well over the last few weeks either. There was something she wanted to tell me on Guy Fawkes night and I never gave her the chance.

On Thursday morning, she had a card from Amy, to tell her that Birmingham was foul. On Thursday afternoon the enquiry was headline news in the local paper. *Local enquiry date set. Campaigners amass evidence.*' The words tugged at her conscience every time she saw them and she saw them everywhere.

As she drove home from Sunday tea — which Maureen had kept pleasant enough despite the underlying tensions — the pressure of her indecision was so great it made her head ache. I must do something about this, she told herself. I can't postpone it for ever. Oh if only I had someone to discuss it with! If only that damn fool man hadn't packed up and left. And at that point, she suddenly remembered Freda, of the woolly hat and the watering eye at the demonstration — and the fur-trimmed coat and careful make-up in the library. 'Phone me,' she'd said, 'if you need any help.' She was just the very person to ask for advice. An old campaigner. If anyone would know what ought to be done, she would. She gave me a card with her telephone number. Now where did I put it?

It took three attempts before she got a ringing tone, which surprised her because Freda had not looked like the sort of woman who spent her life on the phone. However, at last and rather late at night, she got through.

Freda remembered her but sounded rather preoccupied. 'You've caught me at a bad time,' she said. 'We've just had a tip-off that they're going to bring in the earth-movers to start work on the hill. I've been phoning round all evening, passing the news.'

'Oh dear,' Laura sympathised. 'Does this mean they *are* going to start building the road? I thought you were holding them off.'

'So did we,' Freda said. 'But apparently not. They turned down the tunnel. I expect you saw that. Said it would cost too much money and cause too much delay. They've spent £100,000 of public money taking it to the High Court but that doesn't seem to worry them. Now it's gone to the European Commission. Did you know that? In fact it's still being considered so they shouldn't be taking any action yet. Not while it's *sub judice*.'

'But they are.'

'Yes. I'm afraid so.'

'When?'

'Wednesday,' Freda said. 'At dawn. That's when they usually move in machinery. Still I think we've got a reception committee organised for them. We're working on it. How's it going in your neck of the woods?'

'That's what I'm ringing about,' Laura said and told her.

'Ah!' Freda said, after a pause. 'The thing is, Laura, in this movement we don't actually tell one another what to do. That's not the way we work. Every group is autonomous. We support one another but we take individual action. I can tell you what I would do in your situation but that's not a lot of help because I'm not *in* your situation, if you see what I mean.' She made an odd sound as if she was stifling a yawn.

It's nearly midnight, Laura thought, glancing at the clock. I shouldn't be bothering her with my problems at this time of night. 'I'd like to talk it over with you, if you wouldn't mind,' she said, 'but not now. We're both too tired. I'm just about dropping.'

'Me too.'

'I tell you what. Why don't I join your reception committee on Wednesday.' She could get there and back before work, if they really were starting at dawn and she was quick. 'I'll find you there.

Will you be wearing your green bobble hat?'

'Oh yes. I make a point of it. It's my trademark on demonstrations. I'd better warn you, though, it's going to be quite a battle.'

'I'll be there,' Laura promised. 'I can handle it.'

What a long way I've come in the last three months, she thought, as she put down the receiver. In September I wasn't even sure I ought to be going to a demonstration. I thought I was above such things, that it was nothing to do with me. But that was because I was still naive. I thought everybody played fair. I know better now.

It was still dark when the alarm woke her on Wednesday morning and very cold. Ever sensible, she cooked herself a sustaining bacon and eggs for breakfast and made an extra flask of coffee to take with her, as well as her raincoat and a thick cardigan. It was still only five o'clock when she set out on her journey.

Apart from the occasional heavy goods lorry, she had the road to herself. It was rather an unnerving experience but at least it allowed her to drive at speed. The main road west was hung with high globes of orange light which cast a lurid sheen across the tarmac ahead of her. Below their unnatural colour, trees and hedges looked like black paper cut-outs and the Downs were a mere suggestion on the horizon, a smudge against the blue-black of the sky and as vague as a stage backdrop. She drove past towns and villages darkly and silently asleep and she anguished over the problem, on and on and round and round, as the miles raced under her wheels.

It was still completely dark when she arrived at Twyford Down and as far as she could see, the hill looked exactly the same as it had done the last time she was there. The working seemed no bigger, the same yellow trucks were parked on the chalk and the demonstrators wandering about on the dark turf or standing in little groups were the same outlandish-looking people in the same scruffy-looking clothes.

It wasn't until she was walking up the hill and her eyes had adjusted to the darkness that she realised that there *was* a difference and quite a considerable one. For a start there were far more people on the down. Last time there'd been about thirty, if that. Now there were hundreds, so the movement had obviously grown. And this time it was all being filmed. On the upper slopes of the hill there were several young men with camcorders, busily taking pictures. Very professional-looking young men, in flat caps and Barbours as if they were filming a shoot or a race meeting. I wonder who told *them* to come here, she thought. They weren't television crews and yet they looked organised, somehow. And that worried her.

The large crowd presented her with a problem too and one she hadn't anticipated. It was going to be quite a job to find Freda amongst so many people. The sooner she started her search the better. I'll sweep, she decided, from one side of the hill to the other and back again. And I'll ask.

343

They're not moving about much, that's one advantage. I'll find her.

The first group she asked was deep in anxious conversation, all faces tense and much nervous smoking. They broke off to tell her that they knew who Freda was but couldn't see her. The third suggested that she ought to look for 'a girl called Kapok. She'll know. She's got a green mohican. Look for that.'

'Her hair was yellow in September,' Laura remembered. This was the first time she'd experienced the grass-roots communication of a mass demonstration and the easy friendliness of these young people was warming and impressive. 'Thanks!'

'Cheers!' they answered and smiled at her as she continued her search.

There was a green glow on the eastern horizon and as she turned her head from left to right, scanning the crowds for a green mohican, she became aware that the sky was growing short straggling feathers of orange and purple, lovely strong theatrical colours beside the dark turf of the down. Dawn was rising. I shall have to look sharp, she told herself, or the machines will arrive and I shan't have found her. And at that moment she saw Kapok. She was still wearing the same patched overcoat and the same Doc Martens but now she had a cockatoo crest of hair that looked decidedly green even in the darkness. She was bending forward over the dark cup of her mittened hands, lighting a cigarette, the little flame a spurt of yellow that lit up her sharp nose and touched the six rings in her ears with a glint of silver. A matter of yards away one of the young men was filming her, the red light of his camcorder flashing like a star.

So they're not just on the hill, Laura thought. They're taking close-ups too. And at that point the young man looked up from his camera and, with a palpable shock, she recognised who he was. Kevin Marshall. What on earth was he doing filming a demonstration? I thought he was supposed to work for a building contractor. Bridges and blocks of flats and things like that. Wasn't that what Jessica said? But there wasn't time to think about it because Kapok was walking away.

'Kapok!' she called, running after her. 'Just a minute. Have you seen Freda?'

From the corner of her eye, she saw that the red eye of the camera was winking again and suspected that Kevin was filming *her* as well as Kapok. It annoyed her but she hadn't got time to deal with it. Once she'd found out where Freda was she'd go back and ask him what he thought he was playing at. Meantime . . .

'Up there!' Kapok said, pointing uphill. 'Come on. I'll take you.' And as they walked away together, 'I've seen you before somewhere haven' I?'

Freda was in the middle of a large group of elderly protestors who were all waiting stockily and patiently halfway up the hill. She was standing beside a very tall man who had a pair of binoculars strung round his neck.

'Good to see you,' she said. 'You got here just in time. The sun's coming up. It won't be long now.'

'I wish they'd hurry,' one of the men said and joked, 'This is bad for my ulcers.'

There was a movement on the brow of the hill and they all looked up to see what it was. 'Bloody hell fire!' the tall man said.

Rising hideously over the brow of the hill were forty huge yellow machines, so many and so enormous that they covered the hill from one side to the other — great trucks packed with construction workers, like troop carriers full of storm troopers, and the latest in earth-movers, advancing with the inexorable and massive power of a line of tanks. At that moment only the top half of the machines could be seen but the roar of their engines was formidable and, as they rose into full view, the watchers could see that they were escorting a massed line of blue-clad security guards, a hundred at least and more coming up behind, blue helmets glittering in the rising sun, uniforms menacing, black boots trampling, truncheons in hand like an advancing army. There were so many of them and they looked so threatening that Laura was rooted to the spot with fear. This is what it must be like for soldiers, she thought, waiting for a battle to begin, watching the enemy advance, knowing that you're going to be wounded or killed.

'Dear God!' Freda breathed.

The little group bunched together as if they were already trying to protect one another.

'What will you do?' Laura asked. And she was thinking, you'll never be able to stop an army like that.

'What we can,' the tall man said grimly.

'No,' Freda said and her voice was determined, 'we'll do whatever it takes. They won't intimidate us. Come on.' And she walked towards the invaders.'

For a minute or two, Laura didn't know how to react. There were demonstrators on the move all around her, in no sort of order but all marching uphill. I can't go with them, she thought. This isn't my fight. Yet she couldn't walk away. There was something so foolhardy and courageous and touching about those small, dark, individual, unprotected figures. *Marching as to war*, she thought, and the words reminded her of her father and the stories he'd told of his life at sea during the Second World War. She could hear his voice as if he were speaking to her there and then. *We were all in it together you see, Laura-Lou. You can't run away from a war.* No, she thought, you can't. It wouldn't be honourable. And at that, her mind was made up. Even though her heart was pounding with alarm, she set her jaw and began to walk uphill with the others.

Battle was joined the minute the vanguard reached the enemy line. It was more brutal than anything Laura had ever seen. One minute the demonstrators were walking towards the machines and the next they were being manhandled to the ground and pulled out of the way by their jackets, arms, legs, hair or whatever came roughly to hand. The air was full of dreadful sound, the steady roar of the engines, the bullying voices of the guards, screams and shouts. 'Move! Now!' 'Leave her alone! You'll kill her!' 'Move! Now!' And the machines kept coming.

Laura was frog-marched out of the way by two guards. The man beside her was pushed to the ground and kicked. There was so much noise and so much frantic movement all around her that she couldn't see more than a yard or two in any direction. This *is* a war, she thought, as she struggled to the edge of the crowd. These men are fighting ordinary people as if they were an enemy. All we're doing is saying we don't want this hill to be ripped apart and they're treating us as if we're the worst kind of criminals. It's like Hitler and the Jews or Dr Verwoerd and the blacks. And we're supposed to be the cradle of democracy.

Then she saw three young men struggling to carry a woman who looked as if she was unconscious and she ran to them at once to make a fourth.

'Bastards!' one of the men said. 'They've bloody nearly suffocated her.'

They set the woman down gently on the grass, loosened her coat and scarf, smoothed her hair out of her eyes and commiserated with her while she groaned back to consciousness. The fight was still going on a few feet away from them.

'She ought to go to hospital,' Laura said to the nearest young man. And she suddenly remembered Jeff crouched here on this very hillside, tenderly dressing her wounds with those gentle hands of his.

'No,' the woman groaned. 'I'm all right. Really. Just leave me be.'

'I know how you're feeling,' Laura told her sympathetically. 'I was hurt in a demonstration here back in the autumn and I said the same thing. But I *did* need to go to hospital and so do you. Just to be on the safe side. I'll take you if you like.'

Two girls were running towards them, calling, 'Is she all right?' One of the young men looked up to explain.

'She's our aunt,' the taller girl said. 'We'll take her.'

But even with two relations to help them it took several more minutes to persuade their casualty that she needed attention.

How stubborn we are when we're hurt, Laura thought as she watched them stumble away. Jeff should have been here. He would have known what to do and he'd have handled her beautifully. Then she had to look at her watch and check the time because she was suddenly missing him so much. I must go, she thought, or I shall be late for work.

She thought about the demonstration all the way back to Burswood library, burning with anger that such things could be allowed to happen. It was the worst thing she'd ever seen and the most frightening.

We seem to have lost the right to disagree with the government, she thought. And opposition is the essence of democracy, the balance between opposing points of view, the art of compromise, rule by ballot box, the acceptance that we're all different and we all have different needs and opinions. She remembered Voltaire's famous dictum, *I disapprove of what you say but I will defend to the death your right to say it,* and wondered what had happened to the people who used to believe it. How much we've changed since the war, she thought, and not for the better.

The experience had made up her mind for her. Now there was no doubt. This was a war, she was fully involved in it and there was no turning back. She would have to give evidence and go on with her fight. I shall tell David this evening, she decided, as soon as I get back from work.

Chapter Twenty-Two

'Did you see the *Breakfast News*?' Barry Brough asked David as the two of them walked into PPC Pharmaceuticals that morning. 'Your mother's lot are in action again.'

David could feel his heart sinking. 'No,' he said. 'Where?'

'Twyford Down,' his friend told him. 'Right old punch-up apparently. They've been arresting 'em right left and centre.'

'Sorry to disappoint you old son,' David said with relief. 'That's a different group altogether. Nothing to do with my mother, I'm very glad to say.'

'All quiet on the Western Front then?'

'Not so much as a whisper.'

They were entering the foyer. 'Keep up the good work!' Barry advised and punched his old friend on the shoulder by way of encouragement.

David smiled at him to show that everything was under control, but inwardly he was tense with anxiety. The longer he had to wait for his mother's decision, the more despondent he became. If she doesn't phone tonight, he thought, I shall know it's all up with me.

He and Maureen discussed it whenever they could — which usually meant when they were in bed or when the children were both out — but their talk went round and round over the same old ground and was little comfort to him. She was unremittingly optimistic and he was wearily depressed. In his low state he felt it was better to be prepared for the worst and then, whatever happened, you wouldn't get too badly disappointed or hurt. But she would insist on showing him 'the bright side'. Last night she'd listed all the jobs he was qualified to do and when he wouldn't look at it, she'd read them out to him.

'You might get another one you'd like better,' she'd said, running her pen down the list.

'And what if we have to move to get it?' he said miserably. 'Have you thought of that? I can just see our Jessica agreeing to a move with her A levels coming up. Especially if it meant being parted from Kevin. There'd be all hell to pay.'

'She might surprise you.'

'Pigs might fly.'

'Anyway, they wouldn't be parted. He's got a car and there are motorways everywhere. Distance doesn't matter when you've got a car.'

The irony of it made him laugh, a bitter bark of a laugh. 'Mother's driving us all crazy trying to stop a motorway being built through her backyard and you say, never mind, if she gets her own way and you lose your job, we can keep together by using the motorways.'

She took his point with a wry grimace. 'It's a crazy world,' she said.

'It needs changing,' he said. 'It's too confrontational for me.'

And the worst confrontation was still ahead of him. Oh come on, Mum, he urged her silently, make your mind up, for God's sake. This waiting is driving me round the bend.

But when Maureen called him to the phone that evening, knowing was worse than waiting — and he knew from his mother's opening words.

'Is there somewhere quiet and private we can meet?'

'Come here,' he said. 'The kids are out. You won't mind Maureen being in on it, will you.'

So she came to Canterbury Gardens and told them both together. She'd decided to tough it out, no justifications, no arguments, no apologies, just the straight decision and her reasons for making it. 'I've thought and thought about this,' she said when she'd given them the news, 'and I know what an awful decision it is for you but it's the right thing to do. It isn't just the house, you see, it's the campaign. I went to Twyford Down again this morning and what the authorities are doing there has got to be opposed. It simply isn't on to stand back and let them get away with it.'

He sat before her, listening courteously, his face blank. Oh my poor David, she thought, wanting to reach out and touch him. How can I help you to understand? 'It was like a war,' she said. 'They were beating people up. Like the Nazis. I've got to oppose them — and giving evidence at this enquiry is the proper, democratic way to do it.'

'Well that's it,' he said flatly. 'That's the end of the line.'

'Yes,' she agreed. 'I'm afraid it is.'

It was a dreadful moment, because despite his protective pessimism he'd clung on to a small, secret hope that she would see things his way if she thought about it long enough. Now he was defeated and numb with distress. 'Oh well,' he said. 'Thanks for telling me.'

Maureen took his hand and held it as though he were a child. 'Even if the worst does come to the worst, we'll manage,' she promised them both. 'I've got my job. It's not the end of the world.'

But it might as well be, David thought. 'How long have I got?' he asked, withdrawing his hand. 'When's it going to be?'

'It starts just before Christmas. I don't know when they'll call us.'

'And where are they holding it?' If it was far enough away perhaps it wouldn't hit the local news.

'The little Town Hall.'

'Ah!' he said. 'It would be.' They couldn't get anywhere more local than that. And with a great curved drive in front of it all nice and handy for the cameras.

'I must get back,' Laura said sadly. They needed privacy to digest their bad news and get over the first and worst of it. 'I'm sorry it had to be this way.'

'So are we,' Maureen said ruefully and got up to see her out.

They kissed at the opened door, sadly but with affection.

'He doesn't *know* they'll fire him,' Maureen comforted. 'It could be just a threat.'

'God, I do hope so, Maureen.'

'I think you're doing the right thing. So does Jess.'

'But I have to hurt you to do it,' Laura said and despite her determination to be calm and sensible, she began to cry. 'I must go,' she said. 'I've got things to do.' And she walked off quickly so that she could hide in her Land-Rover.

'Look after yourself,' Maureen called after her.

But by then she was crying too much to answer.

Before the advent of cheap foreign holidays, Burswood village had a thriving seaside suburb called Burswood-on-Sea. In the forties and fifties it had been a prosperous resort with several streets full of small hotels and boarding houses, two cinemas, a dancehall and a bandstand. It even had a town hall, a small but rather pretty building on the promenade. Now there is one hotel left and very little bed and breakfast, the cinemas have become bingo halls, the dancehall is gone and the bandstand is a windswept ruin. But the little Town Hall remains, staring bleakly out to sea, and is still in use, as a venue for jumble sales, amateur dramatics and local Conservative Party meetings. It was, as everybody realised, the obvious setting for the public enquiry.

When Laura arrived there with her neighbours on a dark December afternoon, she was nervous even though she was well prepared. She was still torn with distress at what she was doing to David. She'd been awake most of the night, anguishing about it but the only possible compromise she could think of was to take a back seat — or as much of a back seat as she could. The evidence has to be given, she thought, but if I don't say much, maybe it'll keep my name out of the papers. It's the name that Amalgamated Gravels will be looking for. I shall keep quiet and let the others speak.

The town hall staff were as well organised as she was. There were young men in fluorescent jackets to wave them to a parking space, well-placed placards to point the way into the building, and in the foyer, a young man with a clip-board who directed them to a waiting room labelled 'the party from Laura's Way'.

'Now what?' Molly asked, sitting herself at the table.

'We wait I suppose,' Laura said.

'What a bore!' Molly complained. 'What are we supposed to do?' Although it was no more than mid-afternoon it was already too dark to see out of the windows and there was nothing much to look at in the room — just a dusty aspidistra and four yellowing walls. 'I wish I'd brought my knitting.'

'It's always the bloody same,' Joan said, sitting herself squarely at the head of the table. 'They always have to keep you waiting, bloody officials.'

But in fact, had she known it, these officials weren't keeping them waiting unnecessarily. They were taking evidence from Mr and Mrs Todd and their neighbours, listening as one enraged parent after another spoke of the need to protect their children — from asthma and bronchitis, lead poisoning, road accidents.

'It's our kiddies' lives,' Sharon said earnestly.

'We appreciate that,' the chairman told her. 'Are there any other points you wish to make?'

There were and plenty of them, so the session went on a great deal longer than the chairman had anticipated.

After a ten-minute wait, John Cooper heard footsteps approaching along the corridor.

'There's someone coming,' he said, holding up his hand.

'Well that was quick,' his wife smiled. 'You can't complain about that, Joan.'

The footsteps stopped outside the door. They could see a shape peering through the frosted glass at them. Then the door opened and Jeff Turner walked in.

Laura was so surprised to see him that she was momentarily speechless. Where had he suddenly come from? And what had made him turn up just at the very moment they were going to give evidence? Was it coincidence or had he planned it? And if he'd planned it . . . She noticed that he didn't look at her, that he seemed ill at ease and that he was wearing a scruffy leather jacket she hadn't seen before. But in all other respects he was exactly the same, in the same mud-coloured jersey and the same sagging jeans, his hair just as untidy, his beard bristling more than ever. Then she realised how pleased she was to see him again and how very much she'd missed him — and she had to look away for a few seconds to hide what she was feeling.

Her neighbours, having no idea that he'd been lost to her, greeted him cheerfully.

'Welcome aboard!' John Cooper beamed. 'The more the merrier.'

'They said I'd find you here,' Jeff told them. He looked at all of them in turn — except Laura. 'I was afraid you'd be gone before I got here.'

By this time Laura had recovered her composure sufficiently to ask him a question. 'How did you know we were here?'

'Toby told me,' he said, looking at her for the first time. 'He sent me a card.'

Oh did he? Laura thought, resisting the attraction of those tawny eyes. The answer made her cross. And I suppose you phoned him, she thought, or wrote back. You didn't think to phone me. She felt she'd been cut down to size, the person he didn't contact because he didn't need to or didn't want to. It took away all her pleasure at seeing him. Or nearly all her pleasure. Yet he'd come here to be with them and he was smiling at them in his old friendly way. So perhaps she was misjudging him. But where had he been? And why hadn't he got in contact with them before?

There was somebody else casting a shadow on the door — an official of some kind in a grey suit. 'Laura's Way?'

'That's us,' John Cooper said, standing up.

'If you'll come this way.'

'I'll wait,' Jeff said quickly, looking at Laura. 'See how you get on. Good luck!'

The enquiry turned out to be a very low-key affair which wasn't how Laura had imagined it would be. The three officials sat on the stage behind baize-hung tables, while Laura and her friends took their seats in the chilly space of the hall. It made her feel exposed and insignificant out there. And cold.

But the questioning was kindly and attentive. The chairman was a JP, a quiet, grey-haired man with hornrimmed glasses, a small white moustache, and a walking stick propped against his chair. He told them their written evidence had been received and noted and then listened patiently to what they had to say while Laura kept quiet and a stenographer took notes on her clacking machine. However, when they reached a pause, he prompted them with a question directed straight at Laura.

'You say in your covering letter, Mrs Pendleton, that in your opinion this by-pass is not necessary. Could you perhaps elaborate on that?'

At such a direct approach, Laura felt compelled to answer.

'Yes,' she told him. 'Most of the traffic that

goes through Burswood is from north to south and most of it is in the summer time, when the holiday-makers come down to Burswood-on-Sea. There aren't really very many of them these days, so the traffic is never what you'd call bad. It used to be much worse.'

'North-south traffic is outside the terms of reference of this enquiry,' the chairman pointed out.

'Exactly,' Laura agreed. 'We're considering east-west traffic. In our opinion the road that runs east-west is perfectly adequate for our local traffic. We see no good reason to enlarge it and no reason at all to build an entirely new stretch especially if it means destroying an entire community and an area of outstanding natural beauty.'

'So your opposition is on environmental and community grounds?'

'It is.'

'And the community in question is a road called Laura's Way?'

They all agreed to that.

The chairman looked at the papers on the table before him and asked a muffled question of one of the men sitting beside him.

'I believe,' he said, 'that three houses in Laura's Way are no longer in occupation. That is correct is it not?'

Molly Fennimore bristled up at once. 'For the time being,' she said. 'We're waiting for the next tenants to arrive. They won't be empty long.'

'My information is that three houses have been

vacated. Three in occupation, three vacant. That is so, is it not?'

The implication was obvious — that three families had accepted defeat and moved out, leaving the way clear for the road builders. 'None of 'em moved because of the road, sir,' John Cooper said. 'Their reasons was personal.'

'I see,' the chairman said. And returned to his notes. 'An area of outstanding natural beauty,' he prompted again.

They told him about the birds and animals that would be lost if their habitats were destroyed, of the number of wild creatures that had been killed on the existing road, of the trees that would be felled and the wild flowers that would die, and he listened patiently, encouraging them from time to time.

Eventually he told them he thought it might be time to sum up. Laura looked round hoping that one of the others would take on the task but none of them did and the chairman was looking pointedly in her direction. There was a long pause and now they were all looking at her, their expectation so strong it was a physical pressure. She would have to speak, compromise or no.

'We feel very strongly about this,' she said at last. 'We know there are pressure groups who are very keen to build a new superhighway from Folkestone to Honiton, but in our view it is unnecessary and potentially damaging. It will create new hazards, destroy communities, harm the environment and cause noise and pollution. We are totally opposed to it.'

'The road that is under consideration at this enquiry is the Burswood by-pass,' the chairman pointed out. 'The superhighway, as you call it, is outside our terms of reference. I should make that clear to you. We can only deal with the matters that are within our remit.'

'Yes,' Laura said. 'We understand that. But our stretch of road is part of the superhighway, isn't it.'

His answer was spoken soothingly. 'The Burswood by-pass is the scheme that we are considering here today. Do any of you have any further comments to make upon that?' He waited to give them a chance to answer and when they shook their heads, 'No. Then we would like to thank you all for coming here to give us your evidence.' He inclined his head to his colleagues who made murmurs of agreement. The interview was over.

'Well?' Molly said, as they walked down the corridor. 'What d'you think?'

'I think we did rather well,' Laura told her, hoping that her own contribution wouldn't be as noticeable as it felt. 'We said everything we wanted to say. We didn't leave anything out.'

'Are we going back to the waiting room?' Connie wanted to know. 'To see Mr Turner?'

'Well a' course,' her husband said, cheerfully. 'And him waitin'.'

But he wasn't waiting. The room was full of strange men, talking earnestly about haulage.

'They must've moved him out,' Joan said. 'Ain't that just typical.'

'Oh well,' Connie said resignedly, 'we can always see him another time.'

Laura was annoyed with herself for feeling so disappointed. He probably had a long drive home to wherever he was living and there was no real reason why he should have waited for them, especially if he had to hang about in the cold. But even so . . .

'Home then,' Mr Fennimore said. 'I'm getting peckish.'

The hauliers were being led down the corridor.

'You go on,' Laura told her friends. 'I'm going to listen to this lot. I want to know what they've got to say.'

It was persuasive evidence and powerfully presented. Time, the hauliers said, was money. And money was being wasted for lack of a road. They detailed the additional time it took to manoeuvre their heavy goods vehicles through the Burswood streets. They spoke of the number of road accidents and near-misses their company had suffered during the last year, detailed the cost of repairs, spoke tellingly of the proportion of perishable goods that were lost to their customers solely on account of the time the journeys were currently forced to take.

'Can you estimate by how much your journeys would be reduced were this by-pass to be built?' the chairman asked.

The answer was immediate and had figures to

prove it. 'By a tenth.'

'So you would support the building of the by-pass?'

'We go further than that,' the hauliers' leader said. 'We think it's essential.'

Chapter Twenty-Three

It was cold and dark out in the car park and the wind from the sea was full of salt spray. Laura shivered as she ran across to the Land-Rover.

And there was Jeff huddled into his leather jacket, waiting for her.

There was no denying how pleased she was to see him, but the knowledge made her cold towards him. He leaves me high and dry all these weeks, she thought, without a word of explanation and then expects to walk back into my life as if nothing's happened.

'I thought you'd have gone home,' she said, her voice as chill as her hands.

'I promised I'd wait,' he said, 'so I waited. How did you get on?'

'All right, I think,' she said, opening the door. 'The opposition's very powerful though. I've just been listening to the hauliers. They really want this road and I can see why.'

'What sort of questions did they ask *you?*'

The temptation to tell him all about it was very strong despite her annoyance with him. But there were other matters to settle first. 'Haven't you got to get back?'

'I've taken the afternoon off.' And when she raised her eyebrows, 'It's all right. All legal and above board. They've promised not to injure themselves until tomorrow morning.'

'You've got a job then, where you've gone?'

'Gone?' he asked, looking puzzled.

'Where you've moved to.'

'I haven't moved.'

That was such a surprise she had to ask again just to be sure. 'You mean you're still in the same place?'

'Yes. Of course I am. Why do you ask?'

'Still at the flat?'

'Yes. Of course.'

'I thought you'd gone away.'

'Whatever gave you that idea?'

The answer was obvious to them both in the same instance. 'Amy!' they said.

'She told me you'd gone,' Laura explained. 'She said she went to the surgery and they told her you'd left and they'd hired a replacement for you. According to her, nobody knew where you were. I thought you'd got fed up with everything and just cut off.'

So that's why she didn't ring, he thought. Here I've been all these weeks waiting for a call and getting depressed about it and all the time . . . 'That's not my style,' he said. He was shivering, partly with cold and partly with anger. 'I was on holiday, that's all. She was making mischief. She really is bad news.'

'She always was,' Laura said. 'I told you that before.'

He answered her with some warmth. Now that

the truth was out, he could argue with her. 'You didn't have to tell me. I've always known it.'

'On Guy Fawkes night?' she mocked.

'Yes.'

'You could have fooled me.'

'If we're going to quarrel,' he said, 'how about going somewhere warm where we can do it in comfort?'

That made her laugh. The same tender eyes, the same ridiculous sense of humour. The man was impossible. 'Oh all right,' she said. 'You can come home with me and help me cook dinner. But only because I'm freezing to death out here.'

'I thought you'd never ask,' he said.

It was a dark, wet, miserable evening and the wind was tormenting the trees but Laura's Way had never seemed so inviting.

But Jeff took one look at it and was appalled at the state it was in. 'Good God!' he said, squinting across the lane at the boarded windows. 'What's been going on here?'

She'd forgotten what a lot had happened since she'd seen him last. 'All sorts of things,' she said. 'I'll tell you while we're cooking.'

There was so much to catch up on. While they were preparing the vegetables, she told him about the bailiffs and the way the houses had been deliberately left empty. None of it surprised him at all. While the meal was cooking, she told him how the fat man had thrown a wobbly and taken to the attic — which made him laugh out loud. And as they ate their meal, she gave him a blow-by-blow account of the evidence she'd just given and told him how David had been blackmailed to try and stop her, which he said was downright evil.

'You couldn't have done anything else,' he told her. 'As I should know. It was the right choice.'

'But there's a price to pay for it,' she said sadly.

'There always is,' he said. 'That's how they win. Most people give in to the blackmail.'

'I can see why,' she admitted. 'Do you think he really will get the sack?'

'Politics is a dirty business,' he said, 'and this is business politics which is the worst of the lot. It depends how badly Amalgamated Gravels need the contract. And that depends on whether their profits are up or down. This is the market economy we're talking about, don't forget. They worship the great god Profit.'

'That's just what David told me,' she remembered.

There didn't seem to be anything more that either of them could say about it now. What little they *had* said was making her feel depressed. She listened to the wind rattling the holly outside the kitchen window. 'Coffee,' she suggested and went to get the percolator.

The sight of it reminded her of Amy and her endless dirty coffee cups. 'I've got a bit of news about Amy,' she said, cheering at the thought.

He slid her a sideways look that was part suspicion and part apprehension but his voice was casual. 'Oh yes?'

It gave her exquisite satisfaction to enlighten him. 'Mrs Brooke Curtis has got rid of her. Sent her to Birmingham. What d'you think of that?'

'It doesn't surprise me,' he said easily. 'Mrs Brooke Curtis is a lady to reckon with. She virtually runs the firm. She can send staff wherever she likes. It would either have been Birmingham or Edinburgh.'

'But didn't you miss her?' Laura insisted. 'I thought she was always in and out of your surgery.'

'She lives on aspirin, if that's what you mean. Yes, I did wonder where she was.'

Their unfinished row was boiling to the surface. 'I'll bet you did. *"Old Sweetie"*.' She still remembered that cloying endearment, and it still rankled.

He ignored the jibe and went straight to the heart of the matter. 'It was a mistake to cover up for her that night,' he said. 'OK. I'll admit it. It *was* a mistake. Not that it gave you any justification for attacking me.'

'I didn't attack you.'

Now he was mocking her. 'You could have fooled me.'

'Well if I did, you asked for it,' she said and she was only half joking. 'And while we're on the subject, if you've been in the flat all this time, how come you didn't phone me?'

He told her the truth, quickly, before he could think better of it. 'I didn't think you'd want me to. I don't push in where I'm not wanted.'

'Oh how ridiculous!' she said. 'One phone call wouldn't have hurt.'

She was making him feel a coward. 'OK then,' he fought back. 'Why didn't *you* phone *me* if it was so easy?'

'I did,' she said. 'Several times and never got an answer. In the end I gave up. I thought you'd gone.'

That confounded him. He'd spent all these weeks feeling rejected because he thought she'd finished with him and she'd actually been phoning him all that time and he hadn't known it. What a waste! She was right. He *was* a coward. He should have rung. What an appalling waste!

His expression encouraged her and took the sting from her anger. 'You ought to have an answerphone,' she teased, 'then I could have left you a rude message.'

He was cheered by her tone. 'I might just do that — to hear what you'll say.'

She was pouring coffee, and helping herself to milk and sugar. 'So how long *were* you away?' she asked.

'Ten working days. That's all. It was a holiday.'

'And where did you go on this holiday of yours? Somewhere nice?'

'Yes it was, actually. I went to Guildford to see my daughter.'

She paused, percolator in hand. 'I didn't know you had a daughter.'

'There's a lot you don't know about me,' he said, grinning at her. 'I've got two daughters, as it happens, and three grandchildren, two boys and a girl. And an ex-wife, somewhere or other.'

The statement begged a question and he was being so open about it she knew she could ask it. 'You don't see her?'

'We didn't part amicably,' he explained. 'So now we keep out of one another's way. We spend a pre-Christmas holiday with one daughter and Christmas with the other, turn and turn about. That way we see our children and we don't have to endure one another.'

She rejected him, Laura thought, watching him stroke his beard for comfort, and it occurred to her that fear of another rejection could have been the reason why he hadn't tried to contact her in all these weeks. 'It all sounds very civilised,' she said. And was rewarded by a seraphic smile.

They talked into the small hours, sitting one on each sofa in front of the fire with the cats on the cushions beside them and the coffee table discreetly between them, warm and contained and companionable as the rain swooshed against the windows and the wind howled in the chimney. He told her about his grandchildren and showed her a snap of the baby he'd just seen in Guildford and the latest school pictures of the pair from Manchester. She told him about the demonstration at Twyford Down and remembered the young men she'd seen filming.

'It was very peculiar,' she said. 'There were so many of them and they all looked exactly the same.'

'Spies,' he said.

He seemed so sure of it, she had to ask, 'What makes you say that?'

'There've been a lot of rumours,' he told her. 'They say the Ministry are employing private eyes — to film the demonstrators.'

'That occurred to me,' she said. 'But what for? That's what I don't understand.'

'Evidence in court?' he wondered.

'But none of us are trying to deny what we're doing. It's all quite open. Very open, up there on the down.'

'Perhaps it's so that they can identify people and arrest them after the event.'

'That's awful,' she said. 'I do hope not.'

There was something about the tenor of her voice that alerted him. There was more to this than politics. He looked a question at her.

So she told him about Kevin and how she'd seen him filming the girl called Kapok. 'It doesn't make any sort of sense to me,' she said. 'When he first came to Canterbury Gardens, he told David he was a PA, working for a building contractor. We all assumed it was offices and flats and things like that. He never said a word about meeting Jess at Twyford Down. I thought he was being tactful because David had been so cross about her going there. It was a point in his favour at the time. Now I'm not so sure. If he's a PA, then what was he doing filming the demonstrators along with all those others?'

'What if the contractor he's working for is the

firm building the road?'

Laura nodded. 'Yes,' she said. 'I had thought of that. That would account for him being there when we first met him. But if those young men were spies, working for the government, and he's one of them, that changes everything.'

'Have you said anything to Jessica?'

'No,' she said at once, 'and I'm not going to. Nor to Maureen.'

He understood entirely. 'It's a love affair. Right?'

'If I'm any judge.'

'Um,' he said. 'Then I can see the problem.'

'The trouble with families,' she told him, 'is they're so bloody complicated.'

'It's in the nature of the beast,' he told her.

The fire was more ash than flame but there was only one log left in the basket. 'Leave it,' he said, when he saw her thinking about it. 'It's late. I should have gone hours ago.' He stood up and stretched himself, smiling down at her. 'It's been a great evening. Dinner on Saturday?'

They were so easy with one another now. 'Sounds a great idea.'

'Where are you working?'

'At Burswood. All day.'

'I'll pick you up at closing time,' he promised and bent to tickle Ace under the chin. 'Goodnight cat. Look after her.'

She was impressed by how quietly he drove out of the lane so as not to wake her neighbours, his engine making less noise than the wind. And when she shut the door and went back to her dying fire, the cottage felt empty without him.

'That ex-wife of his must have been a fool,' she said to Queenie who had taken full possession of the sofa he'd vacated and was now stretched out on the cushions, yawning widely. 'She doesn't know a good thing when she sees it.'

Dinner on Saturday was followed by dinner on Tuesday and a visit to the theatre on Wednesday. On each occasion he enquired how David was and she was able to tell him that there was no news. As he was driving her home after the show he asked her if she would like to join him at the Beautibelles Christmas 'do'.

She wasn't quite sure about that. Works parties weren't her style.

But he was very persuasive. 'You'll like it,' he encouraged. 'They're a good bunch. The miseries don't come. Wear your pretty shawl.'

'You're turning me into a gadabout,' she protested.

'I'm making the most of you before Christmas sweeps down on us and tears us apart.'

'When are you leaving?'

'Christmas Eve.'

'And how long for?'

'Till New Year's Day. Go on, be a devil. Come to this party with me. Make me a happy man.'

'All right then,' she said. 'Providing David's still got a job.'

He understood her reasoning and approved of

it. 'You're on,' he said.

So, as there was still no bad news from PPC Pharmaceuticals, she went to the party and was surprised by how much she enjoyed herself.

The works canteen was a great deal bigger than she'd expected and full of people, with a bar buzzing at one end, a DJ bellowing among his flashing lights at the other and a sizeable dance floor in the middle. At first she found it rather off-putting but Jeff had everything well under control. He took her by the elbow and steered her to an empty table, greeting his friends all the way. Then he provided her with a gin and tonic and proceeded to hold court, as one after the other his patients came up to the table to wish him merry Christmas and be introduced to his companion. The music was so loud it was hard to hear what they were saying but their smiles and their body cues were so friendly and welcoming that it wasn't long before Laura felt quite at home.

'You're very popular,' she said, leaning towards him so that he could hear.

'That's me,' he agreed. 'They have to make a fuss of me or I'd chop 'em to bits next time they come down to the surgery, eh Jack?'

'He would an' all,' Jack said. 'He's a holy terror with that scalpel.' And he went off chuckling at the joke.

They had the table to themselves for the first time since they'd arrived. 'Do you want to dance?' he asked.

The dance floor was crowded with people all jumping about and making idiots of themselves, so they would have plenty of cover. 'Yes,' she said. 'Why not? I haven't danced for years. It would be nice.'

It was very nice indeed because he was a good dancer, moving to the pulse of the music with a suppleness she hadn't suspected, lithe and light-footed despite his size. So they stayed on the floor for six more records. At which point the DJ announced that he was going to give them all a breather. 'Something slow and smoochy,' he smoothed into his microphone. 'How about that?'

His audience cheered their approval, the lights were dimmed and Jeff held out his arms.

Laura took two steps and was in his embrace, held closely but gently, his arm about her waist, her cheek against his beard, as they swayed from foot to foot. Oh the pleasure of it! It was turning her on most powerfully. And I thought this would never happen to me again, she mused. How extraordinary! It was like being in a trance. As the dance continued she put a tentative hand on his neck and at that he drew her a little closer and began to sing. Is it happening to him too? she wondered. And if it is, will he say anything?

When the record came to an end, he stood still with his arm round her waist and looked down at her. 'Good?' he asked.

She answered him honestly. 'Very.' Now, she thought, he'll say something and I shall know.

But he let her go and looked away from her to

nod at one of his patients at a nearby table. 'I wish it wasn't Christmas,' he said.

That seemed a peculiar thing to say and not what she'd hoped for. He's distancing himself, she thought. I shall have to be careful or I shall end up making a fool of myself. She turned away from him and began to walk back to their table. 'Do you? Why?'

'Because I've got to drive to Manchester first thing in the morning,' he said. But he was thinking, don't turn away. Not when we're starting something. But were they? He didn't dare to ask her. Just in case. This was too fragile and precious to lose by speaking too soon. If only he hadn't ordered a taxi to take them home. If he'd arranged to drive her home himself he might have . . . But he'd left his car behind so that he could drink and now he couldn't drive even if he wanted to — even if he had the car with him — which he didn't. Bloody idiot.

'You'll come back again,' she said, shouting because the next record had begun.

'Yes,' he shouted back. 'I will.'

I shall miss you, she thought, as they reached their table. Perhaps it's just as well it's Christmas and I shall have too much to do to sit around. Images of the pleasures and trials of the season came tumbling and muddling into her mind — the delight of giving presents, days spent cooking, stomachs distended by too much rich food, Jessica tying a Christmas ribbon round Queenie's neck, piles of washing-up in the sink, bundles of balloons on the ceiling, hands playing Scrabble and Monopoly by the fireside, the peace and emotion of midnight mass. And she wished she could share it all with him.

But the party was roaring all round them and she couldn't even talk about it for fear of embarrassing him. Two of his patients were waiting for them at their table. 'We've come to buy you a drink,' they shouted happily. 'What'll it be?'

It should have been champagne, given the secret state they were in, but neither of them was daring enough to admit it. So they settled for beer.

Chapter Twenty-Four

Jessica was on the phone having a guarded conversation with Kevin Marshall. Never the easiest thing to do — there were so many *ears* in her family and they came out on stalks as soon as they knew who she was talking to — and particularly difficult at the moment because she was feeling irritable with him and had to conceal it.

'It's no big deal,' she said coolly, examining her nail varnish. 'I mean, what's Christmas? I knew you'd be away.'

'I'd stay here if I could,' his voice wheedled, 'but you know what parents are.'

'Don't I just,' she said, with some feeling. All bloody ears, that's what *they* are.

'I'll be back for the New Year,' he promised. 'There's a party at Biffin's. Pick you up about nine?'

'Right,' she agreed. It was a consolation. Not much of a one. But better than a kick in the teeth. 'See you around then.'

I handled that well, she thought, as she put the receiver down, but she checked her face in the wall mirror just in case, turning her head this way and that to make sure she looked cool and that she wasn't blushing or anything.

She'd had such hopes of this Christmas holiday

and now they were all wrecked. It was gross. It really was. After all these months, she'd assumed he would invite her home for Christmas to meet the rest of his family — or some of them at any rate. It was the season for parties and meeting people. After all, they were an item now, he'd met all *her* family and it wasn't as if *his* lived at the other end of the world or anything. Portsmouth was no distance. But instead of doing the obvious thing, he'd rung up out of the blue and told her he'd got to go to Wrexham — if you ever heard of such a place — because his stupid parents wanted to spend Christmas with some grotty cousin. How could he be so gross?

His Christmas present had been pretty gross too. He'd given her a compact disc of *his* favourite group — and he should have known what she wanted after all the hours they'd spent discussing the kind of music they liked. She'd given *him* his absolute fave on their last visit to the flat. He'd played it all the time they were there. There were times when she *did* wonder what she'd got herself into.

'Everything all right?' Maureen asked as she came into the kitchen.

Jessica turned on her, sharp faced. 'Why shouldn't it be?'

Oh dear! Maureen thought. So it *was* trouble. 'No reason,' she said as smoothly as she could. 'It was just something to say.'

Jessica tossed her hair. 'Well don't say it then.'

The young are so rude, Maureen thought, and

asked a stinging question to reinstate herself. 'Are you two going out tonight?'

Jessica tried to be nonchalant and failed. 'No, we're not, as it happens. He's got to go to Wrexham. To some cousin or other. It's a real drag but that's parents for you.'

Ah! Maureen thought. I see. 'So what will you do? Your father and I are going to midnight mass with Gran.'

'I expect I shall wash my hair and have an early night or something,' Jessica said coolly. Then feeling she might have been a bit sharp with her mother, she added, 'I'll look after Danny for you if you like.'

'He'll be at church too. He's in the choir. I told you.'

'He would be,' Jessica sniffed and assumed her resigned expression. 'Oh well, I might come with you then. I've got nothing else to do.'

'Good idea,' her mother smiled. 'You never know, you might enjoy it.' And if you don't, at least it'll give you something else to think about. Church was a good place for getting your thoughts straight. It was peaceful there. It gave you time and space away from the problems of your workaday life, the chance to see things in perspective. That was the other reason why she was going there herself.

Of all the many events in the Christian calendar, midnight mass was well and away Laura's favourite and for a whole variety of reasons. It endorsed her belief in the ultimate power of love, it was ritual, thanksgiving and celebration all rolled into one, but best of all it was an expression of hope just when she needed it most, at the darkest month of the year and the darkest hour of the night. This year she was looking forward to it with special pleasure partly because Danny was in the choir and David and Maureen were coming with her, but mostly because there was so much to be thankful for. The enquiry was still going on so nothing could be done about the road, David was still employed and nothing had been said, her friendship with Jeff had reached — how could she put it? — an interesting stage, and Amy had written to say that she was going to spend Christmas 'with friends'.

Christmas Eve was unseasonably mild that year and as bright as if it were early spring so the night was cloudless and sharp with frost. As she walked from the car park to the church with David and Maureen *and* Jessica beside her, the stars over their heads glistened snow white in the black sky and the Great Bear was as clear as she had ever seen it, bold and white and eternal, ploughing its huge unseen furrow in the darkness.

'It's a beautiful night,' she said to Jessica.

And Jessica, caught up in the heightened emotion of an occasion, put her grumpy thoughts to one side and agreed that it was.

It was warm in the church and the pews were packed with smiling faces, the way they always were at Christmas time. Laura sat with Maureen and Jessica on either side of her in a glow of candles and goodwill and let the old familiar phrases lap her about with warmth and reassurance.

The choir boys were singing a carol, faces framed by white ruffs, hair shining clean, pink mouths opening wide and innocent above the scarlet of their gowns. Danny was in the middle of the first row, looking angelic. *'The holly and the ivy now they are full well grown . . .'*

Very appropriate, Laura thought, looking at the holly an inch away from her nose. Whoever had been responsible for decorating the church that Christmas had rather overdone it. There were evergreens at the foot of every column, their branches so thick and their foliage so abundant that they looked more like growing trees than decoration. Above the topmost branches, the columns were twined about with ivy and embossed by sheaves of holly, each spiky leaf sharpened by candlelight, each red berry a tiny globe reflecting its own miniature window of light. It was as if a wood had been transplanted and allowed to grow wild in the aisles.

There were candles everywhere too, some cream coloured, some scarlet, each standing in a pool of melted wax as if it were floating in its own little lake. *'Earth and air and water and fire'*, Laura thought, enjoying them. Her head was bubbling with remembered quotations.

'How far that little candle throws his beams,' she recalled. *'So shines good deed in a naughty world.'*

It seemed to her that the candles were like beacons, lighting the way through the impenetrable darkness of the forest of ignorance. She thought of Blake and his *'Tiger, tiger, burning bright in the forests of the night'* and remembered Isaiah, *'The people that walked in darkness have seen a great light.'* Then she felt ashamed of herself for letting her mind wander and pulled it back to what was going on in the service.

The words were an illumination of her thoughts, as if they'd been chosen for her. *'In Him was life and the life was the light of men. And the light shineth in darkness . . . the true light, which lighteth every man that cometh into the world . . . And the word was made flesh and dwelt among us and we beheld His glory . . .'*

I've had too many quarrels this year, she confessed to her Maker. I've made a decision that I thought was right and I ended up hurting the people I love. I haven't always stopped to see the consequences of what I was doing. I think I need a little of Your light to show me the way.

As they stood for another carol, she turned her head to give some attention to her family. David and Maureen were as deep in their thoughts as she had been but they smiled back at her when she smiled at them — and Jessica, soothed by the untrammelled emotion of the service, slipped her hand through the crook of her grandmother's arm and gave it a squeeze. Yes, Laura thought, as the singing began, this is a beautiful service.

The rest of the Christmas holiday went well

too. They had Christmas dinner in Laura's Way and spent Boxing Day together in Canterbury Gardens. Laura was impressed by how skilfully Maureen was handling this holiday. Not only was the food superb but she seemed to have everything else under perfect control too — especially the conversation. Nobody said anything about the enquiry or David's job or Kevin's absence, they didn't watch the news and any topic that might lead them into difficulties was admirably sidetracked. As a result, the two days passed easily, the presents were a success and they reached the evening of Boxing Day warm, well fed, and rather pleased with themselves.

Then Maureen suddenly startled them all by making an announcement. 'If you're all settled comfortably,' she said. 'I've got something to tell you.' She sounded so serious that they all looked at her at once. 'Something — well really rather important.' They waited, watching her. 'I'm going to apply for a new job. I thought you ought to know.'

The only one who wasn't surprised to hear it was Laura. She'd been half expecting something of the sort ever since their conversation on the way to Twyford Down. But the others were thrown by it, Danny puzzled, Jessica annoyed, David flummoxed.

'What do you mean, a new job?' he asked, frowning at her.

'What's wrong with the one you've got?' Jessica wanted to know. 'I thought you liked it.'

'Our head of department is going to Hong Kong,' Maureen explained. 'He's been offered a job there and he's going to take it. He told us on the last day of term. They want him to start in the middle of January or sooner if he can. It's put the headmaster on the spot.' Then she paused. Midnight mass had given her the strength to make this decision but it hadn't provided her with the words to explain it.

David was still frowning and looking away from her so Laura asked her why.

'Well . . .' Maureen said. 'The trouble is we haven't got a deputy in the department. Not an official one anyway. Ours left at half-term and I've been acting deputy ever since, sort of *protem*.'

The surprise of hearing such a thing made David angry. 'You never told me,' he said, scowling at the carpet.

'It didn't seem worth it,' Maureen told him. 'It was only *protem*. A few weeks, that's all.'

'That school takes advantage of you,' David complained, looking at her sideways. 'Acting deputy. The very idea. Cheap labour, that's all *that* is. You should have told me. I'd have had something to say about it.'

Which is precisely why I didn't, Maureen thought. 'They pay me the going rate,' she corrected. 'I'm called acting deputy because the job isn't permanent, that's all.'

He was mollified. 'Oh well then, that's different. That's all right.'

'The thing is,' Maureen went on, wading into

the complications of her story, 'they advertised for a new deputy but they didn't appoint one. The head said they didn't get any candidates of the right calibre. So once Griff goes there'll be no one left to run the department — until they can appoint a new head. They're not going to appoint a new deputy now until they've got a new head of department. Anyway, the long and short of it is — I'm going to take over the department, temporarily, from the beginning of next term.'

David was exasperated. This was even worse than being a *protem* deputy. 'Oh for heaven's sake, Maur! Now you *are* letting them take advantage.'

Maureen stood her ground although his bad temper was putting her in a flurry. 'Actually,' she said, 'it could turn out to be a very good thing. I've been talking to the headmaster about it, you see, and he thinks I ought to apply for the job.'

'Which one?' Laura asked. 'As deputy?'

'No,' Maureen said giving her a small but decidedly wicked smile. 'As head of department. He said I stood a very good chance. He was surprised I hadn't gone for the deputy's job. I'd have walked it, apparently. I've been in the school for a very long time. I know how it works. It would make sense. So I thought as I'm going to do the job anyway, I might as well apply for it. And if I don't get head of department, I shall apply for deputy.' There, she thought, I've done it now. And she looked around at them, defiant with nervousness.

Laura applauded her at once, before David

could say anything. 'Well good for you,' she said. 'That's out of the kitchen with a vengeance. Joanna Trollope would be proud of you.'

'I've been thinking about her a lot, these past few weeks,' Maureen answered, giving her a fleeting smile. 'It's too good an opportunity to pass up. I might not get either of them because they're open to competition but I'm going after one or the other. I thought you ought to know.'

David couldn't understand what they were talking about and he was so upset he could barely bring himself to speak. 'I suppose this is because I'm going to lose *my* job,' he said miserably. 'That's what it is, isn't it. You think you've got to be the bread-winner.' It was bad enough to have to face the fact that he might be unemployed without being made to feel redundant by his own wife, the woman he'd always thought he could trust to support him and follow him and fall in with his plans.

'No,' she told him, speaking as calmly as she could because she understood what he was suffering and was full of pity for him. 'It isn't. I don't think you *will* lose your job and, if you do, I'm sure you'll get another one. It's got nothing to do with that. That's why I'm telling you now. I shall apply for it and, if they offer it to me, I shall take it no matter what happens at PPC. This is simply my career we're talking about.'

That was such an extraordinary thing for her to say that it made him aggressive. 'Have you thought of all the extra work it'll mean?'

'Yes. And how I'll cope with it. I shall be doing it from the beginning of the spring term anyway.'

'And what will happen if I have to take a job somewhere else? Have you thought of that?'

'No,' she answered him honestly. 'I haven't. And I'm not going to. There's no need to cross that bridge till we come to it. For the moment, I'm going to apply for both jobs and take which-ever one they offer — if they do.'

To be told such a thing, so calmly, was more than David could contend with. 'I don't under-stand you,' he said.

Danny got up and crossed the carpet to sit beside his mother on the sofa. He put his arms round her and gave her a hug. 'Well I think it's great,' he said. 'I hope you get one of them and I don't care which.'

'So do I,' Jessica said, looking a challenge at her father. 'There's only two women with any sort of power in our school. It's high time we had another one. Why shouldn't it be Mum?' She turned to encourage her mother. 'You go for it Mum.'

David had recovered enough to make a heavy joke. 'I seem to be outvoted,' he said. 'That's me for the washing-up I suppose.'

'All taken care of,' Jessica told him lightly. 'It's in the dishwasher. We've done it.'

'If there's any more coffee going,' Laura said, rescuing him, because she could see he wanted an excuse to get out of the room, 'I wouldn't say no.' She waited until he'd taken the empty percolator out into the kitchen before she asked, 'When do you have to put in your application?'

'It has to be decided by half term,' Maureen told her, 'because of people handing in their notice. It's good money. It would pay the mortgage if . . .'

Which has to be a comfort, Laura thought. 'I think it's a very wise decision,' she said.

Maureen made a grimace at the door. 'But will he?' she said.

'In time,' Laura hoped.

'He hates change.'

'I know. But he comes around to it in the end.'

'No he doesn't,' Danny said. 'He just shuts it all out.'

Having attacked her father while he was in the room, Jessica sprang to his defence now he was out of it. 'Of course, you know it all, don't you,' she mocked. 'You're *thirteen*.'

Danny wasn't fazed. 'I know how Dad goes on if that's what you mean,' he said coolly. 'And anyway, I shall be fourteen in three weeks.'

'Change the subject,' Maureen warned them, 'before he comes back.'

But David wasn't ready to come back. He'd left the percolator in the kitchen and was upstairs in his study sitting at the keyboard of his computer. Danny had assessed his reaction very accurately. He'd turned his mind away from his humiliation and now he was taking action to deal with it. He was composing a letter.

In the peace of the church, and just at the very

moment when he was praying most earnestly, an idea had come to him, a way to protect his integrity, to maintain a little pride, to save face if the worst came to the worst. He would write a letter of resignation, something very polite and very dignified, and he would carry it around in his wallet so that when — or if — they called him in to fire him, he could pre-empt them. He wouldn't say anything about it to his mother, naturally, and he wouldn't tell Maureen either — now. She obviously thought he was going to be fired or she wouldn't be rushing off to get a better job. He would write it during this holiday while he had time to think it out. It would be his private insurance policy. Of course, there was a hope that if the enquiry found for the road-builders, his job would be secure. If he was any judge, the SSM was waiting to see whether that was what was going to happen. But public enquiries were unpredictable and it was better to be safe than sorry. I'm not going to be beaten, no matter what.

It took him more than an hour to get the first draft into any sort of shape but it didn't worry him that he was working so slowly. He had the rest of the holiday to get it right — and he *would* get it right. He was quite sure of that. That was the way to deal with problems. Fight back. He could hear the others downstairs laughing at some comedy show and that pleased him because it showed they were back to normal again. He'd go downstairs himself in a minute or two. First he had a phone call to make.

'January could be quite exciting for once,' Maureen was saying, as he walked into the living room. 'Jess should be hearing from some of her college applications then, shouldn't you Jess. And there's Danny's birthday.'

'How about *starting* the year with some excitement?' he said to Maureen. 'I've just been on the blower to Barry Brough. They're giving a party New Year's Eve. He wants us to go. I said we would. OK?'

He was reinstating himself as head of the family — as both women understood. 'Yes,' Maureen said. 'Of course. It'll be fun. I shall wear my new earrings.'

It was the perfect answer as the earrings had been his gift. But she threw a quick glance at Jessica and Danny when she'd spoken and then looked a question at Laura.

'The kids could see the New Year in with me,' Laura offered at once, 'if they'd like.'

'I'm going out with Kevin,' Jessica told them with some superiority.

But Danny said he thought New Year at Laura's Way would be wicked and could he bring his new CDs. 'I could see the fat man in the attic, couldn't I?' he hoped. And Laura laughed at him and said she'd see what she could arrange.

So the evening ended on a good note — even if Laura never got her second cup of coffee — and on New Year's Eve the Pendleton family went their separate ways in remarkably good humour.

Kevin was the first to arrive — in an expensive suit and with an armful of red roses. As soon as they were in the car on their own, he confided to Jessica that he'd had a 'fucking awful time' without her.

'Serve you right,' she said, lifting her hair. 'Don't expect me to sympathise.'

Her insouciance delighted him. 'That's my gel!' he said. 'I knew you wouldn't miss me.'

'Where are we going?'

'The flat first and then on to the party. Oh! I nearly forgot. There's something for you on the back seat. New Year's present. Something to keep at the flat.'

It was a long narrow box labelled *'Naughty but Nice'* and inside was a very sexy black satin nightie. 'Oh I see!' she said, giving him a look to match.

'Thought you might,' he said happily and increased his speed.

After that, the evening was a great success, first with sex and sweet music at the flat, then to the party where they drank a lot, danced a lot and were catty about all the guests, and then on to a second and larger party where they finished the night on a high of extreme excitement and chemical ecstasy.

At his grandmother's party in Laura's Way, Danny was content with a glass of shandy. It made a nice change to be the eldest of all the children there and there were quite a lot of them,

Molly's four grandchildren and two who seemed to belong to Mr and Mrs Cooper and the three Coghlans, come back for the occasion with their mother. He enjoyed the way all the adults spoke so openly in front of him. He learned more about the enquiry in five minutes at Gran's fireside than he'd been able to glean in three weeks at home.

'Once they've made that old report,' Molly Fennimore told him, 'an' everyone knows they're not going ahead, we shall be all right. The colonel'll open up the houses and put more tenants in an' we shall all get back to normal.'

'You think they'll stop the road then?' he asked her.

'Bound to, duck. Stands to reason,' she said cheerfully. 'Might even get your old man out the attic,' she said to Joan Garston who was passing with a plate of sandwiches.

'That'll be the day,' Joan grimaced. 'Want a sandwich Danny? That side's ham, the other's egg and cress.'

Danny took a sandwich and ventured a request. 'Can I come and see him?' he asked. 'Tomorrow, I mean.'

Joan was surprised and looked it. 'Whatever for?'

'He's on the Internet, isn't he? Gran said he was. I'd like to see it.'

'Oh!' Joan said, understanding. 'That! Well all right then, you can if you like. Not too early though. I shall need me beauty sleep after all this malarkey. Midday. How'd that be? That's not to

394

say he'll let you in, mind. But you never know.'

So Danny made his first visit of the new year to Ken Garston's attic. It was — as he told his friends afterwards — really wicked.

Joan Garston was still in her dressing gown when he arrived and surly with hangover but she escorted him up the stairs grumbling all the way.

'He won't see you,' she warned. 'He's like a bear with a sore head this morning.' They reached the door to the attic. 'Here's the boy come,' she shouted.

An equally surly voice shouted back from behind the door, 'Bugger off!'

'What did I tell you?' Joan said.

Danny decided to take matters into his own hands. He had quite a talent for charming difficult adults. 'Are you really on the Internet, Mr Garston?' he said.

Now the voice sounded wearily proud. 'Yeh, yeh.'

'Can you send out e-mail?'

'Yeh.'

'That's great!' Danny admired. 'You must be the only one for miles round here.'

The voice grunted.

'What I mean is, I'd love to see you do it.'

'What for?'

'It's the communication of the future,' Danny told him, quoting his science master. 'We've got it at school. Only everybody uses it, so we have to take turns and we don't send out e-mail. I mean, you're special, having it all to yourself. I think it's wicked! *I'm* going on it when I'm older.'

There was a pause and then the voice asked. 'You've never seen e-mail you say?'

'No.'

'Is *she* still there?'

'No. She's gone downstairs.'

'Hang on a minute.'

A bolt was drawn, the door opened half an inch and a blood-shot eye peered through the crack. 'All right then, you can come in,' the voice said and the door opened to reveal the fattest man Danny had ever seen in his life.

In the weeks since his retreat, Ken Garston had spent all his time sitting at his computer, watching the screen and eating incessantly. Consequently he had put on nearly three stone and even his most roomy clothes were too small for him. His shirt was unbuttoned under a treble chin, his jersey was badly torn, covered in stains and beginning to unravel, and the legs of his trousers were so strained by the flesh that was now squashed inside them that they had burst in various places along the seams like the skin of a cooked sausage. He seemed to have combed his hair now and then, for a comb lay on the bed, trailing strands, but he hadn't washed for weeks — and smelt decidedly cheesy — and he hadn't shaved either so that he had a lopsided, oddly speckled beard. But it was his hands that gave Danny the biggest surprise. His nails were bitten and black-rimmed and his fingers were so fat they looked like pale pink bananas. In fact, the wedding ring on his left hand had sunk so far into his burgeoning flesh that it had almost disappeared.

The room was as dirty and unkempt as he was and smelt like a lavatory that hadn't been cleaned for a very long time. Every single drawer was open and spewing clothes on to the floor and the bed was a wreck. There was a body-sized brown stain on the undersheet and the duvet was all crumpled up and mounded with soiled underwear and dirty socks and shirts. There were stacks of magazines collecting dust in one corner of the room, a fishing rod and cricket bat thrown on top of a pile of old jackets in the other, and garbage littered everywhere, empty beer cans, crumpled cigarette packets, crushed take-away food cartons and, down at the far end of the room, a stinking bucket full of oily brown and yellow liquid. But the fat man made no apologies. In fact, he didn't appear to see anything wrong with it. He had rigged up a desk for himself under the skylight window made out of a large plank and two piles of old biscuit tins and his computer was plugged in and running, its blue screen bright as a jewel in the dark and muddle of the room.

'Come on, there,' he said, rolling towards it, 'and I'll show you what's what. You've got it at school you say? What servers do you use?'

The conversation got technical at once. They played with the computer for nearly an hour, keying in to both Ken's servers and accessing an enormous amount of information. Then he sent a letter by e-mail. Despite the foul air in the room,

Danny was impressed.

'It's very quick,' he admired. 'If you wanted to get a message out to anyone I'll bet you could do it in seconds.'

'So I should bloody think the amount it's cost me. D'you wanna see my *Dangerous Animals*? Sounds and everything that's got.'

'Brilliant!' Danny said, as a tiger roared on to the screen.

'You got the whole world in your room with one a' these things,' Ken told him. 'You don't have to go nowhere. It all comes to you. She don't understand. Bloody idiot she is. She keeps on at me to come out. Bloody ridiculous.'

Danny said yes as he seemed to be expected to say something.

'I shan't come out till they carry me out in my little box. If they want to knock this house down they'll have to do it with me in it. That's the way to deal with 'em. What d'you want to see next? How about scorpions?'

Molly Fennimore was sitting in the kitchen with two of her dogs at her feet when Danny finally went back to Holm End. 'You got in then?' she said.

'It was brilliant,' he told her, stroking the dogs. 'He's got stacks and stacks of programmes.'

'When's he coming out?' she said. 'That's what we all want to know.'

'Never.'

'Did you ask him?'

'No. That's what he said.'

'The man's a fool. He'll have a heart attack, stuck in there with no exercise.'

'It'll be different once they've given their report,' Laura comforted. 'He'll come out then, you'll see.'

'Well I wish they'd hurry up with it,' Molly said. 'How much longer are they going to be?'

'Not long now,' Laura said. 'They must have taken all the evidence they need.' She was warmed to think that their problems would soon be solved. And Jeff would be back by tomorrow. There was a lot to look forward to.

Chapter Twenty-Five

January was a disappointment. It began badly and it got steadily worse. The weather was cold, wet and demoralising, the news predictably bad and predominantly negative. It looked as though there was going to be a war out in the Gulf and at home there were over two and a half million people officially unemployed. At the start of the year the CBI gave out a warning that more job losses 'were in the pipeline' which made David wince. And in Burswood it was announced that the enquiry would continue 'for several more weeks'.

But at least Jeff phoned as he'd promised, as soon as he got back from Manchester.

'How did you get on?' Laura asked him, expecting to be told how much he'd enjoyed being with his grandchildren.

'Dreadful,' he said. 'I've had toothache since Boxing Day.'

'It was nice to see the kids,' she prompted.

But he didn't agree. 'Kids are bad enough when you're fit,' he said sourly. 'When you're in pain they're diabolical.'

That was a side of his character she hadn't suspected. She'd assumed he would like children as much as she did. It gave a sour taste to the rest of the conversation. 'Oh dear,' she said, 'you *are* in a mood.'

'I told you. I've got toothache.'

She didn't give him a lot of sympathy. What was toothache compared to what was going on in the Gulf. 'Then you'd better go and see a dentist,' she said.

He was growling with self-pity. 'I hate dentists.'

She was briskly sensible. 'It's either that or put up with the pain.'

He laughed at that. 'You're a great comfort.'

'That's me.'

'I'll ring you tomorrow,' he sighed, 'when I've sorted something out.'

It wasn't exactly the most romantic of returns. Which just serves me right, Laura thought, for being an old fool and imagining a love affair when there was no such thing. The works 'do' was an aberration. Now we're back to reality. Fancy him not liking children. Or is that just the toothache making him an old grouch? Men can be peculiar when they're in pain. I'll reserve judgment till I see him again.

But when he drove out to see her the following evening, she had to admit that he didn't look at all well. His face was pale and so drawn it looked lopsided, as if the weight of his pain was dragging him down. She wasn't surprised when he said he'd got to have a tooth out.

'I'll cook you something soft,' she said. Sympathy was easier now that they were face to face. 'Stay by the fire. Heat's good for toothache.'

So a dull domestic pattern was set between

them and the month continued in its negative way. It was three weeks before the dentist finished attending to Jeff's teeth and he was either depressed or miserable for most of the time. The enquiry dragged on, there was no news about the road scheme, nothing was said at PPC Pharmaceuticals, Jessica didn't hear from any of the colleges she'd applied to, and there was no date set for Maureen's interview. In fact, as far as Laura could see, the only good thing about the entire month was that Amy wrote to say she wouldn't be coming 'back to the south' for another month or two. So much for looking forward to excitement!

Once his teeth were fixed, Jeff recovered his spirits and took her out to dinner on Saturday evenings. They discussed their work and the appalling tardiness of the enquiry team but, no matter how pleasant the meal, the dizzying intimacy of the works dance wasn't repeated. And the long wait dragged on. David finished composing his letter and worked longer hours than ever. Jessica and Kevin took off for Southampton whenever he could spare the time. Danny did his homework and celebrated his birthday. Maureen ran the department and waited for her interview. Only Laura's neighbours were impatient and they grew more restive by the day.

'I shall be glad when it's February,' Joan Garston said. 'They'll have to tell us then, don't you think.'

Laura couldn't imagine why February should

be any different from the preceding four weeks.

'It's all this hanging about,' Joan said. 'You don't know what to do.'

'I know what I'm going to do,' Laura told them. 'I'm going to put my potatoes to set.'

'But what if we're . . .'

'I am going to put them to set,' Laura said firmly, 'and then they'll be all nice and ready for planting out at the end of March. We can't stop living because we're waiting for a tardy old man to write a report.'

February edged towards March. The first green spears of the daffodils appeared in the flower beds outside Laura's kitchen window. Willow catkins dangled their yellow lambs' tails in the hedgerows. There was enough midday sun to tempt the cats to snooze on the window sills. And then, just as Laura was beginning to resign herself to the possibility that nothing was going to happen for *another* month, Maureen and Jessica both received the letters they were waiting for. They arrived in the same post, one to inform Maureen that she'd been shortlisted for interview, the others to invite Jessica to visit all three colleges of her first choice.

Inevitably, the news caused trouble in Canterbury Gardens. David was delighted to think that his daughter was taking what he called her 'first steps towards a university education' but Maureen's interview plunged him into sulky depression.

'He can hardly bring himself to talk to us,'

Maureen confessed to Laura as they were stacking the dishwasher after Sunday tea. 'Well you saw how he was. I just don't know what to say to him to put things right.'

'Don't say anything,' Laura advised, handing her the milk jug. 'Let him get through it on his own.'

'It makes me feel dreadful,' Maureen said, slotting in tea plates, 'because it's all my fault in a way. The trouble is I've gone too far to pull back now.'

'It makes me feel dreadful too,' Laura told her. 'I was the one who put him in this state in the first place.'

'Do you really think that?'

'I'm sure of it.'

'I think it's more my job than your campaign,' Maureen said. And sighed.

Laura cut through her anxiety to ask the important question. 'Do you still want this job?'

Maureen stopped slotting plates to look up at her. 'Yes. Very much. You know I do.'

'Well there you are then. Nothing's changed. You still want it. He still doesn't want you to take it. He was just the same when he was a boy and I had to go to work. He hated *that*. He used to go off in a huff at the slightest thing.'

'He feels threatened by this, you know.'

'Yes, of course he does. Because he thinks he's going to lose his job. It *is* my fault, you see. He'd feel quite differently if they'd only publish the report and get everything settled.' Oh please God, she thought, let it be settled without any trouble for him. Carrying so much guilt towards him was weighing her down. 'I've got great hopes of this report,' she said, speaking more cheerfully than she felt. 'You mustn't pull back now.'

'No,' Maureen said, shutting the dishwasher and switching it on. 'I know that really. I wasn't going to. It's just it upsets me to see him in such a state.'

'It'll be different when they've published the report,' Laura tried to reassure them both. 'It's unsettling everybody waiting for it like this. You go ahead. And phone me when you know the result.'

'You'll be the first to hear,' Maureen promised. And smiled at her.

Jessica had a problem with her interviews too, although she kept it to herself and her diary. She'd applied to London, Southampton and Lampeter, because that was what her tutor recommended, but once she'd been to Wales and seen the campus at Lampeter she knew there was no other college she wanted to attend. She kept her counsel and didn't say anything until she'd seen all three but she knew all along that nothing could compare with it.

'It's the most gorgeous place I've ever seen,' she told her family. 'The river runs right through the middle of the campus and they've got little footbridges over it, and there's an old fort there next to a very old building they use as a hall of residence for the third years. Just imagine living *there!* It's the third oldest university in Great Britain. Did you know that? And so peaceful. When you look out into the countryside you can see a round mountain with trees on the top. They call it Magic Mountain. Imagine that. And you'd love the library Mum. It's modern, on three levels, with huge windows and you look out over the playing fields and the river. And the course is brilliant. Environmental Geography. Just what I want. I can't wait.' She would have to settle down to some serious study to get the grades she needed but it would be worth it if she could earn a place *there.*

Her relations approved wholeheartedly and David was so cheered that he took them all out to dinner to celebrate.

But, to her crushing disappointment, Kevin sniffed.

'What's wrong with Southampton?' he said.

They'd just had sex and were still sprawled across the bed in their scarlet room, finishing off the bottle of red wine Jessica had bought at the local off-licence. 'Nothing's wrong with it,' she said. 'It's not Lampeter, that's all.'

'Well if you're going to this Lampeter of yours we shan't see much of one another, shall we?'

'Why not? You've got a car.'

He ignored that. 'Southampton would be much better,' he said. 'You could rent a flat. There's plenty round here.'

'At a price,' she reminded him.

'Your dad would help, wouldn't he. He's loaded. It 'ud be great. Just think of it. We could live there together. Play our own music. Eat our own food. No one to interfere with us. Sex whenever we feel like it.'

It was certainly a temptation. A flat of their own where they could be together all the time. But three years at Lampeter was a greater one. 'I'll think about it,' she said.

It wasn't until she'd got home from school on Monday afternoon and was writing up her diary that she realised that what he was proposing was that *he* should live in *her* flat and that he hadn't talked about the economics of it at all. He hadn't offered to go halves with the rent and he hadn't said anything about housekeeping either. Or was she misjudging him? He always paid for their food in the flat and entry to clubs and things like that. But would it be the same if they were living together? She had a nasty feeling that it might not. He didn't pay any keep to his mother and father. She knew that because he'd let it slip quite casually one evening when they were dancing. 'They don't want it,' he'd said. 'They're loaded.' But that was what he'd said about her father. And he wasn't loaded. Very far from it.

This was the third time she'd had cause to think that he might not be quite as charming as she imagined. It was a nasty moment and she couldn't push it aside. She'd been annoyed with him when he went to Wrexham for Christmas, but she'd excused that because he'd done it to please his parents and he'd been extra loving when he got back. She hadn't been too pleased over the CD — but he'd put that right too, with the nightdress. But this was different. After everything she'd said about going to university and all the things she'd told him about Lampeter, it was chauvinistic to ignore what she wanted. Chauvinistic and selfish. She didn't like it at all.

It would be different if she had someone to talk it over with but there wasn't anybody. She could hardly tell Mum, or Emma because she wouldn't understand, or anyone at school because all they were interested in was the sort of course you were going to apply for and whether you were going to get good enough grades. Gran was a possibility, if she could be sworn to secrecy, but she might be a bit too old to understand. Would she have any idea what life could be like when you were seventeen and in love?

'I might go and see her on Thursday,' she mused to her diary, 'and sort of test the water before I see him Saturday. I could ask sort of roundabout questions or something. See what she says.'

But by Thursday evening everything had changed because that was the day the long-awaited report was published.

Laura saw the headline on a placard outside a newsagent's as she was driving home from work. 'Enquiry report. By-pass to be built.' It was so uncompromising and so unexpected that she was sure there must have been some mistake. She stopped her car at once to run into the shop and buy the paper.

There was no mistake. It was all there in hideous black and white. The enquiry had found for the road builders. *'While we have sympathy with the handful of householders who will have to be inconvenienced, we must be aware of the needs of the local population as a whole, for whom this by-pass will provide much-needed relief, and to the many and larger groups who have expressed their opinion that the road is necessary and will ease the burden of traffic through the centre of the village.'*

Laura was so angry she felt as if her entire body was exploding. *'Handful of householders'* she thought, glaring at the words. How dare he belittle us like that! We're not going to be *inconvenienced.* We're going to lose our homes. Wasn't he listening to us? And who are all these local groups who want the road? I know the hauliers wanted it but they're not local. I never saw any local tradesmen out on the streets collecting signatures. We got over six thousand signatures, for God's sake, and he hasn't said a word about *that.* Oh dear God! How could they be so blind? Angry tears sprang from her eyes, hot and pricking. It was a total, terrible defeat. Holm End would be pulled down, Laura's Way destroyed, their beautiful countryside ruined. All their hard work had gone for nothing. And what was worse — oh much, much worse — she'd put David's job at risk, and his house and Jessica's education too for all she knew, and all that was for nothing too.

How *could* they make such a decision? There was no sense or justice in it.

She sat in the car with the paper on her knees and wept with fury and disappointment and an aching sense of loss and injustice. Her life was being dragged out of control in the same terrible way it had been when Pete walked out. All the old familiar feelings returned, as crushing and overwhelming as they'd been then. Failure tore at her brain, grief cramped her guts, she was bowed down by the sense of being abandoned, betrayed, lost, totally powerless.

It was dark before she was calm enough to drive and even then she was in no fit state to go home and face her neighbours. There was only one person she wanted to talk to, only one who would even begin to understand what she was feeling. She found a tissue in her bag and cleaned her face as well as she could, then she drove to Worthing.

Jeff was clearing up his surgery when she arrived and he saw at once that there was something very badly wrong. He left what he was doing and strode across the room towards her, his face full of concern. 'What's the matter?'

She handed him the paper, mutely, and sank into his patient's chair, her legs suddenly too weak to support her.

He read the paper with one hand on her shoulder, as if she really were a patient. 'Ah,' he said. 'I see. Bloody monsters!'

'How could they do such a thing?' she

mourned. 'Weren't they listening?'

'Probably not,' he told her calmly. 'There's none so deaf as them as won't hear. This was always possible, I'm afraid. The Ministry has enormous power.'

'And uses it,' she said. 'Oh Jeff! I shall lose my lovely house.'

He yearned to help her. 'I'll write you a letter for the paper if you like.'

That provoked a bleak smile. It wouldn't do any good but it was kind of him to offer. 'Thanks.'

'What do your neighbours think? I'll bet they're furious.'

'I haven't seen them yet,' she confessed. 'I haven't been home.'

Because you can't face them, he understood. He was aching with sympathy for her. 'I'll come with you,' he offered. 'Bit of moral support. Give me five minutes to clear up here and then I'm all yours.'

So they drove back to Laura's Way in convoy.

The news spread through Burswood all through the late afternoon and evening. David took a call on his mobile as he was driving home. It was Barry Brough, full of excitement because it had 'come out the right way'.

'It's all in the *Evening Argus*,' he said and read out some of the details. 'Ought to let you off the hook, eh.'

It was a great relief to David but he took the news cautiously, knowing how easily hopes can be dashed. 'With a bit of luck,' he said.

'Tough on your mother, of course,' Barry said, 'but there you go. Win some, lose some.'

Jessica was told by her friend Emma, who'd been studying at home that morning and had seen it on the one o'clock news. 'It'll be on again tonight,' she said. 'They were making quite a thing about it. Does this mean they'll pull your Gran's house down?'

'Yes,' Maureen said, when she watched the six o'clock news with her two children. 'I'm afraid it does. Poor Gran!'

'I shall ring her,' Jessica decided, 'and tell her how sorry I am.' Her own problems could wait. 'Poor old Gran. After all her hard work and the petition and everything. I think it's gross.'

But she wasn't able to tell her so because Laura's number was engaged every time she dialled it.

'We'll drop her a note at the library,' Maureen said. Danny had gone upstairs to do his homework and she was busy preparing the evening meal, on edge because she'd lost a bit of time watching the news and she was running late. 'On our way into school in the morning. There's bound to have been a lot of people wanting to talk to her. You think how many there were at that meeting. You can try again when you get in from school. I shall be late don't forget.'

In her annoyance with Kevin and her fury at the report Jessica had forgotten. 'Oh Mum!' she said. 'It's your interview.'

'Everything's happening at once,' Maureen

agreed, peeling the last of the potatoes. 'And here's your father home so we'd better not talk about it.'

'I don't see why not,' Jessica began but her father was already in the kitchen and the expression on his face gave her an answer she couldn't ignore. He was swollen with satisfaction, smug with it, standing tall and straight-spined, his hair smoothed to a dark cap, his eyes full of light.

'Great news for us!' he said. 'Have you heard?'

'Yes,' Jessica said, fighting him at once. 'Poor Gran's going to lose her house.'

'She stood to lose it anyway, Jess,' he told her. 'That was always the risk.'

'It's not fair.'

'Well we must make it easier for her, mustn't we. She can come and stay with us while she's finding somewhere else and you can make a fuss of her. How would that be?'

'I'm off out!' Jessica said, flouncing out of the kitchen before they fought in earnest. How could he be so callous? Poor old Gran! All those signatures and speaking at that meeting and waiting all this while — and then he says she'd have lost anyway.

'Dinner at eight,' Maureen reminded her.

'What a relief eh!' David said when his daughter had gone. 'I doubt there'll be any trouble for us now.'

Not till tomorrow anyway, Maureen thought, but she didn't say anything.

'I need a drink,' David said, heading for the

living room. 'Would you like one?'

'Scotch and soda,' Maureen said. 'I've earned it.' I haven't argued with you. I haven't said anything. Oh yes, I've earned it.

Laura's neighbours came running across to Holm End bristling with newspapers and questions as soon as they heard her car.

John Cooper arrived straight from the cowsheds with muck still on his boots, which he left at the kitchen door; Joan was still in her apron from the farm shop and Molly had been walking her dogs and ran across with four of them behind her, steaming from their exercise, pink tongues lolling. Within seconds the room was full of heat and anger.

Mr Fennimore was the only one who wasn't shouting and he was lugubrious. 'Don't surprise *me*,' he said. 'You ever see a judge that was fair? Eh? Tell me that. You ever seen one come down on the side of ordinary people? They want putting up against a wall an' shooting, that's all I got to say about 'em, the whole damn kit and caboodle.'

But the others were furious and roared their anger at Jeff for several impotent minutes while Laura made coffee.

'They never intended to listen to us,' Joan raged. 'Rotten bastards. It was all fixed years ago, you ask me. All this enquiry business was just a sham. That's all. A sham. They couldn't just ignore everything we said else. Don't you think so Jeff?'

Jeff agreed with her. 'You're up against the

government,' he told her. 'That's the trouble.'

'Bloody government,' she growled.

'They wants putting up against a wall and shooting,' Mr Fennimore said.

'I'd set the dogs on the buggers,' Molly said. 'Wouldn't I boys?' And her four boys looked up at her in their amiable way and thumped their tails on the floor to agree with her.

Eventually John Cooper wondered, miserably, if there was any way they could appeal against the decision and sighed when he was told there wasn't. And Connie asked, very sadly, how long Laura thought they'd got.

'I don't know,' Laura told her. 'Not long I shouldn't think. Now they've got their permission they'll want to start work fairly quickly.'

'Then that's it, I suppose,' Connie said.

Laura's fighting spirit was beginning to return. 'No,' she said. 'I don't think it is. All right, they've declared war on us. There's no denying that. But that doesn't mean we've got to give in. We've only lost the first battle, that's all. There could be others. I don't know about you, but I'm not giving in until this house is actually being pulled down. Not even then, probably.'

'You think we should go on fighting?' Molly said, fondling the ears of the nearest dog. 'Stage a protest or something.'

'Yes. I do.'

'But what would we do?' Joan asked.

'I don't know yet,' Laura admitted.

'Sit down in the road?' Joan asked.

'Carry a banner?' John suggested.

'No. That's been done. I think we should do something different, something out of the ordinary, something that hasn't been done before. Something dramatic or spectacular that'll catch the public eye. Something worth looking at. That's what we need.'

'Gaw dearie me,' Mr Fennimore said. 'You don't want much do you gel. That's a tall order, strike a light if it ain't!'

The word echoed in Laura's brain. Light. *'The people that walked in the shadow of darkness have seen a great light . . . The light shineth in darkness.'* I sat in that church, she thought, and I prayed to be shown the light. The Guy Fawkes bonfire crackled into her memory, shooting flame. The trees were bright with lanterns. Fireworks dropped white stars in the black sky. The church was full of warmth and fire, great candles blazing on the altar, lesser ones glimmering among the evergreens.

'Light!' she said. 'That's it. That's the answer.'

They were mystified. 'What is?' Connie asked.

'Light,' Laura explained. 'We'll hold a festival of lights. A Beltane festival with torches and songs and a bonfire, maybe, to show that we're still here and we haven't given in.'

'Like Guy Fawkes?' John asked, remembering his success with the firework display.

'Like Guy Fawkes only in spring,' Laura said. 'We could hold a torchlit procession all along the route they're going to destroy. Think how spectacular that would look. A long line of flaming torches' all through the Way and into the woods right up to where the footpath joins the road. You would see it for miles. The cameras would love it.'

Once it had been said it was obvious. They decided they would hold it on Saturday week, that Joan and Molly would run off leaflets to hand out over the weekend, that they would phone Toddy and ask him to spread the word, that Laura would tell both local TV companies and that Jeff would get his friend Toby interested. John volunteered to make the torches, 'Nice long staves. Rag heads. Burn up a treat they will. See 'em for miles.' And Molly offered to buy soup at the cash and carry 'to warm us all up come the finish'.

As they made their plans, the phone began to ring, first Toddy who agreed to hand out leaflets outside the school, then one of their allies after another, all glad to hear that they weren't giving in and all offering help. After the third call, Molly appointed herself telephone operator.

'There you are,' she said triumphantly after the sixth call. 'It's not the end by any manner a' means and they needn't think it. You just wait till they see our torches.'

' *"Earth and air and fire and water",*' Jeff said. 'You know where we ought to end this demonstration. Up by the pond with all the torches reflected in the water.'

The mere thought of that dreadful black water

made Laura wince. 'It would be in the dark,' she said.

He looked across at her, half anxious, half hopeful. 'It would make a wonderful picture,' he urged.

Joan and Molly were instantly enthusiastic about it. What did they know about how danger-ous water could be? 'Wouldn't it just!' Molly said. 'That's brilliant, Jeff. Perfect.'

'We could all stand round in a circle,' John Coo-per said, 'and hold our torches up high. You'd get a cracking reflection that way. There's a mound on the far side, where the ash trees are. We could go all along the top a' that. I can see it now.'

Fear was like a cramp in Laura's chest but she couldn't say no to them. Not when they were so full of hope and enthusiasm. It was time to face this silly phobia of hers and put paid to it once and for all. It was only water — and she didn't have to go right up to the edge. She ought to be able to cope with it. Dammit, she *would* cope with it. 'Well, yes,' she said. 'I suppose we could.'

'It'll be terrific,' Molly applauded. 'So that's settled then.'

Laura tried to turn her fear away by joking. 'The things you let me in for,' she said to Jeff, as they all said goodnight to one another on the doorstep.

There was no mistaking the admiration on his face. 'You're a woman and a half,' he said.

Chapter Twenty-Six

For the first time in more years than she cared to remember, Maureen Pendleton was giving thought to her appearance. David's selfish reaction to the report had hardened her mind and stilled the last niggle of doubt. She wanted this job, she was right for it, and she was going to pull out all the stops to get it.

When she'd first put in her application, she'd toyed with the idea of indulging in a shorter hairstyle for the interview, but had decided against it as being a bit extreme and because it would take time to put right if she didn't like it. However, a new suit was another matter. She'd driven to Worthing one day last week instead of coming straight home from school and treated herself to a cream wool, with a short, straight skirt and a long, easy jacket. It was very stylish and horribly expensive and she was pleased with it on both counts but until that moment she hadn't been quite sure about her right to wear such a thing.

Now, on the fateful Friday morning, as she assessed it in her wardrobe mirror, she decided that it had been exactly the right choice. It made her look professional and confident, just the sort of woman who ought to be the new head of department. She would take a cardigan to wear while she was teaching and leave the jacket hanging in the cloakroom so that it would be pristine for the interview. Stud earrings and her engagement ring as jewellery. Comfortable shoes to show she wasn't a bimbo. Her dependable bag. Yes, she thought, as her image was finally assembled. I've done the best I can.

David had gone rushing off to work as soon as he'd finished breakfast and Jessica and Danny had both decided to cycle to school that morning, so she'd had ten precious minutes to prepare. She ran a last minute check — make-up, tissues, red pen, good-luck charm. She hadn't forgotten anything. Well, she smiled at her reflection, this is it!

It was a beautiful day, warm for late February and more like spring than winter. The earth in the flower beds looked richer than usual and the daffodils were all in bud. Whatever happens, she told herself as she drove to school, this is going to be a very good day.

It was certainly a very busy one, with far too many things to attend to. Two of the English teachers were off sick so there was work to provide for their classes, there were book orders to check in and exam entries to check out, and, on top of that, she also had to look after the other four candidates during the lunch-hour. It was a very odd experience for, although they were polite and affable to one another, there was no denying that they were also rivals and that put a strain on everything they said. She was relieved when the school secretary came across to her classroom halfway through the afternoon, to tell her that the governors were ready for her.

There was no time to adjust her make-up but no time to get flustered either. She put on her jacket, ran a quick comb through her hair, and set off at a brisk pace to the library.

There were more people in the room than she expected, the headmaster and both his deputies and four of the governors, which made her quail a bit. But their questions were asked in a kindly way, even if they were searching, and when she emerged to a darkening sky at the end of her half-hour grilling, she felt she'd acquitted herself as well as she could.

Then there was nothing to do except sit around in the staff room with the other candidates and wait for the result to be announced. The final bell rang, chairs scraped in every classroom, feet tramped and scuffed in every corridor, the air was full of yells and calls and the chatter of excited voices, and soon groups of children began to stroll and gossip past the windows on their way home and the rest of the staff drifted into the staff room, packed their bags and went home too. Then the hubbub subsided and the campus settled into the unnatural calm of early evening.

'This is the worst bit,' the other woman candidate observed. 'Waiting.'

'It feels like a cattle market,' Maureen said and tried a joke to cheer them up a bit. 'I keep thinking someone's going to come in and staple a plastic button through my ear.'

But it wasn't a cattle-man who arrived. It was the school secretary.

'Mrs Pendleton,' she said. 'If you'll just come this way.'

It was the signal by which all successful applicants were greeted. I've done it! Maureen thought, as the others leaned across to congratulate her. I've got the job!

She went through the formalities of acceptance in a daze, drove home still in her interview suit and ran into the house. She couldn't wait to tell the children. Wouldn't they be thrilled!

But they weren't at home. There was only David, slumped in his armchair gloomily watching television.

'They're out,' he said. 'There's a message for you on the answerphone.'

Jessica's cool voice spoke from the machine. 'We're at Gran's. We thought we'd give her a bit of commiseration because she's only a dear old granny.' Laura was chuckling in the background and she and Danny were talking happily to one another. 'So we cycled over. Anyway, shan't be long. Back in time for dinner. I've done the potatoes. Hope you got your job. See yer!'

It was a miserable anti-climax and it cast Maureen down even though she tried to be sensible about it. Naturally they'd go and see their grandmother after that awful report. They were being kind to her, cheering her up. That was the way she'd brought them up to be. But why did they have to do it on this day, of all days, when she needed them here?

'Oh well,' she said, flatly, 'I'll get on with the dinner then.'

The flat tone caught David off balance. He'd been sitting in the semi-darkness trying to think out what to say to her when she got back — something comforting if she hadn't got the job or some sort of congratulation if she had. Despite his annoyance with her, he wanted her to be chosen. Even now he felt a sort of grudging pride in her success. But she'd wrong-footed him by being miserable and now he couldn't think of anything to say at all.

His long silence annoyed her. 'Aren't you going to ask me how I got on?' she said and her voice sounded irritable.

'I know how you got on,' he said shortly. 'It's written all over your face.'

The nervous irritation she'd kept in check all through that long difficult day was suddenly beyond her control. 'Well go on then,' she said angrily. 'Say it! Why don't you?'

'There's no point in me saying anything,' he told her, with chilling mildness. 'You'll do what you want no matter what I say.'

The sheer unfairness of it made her gasp! 'Now look,' she said angrily. 'We've been married eighteen years and in all that time I've never opposed you once, not once, in anything. You've always had your own way. This is the first time I've ever asked for anything for myself.'

All the kind words he'd been planning were

frozen away. Now he was angry and his anger was ice cold. He turned his head away from the television to glare at her. 'Now *you* look here,' he spat at her. 'I've turned myself inside out to provide for you and the kids. I've worked all hours. Taken on any job, no matter how unethical — and some of them have been pretty near the knuckle I can tell you. Done anything. Kowtowed to anyone.'

She stood her ground, pink-cheeked against the magnolia wall. 'I'm not saying you haven't.'

'Well then you just remember it before you start calling me selfish.'

'I didn't call you selfish.'

'You've got a good home, washing machine, dishwasher, built-in furniture, nice car. I haven't stinted you, any of you. It hasn't been easy, let me tell you that, but I've done it. Holidays abroad, books for school, good clothes. I've provided you with every mortal thing you could possibly want. Haven't I? Admit it. Every mortal thing. I've always been here for you. What more do you want?'

The anguish on his face and those awful staring eyes touched her pity, despite her annoyance. 'You've been a good husband,' she reassured him. 'Nobody says you haven't. A good husband and a good father. That's not what we're talking about.'

'Yes, it is,' he insisted, still glaring. 'That's exactly what we're talking about. You think I'm going to get the sack. That's it isn't it. You think

I'm going to get the sack so you've gone off after some stupid job so that you can be the breadwinner when I'm redundant. The next thing you'll be asking me to leave. I shall be redundant in my own home as well as the office. That's what'll happen.'

That was so far over the top that her pity dissolved. 'Don't be so bloody ridiculous.'

'Ridiculous is it?' he yelled at her, shouting because he *knew* how ridiculous it was. 'Well we shall see, won't we.'

'I've taken this job because I want it,' she said, being as calm as she could. 'That's all there is to it. I want it. Not for you. Not for the kids. For me.'

'Look who's being selfish now!'

'Yes,' she admitted, 'I am. But it's the first time in eighteen years, that's the point. I've gone along with everything you wanted for eighteen years. Now I think I've earned the right to a life of my own.'

'Gone along with everything I wanted!' he mocked. 'Like what, I should like to know.'

'Like taking finals six months pregnant,' she said, the old resentment bubbling to the surface. It wasn't fair to rebuke him with that and she knew it. She'd always vowed she would never do it. But it was out now and she couldn't unsay it or stop it. It *had* been awful and it was about time he knew it. 'Like giving up my career before I'd even started. Pushing a pen one day and a pram the next.'

'I knew you'd throw that in my face one day,' he said sullenly. 'It couldn't be helped. We agreed about it. We weathered it. You wouldn't want to be without our Jessica would you?'

'All right then,' she said, because that was unanswerable. 'Like moving to Birmingham the minute she was born. We didn't agree about that.'

'That was for my job. There wasn't any option.'

'Like hosting all those awful dinner parties.'

'I didn't enjoy them any more than you did. They were a means to an end. You knew that. And don't tell me you didn't.'

'All right then,' she said wildly, 'like all these years living in an igloo.'

That startled him. 'What are you talking about?'

She waved her arms at the walls. 'All this white everywhere. Your bloody awful black and white.'

He touched the back of his hair for comfort. 'But you like it.'

'No I don't, as it happens. I like a bit of colour.'

'You never said you didn't like it.'

'You never asked me.'

'Oh come on! I consulted you. I consult you about everything.'

She fought back hard. 'No you don't. You assume I'll agree with you. That's not the same thing.'

David passed his hand over his eyes, pressing his eyeballs with his thumb and third finger. The white walls were beginning to shimmer and fracture at the edges of his vision. How did we get

426

into this? he wondered, recognising the start of a migraine. Why are we talking about the decorations? The conversation was out of hand and he was losing the will to fight back. Why didn't she say all this before? She only had to say.

The front door was opening. There were voices in the hall, Danny gruff and cheerful, Jessica light-toned and laughing. The patterns on the white wall stabbed and zig-zagged, bright as a laser beam — and they were still there when he shut his eyes. Oh Christ, what timing! What bloody awful timing!

His children strode into the room, still talking, their faces full of good news. Jessica picked up the atmosphere at once and looked a question at her mother, who sent back an equally rapid message, eyes narrowed, head given an almost imperceptible shake. But Danny was too excited to notice what was going on.

'You'll never guess what she's going to do,' he said.

'Who's "she"?' David rebuked automatically.

'Gran,' his son said, unabashed. 'She's going to hold a torchlight procession. The fight goes on!'

David groaned.

'Come into the kitchen and tell me all about it,' Maureen said, trying to intercede.

But David insisted on being told there and then. If news was bad it was better to hear it at once and deal with it.

They told him in much excited detail.

'They've been printing off leaflets all after-noon,' Danny said, producing one and handing it to his father. 'See. Isn't it brilliant?'

David took the leaflet and read it, eyebrows raised. 'But she can't do this!' he said.

'She's doing it,' Jessica told him. 'You can't stop her.'

For once he didn't check her rudeness because he barely noticed it. He was overwhelmed by the foolhardy, ridiculous courage of his mother. 'It says here they're going to end at the pond. She'll be up there by that pond in the pitch darkness. She can't do it.'

'Why not?' Jessica dared him.

'Because she's terrified of water,' he said. 'That's why not. She couldn't stand it.'

Jessica's defiant tone changed to concern. In the excitement of the moment she'd forgotten her grandmother's phobia. 'She didn't say anything.'

'No, well she wouldn't, would she.'

'She'll be all right,' Danny said stoutly. 'She'll have lots and lots of people round her. They won't let her fall in. It's going to be tremendous.'

David's migraine was beginning to pound. He stood up heavily, his forehead wrinkled against it. 'I'll have to go and get one of my tablets,' he said to Maureen. 'I've got a migraine coming.'

'Would you like a cup of tea?' she offered, feeling she ought to make some sort of amends.

'No,' he said, adding pointedly, 'All I need's a bit of peace and quiet. That's all I've ever needed.'

'It was horrendous,' Jessica said to Kevin when she'd told him all about it on Saturday evening. 'They were in the middle of a row when we came in. You could tell. Well I could. Danny missed it, but then he misses everything.'

'Have you got one of the leaflets?' Kevin asked ingenuously. 'I'd like to see it.'

There were still two or three in the pocket of her new leather jacket. 'There you go.'

Unlike her father, he read it with interest and admiration. 'She's a feisty old lady,' he said. 'Didn't I always say so.'

His praise pleased her. 'You did.'

'Is she really all that afraid of water? I mean seriously afraid?'

'Terrified, according to the old man. She doesn't say much about it herself but we all know she's frightened.'

'I suppose you'll all be going with her?'

'Mum says not. She says we're not to take sides. I can't see why we shouldn't. Danny's going. I shall be with you though, shan't I?'

'Well no,' he said, looking at the leaflet. 'No, actually, as it happens. I've got a job on Saturday. It'll have to be a different day next week.'

It annoyed her that he was so casual about it. 'It'll have to be Thursday then,' she told him. 'That's the only evening I've got free.' And she looked at the leaflet, thinking, if I'm not going to be here on Saturday, I shall go with Danny and see what Dad has to say about *that*.

He threw the leaflet into the waste paper basket and came and stood behind her, to kiss her neck and stroke her thighs. 'Gorgeous!' he said. 'That's what you are. Fucking gorgeous!'

She felt gorgeous and glancing at herself in the dressing table mirror she knew that she looked it too. He was like a chameleon. He could change his mood and her opinion in an instant. 'Is there a party tonight?' she asked, leaning back against him.

'Two,' he told her. 'The first one's starting now.'

The leaflet had a wide distribution that week. By Thursday it had reached the Leader of the Council.

'Look at that, Mr Cranbourne,' he said, tossing the wretched thing across the board-table. 'That damned librarian of yours is getting out of hand.'

'She's not my librarian,' Mr Cranbourne demurred, alarmed by the Leader's aggressive tone. 'I'm not Libraries.'

'Perhaps we ought to bring the work forward,' Councillor Mrs Smith suggested. 'If it's possible.'

'A wise suggestion,' the Leader agreed. 'The sooner this is over and done with the better. There's been altogether too much fuss about it, if you want my opinion. The road's got to be built, when all's said and done. We can't put it off for ever.'

Chapter Twenty-Seven

Preparations for the torchlit procession were almost complete. The borrowed vat was full of hot soup and being watched over by Connie Cooper, Jessica and Danny had cycled over and were busy setting out plastic cups, Laura was swathed in her shawl ready to greet the television crew, the cats were safely locked away in the bedroom, and Molly had been manning the phone since four o'clock. Outside, John Cooper's torches were heaped under the oak trees like a gigantic pile of kindling, and Toddy, Sharon and four of their friends were in position in the lane ready to show the car drivers where to park. The only member of the team who hadn't turned up was Jeff Turner and they were all sure he'd be along at any minute.

Laura was lurking by the window watching out for the arrival of the TV van, when the phone rang. She was surprised to hear it was Jeff.

'I'm ever so sorry,' he said, 'but I'm going to be a bit late. I've just had a call from my daughter, Sally. The one in Dorking. The younger one, you remember. Her car's broken down. I said I'd fix it.'

Oh for heaven's sake! Laura thought. How feeble of her. 'What's wrong with her partner? Rory,

431

or whoever he is. Can't he do it?'

'He's in Ireland,' Jeff said and his voice sounded apologetic. 'She's on her own with the baby. That's why she rang me. I can't let her down. She's depending on me.'

The black waters of the pond lunged into Laura's mind, unfathomed and threatening. I was depending on you too, she thought, for a bit of protection. Didn't you realise it? I was going to hide behind your back when we got to the pond. Well serve me right for being feeble myself. 'You're a fine one!' she joked. 'You let me in for all this and now you're chickening out.'

It upset him to be mocked. 'I know,' he said. 'I wouldn't do it if it was anyone else.'

'We're nearly ready for the off,' she told him. 'Will it take long?'

'No idea till I've seen it.'

'Where is she?'

'In a Little Chef just outside Horsham, so she says.'

'It'll take you an hour to get there and back,' she said, her annoyance growing.

'I'll drive like the clappers.'

Two large, dazzling lights were swinging in through the gate. 'Here's the TV people come,' she said. 'I'll have to go. See you when you get here.' She expunged her irritation by hanging up on him. Then she took a deep breath and went out, smiling, to greet the television crew.

There were lights in every window in every occupied house, the grass verges were already lined with parked cars and the lane was full of people, men and women of all ages, children, dogs, even an old lady in a wheelchair. All these people, fighting back, Laura thought, and all because of our leaflet. She recognised some of them from the meeting and some of them she'd met at one or other of the libraries but others were strangers to her. How wonderful that strangers have come to help us. She tried to estimate how many people there were. Fifty? A hundred? It was impossible to say. There were more cars arriving as she watched and they all seemed to be full. She remembered some silly joke about counting legs and dividing by two and knew that she was feeling excited and honoured as well as nervous.

Danny and Jessica were at her elbow.

'What a lot of people!' Jessica said. 'Isn't it brilliant!'

Danny was more interested in the torches. 'Can we go and help Mr Cooper?' he asked. The thought of seeing them lit was making him bright-eyed with excitement. If he were allowed to help he might even get to light a few himself.

'Go on then,' she said. 'Tell him I'll be up presently.'

The producer was walking towards her, ready to introduce himself. 'You've got a good turnout,' he smiled at her.

'Yes,' she said proudly. 'People care, you see.'

'We're going to do a piece to camera,' he explained. 'We've got a quote from this week's *Economist*, rather apposite, we think. Then we'll film the interview with you. Just a short piece — why you're doing this, how you started, what you hope to achieve, that sort of thing. Then we'll take a shot of the march. You're going to end up by a lake of some sort, right?'

'A pond,' she said — and at that the waters of the pond swelled about her feet, pulling her down and down into the abyss and roaring in her ears. She shuddered despite herself. This won't do, she thought. There's nothing to be gained by thinking about it. Concentrate on the matter in hand. But water was waiting for her just the same.

At the far end of the way, Danny and Jessica were handing out the first batch of torches, and John Cooper was giving instructions in his slow careful way. 'Hold 'em up, see. Like this. Otherwise you'll set fire to the trees. They'll spark a bit when I light them an' you'll feel quite a bit of heat, so keep 'em away from anything you could burn.' He looked across at Laura. 'Ready when you are!' he called.

If Jeff doesn't get here in time for me to hide behind him, she thought, I'll keep out of the way behind the crowd. If I'm going to do this interview first I've got a good excuse not to lead them. 'Light up!' she called to John. 'Jess and Danny will help you.' And turned her attention to the producer.

So the torches roared into light as the presenter faced the camera and spoke her set piece.

'According to *The Economist*,' she said, ' "Protesting about new roads has become that rarest of

British phenomena, a truly populist movement draw-ing supporters from all walks of life. " I don't know about the rest of Great Britain, but that is cer-tainly true of the people of Laura's Way in West Sussex here tonight. Led by their local librarian, Mrs Laura Pendleton, they are gathering for the start of a torchlit procession to show their disap-proval of a plan to build a by-pass round their village or, as they claim, part of the Folkestone to Honiton superhighway. Mrs Pendleton, can you tell me what first made you decide to chal-lenge this road?'

At which point a dog walked into shot and lifted its leg against the hedge — to applause and laugh-ter.

'Oh dear,' Laura said, laughing too. 'I *am* sorry.'

'Happens all the time,' the producer told her. 'Never work with animals. Take it from the ques-tion, Felicity.'

The animal's intervention had released Laura's tension. 'We don't want this road,' she said, pleased by how calm she sounded. 'There isn't the traffic to justify it.'

'Is there another route you would prefer?' Fe-licity asked.

'No,' Laura said firmly. 'We don't want any route. We don't believe that a by-pass is neces-sary. It would just cause more congestion wher-ever it was built.'

'Then there *are* the cars to fill it? Doesn't that presuppose a need?'

Who's side is she on? Laura wondered. Or is she playing devil's advocate? 'No,' she said firmly. 'Not at all. If a road is built people will come out in their cars and drive along it. Roads attract cars.'

'But having said that,' Felicity observed, 'you have to admit that your supporters have driven here in *their* cars —' the camera was turning to look at them — 'in order to join your march.'

'Yes,' Laura agreed. 'Ironic isn't it. But they wouldn't have come here if it hadn't been for the threat of this superhighway. Normally we're very peaceful here and that's how we'd like to keep it.'

'You don't see this road as progress?' Felicity prompted.

'No, I don't. I see it as entirely regressive. I think the Red Indians have got the best approach to this sort of thing. They have a saying, *"Tread lightly on the land and leave it as you found it."* Farm it, yes, conserve it, but don't smother it in concrete. Once you've done that you've soured it for ever.'

'Great!' the producer said. 'You're a star!'

'Can we get started?' she asked him.

He doffed an imaginary cap and bowed towards her as if she were royalty. So the procession set off, with John, Danny and Jessica happily leading the way.

It was every bit as impressive as Laura had hoped. Her fifty torches were very bright indeed and very theatrical, their long flames feathering sideways in the evening breeze and spitting red

436

sparks as the procession set off along the footpath towards the pond. Soon the wood was full of leaping fire, golden and primitive among the silent branches, and the marchers were obscured by the comparative darkness below so that all she could see of them was a moving column of dark heads and faces gleaming like mother-of-pearl.

'Is it far to this pond of yours?' the cameraman asked, shifting the weight of his camera on his shoulder.

'Four hundred yards,' she told him. 'The head of the column should be there already.'

A girl in a greatcoat and a bush hat was running down the path to catch up with them. 'Mrs Pendleton!' She was carrying a camera too, slung round her neck like a baby-carrier.

'Anna Mays,' she introduced herself, 'from the *Gazette*. Toby Fawcett sent me.'

'Is *he* coming too?' Laura asked.

'He said to tell you he'd phone you in the morning.'

They rounded the bend, walking slowly because the march was coming to a halt. And suddenly there it all was, the picture they'd planned, magical in the mysterious darkness of the wood and even more spectacular than she'd imagined. The marchers were massed about the pond, up over the mound and down the other side, in a solid phalanx of thick coats and determination. They held their torches before them so that the flames were reflected in the black water and the twin arches of light formed a perfect golden ellipse. Above their heads the light silvered the burgeoning foliage of the trees, beside them children held gloved hands, awed and round-eyed, at their feet the dogs sat patient and primitive as if they'd been trained to the occasion.

'Great!' the producer said. 'What a picture! Let's have you right in the middle shall we.'

Laura opened her mouth to protest but Molly was already pushing her towards the mound. 'Make way!' she cried. 'Let's have a bit of room. We want our Laura in the middle.' And her cry was taken up on every side. 'Come on Laura!' 'Good old Laura!' 'Right in the middle. That's the style!'

There was nothing Laura could do to stop them. She was urged and jostled to the very edge of the pond, had a torch thrust into her hand, stood clutching it while photographs were taken and the camera rolled. The horror of the pond was inches away. Nobody knew how deep that water was, nor what terrors were lurking in the depths, what terrible secrets lay like traps, hidden in its impenetrable gloom, what deaths had been endured there — drowned bones lustrous in a debris of leaves and slime. She smiled until her jaw felt frozen. She could feel the water sucking at the earth under her feet, pulling her down. The filming went on and on. Time seemed to have stopped. If I fall, she thought, I shall sink into the darkness and never come up again. She could feel the water pounding against her spine and hear the roar of it in her ears. Her forehead was dank with sweat. She was beginning to pant. Dizziness was pulling her forward. I'm going to faint, she thought. Oh dear God, if I faint, I'm lost.

There was a movement in the crowd beside her, someone pushing his way through, an arm firmly round her waist, a voice saying, 'It's all right. I'm here.' And she turned in relief to whoever it was and for a few dizzied seconds she thought she was looking at Pete and that he'd come back to her after all these years. Then she realised that it was David who was holding her and she clung on to his arm and began to shake.

'Oh David!' she said. 'I *am* glad to see you.'

Molly pushed in beside him. 'Are you all right?' she said to Laura, broad face wrinkled in concern.

'A bit dizzy,' Laura admitted. 'Nothing really.' David still had his arm round her waist, holding her firmly as he led her away from the water's edge.

'You've finished here now, haven't you?' he called to the TV crew.

Apparently they had and so had Anna Mays. He seemed to have everything under control. Molly was told to organise the return of the marchers, Jessica to run on ahead and put on a kettle, Danny to hold on to his grandmother's other arm.

Within seconds they were on the path and heading towards the lane.

'Better now?' he asked.

She said she was, but in fact, she didn't feel better until she was in the cottage, sitting by the fire with Ace on her lap and a double brandy in her hand.

'Total madness,' David said, as Jessica made tea. 'What were you thinking of to hold it by the pond?'

'It was for the reflection,' she said. 'We thought it would make a good picture.'

'It did too,' Danny assured her. 'It was brilliant.'

'But that pond,' David insisted, 'of all places. The one place that's always scared you rigid.'

The evening was full of surprises. 'How did you know that?' she asked him. 'I never told you.'

'You didn't have to, old thing. It was all subliminal. You used to say, *"Don't you go near that pond."* Every time I went out to play it was always the same. *"Don't you go near that pond."* You were terrified of it. I've always known that. And then you go and hold a demonstration right at the water's edge. It's a wonder you didn't give yourself a heart attack.'

She'd recovered enough to joke. 'I'm not that fragile.'

'They're coming back,' Jessica said, glancing out of the window. 'Shall I start dishing up the soup?'

'Three quarters of a cup each,' Laura instructed. 'There's so many of them it won't go round otherwise. I'll give you a hand. I'm quite all right now.'

'You'll sit by the fire till they're served,' her son said. 'You've done enough for one night. You can come out and say goodbye to them when they're all feeding.'

It wasn't like Laura to be submissive but, for once, she did as she was told. His concern for her was so comforting and she knew she needed comfort. So he and the children dished up the soup, the neighbours bustled out with trays full of paper cups, and the returning procession made a cheerful noise in the lane and the garden. It seemed to be a jolly gathering and Jessica said the soup had been an inspiration. It certainly took a very long time to serve it all and by then Laura was much better and went off into the garden feeling she could face anything.

It was like a party out there. Nobody was in a hurry to rush off. They were all too excited and they all felt the evening had been a triumph. She walked from group to group, greeting old acquaintances and agreeing with their opinion.

'It was splendid,' she said. 'We couldn't have improved on it. Look out for us on the late night news.'

When the cars finally began to drive out of the lane, David decided she'd recovered enough for him to leave her. 'Come on you two,' he said to Danny and Jessica, 'or your mother will wonder where we are.'

Laura kissed them. 'Thanks ever so much for all you've done,' she said. 'I do appreciate it. Especially . . .' And she looked at David, not needing to finish the sentence. 'I don't know what I would have done without you tonight.'

He was embarrassed to be praised out there in the open in front of everybody. 'Yes, well,' he said stiffly. 'That's what sons are for. I couldn't let you face — that — on your own.'

There was so much she wanted to say to him but this was neither the time nor the place. 'I had to do this, you know,' she felt she had to explain.

'Yes. I do know,' he said, adding confidentially, 'Actually, I admire you for it.'

His generosity made her ache for him. After she'd deliberately put his job at risk, he could say a thing like that to her! 'I do hope it doesn't cause trouble. At PPC, I mean.'

He made a little grimace. 'It's a bit late to say that now,' he said. 'But don't worry. I'm ready for it.' If only they hadn't been in the garden he would have told her about the letter.

But they *were* in the garden and that photographer from the *Gazette* was lurking near by. 'Could I just have one last picture of you, Mrs Pendleton?' she asked. 'With your neighbours.'

The conversation would have to be abandoned. 'I expect so,' Laura said. 'When I've said goodbye to my family.'

So David drove away, the neighbours were rounded up and they all went into the cottage and posed around the fireside. It wasn't until several pictures had been taken that they realised that Joan Garston was missing.

'Where's she got to, daft ha'p'orth?' Molly said. 'Trust her to miss the boat.'

'She was gathering up the torches last I see of

her,' John said. 'Up by the pond.'

'Could someone go and get her?' Laura asked. 'We can't have her left out of the picture. Not after all the work she's done.'

Joan Garston was still cheerfully busy, gathering up the spent torches and stacking them on the trolley she'd 'borrowed' from the farm shop for the purpose. She'd had a really happy time at Laura's demonstration, out in the open, among friends, being valued for what she was doing. It made a nice change from lugging food up the stairs to that lazy great lump in the attic. Now she was singing as she worked, her voice flat and croaky but who cared when there was no one near to hear her? *'We shall not — we shall not be moved. Just like a tree that's standing by the wa-a-ter, we shall not be moved.'*

It was very dark in the woods now that the marchers were gone and the torches were all out. There was a full moon but that wasn't much help. Moonlight cast eerie shadows in woodland and especially among the half-fledged trees of early spring. It could shift from a ghostly dapple that vanished as soon as you looked at it, to black shapes so solid that you could almost imagine they were men lurking among the branches. That one on the mound looked just like a man in a black jersey and a balaclava helmet. She could see the glint of his eyes and the pale gleam of a white hand, holding up an overhanging branch as he ducked underneath it.

Jesus, Mary and Joseph! It *was* a man and there was another one beside him and they were both charging down the mound towards her. She was frozen to the spot and struck silent, too frightened to scream.

'That's her!' the taller man said. 'Grab her!'

She was seized by the arms and pushed back against a tree. 'Let go!' she said, finding her voice. 'What d'you think you're playin' at?' She tried to struggle away from them and couldn't do it because all her strength had drained away — and that frightened her even more.

The tall man tightened his grip. 'Oh we're not playing,' he said, glaring at her through the slit in his balaclava. 'We're in earnest. You'd better believe it. We got a message for you.'

She looked from one pair of hard eyes to the other. 'What message?' she said. If she could keep them talking she might just get back enough strength to make a bolt for it.

'You're to go home and stop all this fucking nonsense,' the tall man said, prodding her to emphasise the words. 'That's the message. Stop all this fucking nonsense. It won't get you nowhere. Right? This road's gonna be built. Got it?'

'There's hundreds a' people just down there,' she said, waving a weak hand in the direction of the lane. 'You going to stop all a' them are you?'

'You've got too much mouth,' the shorter man said. 'Perhaps we ought to wash it out for you. How'd you like that? Eh? In the pond. Under the water.' There was something sinister about the

444

way he said that. 'Under the water.'

She was doubly frightened, her heart pounding in her throat like a hammer. Were they threatening to drown her? 'Get off!' she said, making another attempt to wrench free.

'Under the water,' the taller one repeated. 'You won't like that will you? Oh no! We know about you and water.'

The shorter man pinned her arms to the tree and thrust his face so close to hers she could feel his breath. 'So how about it?' he said. 'D'you promise?'

She was paralysed with fear but she managed to speak. 'No, I don't!' she said, spitting the words at him through clenched teeth. 'I don't.'

'Right,' he said. 'You've asked for it.' And before she could yell they pulled her away from the tree, seized her by the arms and legs and threw her into the pond.

The water was ice cold and evil tasting but its impact galvanized her into action. She struggled to the surface, lungs bursting, swam to the far bank, her skirt dragging about her legs, scrambled out. Then she ran, faster than she'd ever done in her life, panting and sobbing, her heart swelled to bursting and her wet clothes sticking to her skin.

John Cooper met her halfway back to the lane.

'Good God alive gel!' he said. 'What's happened to you?'

'I been mugged,' she wept. 'That's what's happened to me. I been mugged.'

Chapter Twenty-Eight

Maureen had spent most of Saturday evening cooking pies and flans for the freezer. She had a lot of school work to do but she'd decided that she would devote that particular evening to something that was manifestly domestic. It would be a way of demonstrating to David that she wasn't taking sides, that the new job wasn't dominating their life, that she was still a caring wife and mother. And besides, the freezer was virtually empty.

She *had* hoped that the family would drift in and out and talk to her while she was cooking, which was what they usually did, but Danny and Jeff went rushing off to their grandmother's as soon as they'd had their tea, and David put his head round the door an hour or so later to tell her he was 'just popping out for a few minutes'.

I might as well not have bothered, Maureen thought, as she took the last pie out of the oven. She went back to the empty living room to watch television on her own, feeling decidedly disgruntled.

David's few minutes extended into an hour and a half and she was beginning to wonder where he'd got to when a car crunched into the drive and all three members of her family burst in through the door with their faces full of excited news.

They gave it to her in such a babble she could hardly take it all in, how the procession had been brilliant, how Danny lit the torches and Jessica served the soup, how the TV people had come and interviewed Gran in the garden, how a woman from the *Gazette* had taken pictures of *'everybody'* and, finally, how Gran had got scared by the pond and Dad had appeared out of no-where — 'We didn't know he was there' — to look after her.

'So *that's* where you were,' she said to him. What a loving thing to have done!

He received her affection proudly, knowing how well he'd deserved it. 'I couldn't let her face it on her own,' he explained.

In that second, the eighteen-year-old that Maureen had fallen in love with all those years ago suddenly smiled at her again. The years of salesman suavity fell away, the obsessive tidiness and black-and-white certainties were gone, the thickened flesh of affluence dissolved into the air, and there he was as she remembered him, skinny and proud, idealistic, pig-headed, vulnerable, his hair too thick and flopping over his forehead, his neck too slender, his eyes full of ardent tender-ness, just as he'd been when she'd marched through the streets, carrying the banner against the Vietnam war, and he'd come to watch her. She put her arms round his neck and kissed him full on the lips. 'You're a good man, David

Pendleton,' she said. 'Haven't I always said so.'

'Come on you,' Jessica said to her brother. 'We're setting the table.' And she dragged him into the dining room, quickly, before he could say something and spoil it. 'Wasn't that sweet!'

Danny had found himself very nearly moved to tears so he screwed up his face in mock disgust and was scathing. 'Yuk!' he said. 'Makes you sick.'

They set the table with the best china and dinner was a celebration. It was a splendid homecoming.

Jeff Turner's evening wasn't anywhere near so pleasant. He'd found the Little Chef easily enough, driven up alongside his daughter's non-functioning Peugeot and been welcomed with obvious and flattering relief but when he examined the car he was very angry.

'Oh Sally, for heaven's sake!' he said. 'It's out of petrol. That's all. Why didn't you check it, you stupid girl? You've had me all this way just to fill a petrol tank.'

Sally stood beside him, biting her lip. 'I didn't know,' she said. 'Honest, Dad. It just stopped. I thought it was something awful. I had to push it in here. And with Tabitha asleep and everything, I didn't know what to do.' Her two-year-old was still fast asleep in the car seat, with her head on one side and her thumb in her mouth.

She *is* feeble, Jeff thought. Laura was right. She ought to have seen to it herself instead of dragging

448

me out all this way for nothing. But it was partly his fault and he was honest enough to admit it. When she'd been a little girl her dependence on him had been so charming that he'd encouraged it and never seen the need to wean her away from it. So he could hardly blame her now, when it was a nuisance. Oh well, he thought, I've come here, so I might as well help her. He put his angry feelings to one side and set to work.

First he siphoned petrol from his tank into her virtually empty one, then, when the engine wouldn't fire, he cleaned her spark plugs and finally, as it was still lethargic, he gave the wretched thing a jump-start to get it going.

'Fill the tank,' he instructed, as his daughter climbed back into the driving seat. 'And get that battery looked at. It's clapped out. You'll probably need a new one.' Work had restored his good humour as it usually did.

Sally leaned out of the window to say goodbye and thanks. 'I don't know what I'd have done without you tonight,' she said, looking at him with her mother's blue eyes.

'Stayed at the Little Chef and phoned a garage in the morning, I expect,' he said.

'I couldn't have done that. Not with Tabitha. I didn't have her nappies or bottles or anything. I do appreciate it Dad. You are good. Especially when you've had all that toothache and everything. Fran told me how bad you were over Christmas.'

Being reminded of how bad he'd been, renewed

his ill temper. He was tired, disappointed, covered in grease and it was much too late for him to get back to Laura's Way for the demonstration. Even if he *did* drive like the clappers he wouldn't even see the end of it. He found a rag in his glove compartment and did what he could to clean his hands. 'I hope you realise I've had to stand someone up because of you,' he complained.

Sally decided not to take the complaint too seriously. One scolding was enough. 'Oh dear!' she grimaced. 'He won't mind, though, will he? If you explain.'

'She might.'

That surprised her. 'Oh,' she said, 'it's like that is it?'

'I shall never know now, shall I?' he said. 'You've buggered it all up.'

'There'll be another time, though, won't there?'

He was too cross to be truthful. 'How should I know?'

'I'm sure there will,' she said, slipping the car into gear. 'I'm glad you've got someone else. It's about time.' Her mother had been remarried for nearly five years and she and Fran had always felt he shouldn't be alone. 'What's she like?'

'She's an anti-road campaigner,' he said. 'Very tough. She's on a demonstration this very minute. I should have been with her instead of siphoning petrol into your car.'

'You ought to be the perfect pair,' Sally said and drove away before she could be rebuked for being cheeky.

'No such thing,' her father called after her, as he watched the Peugeot's tail lights turning out of the car park. 'I only wish there were.'

There was no point in rushing back so he took his time on his return journey and headed straight for Worthing and his local. He'd have a quick one to cheer himself up, then he'd phone her. There was nothing else he could do.

The pub was full that night and very noisy, which pleased him. A convivial atmosphere was the best cure he knew for the blues. He found two of his cronies and joined them for a pint. It wasn't long before their raucous argument made them the focus of an exuberant crowd. Having analysed the state of the nation, they were just about to tackle the state of the world, when Toby Fawcett and his partner strolled across to join the party.

'Nasty business about the mugging,' Toby said.

Jeff wasn't really interested in local crime but he felt he ought to ask. 'What mugging?'

'In Laura's Way, after the demonstration. Weren't you there?'

Jeff's heart skipped a beat. 'No. I missed it.'

'Anna phoned in just before we left. Apparently there was a mugging up by the pond.'

There was only one question Jeff wanted answered now. 'Who?'

'Your anti-roads woman by the sound of it. One of the organizers, Anna said, so it must have been her. I thought you'd have known.'

'Oh Christ!' Jeff said, on his feet and pushing

his way to the door. 'I should have been there. Make way, some of you. 'Scuse me! Oh come on, get out the way!'

He was in his car and squealing out of the car park before he realised he hadn't asked how badly she'd been hurt. Bloody fool! he swore at himself. Stupid, bloody fool! Now he'd have to wait to know until he got there and he'd be thinking the worst all the way. He drove irritably, fretting at every hindrance, swearing and drumming his fingers on the steering wheel when the lights were against him, taking risks out on the open road, his heart pounding with anxiety. Oh come on, come on, get out of my way!

Laura's Way was ominously quiet and completely empty except for a dark car parked by the terraces. No sign of the police. No ambulance either, so it must have been and gone. He skidded to a halt outside the kitchen door and hurtled into the house.

'Oh it's you,' Molly Fennimore said. 'I thought you was the police coming back.' She and Connie Cooper seemed to be cleaning up the kitchen. The sight of their mops and floor cloths sent him into a panic. Was it because there'd been so much blood? God, why hadn't he asked? There was no sign of Laura.

'Where is she?' he asked.

'Upstairs,' Molly said and opened her mouth to tell him the story but he was out of the room before she could say another word.

Bed-rest at home was better than being taken

to A and E. She couldn't be too badly injured if they were leaving her at home. He charged the stairs, banging his knees against walls as he turned the corner, flung doors open. Not there. Not there either. How many more bloody doors are there? Here then — and there she was standing by the open wardrobe with her back to him, no dressings that he could see and no sign of blood.

He was into the room in a single stride, had caught her by the shoulders, turned her so that she was facing him. No injuries to her face. 'Oh thank God!' he said, pulling her into his arms. 'Thank God! You're all right.' He was kissing her cheeks and her hair in an anguish of relief and affection. 'My dear, dear girl. I thought you'd been hurt. I should have been here with you. You *are* all right aren't you?'

His onslaught was so sudden and so unexpected that Laura had to put her hands on his chest to steady herself. I was right, she thought. This *is* a love affair. It's as strong for him as it is for me. There was no doubting the strength of his feelings. They were clear in every line and movement of his face. But what a time for him to tell me, after all the things that have been happening here tonight. 'I'm fine,' she reassured him, smiling into his eyes. Such loving eyes, their tawny depths darkened by emotion. 'What made you think I wasn't?'

He tucked her head under his chin and held her in his arms, close and safe while he digested what she'd said. He was so glad she hadn't been hurt he felt dizzy. 'The mugging. Toby told me. He said you'd been attacked.'

She laughed at that. It probably wasn't the right thing to do but she couldn't help herself. 'Oh Jeff,' she said, putting her arms round his neck. 'It wasn't me. It was poor old Joan. They threw her into the pond. She's in ever such a state. We've had the police here questioning her.'

He was still so dizzy with relief that he didn't take it in.

'The doctor's with her now. Didn't you see the car? She's having a bath to ease the bruising. I've come back to get my bathrobe for her.' She held the bathrobe up for him to see.

But he didn't look at the robe. His eyes filled with tears.

She put an arm round his shoulders. 'Hey!' she said. 'We're all right. All of us.'

'But you mightn't have been,' he said. 'I should have been here. I left you to all that. I should have been here.'

'You wouldn't have been able to do anything if you *had* been,' she said. 'It all happened up by the pond and they waited until she was on her own up there.'

He blinked the tears out of his eyes and turned his head away from her, feeling angry with himself. 'It could have been you. Dear God, woman. It could have been you.'

'From what Joan told the police I rather imagine they thought it *was* me,' she said. 'They told her to call off the demonstrations for a start and when she wouldn't agree they threw her in the pond because they thought she was afraid of water.'

'Christ!'

'Exactly.'

'How did they know that?'

'That's what I should like to know. If they're using spies they're very well informed.'

'Could it have been Kevin? Would Jessica have told him?'

'It's not a very nice thought, but it's possible.'

'What are you going to do about it?'

'I don't know yet. I haven't thought it out. She doesn't know I saw him filming. Look, I'd better take this robe across or they'll be wondering what's happened to me.'

'I'll come with you,' he said, stockily determined. 'You're not going out there on your own with muggers about.'

So they went together, taking Molly and Connie with them. He took a professional interest in Joan's injuries and congratulated her on putting up a fight. 'You're over the worst now,' he said. But once he and Laura were back in the cottage, he locked the kitchen door.

'What are you doing?' Laura said. 'I never lock my door.'

'You do now,' he told her grimly. 'This is getting nasty.'

It was an unpleasant thought but she accepted it — with a sigh. 'I suppose you're right.'

Her resignation saddened him and made him

aware of what a lot she'd had to contend with.

'I'm sorry to have made such a fuss earlier,' he said. 'I feel a fool getting hold of the wrong end of the stick like that.'

She put her arms round his neck again and kissed him — briefly but on the lips. 'Don't apologise. I'm touched.'

There was no need for pretence now. He could tell her the truth without fear of the consequences. 'I love you too much to be sensible.'

'Did I ever say you'd got to be sensible?'

'You know what I mean,' he begged.

Yes, she did but she was still bemused by the pace of the night's events. 'It'll take a bit of getting used to.'

'Don't you want to be loved?' he asked, his eyes offering kisses.

'Yes. I do,' she said, accepting them. 'Um. Very much.'

Several kisses later he asked, 'Didn't you ever suspect what I was feeling?'

'Yes. I did once.'

'When?' He already knew — being all instinct now — but it would be wonderful to be told.

She obliged — although she knew that he knew. 'When we were dancing. You turned me on rotten. I thought you knew.'

He gave her an honest answer. 'No. I didn't. I didn't even dare to hope in those days. Anyway, I was too busy coping with what you were doing to me.'

'I'm doing it now, aren't I?'

To be so close to the lovemaking he'd wanted for so long made him as breathless as a boy. 'Christ, yes.'

She kissed him again. This time lingeringly. 'Then I think we ought to go to bed,' she said.

He just about had enough of his wits left for their joke. 'I thought you'd never ask!'

Upstairs, she switched off the lights to give them the necessary darkness to hide their imperfections, removed Jack and Queenie from the bed and took off her shoes.

Now that the moment had come he was diffident. 'Am I allowed to undress you?'

'I was just going to ask you the same thing.'

'I've got a beer belly.'

She laughed at that. 'So who's perfect? I've got three cats and they sleep on the bed.'

'I thought I should warn you.'

'I'm warned,' she said and unbuttoned his shirt.

He was a gentle lover and a patient one so it surprised her that they didn't sleep afterwards. She lay in the curve of his arm, breathing in the scent of his skin and they talked.

'This is a lovely room,' he told her. He was observing it bit by bit, the oval mirror on her wardrobe door silvered by moonlight, the faint gleam of cream-coloured walls between the darkness of beams and the mysterious squares of prints and pictures, the crammed untidiness of it, the crowded bookcase tumbling books and papers, beads hanging on a cork board, clothes slung across the chair, boots waiting in the corner, one lolloping against the other like two old friends. A warm, comfortable, welcoming room, like its owner.

'Yes,' she said, enjoying the sight of it too. 'It is. I've got it the way I like it.'

'There's so much I want to know about you,' he said.

'Like what?'

'All sorts of things. Like why you're on your own, for a start. I've never been able to understand that. You're not the sort of woman who ought to be alone. There's too much affection in you.'

'That's simple,' she said bluntly. 'I'm alone because my husband walked out on me.'

'Yes, I know that. Amy told me.'

'She would!'

'So are *you* divorced too?' It would be comforting to know that they shared the experience.

'No,' she said and told him the story, from the moment of Pete's departure, all through her long search to the moment when she accepted that she wasn't going to see him again.

'So he could still be alive,' he said, when she'd finished.

'For all I know.'

'It must have been difficult.'

'No not really. It was too gradual. I got used to the idea by stages.'

'I think we all do that,' he said. 'Even with a

divorce. You know you're not wanted but you accept it by fits and starts. You don't take it all in at once.'

'Was it that bad?'

'I brought it on myself really,' he admitted. 'By whistle-blowing.'

She waited.

'I was the charge nurse in a big teaching hospital,' he said, beginning *his* story. 'Good reputation, prestigious building, award winning car park, that sort of thing. It should have been a wonderful place to work in. It was when I first went there. But it changed when the cuts started. We were chronically understaffed, you see. That was the trouble. And as the years went on it got worse. Nobody was allowed to say anything about it because of our image but by the time I left it was really dreadful. There were nights when I was the only fully qualified member of staff on the ward. Twenty-six geriatric beds and only me and a ward orderly to look after them. Ridiculous.'

'So you blew the whistle on them,' she prompted.

'Not straight away. I tried going through the proper channels, bringing things up at department meetings, sending notes to the management, that sort of thing. But it was a waste of time. They kept saying they were looking into it but they never did anything. We were still understaffed. In the end I thought the situation had reached danger point and I wrote to the papers.' He gave a short bitter laugh. 'It was the start of my letter-writing career.'

'And?'

'The beginning of the end, although I didn't realise it at the time. From that moment on they made it their business to get rid of me, although I didn't realise *that* at the time either. Like I said, you come to things by fits and starts. I was shoved from one ward to another, forbidden to contact anyone in the media, not allowed to speak at meetings. In the end they held a tribunal — well a kangaroo court really — and I was dismissed.'

'For telling the truth about what was going on?'

'Yes.'

She burned with pity for him. 'That's monstrous.'

'Yes,' he said calmly. 'It was. I've lived through it now but it was. And of course it made me monstrous too. Eve used to say I had no time for anything but fighting the authorities and she was right. I don't think I noticed what was going on at home. Being persecuted consumes you. You think about it every waking moment, trying to get back at them or to work out what they're going to do next. And it's all a total waste of time because they hold all the trump cards.'

'So she walked out on you, is that it?'

'We parted by mutual agreement,' he said, and now there was no mistaking how bitter he was. 'I let her have the house, because Sally was still living at home, and I took my savings and came down here to get away from it all. I had to take whatever job I could. I was lucky this consortium took me on. They were the only ones to offer.'

'I think that's really awful,' she said.

He grinned at her in the moonlight. 'But then if I hadn't come down here, I shouldn't have met you,' he said, 'so it's not all bad. Do you realise your cat's lying on my feet?'

'You're honoured,' she said.

'My toes are going to sleep.'

'Only your toes?'

'Yes,' he said. 'You're right. We should be sleeping. We've been talking for hours. Good job it's Sunday. At least we can have a lie-in.'

'Goodnight then,' she said to him, nuzzling his shoulder.

'Love me?'

'Just a bit,' she teased.

'That'll do to be going on with,' he said, drowsy at last. Oh it would more than do to be going on with.

Chapter Twenty-Nine

Jeff and Laura weren't the only couple to indulge in a long lie-in that Sunday morning. After the celebrations and triumphs of the previous evening, David and Maureen had happy excesses to sleep off too. In fact nobody stirred in Canterbury Gardens until well after eleven o'clock and then the first riser was Danny.

He crept into his sister's room, rather daunted by the silence in the house. It wasn't like the parents to sleep all morning — even on a Sunday.

'It's ten past eleven,' he said, when he'd nudged Jessica back to consciousness. 'Do you think they're all right?'

She groaned. 'Go and look, if you're so worried. They're most probably tired, like I am.'

Danny wasn't too sure about invading the privacy of the master bedroom, but he inched the door open, very very gently, and satisfied himself that both his parents were sleeping peacefully. Then he went downstairs to get himself something to eat. By the time he'd made a pot of tea and burnt two lots of toast, Jessica came yawning into the kitchen to join him.

'Ought we to wake them?' he wondered.

'No. Leave them be.'

'What about our bikes?'

'*What* about our bikes?'

'They're at Gran's. Mum said she'd drive us over to collect them.'

'No problem. We'll walk over and get them.'

Danny was horrified by such a suggestion. 'Walk!' he objected. 'But it's miles!'

His sister gave him a scathing look. 'You are a wimp!' she mocked. 'Your feet haven't fallen off, have they. It's four miles, that's all.'

'It's miles more than four!'

'Four and a half then. Don't whinge! It'll do you good.'

So they walked to Holm End. And were surprised to find that their grandmother had only just got up too. The cats were in the kitchen, happy at their bowls, the table was set with her nice green cloth and there was a brown vase full of daffodils next to the milk jug. Jeff Turner had come to visit her and was cooking the breakfast, which Danny thought really nice of him. Bacon and eggs. It smelt really appetising.

'Have you had breakfast?' Jeff asked, noticing the appreciative sniffing.

'Only toast,' Danny said, eyeing the bacon.

'And he burnt *that*,' Jessica told them.

So they had bacon and eggs with the others, sitting in the midday sun round Laura's loaded table, and Laura made a pot of coffee just for them. All three cats came to the table to mump for bacon rinds and Queenie condescended to sit on Jessica's lap. It was a happy family meal. And naturally they talked about the procession.

'It was on the ten o'clock news,' Danny said. 'Did you see it Gran? Dad let us sit up. It was a bit dark but you could see all the torches and the reflection in the pond and everything. And they showed a bit of you talking.'

Laura sent a quick eye message to Jeff, who responded equally quickly. 'No,' she admitted. 'I forgot all about the news.'

'Never mind,' Danny said, helping himself to more coffee. 'We've got it on video. You can see it at tea-time.'

But Jessica had intercepted the messages. 'Why didn't you see it last night?' she asked, eyebrows raised.

'We had a mugging,' Laura explained. 'I'd forgotten you missed it. I was assuming you knew.' And she told them all about it.

They were deeply impressed and Danny pressed for all the gory details. Did they hold her under? Was she unconscious? Did she have to have stitches? Did she recognise them? Were they masked? Did they have guns? What did the police say?

'Don't tell your father,' Laura warned, 'or he'll have kittens.'

'Don't worry,' Jessica said. 'We won't, will we Danny. Poor Mrs Garston! She must have been upset.'

'I ought to go over the road and see how she is,' Laura said. 'I feel a bit guilty really getting up so late.'

'We'll all go,' Danny offered.

But at that point the dogs began to bark.

'What a racket!' Jeff said.

'It's only Molly's dogs,' Laura told him. 'They always bark at strangers. She'll quieten them in a second.'

But several seconds went by and the barking grew louder and markedly more frantic.

'You don't think the muggers have come back,' Danny hoped.

The thought had occurred to Jeff and Laura. 'You stay here,' Jeff said, 'and I'll go and see.'

He was halfway across the lane when Mr Fennimore came out of his front door with a stick in his hand.

'Damned varmints!' he shouted.

'Have you seen them?' Jeff shouted back.

'They wants locking up, the whole damn lot. She's out there looking. I'd set the dogs on 'em.'

Molly was in the compound at the far end of their scruffy half acre, calming her animals. There was no sign of any muggers and now Jeff could hear what the problem was. Engines.

'They're up the other end of the footpath,' Molly said, patting the head of the nearest growling dog. 'Where it comes out on the road. Shush, shush, shush, Merry. You're all right. That's a good gel. You don't reckon they're starting work on this road, do you?' Her round face was wrinkled with anxiety.

'We'll go up and see,' Jeff said.

They went as a group, for safety and mutual encouragement, Jeff and Laura leading the way.

What they found cast them into despair, even though they were partly prepared for it. The end of the footpath had been roped off, there were traffic cones all along one side of the main road and two JCBs were already gouging out a deep trench on one side of the adjoining field. They'd knocked down the old stile, and tipped a telegraph pole out of alignment, and now they were tearing out the hedges and ripping through the edge of the cornfield, in a careless orgy of mechanical destruction.

The little group watched in silence for a very long time, appalled at the speed with which a machine could devastate their landscape. We declared war on them last night, Laura thought, and this is the answer. Now we're in the firing line. Her stomach knotted at the thought of all the dreadful things that would happen when the battle began, of bodies being dragged from the machines and hurled to the ground, of flailing limbs and screaming mouths, of heads bleeding and faces white with shock. But it would have to be done. They were committed to it now, hideous though it was.

Jeff watched her face, knew what she was thinking and put an arm round her shoulders to comfort her. 'I *did* warn you,' he said.

'I know,' she said. 'I never take any notice of warnings though, that's my trouble.' She was still looking at the earth-movers. 'It's such a wicked waste. All those years to grow a tree and they root it out of the ground and kill it in seconds.'

A blackbird was piping his frantic, useless warning from a neighbouring ash and a flock of finches watched anxiously from the lower branches, for the hedges had just come into leaf and there were new nests among the fallen branches.

'Poor things,' Connie murmured. 'All their hard work gone for nothing.'

'And ours,' Mr Fennimore said. 'That hedge took upkeep.'

Joan Garston touched the tender skin around her black eye. Now that her bruises were coming out she felt better than she'd done the night before and more angry. 'What buggers they are,' she complained. 'I never thought they'd start so soon. They don't give you a chance to breathe.'

'It'll be us next,' Molly said sadly. 'What *are* we going to do?'

Laura's anger had solidified into determination. She thought for a few minutes, taking stock of the situation. 'They'll have to cut all the trees down that side before they get to us,' she said, 'so we'll build tree houses and put people up there to stop them.'

'People?' Mr Fennimore said. 'There's only six of us, gel. We'll never stop those things with only six of us.'

'I'll make some phone calls,' Laura said. 'We're not the only ones opposed to this road. Look how many were here last night.'

Mr Fennimore snorted. 'Walking about with a candle's one thing, living up in a tree's another.'

467

Laura was already on her way back to the cottage. 'I can but try,' she said. 'I shall phone Freda for a start.'

But Freda's phone was heavily engaged that afternoon and after dialling four times without success she started to ring round to other people too. And began to suspect that Mr Fennimore's opinion could well be right. Most of the people she talked to were sympathetic but none could help her, for various predictable reasons.

Toddy said he'd come if he could but he couldn't leave the kids to Sharon all the time. 'I'll tell the others,' he promised Laura. 'Pass the word, sort a' thing.' But his friends were all parents too as Laura knew only too well. The lollipop lady said she'd *love* to join them but with an arthritic hip she didn't think she'd be able to climb very far. 'I'll make tea and soup if you like,' she offered. 'I really enjoyed that soup last night.' Toddy's next-door neighbour offered to send his fourteen-year-old son but said he couldn't do much himself. In the entire afternoon she only found one couple who were prepared to help, and even they said it would have to wait until they got home from work on Monday evening.

Although she put a brave face on it, Laura was depressed by so many refusals. But at last she got through to Freda.

'I *am* sorry to hear that,' Freda said. 'You're right of course. You must take to the trees. They don't like felling trees when there are people in them.'

'Could you send someone to help us?' Laura hoped. 'I'll do what I can but all this is new to me and I'm sure there's a right way to set about it.'

'Kapok would be the best,' Freda said, 'but I don't know where she is at the moment. I'll do what I can but we've got horrendous problems here — I expect you've heard about them — so I can't promise to be very quick.'

'No. I haven't heard,' Laura said, heart sinking. 'What problems?'

'The Ministry are taking us to court,' Freda told her. 'Seventy-six of us. They say we owe them £1.9 million.'

Laura was horrified. 'Good God, whatever for?'

'Delays and damages, would you believe.'

'But that's monstrous. You can't possibly pay a sum like that.'

'No, of course we can't. They're intimidating us. We all know that. But it's very worrying. Most of us have got houses, you see, and they might force us to sell to realise the capital.'

'What are you going to do?'

'We don't know yet,' Freda said. 'We're working on it.'

Which is why you were so difficult to reach, Laura understood. And why you won't have time to help us now.

'We're on our own,' she said to Jeff when she put the phone down.

'So I gather.'

She was looking at the clock. 'You children ought to be getting back,' she said, 'or your

469

mother will wonder what's become of you.'

'Are you coming with us?' Danny wanted to know. 'It's Sunday tea.'

Laura rubbed her face, wearily. She'd forgotten. She'd actually forgotten Sunday tea. 'No, I'm sorry, Danny. I don't think I can. Make my excuses, will you. Tell them what's going on. They'll understand.'

Jeff was worried by her weariness. 'Come out for a walk,' he said. 'You could do with a breath of fresh air. You've been bent over that phone all afternoon.'

'I'll just see the children off,' she said. 'Then I might.'

'They can see themselves off,' Jeff said firmly. 'Can't you, kids? Right. Get your coat and we'll go out through the back gate.' That route would put two fields of peaceful countryside between her and the roadworks — and give them the chance to be alone together.

It surprised her grandchildren that she didn't argue with him, but found her wellies and put on her coat and hat as obedient as a child.

'She *is* down,' Jessica said as they wheeled their bikes into the lane. 'Poor old Gran!'

'That's because they're all letting her down,' Danny said. 'I think they're scumbags, the way they're all going on.'

'So do I,' Jessica told him, 'but what can *we* do about it? I mean, we'll help her but she needs hundreds of people — well, scores anyway — and we can't do much about them.'

'No,' Danny admitted, 'but I know a man who can. Come on.'

'Where to? I thought we were going home.'

'The fat man's.'

'Why?'

'He's on the Internet.'

The fat man's house looked dark and unoccupied but after a few minutes Joan Garston came shuffling to the door to let them in.

'I thought you'd've gone home long since,' she said.

Danny explained what they wanted but she trailed back into her narrow kitchen as though it didn't concern her. She seemed to be cooking a late Sunday dinner. 'I'm all behind today,' she explained as she basted the joint. 'Like the cow's tail. He won't let you in. Not after last night.'

'Can I try?'

Joan wiped her nose on the back of her hand. 'If you like,' she said, adding dourly, 'Won't do you no good though.'

Sure enough, the fat man was surly and wouldn't answer the door.

'I'm starving,' he growled. 'You go down an' tell her. I want my dinner. Ask her what she's playing at?'

'She's just dishing up now,' Danny said, craftily. 'She said I could come up and ask your advice while she was making the gravy.'

'What advice?'

Danny grinned at his sister. 'If you let me in I'll tell you.'

'How long's she going to be, damned woman?'

'Five minutes,' Danny lied. 'Just nice time.'

The door was opened, not just grudgingly but with considerable difficulty. In fact there was only just enough room for Danny to squeeze through the crack and he had to kick a mound of discarded tins aside to be able to do that. Jessica stood on the landing wrinkling her nose against the stink.

Ken peered out at the pale gleam of her blonde hair. 'Who's that?' he wanted to know.

'Only my sister.'

'Tell her to bugger off,' Ken growled. 'I'm not a peep show.'

'I'll wait for you downstairs,' Jessica said. 'And don't be long or you'll catch something nasty.'

'Good riddance,' Ken said as he pushed the door shut again. 'We don't want women in here. This is man's work.'

'Right!' Danny agreed, finding a clear bit of floorboard to stand on. 'Now, you know you showed me how quickly you could get a message out on the Internet. Well . . .'

Left on her own on the musty landing, Jessica tossed her hair and felt annoyed. What a disgusting man! she thought. A real male chauvinist pig! *'We don't want women in here.' He's* pigging it in a stinking attic and *she's* downstairs cooking food for him, stupid woman. I'd let him starve and see how he liked that.

Joan was prodding potatoes and grumbling to

herself in the kitchen. 'Well?' she asked.

'He said yes.'

'Wonders'll never cease.'

Now that she'd smelled the attic, Jessica was curious about its occupant. 'Doesn't he ever come out of there?'

'Nope,' Joan said shortly. 'Take an earthquake to get him out now. Well look at the way he went on last night. Wouldn't so much as put his head round the door to see how I was an' he must've heard the doctor come.'

Jessica disliked him even more. 'It must have been awful,' she said.

Sympathy was enough to launch Joan off into her recital. She'd told the story so often now — to the police, the doctor, and twice each to all her neighbours — that she had it down to a fine art. She knew when to pause and look knowing, when to sigh and look pained, how to end on a flourish. 'It's a wonder I wasn't killed.'

Jessica listened politely, as she observed the greasy squalor of the kitchen and felt sorry for the woman working in it. Poor Mrs Garston, she thought, noting the lank hair and the sallow skin, the awful mauve cardigan. 'Good job you got away from them,' she said.

'Well, between you an' me,' Joan told her confidentially, 'I don't think they were very bright. They'd got it into their heads I was afraid of water, see. Kept telling me they were going to drown me. Daft beggars. They thought I'd give in if they said they were gonna throw me in the pond. One of 'em kept saying, *"You won't like that."* Daft. I'm a good swimmer, though I sez it as shouldn't. When they threw me in, I just swum to the other side. That's how I got away.'

'Perhaps they mistook you for my gran,' Jessica said. 'She's afraid of water.' Then she thought that sounded disloyal and amended it. 'Well not afraid, exactly, but she doesn't like it.'

Joan wasn't interested. This was her story and her adventure. 'Is she?' she said vaguely. 'No. It was *me* they wanted. The police reckoned they lay in wait up there 'til I was on my own. It was *me* they were after, right enough.'

Danny was in the doorway, looking pleased with himself. 'Well that's done,' he said cheerfully. 'Come on, Jess. Thanks for letting us in Mrs Garston.'

Jessica followed him, thinking hard. What if they had been after Gran? What if they came back? We ought to warn her. She's safe for the moment because Jeff's with her but she never locks the door. People wander in and out all the time. They could get in whenever they wanted.

'Look,' she said, as they pedalled to the end of the lane. 'I think we ought to go back.'

Now that his mission was accomplished, Danny was eager to get home. 'What for?'

'We ought to warn her to keep her door locked. What if the muggers came back? She's all on her own up there.'

'No, she's not,' Danny said easily. 'She's got Jeff with her. He'll keep the door locked. Anyway

474

there'll be hundreds of people with her in an hour or two.'

It sounded comforting but highly unlikely. 'You're so thick sometimes,' she said. 'How can you possibly know that?'

They'd reached the end of the lane and were negotiating the intersection. Danny balanced one foot on the tarmac and peered to left and right. 'Thick yourself!' he said. 'The fat man got through.'

Out in the darkening fields, Laura and Jeff were strolling arm in arm along the narrow footpath towards the farm-shop where Joan Garston worked. Ever since the mugging, Jeff had been feeling very protective towards his new love and, now that there was no one else to hear her, Laura could admit how depressed she was.

'You chose a hell of a time to get involved with me,' she said.

'I think the time chose us,' he told her, 'not vice versa.'

'Well whatever. I shall be terrible company for you.'

'Let me be the judge of that.'

'No really,' she said. 'It's knocked me sideways that no one will help us. I suppose I'm facing up to the fact that we might lose. I've never let it enter my head until this afternoon, you see. But Mr Fennimore could be right. What can seven people do against the Ministry of Transport?'

'This is a war,' he said, 'and there's pattern to

life when you're at war. I know. I've been there. You get obsessed.'

'Tell me about it!'

'Exactly. And when you're obsessed you don't see straight. Eve was always telling me that and she was right. Most of the time you fight without thinking about anything except the next battle. If you think of defeat, you're halfway to being defeated. So you just keep off. It's only now and then you face all the possibilities. And then it's very hard. But you get over it. By tomorrow you'll be fighting again and your doubts will be behind you. Believe me. You won't have forgotten them but you'll have absorbed them.'

'You were defeated,' she remembered.

'I lost my job,' he corrected her. 'That's all it was really, when it came down to it. *I* wasn't defeated. They just pushed me out of my job. I came here. Got another one. Met you. Even if the worst comes to the worst, you'll still be alive, you'll still have your family and your friends, you'll still be a good librarian, you'll still have me — if you want me.'

It was a comfort of sorts but a very marginal one and the smile she gave him was bleak. 'I've always thought I led a charmed life,' she confided. 'After I nearly drowned that time, people used to say I'd been saved for a purpose, and I believed them. And then, when this road business began — I know it's probably vain and stupid to say so — but I thought *that* was the purpose. Yes, I know. It *was* vain. So it serves me right now it's all going wrong.'

'It's not going wrong,' he corrected. 'You've hit a set-back, that's all. There are always set-backs.'

Reason told her he was probably right but she was too down to accept it. 'If I can't get someone to come out tonight and help us, they'll have those trees out of the ground tomorrow morning before we can blink and then there'll be nothing to stop them knocking down our houses. After all our hard work and all our effort, we shall lose. It's brutal.'

'Authority *is* brutal,' Jeff said. 'I've known that all my life. Brutal and untrustworthy. The only authority you can actually depend on is your own. If I've learned nothing else in fifty-seven years, I've learned that.'

She gave his arm a squeeze. 'Is that how old you are?'

' 'Fraid so.'

'What am I going to do, Jeff?'

'Fight on.'

'Yes.' That was obvious. There'd never been any doubt about it.

'Let me look after you?'

'You can't stop the road for me though, can you?'

He stopped walking, turned her towards him and kissed her. 'I would if I could,' he said. 'I'll do my darnedest. You know that.'

She did and was touched by the knowledge.

'We'll get some sort of tree-house fixed up between us,' he said. 'You'll see. And if the worst comes to the worst, we'll chain ourselves to the trees.'

Yes, she thought. That was possible. Maybe he's right.

He kissed her again, holding her quietly as the new leaves shushed in the darkness. She stood in the circle of his arms and gave herself up to the illusion of being protected. It was an illusion, however much they would like it to be otherwise. She knew that. Who better? But it was comforting just the same. They *could* build a tree-house, somehow or other. They *could* chain themselves to the trees. The fight *would* go on.

'It's not over till the fat lady sings,' she said.

'Right!'

'Let's get back to the house,' she decided. 'I've thought of some other people I could phone.'

There were two scruffy strangers waiting for her in the garden, sitting side by side under the oak, bulky in army greatcoats and huge boots, the pale blue smoke from their cigarettes spiralling into the darkness of the branches. Not muggers — they were far too quiet for that — but not two of last night's demonstrators either.

'Hello!' she called to them.

The nearest figure stood up, brushed down its jeans and strode towards them. Now Laura could see that its hair was pillar-box red and that there were silver rings in its ears. 'I hear you got a problem,' she said. It was Kapok.

Laura had never been so pleased to see anyone in her life. 'Hello,' she said again. 'Did Freda tell you?'

Kapok turned to her companion who had ambled up to join her. Despite the bulky greatcoat, he turned out to be a gentle young man, tall and slight, with fair hair, freckles and the mildest of expressions and, as far as Laura could see in the half light, he seemed to be dressed entirely in green. 'It was e-mail, wasn't it Barney? This is Barney.'

'E-mail,' Laura said, astounded to hear it. 'Good God!'

'We use it all the time,' Barney smiled. 'It's our secret weapon.'

Jeff was introduced as Kapok lit another cigarette, shielding the flame in those familiar mittens of hers. 'Right,' she said, 'We'll get the others.'

This was getting more hopeful by the minute. 'Others?' Laura asked.

'There's seven of us,' Kapok told her. 'The rest are in the van. Can we park it in your drive? It's a bit obvious in the lane.'

It was a rusty transit, seriously overloaded, badly battered and caked with road dust. It had once been white but now it was covered with hand-painted rainbows, variegated flower-heads and doves of peace bearing olive branches. In short, it was the sort of vehicle that Laura would have recoiled from in horror less than a year ago. Now she opened the double gate to let it through, and stood back as the occupants scrambled out, feeling light-hearted with renewed hope.

They were dirty, scruffily dressed and full of energy, three young men, two young women and a baby called Jasmine, who was warmly asleep in a sling on its mother's back, like a papoose.

Kapok introduced them as they emerged, Vinny, a stocky Liverpudlian with the biggest boots and shortest haircut Laura had ever seen, Hen, a tall West Indian, who wore a Rastafarian beret balanced on top of an impressive set of dreadlocks, Chris, who carried the sleeping baby and was young, blonde and grubby, in dungarees and a holey jersey, Aysha, who wore a long flowery skirt, was small and wiry and spoke with a Birmingham accent. And finally . . .

'This is Rad,' Kapok said.

The man who stretched his long legs out of the van was tall and looked taller because he was wearing a long leather coat over patched jeans and a torn, grey vest. He had a walkie-talkie round his neck, designer stubble on his chin and light brown hair twisted into stringy dreadlocks. Laura recognised him at once. He was the man whose appearance had horrified her so much when she first saw him, the man who'd been organising the demonstrators at Twyford Down on her first visit there.

She held out her hand to welcome him. 'I'm very glad to see you,' she said.

He started organising them the minute he'd been introduced. 'How many of you are there?'

'Seven,' Jeff told him.

'That's good,' he said. 'Fourteen'll make a good team. Can we put our benders in your garden? Right. Then let's have a look at these roadworks.'

Jeff and Laura led their new allies through the darkness under the trees, past the black pond to the scar on the landscape.

'This is going to be a roundabout,' Rad said. 'They'll probably get that built and out of the way first, which will give us a bit of leeway. On the other hand they might be going to work from both ends. Have you had your compulsory purchase order? No. Right. That's good. It buys time. And that's what we need at the moment. So. We'll have a look-out built here first. What d'you think Barney?'

'With fourteen of us, we can have that up tonight,' Barney said. 'No problem.'

Laura could feel her energy returning in full force. 'Show us what to do,' she grinned at them, 'and we'll do it.'

Chapter Thirty

'What the hell is that?' the truck driver said. It was early Monday morning and the contractors were gathering for work. He had just climbed into his dumper truck and given his customary quick glance round the site before he switched on the ignition. Now he was staring up at a chestnut tree at the edge of the wood, where the new look-out post was wedged in a precarious and ungainly position.

'Bird's nest?' his mate suggested. He had a point. It was a ramshackle affair of old planks and dead wood and, from a distance, not unlike a rook's nest.

'Fucking kids.' another driver offered. 'That's what.'

The foreman was none too pleased. 'It's a bloody hippy,' he said. 'That's all we need. I can see him moving about, under the tarpaulin. Where do they get all their bloody junk from? He's got that bloody awful stringy hair. Look! There he is. See him. A bloody black hippy.'

'Shall we call Security?' the truck driver asked.

'No,' the foreman decided. 'Leave him be. He might pack up and go of his own accord. You never know. He'll be easy enough to shift if we have to. That lot 'ud fall down if you fucking sneezed at it.'

The bloody black hippy was using his mobile phone to report back to Rad. 'They seen me, man,' he said laconically. 'They t'inking about it.'

Rad was squatting just inside the entrance to his bender. 'No action?' he checked.

'No. Jus' t'inking.'

'Keep me posted,' Rad instructed. 'Barney'll be up presently with the rope ladder. Your breakfast's cooking.'

The benders were the first things Laura saw when she drew the bedroom curtains that morning. There were three of them, set side by side, and looking like gypsy caravans without their wheels or miniature versions of the Nissen huts she'd seen on army camps just after the war. But, as she knew having watched their assembly, their outward appearance was deceptive. Inside they were neat and well equipped, with carpets and cooking pots, a carry-cot for the baby and even a miniature television set run from a battery.

She was stiff from all the hard labour of the night but not tired, which was a surprise. It had lifted her to build that look-out post, out there in the dark, with Jeff and her neighbours working alongside her, hauling dead branches and carrying up ropes and sheets of cardboard, while Rad, Hen and Kapok hammered and assembled. Even though it was a bit rickety and Rad said it would have to be improved in the morning, she thought it was a job well done. Now she was alive with energy and her head was full of plans.

'I've been thinking,' she said, as she and Jeff ate their breakfast. 'There's a lot of wood going spare on all those boarded up windows. It's not particularly good but we could use it for the tree houses.'

'So it's vandalism now, is it?' he teased.

'Why not?' she said, drinking tea. 'It's only a keep-out sign and nobody round here needs to be told to keep out. The Colonel doesn't want it. He's shut those houses down.'

'I shall have to go to Worthing to get some clean clothes,' Jeff said, 'or I'd stay here and help you prise it off.'

The postman was walking by the kitchen window, waving a brown envelope and pointing at the kitchen door. 'Hang on!' she called to him and went to open it.

'I reckon this is from the council,' he said, putting the envelope into her hand. 'Could be your compulsory purchase.' And waited while she opened it.

It was a shock even though she'd been expecting it. She read the words, her heart suddenly racing. The council were sorry to have to inform her that her house was now the subject of a compulsory purchase order. They would be grateful if she would vacate the premises by . . . The date swam sideways from the paper. That's Wednesday week, she thought, a momentary panic squeezing her chest. Two days before Good Friday. That can't be right. They can't expect us to move just before Easter. But they did. There was no doubt about the date. They wanted her to be out of her house in nine days.

'Bad news?' the postman commiserated.

'If I take it seriously,' she told him, 'which I'm not going to do.'

'Quite right,' he agreed. 'You fight the buggers. If you'll excuse my French.'

But nine days, she thought, as she closed the door and took the letter to the table to show Jeff. 'How could I possibly get out in nine days?' she said to him when he'd read it. 'It would take me longer than that to pack. And it's Easter.'

He took the news calmly. 'But you're not going to get out, are you,' he said. 'They've forewarned you, that's all. You know when they're going to arrive which is all to the good.'

'Here's the others coming,' she said, glancing out of the window. 'I hope they're not too upset.'

But she needn't have worried about them. Although they arrived waving their letters, like her, they'd decided to ignore them.

'We won't have to move will we?' Connie asked. She couldn't help being anxious despite the energising fury all round her. 'I haven't told my John yet. He's gone milking. We won't have to though will we?'

'Not once the barricades are up,' Laura told her.

'They can't knock my house down,' Joan said grimly, 'not with *him* in the attic. I shall tell 'em *that* an' see how they like it.'

485

'Don't take any notice of 'em,' Molly advised. 'Saucy beggars! If they think I'm getting out by Wednesday week they got another think coming. I shall set the dogs on 'em.'

'They wants shooting,' her husband growled. 'The whole damn kit and caboodle. I wish I'd kept my gun.'

'I'd rather have a crowbar than a gun,' Laura said. 'You haven't got one of those have you?'

He had and was delighted to say so. And when she told then, what she needed it for he was even more delighted. 'That's the style,' he said. 'Beat 'em at their own game. They put the damn things up so we'll take 'em down. I'm all for it.'

'I'll go out presently and tell the others,' Laura said, checking the time.

Joan looked at the clock too. 'I've got to be at the shop in ten minutes,' she said. 'Tell 'em I'll be back as soon as I can make it.'

The demands of the day drove them on, Jeff to Worthing, Molly to feed her dogs, Connie to cook breakfast for her returning dairyman, Mr Fennimore to find his crowbar.

'You've got a date now,' Jeff reminded them as he left. 'You can plan your campaign.'

That was Rad's opinion too when Laura took her letter down to the benders. 'They haven't given us very long,' he said, 'but it's long enough.'

'We've done a recce,' Kapok told her, 'and the situation is this. They'll have to cut a swathe of trees from the edge of the wood right down to the lane. There's an oak in the garden at the far end that ought to be protected . . .'

'That's the Fennimores',' Laura said.

'Who owns the house?' Rad wanted to know.

'He does.'

'Great. Then that's where we'll start. If he owns the house and garden, he owns the tree, and if he owns the tree, he's got the right to put a tree-house in it.'

'There's a horse chestnut at the other end of the terrace,' Kapok said. 'Who owns that?'

'The Garstons.'

'Perfect,' Rad said, giving them a devilish grin. 'Then we'll use that too.'

'I've got to go to work now,' Laura told them. 'But I'll see if I can take some time off this week and I'll definitely be off on the Wednesday. I've got some leave owing so it shouldn't be too difficult.'

'What will you do if they say no?' Kapok asked, grinning.

'Be ill,' she said succinctly. 'There's my phone number in case you need it. You've got a mobile, haven't you. I shall be back about six. I'm going to Sainsbury's to stock up the freezer and buy something tasty for supper tonight. I shall cook a meal for you all every evening and you're to be my guests. It's the least I can do the way you're all helping me.'

'Thanks,' Rad said, rubbing the stubble on his chin and smiling at her. 'We appreciate it.'

She checked her watch. It wouldn't do to be late if she was going to ask for time off. 'Is there anything else you need while I'm shopping?'

The answers came very quickly. 'Nails, planks, rope.' And Kapok added, 'Ciggies.'

'Give me a list of what you want,' she offered, 'and I'll get it for you.'

It took more time and was a longer list than she expected, for once they started to write it, they thought of all sorts of other things they needed too, like baby milk and nappies, and tea and potatoes.

'Good job I've got a Land-Rover,' she said to them, thinking she'd let herself in for considerable expense. But you don't stint expenses when you're at war and any outlay would be worth it for their expertise alone.

They came to the gate to see her off, waving to her cheerfully.

'See you tonight,' they called.

'You won't know the place,' Kapok promised, waving a mittened hand.

Never a truer word spoken. By six o'clock when she finally drove her loaded Land-Rover into the drive, the trees at either end of the terrace were full of constructions, two tree-houses, well under way, several rope ladders and a walk-way swinging precariously from the chestnut out into the woods like something from all old Tarzan movie. Kapok and Barney took her on a tour of inspection, well pleased with their work.

'The boards were a godsend,' Kapok told her, 'and we've taken the back doors too.'

Oh dear! Laura thought. Now that *is* vandalism. But she didn't comment. Worrying about it was simply the residue of her middle-class morality and she'd left all that behind when she took on the campaign. Besides, all's fair in love and war.

'How d'you get on with your leave?' Kapok wanted to know.

'It was a compromise,' Laura told her. 'I've got Wednesday and Thursday off this week and I'm running a bit of my annual holiday into Easter. It's the best I can manage.'

'Your neighbours have been up and down all day,' Barney told her. 'Joan's brought us all sorts of stuff from the farm-shop and Mr Fennimore's a star. He's been in the trees all day.'

And there he was, still in the trees, even though it was nearly dark, and grinning all over his face. 'Works a treat, does this!' he called to her and swung down along the rope ladder, nimble as a monkey. 'I'm on look-out duty tonight. What d'you reckon to that?'

'What can I say?' she laughed back at him. At which point there was a clink of harness and Vinny, the dark-haired Liverpudlian, went abseiling immediately above their heads. 'Good God!' she said.

'It's quite safe,' Barney reassured her. 'He knows what he's doing. He's a mountaineer.'

But of course, Laura thought. Nothing would surprise her about these new friends of hers now. 'And what are you?' she asked him. 'When you're not fighting roads.' He had such skill with ropes

and tackle he had to have learned them somewhere.

'A boat-builder,' he told her. 'Till they closed
the yard. They don't want boat-builders nowadays. All the work goes to Germany.'

Such an assembly of unwanted talents, Laura
thought. 'Well you're very much wanted here,'
she said.

'Go on then,' Kapok grinned. 'Ask me what *I*
was.'

Laura accepted the challenge. 'What were you?'

'A nanny!' Kapok crowed. 'Dirty bums and
temper tantrums. Randy old dads. Mums with
plums in their mouths. The lot. A nanny. I'll bet
you never imagined that.' And she laughed for a
very long time.

Despite her misgivings about cooking for such
a large number of strangers, Laura's first meal
was a great success. Aysha and Kapok came over
to help her with the vegetables, Hen carved the
joint — *'used to be a chef, man'* — Jeff arrived just
in time to be served, baby Jasmine sat on her
mother's knee and ate tit-bits and the entire party
did the washing-up.

Just as they were settling down in front of the
fire for a final cup of coffee, the baby was enjoying
her bottle and Hen had teased all three cats back
into the room and was nursing Ace, Molly and
Joan arrived to tell them what an amazing day it
had been.

'Did you hear about *our* tree-house?' Joan
asked, pink with remembered excitement. 'The

door fell right out the tree just as Vinny was fixing a rope. Left him swinging on the end of it, didn't it Vinny?'

Vinny laughed at that, showing his white teeth. 'All in a day's work,' he joked.

The history of the day was still being told when two cars suddenly turned into the drive. It was Toddy with four of his neighbours come to see how they were getting on and to offer to lend a hand.

'Couldn't let you face all this on your own,' he said to Laura. 'Sharon's been on at me all day.'

'Not a lot you can do at the moment,' Rad told them. 'But you can help man the barricades when the troops move in.'

'Do we know when that'll be?' Toddy asked.

'Wednesday week,' Laura told him.

'What time of day?'

'They didn't say.'

'Early,' Rad told them, 'if I'm any judge.'

'We'll be there at the crack a' dawn,' Toddy promised. 'I'll spread the word. I got a mobile.'

But in the event, television did the job for him. On Wednesday afternoon, while Laura was helping to erect a third rope ladder — feeling quite at home in the branches — and Hen and Rad were fixing a tarpaulin over the first tree-house, the cameras arrived. They filmed the tree-houses and the walk-ways, the baby being fed up aloft, Hen in his Rasta beret, Aysha in her Indian skirt, Barney green among the leaves, Vinny ab-seiling through the branches, and down on the

ground, they questioned Laura and her neighbours about what they were hoping to achieve.

They got a five-minute slot on the evening
news. And not long afterwards, the phone began
to ring with offer of help.

'If this goes on, I shall have to take over as
permanent telephone girl,' Molly said, as she left
the cottage much later that evening.

'If this goes on,' Jeff said, when he'd taken yet
another call after all their guests had gone, 'I shall
take the damn thing off the hook.'

'I think it's marvellous,' Laura said. 'If only half
of them turn up on Wednesday we shall be well
away. You're just an old grouch, that's your
trouble. First you tell me you don't like kids and
now you've taken against phones.'

'It's all very well for you,' he grinned at her.
'You're running on neat adrenaline. I need my
sleep. And if that's being a grouch, OK, I'm a
grouch.'

The phone didn't ring quite so much the next
day. Molly stayed on duty most of the morning,
just in case, but after they'd had their midday
picnic crouched around Kapok's camp fire in the
clearing above the pond, she decided to join the
workers up aloft.

It was the first time she'd been up in the trees.
She was charmed by the view and spent a long
time spying out the land in all directions, declaring that she'd never realised how much ground
her half-acre covered.

'I can see all my dogs,' she said to Chris, who

had left her baby with Kapok and was now weaving a canopy for the look-out post. 'There they are look. Down there. Hark at 'em bark. Do you think they can see me?' But then she saw something that put her in a fury. 'Oh no!' she said, 'this I will *not* have.' And she went wobbling off along the rope walk as quickly as her bulk would allow, calling as she went, 'Dirty beggar! Laura! Come and look!'

'What is it?' Laura asked. She was perched in the fork of a tree hauling up a rope that Barney had just thrown up to her and she didn't want to be interrupted. But Molly was so insistent that in the end she handed over to Vinny to finish and joined her on the walk-way to see what was the matter.

Molly didn't tell her. 'Come on!' she panted. 'We're going down. Dirty beggar.'

They climbed down the rope ladder, ran along the lane and into Molly's garden, where the dogs were still barking the alarm.

'There you are!' Molly said, pointing at the bushes that edged the half acre. 'Look at that! Dirty beggar!'

One of the workmen was crouched in the bushes. At first Laura couldn't make out what he was doing. Then she realised that his jeans were heaped about his ankles and that he was relieving himself on the grass verge.

'Bloody sauce!' Molly hissed. 'I'll teach him to crap in my garden.'

They had reached the gate to the compound

and the dogs were running towards them, tongues lolling. 'Get'im!' she commanded and slipped the gate open.

The dogs were off in a split second, running and baying towards their quarry, golden fur rippling. Laura had a brief glimpse of the man's horrified face and then they were on him, tearing at his jeans, and snapping at his flailing arms and his bare backside. He hopped out of the bushes. 'Call 'em off, missus, fer fuck's sake. They'll do me a mischief.'

'Good!' Molly shouted. 'Serve you right, you dirty beggar!'

He was struggling to pull up his jeans and run at the same time. 'Call 'em off. They're fucking killing me.'

But she didn't call them until he'd pushed his way through the gap in the fence and was off her property. By then she was laughing so much it was all she could do to whistle.

'Oh my dear life!' she said. 'I 'ent seen anything as funny as that for years! Didn't he run! He won't do that again in a hurry. Wait till we tell the others.'

The story went the rounds all afternoon. And was told again after the evening meal because John and Connie, Jeff and Joan had been at work and missed it. It was much enjoyed and Molly told it well, with suitably vulgar gestures. Her imitation of the man hopping away with one hand clutching his jeans and the other doing duty as a fig-leaf was a sight to see.

So naturally when Danny and Jessica turned up it had to be told yet again for their entertainment. Danny thought it was wicked and laughed uproariously.

'I'd have loved to have seen it,' he told them.

'You should have filmed it,' Jessica said. 'You could have sent it to Jeremy Beadle.'

'We don't run to cameras on *our* side,' Kapok told her, snorting smoke out of her nose like a red dragon.

Jessica picked up the inference very quickly. 'You mean the other side do?'

'Right,' Kapok said. 'Use them all the time.'

'Like spies?' Danny asked.

'That's what they are,' Kapok said, curling her lip with scorn. 'The government hires them to spy on us.'

Jessica was beginning to get agitated. 'How do you know?' she asked.

'Everybody knows,' Kapok told her calmly. 'It's all quite open. They come from a detective agency called Hays. They've got branches all over the place. They're even in the Yellow Pages. You can look 'em up if you like. There's no secret about them. The government hires them to spy on us. They've been filming Twyford Down for years.'

Laura had a sudden vision of Kevin Marshall wielding his camcorder and wondered whether this was the right moment to say something about it. But the expression on Jessica's face made her think better of it. She looked guarded, as if she was aware she might be caught out, guarded and suspicious and agitatedly interested. She knows, she thought. Or she suspects. Oh poor girl.

'There's a court case coming up in a few weeks' time,' Rad was telling them. 'In Winchester. We're going there to give evidence for the defence. If they'll let us. The case for the Crown is almost entirely based on film evidence. They even used film to justify the arrests they made.'

'Like *Crimewatch*,' Danny offered, feeling he understood. 'People doing crimes.'

He was corrected gently. 'No,' Rad said. 'People on protest marches. People walking about on the Downs saying they don't want this road to be built. Ordinary people, like you and me and your gran. People who don't agree with what the Ministry of Transport are doing.'

Danny was puzzled. 'But that's not a crime.'

'It is now,' Kapok said. 'They're bringing this case to prove it.'

Jessica's wariness had broken into anger. 'But that's awful!' she said. 'What scumbags! Governments aren't supposed to spy on their own people. They're supposed to look after us, represent us, that sort of thing. Not spy on us. Can't somebody stop them?'

'Only by ballot box,' Barney said in his gentle way. 'And that's months away.'

'Gaw dearie me,' Molly Fennimore said, standing up and brushing down her skirt. 'Aren't you all serious! Who's for more coffee? Tell you what, Barney. Why don't you get your guitar and give us a tune? We need cheering up.'

So the evening shifted into music and song and politics were temporarily forgotten.

'I feel as if I've had four parties in a row,' Laura said when their guests had finally gone and she and Jeff had the cottage to themselves. She was sitting at her dressing table in her nightdress, brushing the tangles out of her hair. Her head was bent forward so that the debris from her day in the trees would fall into her lap and she was wielding the brush so vigorously that her hair crackled.

Jeff was already in bed, watching her from the pillows. 'Well you have,' he said.

She paused in her work and looked across at him, her hair brushed about her face. 'I know this is going to sound like a silly thing to say,' she told him, 'but I'm actually quite enjoying this. I know it's going to be dreadful when the bailiffs move in and I'm worried about that, naturally — even a bit frightened sometimes — but the preparation for it is marvellous. I wouldn't have missed it for worlds. It must have been like this during the war, this sense of being part of a community all working for the same ends, singing songs and sitting round a camp fire, sharing things.'

'Danger sharpens your senses,' he told her.

'Yes,' she said, brushing her hair to rights again. 'I suppose that's it. We're all experiencing everything in sharp focus. It gives a zest to things.'

'You're a beauty,' he said, admiring her. 'Do you know that?'

'I have my moments,' she agreed, enjoying the admiration.

'Come to bed and have another moment then,' he suggested.

Chapter Thirty-One

His mother might be enjoying her new eventful life among the tree-houses but to David Pendleton that week was one of the longest and most difficult he'd ever known. The nearer she was drawn to conflict, the more distressed he became, driving in to work every morning wondering whether or not he would be fired during the day, driving back every evening, still hired but worn to a frazzle. While he was out on the road or pressurising his clients to buy more than they intended, his life felt normal if increasingly unethical, but in the office he lived on tenterhooks, pretending to work but actually waiting for the moment when Mr Cosgrave would sidle by his desk and ask him if he *'had a minute'*. It was impossible to concentrate on his accounts, which all had to be done three times to check for errors, and his order book was a shambles. He was short-tempered with his colleagues and irritable at home.

On Wednesday evening, when he watched the news and saw his mother's interview and all those ghastly hippies parading about in the trees in their ghastly clothes, his heart sank with the certainty that his career was over. On Thursday when *'Laura's struggle'* was front-page news in the local paper, the words shattered into a migraine as he read. By Friday afternoon he was so tense his hands were shaking as he typed.

It was almost a relief when Mr Cosgrave arrived with his inevitable request. He followed the man into his office like a sheep to the slaughter.

'Do sit down,' Mr Cosgrave said, giving him his artificial smile.

David sat heavily, automatically smoothing the short hair on his neck. This was it, the moment he'd been dreading all week. The moment he'd been dreading since September. He was for it now.

'I've asked you to see me,' Mr Cosgrave began, 'because the management would like me to tell you that they feel the time may have come for you to review your career prospects with this company. This is in no way a reflection on the quality of your work within the company you understand . . .' David nodded bleakly. 'It is more a question of your suitability for this particular environment, where an unequivocal acceptance of company policy is of the essence.'

The words arrived in David's ears and slid away from his understanding. He felt in his pocket for the reassuring oblong of his letter, drew it out and laid it on the desk before him, ready. He hadn't got the energy to interrupt Mr Cosgrave in full pompous flow. He would wait for a pause.

Mr Cosgrave oiled on. There was a fly crawling across the grey top of his computer screen. It stopped halfway, balanced itself delicately on its four hind legs and began to clean its head, rotating it vigorously between legs like small thorned twigs. I never realised flies had spikes on their legs, David thought, observing it. Nor that their wings were such pretty colours, fluorescent green, like petrol in a puddle. It's giving that head a real going-over. Then he realised that the weight of his long subservience to the firm was lifting as he watched. I shall never have to agree with this man again, he thought. Never take another of his fatuous orders. Never sit through another diatribe. Never watch those irritating fingers propped under that irritating nose. I can tell him what I think. He may be giving me the sack, but once it's done I'm free of him. I'm being liberated.

'We felt you should know our feelings,' Mr Cosgrave said. 'In your own interest naturally.' And paused.

David picked up the envelope and pulled out the letter. He was working slowly as if his fingers were made of lead, but he was quite calm. 'This is my letter of resignation,' he said, handing it across the desk. 'It makes my position quite clear, as you'll see. You are quite right. I don't see eye to eye with the policy of this firm. I know we produce some excellent products but I've never been happy about high-pressure selling. I do it well but it's against my nature. Trade by half-truth and exaggeration has always seemed unethical to me. If there are known adverse side-effects to our products then I believe we should be open about them. Anything less is trickery. It's all in the letter.'

Mr Cosgrave's irritating jaw dropped visibly but his recovery was swift and brutal. He took the letter and read it briefly. 'Right!' he said. 'That's all perfectly clear. There's nothing more to be said, is there. I should be obliged if you would clear your desk by six o'clock this evening.'

And that was that. After months of anxiety and head-searching, it was all over in less than a minute.

'Well?' Barry Brough asked when he got back to the office. 'What happened?' All work stopped while they waited for his answer.

'I handed in my letter of resignation,' David told them. 'I preempted him. I've got to clear my desk by six this evening.' He felt deflated and completely exhausted.

'Christ!' Barry said, as the room erupted into horrified exclamations. 'What? Tonight you mean? Christ! They don't waste any time.'

David was already clearing his desk. It didn't take him long because it was always neat and well ordered. Personal files into his briefcase, framed portrait of Maureen and the kids, wrapped in paper to protect the glass and eased into the inner pocket, a quick flick-over with a duster and it was done.

'We'll have a quick one after work,' Barry commiserated. 'Eh fellers?'

The fellers thought a piss-up was called for. 'A proper send-off.'

'Maureen won't mind will she?' Barry checked. Being made much of had comforted David quite a lot, but the thought of Maureen brought him back to painful reality. When they met, he would have to face all the consequences of this dismissal, unemployment, job hunting, being on the dole, trouble with the mortgage. But he would face them later. When he got home. For the moment he would have a few drinks with his colleagues and forget it all. 'No, 'course not,' he said. 'It's her night for Sainsbury's.'

Since she'd taken up her new job, Maureen's weekly trip to Sainsbury's had become more and more of a chore. She usually managed to check the cupboards and write a list before she went to work on Friday morning but because this Friday was the last day of term, she'd been in such a rush she hadn't had time to do it.

It had been a difficult day, with far too many things to attend to after the kids had gone home, which they did at half past two at Burswood School on the last day of term. By half past five, when she finally got to the store, she was too tired to think straight — too tired to face shopping if the truth be told. She dithered by the breakfast cereals trying to remember whether it was Honey Nut Loops or Weetabix that was running short.

'Hello!' a voice said. 'Long time no see!'

She turned, blinking away her fatigue, to see a familiar face smiling into her line of vision. It was Kitty Ravelle, Emma's mother.

'Kitty!' she said. 'I haven't seen you in ages.'

'How's it going?' Kitty said. 'We were ever so pleased when you got the job.'

'It's hard work,' Maureen told her. 'I never get a minute to myself.'

They exchanged pleasantries while the other shoppers pushed their trolleys round the blockage they were causing — or into their legs.

'I really ought to have phoned you,' Maureen confessed. 'I've been meaning to for weeks. To thank you.'

Kitty looked surprised. 'Well it's nice to be thanked,' she said, 'but what am I being thanked for?'

'Putting up with Jessica,' Maureen explained. 'I mean, she virtually lives at your house these days. It's very good of you.'

Kitty didn't seem to have received the message. She stood quite still with one hand on the handle of her trolley, looking at Maureen thoughtfully, her head inclined, as if the weight of her auburn hair were tipping it sideways.

'Remind me,' she said. 'When was the last time?'

'The Saturday before last,' Maureen told her. 'She must have been good if you've forgotten so soon.'

'I haven't forgotten,' Kitty said. 'Oh dear, how can I put this. I haven't forgotten because she wasn't there. We haven't seen her for months. Emma's been quite cut up about it.'

'She's not been with you?'

'No. Sorry.'

Suspicion crawled into Maureen's belly and wriggled there. 'When was the last time she stayed over?'

'Way back. Before Emma's birthday and that was October. She's been telling you porkies.'

Maureen tried to pretend it didn't matter. 'Naughty girl.'

'A boyfriend?' Kitty asked.

'Oh I expect so,' Maureen said lightly, trying to sound as though it didn't matter. She was terribly upset, ashamed to have her daughter's faults revealed to a neighbour — even one as friendly as Kitty — disappointed that Jessica should go so far as to lie to them, angry and afraid at the thought of what she must have been doing. If she was lying, it had to be because she was out all night with that boy Kevin, and that could only mean sex. And wasn't that what she'd feared and dreaded all along?

'Sorry to be the bearer of bad tidings,' Kitty was saying.

'Not to worry,' Maureen smiled at her. 'It was bound to happen sooner or later.' But despite the smile she was seething.

She struggled on with her shopping but neither her heart nor her mind was on it. She simply wanted to get it finished so that she could get home and have it out with Jessica before any more harm was done. How could she have been so deceitful? she thought, as she hurled four tins of beans into her trolley. Or run such risks? The stupid, stupid girl! Sugar! Where's the sugar. I thought it was here. Don't forget the bacon. Soap. Oh God! Look at the queues at those checkouts. I shall be hours. Stupid, stupid girl!

The stupid girl had been at home all afternoon, up in her bedroom. As luck would have it, Danny had been out with his friends most of the time. He and Charles had come in at tea time to wolf their way through the biscuits but they weren't around for long and now they'd gone chattering off to their choir practice. So she was alone with her thoughts, sitting on the bed with her diary open across her knees and her long hair dangling on the page. She looked like a dreamy mermaid, but in fact, she was wrestling with her conscience.

The suspicion that Joan Garston had triggered in her mind in that horrid greasy kitchen had grown uncomfortably since last night's conversation with Kapok. She knew very well that the only people who knew about Gran's fear of water were the four members of her family. Five if you counted Amy, because she was family and probably knew too, but she wasn't there. Five, and one of them had talked. Not deliberately, she was quite sure of that, but sort of accidentally, in a conversation or something. It was an awful thing to have to face but if the muggers really *had* found out about it, it had to be through one of them. Knowing about the spies had clinched it. It hadn't occurred to her that the government would sink so low as to use paid spies against their own people but it was possible. And the more she thought about it, the more she realised that there was only one person who might have been told and that was Kevin. Because *she*'d told him. She was sure of it. She couldn't remember when, or why, but she knew she had.

It had worried her all day. What if it *were* Kevin. He'd shown a lot of interest in Gran. I thought he was being nice but what if he'd told someone else? He could have done. He might not have meant to make mischief — I'm sure he didn't — but he could have passed it on, sort of casually. The longer she worried the more likely it seemed. And she didn't want it to be likely.

As soon as she got home she went upstairs and began to check her diary. It was a bitter-sweet experience because she'd poured out her heart to that little green book and every page reminded her of how much she loved him. But some of the entries seemed ambiguous now.

'We went up to the pond and kissed among the trees. Very spooky. He took lots of pictures. He's going to give me one for a special Christmas card for Gran.' Now what happened to *that*? To be fair, she had to admit that she'd forgotten all about it, so she hadn't asked him for it, but he hadn't *offered* it. And they *had* talked about Gran's phobia. Nudged by her written word, she remembered it quite clearly.

She was balancing a bottle of nail varnish on her knee and painting her nails as she read. She took a brief pause from her investigations to enjoy the colour, a nice bright pink to match her earrings. If he loved me, she thought, he wouldn't be spying on my grandmother. And he did love her. There was evidence of that on every page.

There's probably some perfectly innocent explanation, she thought, stretching out the middle finger of her right hand and dipping the little brush awkwardly into the bottle with her left.

Just at that moment, the phone rang. The noise was so sudden and she was so tense that it made her start. Before she could prevent it, the varnish bottle tipped off her knee and drooled a long pink stain across the white duvet.

'Oh shit!' she said, caught between the need to answer the phone and the need to clean up the mess as quickly as she could. She seized a towel and dabbed at it, wild with guilt. Dad'll go spare when he sees. How do you get varnish off? What if it's gone through? The more frantically she worked, the worse she was making it. The colour was all over the towel, the stain on the duvet was twice its original size, and the phone was ringing like a mad thing.

She flung the towel over the stain and ran into her parents' bedroom to answer it.

'Hello gorgeous!' Kevin said. 'I thought you'd gone out.'

After an afternoon remembering him, the sound of his voice made her feel weak. He couldn't be a spy. It wasn't possible. 'No,' she said, breathlessly. 'I've been in all afternoon.'

'How about coming to Southampton?'

'When?'

'Tonight. I've been given a bonus.'

'What for?'

'Because I'm brilliant. What d'you say? Shall

508

we? We could go to a den of vice and spend all my ill-gotten gains on a night of debauchery and passion.'

'Yes,' she said, making rapid plans. I'll leave Mum a note. Put a pile of towels over the stain. I can clean it up when I get back. Yes. Yes.

'Be with you in five minutes,' he said.

He was at the house so quickly she'd only just had time to paint the two remaining nails and pack what little she needed in her overnight bag. She was wriggling down into the passenger seat before she remembered her coat and by then it was too late because he'd already put the car in gear. But it didn't matter. It was warm in the car. It was so good to see him that nothing else mattered in the world. He was the man she loved, admiring her with those odd pale eyes of his, licking his lower lip as though he was eating her in imagination, showing those straight white teeth. He took his hand off the gear-stick and pulled her towards him to kiss her. 'You look fucking gorgeous,' he said. No, he couldn't possibly be a spy.

He drove to Southampton at fantastic speed and they had sex as soon as they got to the flat. Afterwards, she lay in the tumbled bed feeling sleepy and satisfied while he went off for a shower. The rich reds of the duvet were a joy to look at. Beautiful and decadent. If my duvet had been this colour, she thought, no one would notice a little pink stain. And she hoped nobody *had*. Better not think about that.

'What are we doing tonight?' she called.

'Concert,' he called back.

'Where?'

'Tickets on the table,' he called above splashes. 'Have a look.'

There were no tickets on either bedside table, just his watch and a handful of coins and his wallet. But there was a piece of pinkish paper protruding from the wallet so she opened it out. It wasn't the tickets she expected but a cheque, a very large cheque, for £400, made out to K.K. Marshall and paid from the account of Hay's Detective Agency, Southampton.

She surprised herself by how cool she was. 'Kevin,' she called, casually. 'You know that bonus you told me about.'

'Yeh!'

'Have you really won it or were you kidding?'

'No. I won it. I told you.'

She kept her tone casual. 'Was it a lot?'

The chance to brag was too tempting. 'Four hundred.'

'Paid by Hay's Detective Agency,' she said, her voice suddenly flat with loathing. 'You're a spy.'

The taps were turned off. She could see him through the reeded glass, wrapping himself in a towel. 'Yes,' he said, stepping out of the shower. 'So?' There was no point in denying it. She was holding the cheque in her hand. He would just have to brazen it out.

She glared at him above the reds and blues of the duvet, her face pale and determined. 'You

510

said you worked for a construction firm.'

'So I do,' he said, drying his back. 'They hire me from the agency. It's no big deal.'

She sat among the violence of reds and blues, clutching the duvet to her nakedness and fought him angrily. 'You're a spy.'

He began to dress as though there were nothing the matter. 'I provide information. Right?'

'You're a spy.'

'Look,' he said, zipping up his jeans. 'I provide information. They pay me for it. Period. I don't ask them why they want it. I'm not interested. It's a job.'

'Do you ask them what they're going to do with this information?'

'No.'

'Don't you think you should?'

'No. I told you. It's up to them what they do with it. It's no concern of mine. I'm not interested.'

'Well I am,' she said fiercely, hugging her knees as though they were a shield. 'You told then my gran was afraid of water, didn't you? You told them she was afraid of water and they sent someone to the pond to threaten to drown her. That was *your* information.'

Being attacked made him insolent. 'So?'

'So? So? Is that all you can fucking say? My gran could have been drowned.'

'But she wasn't, was she?'

'No thanks to you.' She scrambled out of bed and began to dress, throwing on her clothes so rapidly that she pulled a button off her shirt.

'Now what?' he said.

'I'm going home,' she said. Her fingers were so stiff with fury that even the simplest action was hard. She hauled at the zip on her skirt, fought the arms of her jersey. 'I'm not staying here with you. You're a spy.'

'What about the concert?' he said.

She was dressed at last. 'Fuck the concert and fuck you,' she said, crammed her things into her bag and left. It was a terrible, inevitable, glorious moment.

It was only when she was halfway down the street that she realised she hadn't got the faintest idea where she was going and that she was very cold without a coat. But her fury had receded sufficiently for common sense to return. She remembered what her Geography teacher was always saying, *'All problems are capable of solution.'* She would have to catch a train, providing she had enough money for the ticket. It was ages since she'd last travelled on a train and she hadn't got any idea what the fares were, nor where the station was either. But there had to be road signs.

It took her a long time and a lot of walking before she reached the station which was down a long incline below a vast roundabout. By dint of scraping together all the coins in her purse, she managed the fare too. But it was a long wait for the next train to Worthing and by then she was shivering with cold.

There was a cafe but she didn't have enough

512

money to buy anything so she couldn't go in there: there was a waiting room but it was full of schoolkids giggling and being stupid, so she certainly wouldn't go in there either. She sat on the platform and watched the screens as they announced one train after another that wasn't any use to her. Her bare legs were covered in goosepimples, her fingers white with cold. She wanted to cry but it was too public for that. She wanted to go back to the flat and scream abuse at him for being such a shit. She wanted to go home.

Chapter Thirty-Two

It was just before seven o'clock that evening and spitting with rain when David and Maureen met on the doorstep, he flushed with distress, she dark with suppressed fury. They greeted one another with the same breathless words.

'I've got something to tell you.'

David deferred to his wife at once, glad to put off his confession and — although he would have been ashamed to admit it — secretly hopeful that her news would be bad enough to put his into a better perspective. She told him what she'd heard as they unpacked the groceries from the boot of her car and carried them into the kitchen. He was even more angry about it than she was, turning the rage he'd felt against his callous treatment into furious grievance against the weight of supporting two teenaged children.

'You slog your guts out to do the very best for them,' he said, as he put the heaviest box down on the kitchen table, 'and this is the way they repay you. Where is she? Sprawled in front of the telly I suppose, or upstairs playing that awful jungle music of hers.'

But there was no sound of her, sprawled or otherwise. Only a note written on her blue notepaper and propped against the white clock on the mantelpiece.

'Gone out with Kevin and the others. Will probably sleep over at Emma's. See ya. Luv, J'

Maureen was tense with anger and anxiety. 'There you are!' she said. 'She's doing it again. *"Sleep over at Emma's."* It's so bare-faced. And she'd been doing it for months. Ever since Christmas Kitty reckons. I thought we'd brought her up to be more honest than that.' And sleeping with Kevin all that time too. What if he's got her pregnant? Or given her some disease? It was too awful to think about. I thought I'd brought her up to be more honest than that.

David had noticed that his other child was missing too. 'Where's Danny?' he wanted to know. 'I suppose he's gone off somewhere too. They treat this house like a hotel.'

Maureen wasn't worried about Danny. 'Choir practice,' she said. 'It's Friday. He'll be back in time for dinner. He's no problem. *She* doesn't even bother to tell us when she's coming home. Just *"See ya!"* ' She felt so hurt by all this. To find out that her daughter was capable of deceiving her had been bad enough but to know that she could do it so easily was making her ache. 'It's so casual.'

'And ungrammatical.'

They put the groceries away, complaining all the time, but complaint was less and less comfort to them. Then Maureen went upstairs to put fresh soap and tissues in the family bathroom and on impulse, she checked Jessica's room to see what sort of state she'd left it in. She was annoyed to see a heap of used towels lying on the bed.

'Towels all over the duvet,' she grumbled, 'and I'll bet they're damp. She never stops to think.' She picked them up automatically, checked to see whether they'd been used or not, and started to fold them, ready to put them back in the bathroom. Then she saw the stain.

It was the last straw. 'Oh no, really this is too bad!' she cried. She was so upset, she was ready to weep. 'David! David! Just come and see what she's done now.'

'Totally selfish, that's her trouble,' David said, when he arrived in the room and had inspected the damage. 'She's got no idea of the price of things Never has had. We've spoilt her, Maur, let's face it. We should have taken her in hand years ago. Top of the range and she throws nail varnish all over it. Well it's got to stop, that's all. I shall have something to say to her when she gets back.'

'*When* she gets back,' Maureen said. He was right. They would have to make a stand.

Meantime there was a meal to cook although neither of them had any appetite for it. It was just as well that Danny came home from his choir practice saying he 'could eat a horse'. Neither of them said anything about Jessica as the meal proceeded. There was no need to burden him with their worries. He was too young to understand them in any case. Besides, it wasn't his fault she was behaving so badly.

'Would you like a second helping?' Maureen was saying to him, when there was the sound of a key in the front door and Jessica came dripping into the dining room, white with cold and looking very sorry for herself.

Her parents fell on her. 'What time do you call this?' David shouted. 'Have you any idea what a state your mother's been in?'

Danny was astonished by the onslaught. He looked at Jess to see how she would take it and was surprised to see that she was biting her lip and glancing rapidly from one parent to the other as if she was afraid of them. Why were they so angry? What was going on?

'Where have you been?' Maureen said. 'And let's have the truth this time, shall we.'

Jessica hesitated. She could ignore her father's red-faced rage but her mother was icy and that was dangerous. It was obvious that she'd been found out, that lying wouldn't work any more. She shrugged her shoulders and told the truth. 'Southampton,' she said. 'If you must know.'

'Yes, we *must* know,' her father shouted at her. 'You've told your last lie my girl, understand that. We know what you've been up to.'

Jessica was too depressed to be diplomatic. She fought back in the only way left open to her, by daring and rudeness. 'So I don't need to tell you then, do I?' she said, sticking her chin in the air.

The effect on her father was predictable. 'Don't you take that tone with me.'

'What tone should I take then?'

'Who were you with?' her mother said and her words were still weighted with ice.

Again the shrug. 'Kevin.'

'Damned little fool!' her father roared. 'You haven't got the sense you were born with. What's the matter with you girl?'

'I thought you liked him.'

'That's got nothing to do with it. There's a right way and a wrong way to behave, in case you're not aware of it. And you've been behaving in the wrong way.'

'Can I go and get changed?' Jessica said, as if the subject bored her. 'I came home on the train and I'm soaking wet.'

'And that's another thing,' David roared. 'You've ruined that duvet cover, I hope you realise. What were you thinking of to put nail varnish on your duvet? You must have been out of your mind.'

'I didn't put it on, it fell.'

'It shouldn't have been anywhere near the duvet. Have you any idea how much that cost?'

'I'll pay it back.'

'Pay it back!' he mocked. 'You couldn't begin to pay it back. You're a schoolgirl, let me remind you. Where would you get that sort of money?'

Tears pricked behind Jessica's eyes but she held her face rigid, determined not to weep. After all the awful things that had happened to her that evening, a fuss about a little spilt nail varnish seemed petty beyond words — and unkind, because she hadn't done it deliberately. All through

518

her miserable journey from Southampton and the long wet walk from the station, she'd buoyed herself up by thinking of home and how she'd be warm and safe once she got there. And this was the welcome she got. Well, he needn't think he can browbeat *me*, she thought. 'I could go on the game,' she said.

He was so angry to hear her say such a thing that he got up, walked round the table to where she stood and slapped her hard across the face. 'How *dare* you talk to me like that!' The echo of the slap resounded in his black and white room like a gunshot. It was the first time in their lives that he'd ever hit her and he was as shocked by it as she was.

The tears welled into Jessica's eyes but she still didn't weep. She lifted her damp hair away from her face and raised her chin in defiance. 'That's it,' she said. 'I can see it all now. You hate me. All right then. I'll go. I'll leave you. You needn't ever see me again if you hate me so much.' Then she was out of the room and out of the house before any of them could draw breath to answer her.

'Oh David, stop her!' Maureen said. 'She can't go running off like that. She's soaking wet.'

He was adamant. 'She should have thought of that.'

Danny had pulled the curtains aside and was looking out of the window. 'She's taken her bike,' he reported.

'She'll get run over,' Maureen worried. 'Going

off in a state like that. Don't you think we ought to go after her?'

David was so far into his rage he was beyond reason or compassion. 'No, I don't,' he said. 'She's made her bed now she must lie on it.'

'It's *pouring* with rain,' Danny reported from the window.

'Good. Let her get wet. Maybe it'll bring her to her senses.'

'But . . .' Maureen began.

'She'll be back,' he interrupted with a confidence he didn't feel. 'She can't stay out for ever. Let's finish our dinner, eh. Danny was going to have second helpings, weren't you old son.'

His bonhomie fell flat. 'Well no,' Danny said. 'I don't think I will thanks.'

'Then we'll clear the table,' David said. Tidying up always made him feel easier no matter what the problem.

But that evening neatness was no comfort to him. The table was cleared, the dirty dishes hidden away in the dishwasher, they took up their usual positions in the living room ready for an evening's television and he was still aching with the distress of what he'd just done. He'd hit his daughter. His own daughter. The baby he'd loved and cherished all these years. How could he have done such a thing? First the job, he thought, and now this. Her voice echoed in his mind. *'You hate me!'* But it wasn't true. He didn't. He loved her so much he wanted to cry.

Danny sat in the chair allocated to him and

tried to interest himself in the comedy pro-
gramme guffawing on the screen but he couldn't
do it either. Jess was out there in the pouring rain,
cycling about, thinking they all hated her. *He*
didn't hate her. He'd go out and find her and
bring her back if they'd let him. Somebody ought
to. It wasn't fair just to sit here and do nothing.
But Dad was in such a foul mood he couldn't say
anything.

Maureen watched their grim faces and decided
she would have to try to make conversation. If
she could get David halfway back to normal she
might be able to persuade him to take the car and
look for poor Jess. It wasn't like him to be cruel.
He'd have to come round sooner or later. I wish
I hadn't shown him that wretched stain, she
thought. That's what set him off. But it was too
late now. The damage was done. And in the
meantime Jess was out there in the dark, cycling
about on those awful dangerous roads where anything could happen to her. She turned her attention and hope to Danny. 'How did you get on at
choir practice?' she asked.

'Not bad,' Danny said and looked at his father
anxiously. He had something to tell them both
and he wasn't sure whether this was the best or
the worst time to do it. 'Actually,' he ventured,
'as it happens, I'm giving it up. That was my last
practice.'

David exploded into the second rage of the
evening. 'What's the matter with kids today?' he
roared. 'Can't they stick at anything? All these

months and you just throw it away. Where's your stamina, for God's sake? You're as bad as your sister.'

Danny was scarlet. 'Actually,' he said again, his voice husky with distress, 'I'm not giving it up, as it happens. I can't do it any more. Mr Thomas said so. My — my — my voice is breaking, if you really want to know.' He was hot with embarrassment and there were tears in his throat. If he didn't get out of the room he'd be crying in front of them. ' 'Scuse me!' he said. And fled.

'Oh for God's sake!' David said, flicking channels irritably. 'What's the matter with them all?'

Maureen was furious with him. It was monstrously unfair to round on Danny, poor kid. It was nothing to do with him. But she kept her anger dampened down and tried to be reasonable. They were in enough trouble as it was without her losing her cool. 'Leave him be,' she advised. 'He's embarrassed that's all.'

'Embarrassed?' his father said, watching the screen. 'What's he got to be embarrassed about?'

'His voice breaking,' Maureen explained. 'He's very self-conscious about it. Boys are. Or don't you remember?'

He did, suddenly and most painfully, with a jolt that deflated his anger like a burst balloon. 'Oh Christ, Maur,' he said. 'I'm a total failure.'

She comforted him automatically, her mind still anxiously concerned with Jessica. 'No you're not,' she said. 'You've had a row with your kids, that's all. Once we've been out and found

Jessica you'll be . . .'

'No I shan't,' he said wearily. 'It isn't just the kids. I've had an absolute pig of a day. I've failed at everything.'

She was still caught up in the need to control herself and wasn't really listening to him. 'Um,' she said vaguely.

So he told her, flatly and furiously. 'I've lost my job.'

The words caught her attention but not in the way he expected. 'Ah!' she understood. 'So *that* was what it was all about.'

'What's that supposed to mean?'

'You get the sack so you take it out on your children.'

'I didn't get the sack,' he corrected her. 'I handed in my notice, the way I told you I would. I didn't have any option.'

'And then you came home and hit poor Jess.'

The unfairness of it was more than he could bear. Even in his present depressed state he had to fight back against an accusation like that. 'Oh it's poor Jess now is it? Let me remind you that when I got home you were ready to turn her out On the streets.'

'I was *not*. I was cross with her, I'll admit that. I was going to tell her off. But not this. I never wanted this to happen.'

'And I did?'

'You made it happen. You hit her.'

'Christ Almighty, Maur! I'm not a saint.'

'Evidently.'

'I've lost my job,' he said, speaking slowly because it was imperative that he made her understand. 'I've been out of work since six o'clock. Out of work. Do you hear what I'm saying? I can't support my wife and family. And that's the one thing I've always been determined to do properly. Once I've had my last pay cheque I shan't be able to pay the mortgage. I'm going to lose all the things I've worked for all these years. Everything. I'm a total, unforgivable, God-awful failure. Just like my father. I might as well give in and walk out on the lot of you now, like he did. All these years I've struggled not to be like him and when it comes down to it we're just the same.'

Now and at last Maureen understood his distress. She crossed the room and sat beside him. 'No, you're not,' she said. 'You're a good man. You've always done the best for us. Always. We'll come through it. You'll see.'

Her sympathy, slight though it was, broke down the last of his control. He put his face in his hands and wept.

Always that damned father of his, she thought, round his neck like a millstone, weighing him down. The search for Jessica would have to wait until he'd got all this off his chest. After all, it wasn't as if she was a child. She was old enough to look after herself and she *had* gone steaming off on her own accord. She would have to hope he was right about her and that she'd just ride around for an hour or so and then come back.

For the moment his needs were more pressing. She put her arm round his neck. 'We'll come through,' she repeated. 'You'll see.'

Upstairs in the empty tidiness of his white bedroom, Danny was dressing himself for wet weather. This time his father had gone too far. They could sit down there and talk if they liked, *he* was going to find his sister, which was what they ought to do if they had any affection in them. But they hadn't. Or at least Dad hadn't. We're just exam-passing machines to him. That's all. Well it's gone on too long. It's time I showed him we're made of flesh and blood.

He wrote a note to tell his mother where he was going, left it on his pillow and made a gentle exit, tiptoeing down the stairs. As he passed the living-room door he could hear the sound of crying. Poor Mum, he thought, pitying her. Now he's made *her* cry too. But he didn't go in and he didn't turn back. He walked into the kitchen and went out through the back door, closing it discreetly behind him.

Chapter Thirty-Three

In Laura's kitchen at Holm End it was Chris and Vinny's turn to help with the evening meal and Jeff had gone off to the nearest off-licence, which was three miles away, to buy some wine. The meal was well behind schedule because the joint was taking such a long time to cook and Chris and Vinny were both so busy that they didn't see Jessica looking in through the window at them. But Laura did and recognising trouble, went to open the door to her at once.

'Come in quick!' she said. 'Aren't you wet!'

Jessica dithered on the doorstep, wearied by travel and emotion. 'My bike . . .'

'Vinny'll put it away for you, won't you Vinny.' Of course he would. 'You just come into the warm. Your hands are like ice.'

Once in the living room and by the heat of the fire, Jessica began to shiver. 'Oh Gran!' she said. 'It's awful. I've run away from home. What am I going to do?'

'Have a warm bath, for a start,' Laura told her, 'and get into some dry clothes or you'll catch pneumonia.'

Her grandmother's practical kindness triggered the tears that Jessica had been holding back all evening. 'I haven't got any dry clothes,' she wept.

Laura put an arm round her shoulders and guided her towards the stairs. 'Then you'll have to wear some of mine. You'll be a sight for sore eyes. Come on.'

The bath was run and perfumed with bath salts, the wet clothes removed and hung on the towel rail, and Jessica slid into the water with a sigh and closed her eyes.

'That's better,' Laura said, perching herself on the stool. The bathroom had been converted from an eaves cupboard and there was very little room in it. The bath itself was so close to the slope of the eaves that only a very small child could stand up in it and anyone who used it had to get in and out with caution. The very oddity of the little room had always been part of its charm for Jessica and Danny. It was the perfect place for the sort of intimate conversation that was needed now.

'Don't you think we ought to tell your mother where you are?' Laura suggested.

'No! Don't!' Jessica said wildly. 'I couldn't bear it. If you ring I shall get out of the bath and go.'

'All right, all right,' Laura soothed. 'I won't do it if you don't want me to.'

'He said he hated me,' Jessica wept. 'He hit me. Right round the face.'

'Who did?' Laura asked, keeping her tone mild. 'Kevin?'

'No. Dad. Isn't that gross! My own father.'

Laura found that shocking and very unlikely, but she didn't say so. 'There must have been a reason for it,' she said, still mild. 'I can't imagine your father hitting anyone without reason.'

'I told him I was going on the game.'

'Oh Jess, you dreadful girl!' Laura laughed at her. 'I should think he *was* cross. Whatever made you say a thing like that?'

Jessica was glad of the laughter because it showed that Gran at least wasn't taking her threat seriously but she didn't know where to begin to explain what had happened. 'I've split up with Kevin,' she said. 'He's a spy. He told them you were afraid of water.'

Laura took that calmly too. 'It doesn't surprise me,' she said. 'He was taking pictures of the demonstrators at Twyford Down the last time I saw him.'

The tears were staunched. 'When was that?'

So Laura told her all about, while Jessica lay in the scented water and grew warm again. Afterwards, she was thoughtful for a long time. 'Why didn't you tell me this before?' she asked.

'It wouldn't have done much good, would it?' Laura said. 'You were in love with him. I don't know whether you still are . . .' Jessica shook her head '. . . but you certainly were then. You wouldn't have believed it, would you? No. And you'd have hated me for telling you. We don't see straight when we're in love.'

'You're right,' Jessica said, amazed that her grandmother should understand so well. 'We don't. I was in love with him. I'm not now. I think he's a scumbag.' The words reminded her of how awful everything was and she began to cry again. 'Oh Gran I loved him so much. I thought he was wonderful. I'd have done anything for him. Anything. I told lies to Mum because of him. It was gross but I did. I was going to refuse a place at Lampeter. And he was a spy all the time, spying on you. He never worked for a contractor. That was all lies. He couldn't even tell me the truth about his job. And that's another thing. When I told him Mrs Garston had been thrown in the pond because of him do you know what he said?'

' "I provide the information, it's up to them what they do with it," ' Laura guessed.

'Yes,' Jessica said with increased amazement. 'You're so clever. You *understand*. I could tell you anything.'

Which she did, in tearful detail and with much painful repetition, while Laura encouraged her to wash and dress — in an accommodating petticoat, a white blouse and a skirt safety-pinned to fit. She talked as she dried her hair — peering through the wet strands — and sat on Laura's bed with her arms round her knees and Laura's beautiful shawl over her shoulders, still talking.

'Love is so gross,' she said. 'Everyone says how wonderful it's going to be and you believe them, don't you. And then you fall in love and everything goes wrong. You tell lies to your mother and you pretend it's all wonderful when it isn't really. And then he turns out to be a scumbag and you find out he's been telling lies to you all along.'

529

'It isn't always as bad as that,' Laura smiled at her. 'There are some very nice men around. You just happened to pick a bad one.'

'I shan't pick another one,' Jessica told her, bitterly. 'Once is enough. Oh Gran, how *could* he have been so vile?'

'It's a hard lesson to learn when you're only seventeen,' Laura said. 'Still, at least you had the good sense not to get pregnant. You're not, are you?'

'I may be stupid,' Jessica said, 'but I'm not *that* stupid.'

There was a timid knock at the bedroom door and Chris put her head into the room to tell them that Jeff had come back with the wine, that dinner was ready, and that Danny had turned up and wanted to know how his sister was.

'Oh!' Jessica said, springing up at once, much cheered. 'Isn't that sweet of him. *He* loves me even if Dad doesn't.'

But he was in a very bad state, talking wildly about not being a machine and how he was the only one to stick up for his sister and saying, over and over again, how gross his father had been. It took Laura quite a while to calm him down, while Jeff and the cooks took themselves off to the kitchen and were carefully discreet.

When the rest of the party arrived he made a great effort to control himself and things got easier when the meal was served, especially as the talk round the table was all of tree-houses and contractors and what was likely to happen on

530

Wednesday. Laura watched over both her grand-children and was relieved to notice that although Danny ate very little — saying he'd eaten already — Jessica sat happily between Barney and Kapok and made a good meal. If she's got her appetite back, Laura thought, she's on the road to recovery.

That night, partly because the meal was late and partly because Rad had sensed an atmosphere, he and his friends went back to their benders as soon as the washing-up was done. For once Laura was glad to see them go.

'Now,' she said, as she closed the door after them. 'We've got some decisions to make.'

'I'm not going home,' Jessica said. 'Not after the way he treated me. And that's flat.'

Now that he was settled, Danny decided to opt for fraternal solidarity. 'Nor am I,' he said. 'We could stay here for a little while, couldn't we?'

'It *will* be a little while,' Laura told them. 'I might not be here myself after Wednesday. They've had a row with their father,' she explained to Jeff.

'Well that's par for the course,' he told them amiably. 'Most teenagers have a row with their fathers sooner or later.'

Jessica gave him a withering look. 'Ours was different,' she said.

'They're all different,' he said, grinning at her. 'As you'll discover when you're a parent yourself.'

'If *I* have kids,' she said fiercely, 'I shall treat them properly.'

'The thing is,' Laura said, taking the conversation back into her control again, 'we've got to decide what we're going to do now.'

'We *can* stay here can't we?' Danny asked.

'While I'm still the owner of the place,' Laura said. 'But that might only be until Wednesday and Wednesday's only four days away. You're welcome to stay until then. But after that we might all have to think again. Heaven help us! And I shan't be here all the time. You realise that don't you? You'll be on your own here tomorrow because I shall be at work all day.'

'That's all right,' Jessica said, earnestly. 'Really. We'll help with the work, look after the house, anything you like. Only we can't go back.'

'And what about your parents?'

That made Jessica aggressive, '*What* about them?'

'Well don't you think you ought to tell them where you are?'

No, she didn't and said so furiously. 'He can stew in his own rotten juice.'

'And your mother?' Laura asked.

'We ought to tell *her*,' Danny urged, remembering the sound of her crying. 'She'll be worrying.'

'You could phone,' Laura offered.

But Jessica wouldn't hear of it. 'Oh no,' she said. 'I'm not talking to them. Either of them. They'll try to get round us.'

Jeff had been watching and listening, stroking his beard contemplatively. 'I tell you what,' he

532

said. 'Suppose I drive over and just let them know you're here and safe. I could tell them you're not coming home for a few days. What do you think?'

'Tell them I'm never coming home,' Jessica said.

'OK. If that's what you want.'

'You'll need your clothes too,' Laura pointed out.

'That's settled then,' Jeff said. And rather to his surprise was thanked by both absconders.

'Can we sit up 'til you get back?' Danny asked.

'No you can *not*,' Laura told him firmly. 'It's time you were in bed. You're all eyes, the pair of you. We'll tell you what's happened in the morning. I'll just see Jeff out and then I'll come up and kiss you goodnight.'

Jeff turned up his collar ready for the sprint to his car. 'And you wonder why I don't like kids,' he said.

'It's Maureen I'm thinking about,' she told him. 'Tell her they're all right and say I'll phone her tomorrow.'

By the time David had talked out his distress and was more himself again, Jessica had been missing for over an hour and a half, as Maureen knew because she'd been watching the clock.

'I really think we ought to go and look for her,' she said tentatively, 'don't you? Or make a few phone calls or something. It's getting late.'

This time David could see the sense of it but he drew a line at phone calls. 'We'll drive round the village,' he decided. 'She can't have gone far. Probably sitting on a wall somewhere, feeling sorry for herself. There's no point in phoning anyone yet. It would only alarm them.'

'What about your mother?' Maureen asked. 'She might have gone *there*.'

'Least of all my mother,' he said. 'If she'd gone there, she'd have rung by now.'

'But . . .'

'We'll drive round,' he said and tried to be optimistic because he was as worried as she was, now that he'd seen the time. 'We'll find her.'

So Maureen went upstairs to let Danny know. She was down almost immediately, her face paper-white. 'He's gone too,' she said, passing him the note.

He tried not to show how upset he was. 'Then we'll look for them both.'

It was an anguished search through largely empty streets and it became inexorably more and more frantic. There were a few cars about and one or two cyclists but none of them riding the familiar mountain bikes. Once, as they turned into the village square, they saw a group of teenagers outside the pub and took momentary heart. But Jess and Danny weren't among them and there was no sign of them anywhere else, although they drove up and down every single street in the place.

'Let's go home,' Maureen said at last. 'I'm going to phone round. We can't go on like this. Something could have happened to them. I think

534

we ought to phone the hospital.'

'One more turn round the village,' David urged. 'We might have missed them the first time. They could have been riding down one street while we were driving up another one. That could easily have happened. One more turn. *Then* we'll go home.'

'And phone?' Maureen insisted.

'If they're not there waiting for us.'

But it was Jeff's car that was waiting for them. He'd been in the drive for nearly ten minutes and had decided to give them half an hour. There were lights on all over the house, so when he'd rung the doorbell and got no answer he'd guessed they were out searching.

'Oh my God!' Maureen said, struggling out of the car. 'They're hurt!'

Jeff got out of his car too. 'It's all right,' he called to her. 'They're with Laura.'

'Oh, thank God!' she said. She felt weak with relief, leaning against David's chest as he stood behind her. 'They're with your mother. Didn't I say we ought to ring her?'

By now David was grey with fatigue and stress but he remembered to be polite, opening the door and welcoming his visitor. 'Do come in Jeff. It's very good of you to come over.'

'Are they all right?' Maureen wanted to know, leading the way into the living room.

'They're in bed,' Jeff told her diplomatically.

David was recovering now that he knew they were safe. 'What will she do?' he asked, trying to sound casual about it. 'Bring them home tomorrow on her way to work?'

'Let's sit down,' Jeff said.

Maureen's fear flared at once. 'Jess is hurt.'

He reassured her quickly. 'No. I told you. They're all right. They're just not coming home for a little while.'

Ordinarily David would have insisted that they be made to mind and brought back to him at once. Now, after so much exhausting emotion, he merely accepted what he was told. 'Ah!' he sighed.

'They're in a bit of a state,' Jeff explained. 'Typical teenagers. We thought a few days in the sticks would calm them down. Laura says she'll phone you tomorrow.'

'How many days?' Maureen worried. 'They won't be there on Wednesday will they? I wouldn't like them caught up in all that.'

'That's four days away,' Jeff said. 'A lot can happen in four days.'

'Let's hope so.'

'Meantime,' he told her, 'they haven't got any clean clothes. Laura said I was to tell you that too.'

'I'll pack a case,' Maureen decided, cheered to have something practical to do. 'They haven't got their toothbrushes either. Or pyjamas or anything. Running out like that!' And she went to attend to it.

'Whisky?' David offered, when she'd gone.

'No thanks. I'm driving.'

'Of course. Can I offer you anything else?'

'No thanks.'

'You won't mind if I do?' David said pouring himself a double. 'I've had a pig of a day. Bad from start to finish.'

The size of the drink and the tone of his voice revealed more than he knew. He's lost his job, Jeff thought, watching him. 'Some days are like that,' he said noncommittally.

'An absolute pig.'

'Work?' Jeff asked.

'Or lack of it. It comes to us all I suppose.'

'Ah!' Jeff understood. 'It happens to the best of us. I lost my job too, some years back.'

'It's a tough world.'

'If it's any consolation to you,' Jeff said, 'there are plenty of people around who could give you all sorts of reasons why people lose their jobs. Sometimes it's simply because the boss wants to get rid of you. I was kicked out for being too conscientious.'

David was interested despite his gloom. 'Is that right?'

'Believe me.'

'If you don't mind me asking, how long did it take you to get another one?'

Jeff told him the truth. 'Three months and it felt like a lifetime.'

'I'll bet,' David said and smiled at his guest. It was a small smile and a rather bleak one, but it *was* a smile, because he recognised that, as one man to another, he was being helped and encouraged.

Laura was waiting up to hear how they'd got on, her face anxious.

Jeff went to the nub of the problem at once, his nursing instincts telling him it was necessary to be cruel to be kind. 'He's lost his job,' he said. 'That's what this is all about.'

It was no surprise to her. 'Oh God!' she said. 'Then it's all my fault.' It was a horrible responsibility to have to accept.

'Yours or the Ministry of Transport's,' he agreed. There was no point in trying to soothe her either. She was too honest for that. 'It depends how far back you go.'

'Mine,' she said. 'It was my choice. I've known it could happen all along. We all have. My poor David. How's he taking it?'

'Not as badly as you'd think. Maybe you underestimate him.'

'I hope so,' she said. 'Because it's hurt Jess and Danny too. How was Maureen?'

'Worried but sensible,' he said.

'I wish I'd never started this now,' she sighed.

'You've gone too far to do anything about it now.'

'I know. That makes it worse.'

Jeff decided to change the subject. 'I think I shall go back to the flat after work tomorrow,' he told her. 'Stay the weekend and clean it up a bit. Catch up with the washing, that sort of thing. Otherwise I shall have my neighbours calling in the Health Inspector.'

'Back on Monday?' she hoped. She needed his support more than ever now.

'Yes,' he assured her, 'and I shall arrange for Sister Hughes to cover for me on Wednesday.'

'Thanks.'

'Your eco-warriors should be back by then.'

'Back?' she said. 'Are they going away?'

'They're going to Winchester for a couple of days.'

That was news to her. 'Are they?'

'So they say.'

'What all of them?'

'Rad and Kapok anyway. Vinny and Hen said they might tag along as moral support. They were telling me about it at dinner. It's to do with this trial that's coming up. There's some sort of pre-trial meeting about it.'

'What trial?'

'Criminal damage. You know. The one your friend Freda's involved in. Apparently they're being sued too.'

'What? For the two million? How ridiculous!'

'Yes. Isn't it.'

'The official mind is beyond my under-standing,' Laura said, glad to have something else to take her attention. 'It's stupid enough of them to expect Freda to pay. They ought to know she won't do it. But at least she's got some capital so there's a *bit* of sense in it from their point of view. This lot haven't any money at all. It's almost a point of honour with them. They live from one casual pay packet to the next. What they earn they spend. What *is* the point of suing them?'

'None whatsoever.'

'It's very difficult to fight people like that,' she said. 'They don't accept the normal rules of human conduct. Poor David. What *will* he do without his work?'

'He'll cope,' he reassured her, 'like we all have to. Unemployment's not uncommon.'

'It will be to him,' she said. 'Work's the most important thing in his life.'

Chapter Thirty-Four

'This is the end!' Joan Garston said in a voice of doom. 'We've had it! They've beaten us hands down. We can't go on!'

It was late on Saturday afternoon and already growing dark. Laura had been at work all day. Now she was tired and yearning for a pot of tea. But her neighbours had run across the road as soon as she drove through the gate, and their expressions were so fraught that she was alerted to trouble at the mere sight of them.

'She's right,' Connie said, joining in the conversation as she joined the group. 'We can't do without water, can we.'

'Rotten buggers!' Mr Fennimore scowled. He was munching with annoyance and that fleshy nose of his was an angry purple. 'They're bloody inhuman, that's what they are.'

'What are you talking about?' Laura asked, extricating herself from the driver's seat. 'What's happened?'

'Yours'll be inside,' John told her. 'We had ours this morning.'

A letter, Laura understood, and bad news, obviously. She tensed herself ready to receive it.

'They're from South Downs Water,' Molly explained as Laura led them all into the kitchen.

'They're going to cut us off.'

Laura put down her bag and turned to look at their anxious, angry faces. 'They can't do that!' she said, shocked at the very idea. 'It's not legal. They've got to provide us with water.'

'Legal or not, they're doing it,' Joan said. 'I told you. We're finished. They got us by the short an' curlies.'

'Read the letter,' Molly said, offering hers.

It was brutally explicit. Having been reliably informed that the above-named property was under a compulsory purchase order and due for demolition, South Downs Water was writing to inform the occupants that the water supply to the property would therefore be disconnected at 08.00 hours on Wednesday morning.

'That's blackmail,' Laura understood.

'It gets worse,' Joan said. 'Molly rang them up about it, didn't you Molly. Straight away. And d'you know what they said?'

'Surprise me,' Laura invited.

'Apparently,' Molly told her, 'the pipes are falling to pieces anyway. If we want them to continue the supply they say it'll cost £70,000 per house to put in new ones.'

'What are we going to do?' John asked. 'I mean to say, we can't live without water. An' seventy thousand pounds, I mean to say . . .'

'The farm-shop might help us out,' Connie said. 'I asked an' they said they'd try but they're more than two miles away.'

'No good,' Joan said. 'You think a' the weight

a' carrying all that water all that way.'

'We could fill the baths before they cut us off,' Molly suggested. 'But how long would it last?'

'No time at all,' Joan said. She seemed to be taking a perverse delight in knocking down every suggestion. 'You think a' the amount of water we get through. An' there's the hippies.'

'Do they know?' Laura asked.

Molly had told them. 'They been ever so good,' she said. 'Up in the trees an' workin' all day regardless. Barney said they might as well because Wednesday'll happen whether there's any water or not.'

'And what about Jess and Danny?'

'They've been with them,' Molly said. 'Working like Trojans.'

'It's a bloody shame,' her husband growled.

'If only that Rad feller hadn't gone to Winchester,' John said, 'he might have thought of something. We've been at our wits' end.'

'There's nothing you *can* think of,' Joan told her sourly. 'They got the trump card an' they've played it. We're stymied. And I can't see it's anything to laugh at,' she added, glaring at Laura.

But Laura was grinning all over her face, her wide mouth spread until it ached. 'I'm sorry!' she said. 'But there's a very funny side to all this, if you did but know it. A very funny side. Come with me and I'll show you.' She was looking in the kitchen drawer for a torch and her bag of tools. 'They may have played their trump, Joan, but we've got the ace.'

They followed her down the garden, past the benders — where Barney was playing his guitar and the others were sitting in a circle listening to him and they all got up to follow her — past the vegetable garden — and how I've neglected *that* this year — right down to the patio she'd built for their barbecues all those years ago. 'There you are!' she said.

'There you are what?' Joan asked.

'That's the answer.'

'That table?' John said. There was nothing else and that's where Laura seemed to be looking. But how a round wooden table top built over a low brick wall could possibly be the answer was beyond him.

'That table, John,' Laura said with splendid triumph, 'is a well.'

'So it is,' Molly said. 'Bless me! I'd forgotten all about it. It was all well-water round here one time. Does it still work?'

'There's only one way to find out,' Laura said.

The wooden cover had done duty as a table for so many years that it was a hard job to prise it loose, especially as it had to be done in semi-darkness. But at last it gave, with a great creaking of timber. Then there was a rush of hands to lift it clear.

'Is there any water?' Danny asked, leaning over the wall to peer down.

'Course there is, Lame-brain,' his sister said. 'It's a well.'

Laura shone her torch into the well-shaft but

544

nobody could see anything.

'We need a bucket,' Molly said, 'and a length of rope.'

Barney could provide both and went back to the camp at once to get them.

'It smells damp,' Danny said, still hanging over the edge.

'You used to have a pulley here one time,' Molly remembered. 'It's all coming back to me. An' we had a well an' all, at the end of the terrace, where you've got that funny old rustic seat of yours, Joan.'

Laura was caught up in memory too. She was a child running out into the garden at the start of the summer holidays to draw water for their first pot of country tea. She was newly married and pregnant and Pete was pulling up the bucket with a frog in it and someone was saying, *Put it back, my dear. It'll catch the insects.*

'Lovely water that was,' Josh Fennimore was remembering. 'Sweet an' cold. Used to come up out the earth sweet an' cold, even on a summer's day. D'you remember that, Molly? Lovely water. Not like the rubbish you get out the tap. No chlorine in that there wasn't. None a' this fluoride muck they will keep putting in everything. Just good sweet water.'

Barney was back with a pail and a length of rope. And there *was* water there. They all heard the splash.

'Pull it up! Pull it up!' Danny urged.

'Lovely sweet water,' Mr Fennimore said.

It was full of floating debris, smelt brackish and looked decidedly green.

Danny was horrified. 'Ugh!'

'It was always like that in the first two or three bucket loads,' Laura told him. 'Once we've cleared it, it'll be quite different. There's water there. That's the main thing.'

Barney was lowering the pail again. And sure enough, after the sixth bucketful the water was almost clean. The seventh was greeted by a cheer.

'Eat yer heart out South Downs Water!' Josh Fennimore said gleefully.

'You clever, clever thing!' Molly applauded.

'I shall phone the National Rivers Authority on Monday morning,' Laura said. 'Just to be sure it's all still legal. We'll draw out some more tomorrow morning. Another two or three buckets and it'll be ready to drink. We're on chalk you see and water's always good from chalk.'

They went back to the cottage rejoicing.

'You ought to look under that seat of yours,' John said to Joan. 'Maybe you got a well there an' all.'

Molly thought it was possible. 'I can't remember it ever being filled in,' she said.

'I'll get on to it first thing,' Joan decided.

'We all will,' John said. 'Eh Laura?'

But Laura had other plans. 'No,' she said. 'I'll give you a hand in the afternoon but in the morning I'm going to church.'

'Very good idea, with Wednesday coming,'

Molly said. 'Prayer before battle, sort of thing. I think we should all go.'

Rather to Laura's surprise, they all agreed, with the exception of the eco-warriors who said they were still building the last barricade, Mr Fennimore who growled that religion was all mumbo-jumbo and Ken Garston who was still locked in his attic. So it was quite an excursion that set out that Sunday morning.

It was calm in the Church of St Mary and the light that filtered through the stained-glass windows was hazy and soft as water. The place was decorated with spring flowers, their bright white, orange and gold, bold against the quiet stone, and there were friends and neighbours to greet her and wish her well at every step. It was the season of death and resurrection, of sorrow and hope, the time when prayer was most intense.

Laura began to pray most earnestly as soon as she knelt in the pew. She knew that she needed a very special grace and strength to carry her through the next few days. Strength to withstand whatever was going to happen, to endure rough handling, as that seemed to be almost inevitable, to cope with loss, if the house really had to be lost, to comfort those who were hurt, if things degenerated to a fight. And grace too, to reconcile her son and grandchildren, if it was within her power, or to stand back and allow them to do it for themselves if that was the better way.

My life gets more complicated the older I get, she thought. But prayer was calming and sustaining. And the words of Isaiah sang in her ears. *'The Lord God will help me, therefore I shall not be confounded . . . He is near that justifieth me; who will contend with me? Let us stand together; who is mine adversary? . . . Behold, all ye that kindle a fire, that compass yourselves about with sparks; walk in the light of your fire, and in the sparks that ye have kindled . . .'*

By the time the service was over and she was walking back to the Land-Rover, she felt she could cope with anything.

Danny was melancholy on the way home. 'That was my last time in the choir,' he said sadly.

'You can go back when you're a baritone,' Jessica told him.

But he wasn't comforted by that at all. 'Well thanks.'

'You can help me cook the dinner,' Laura offered, feeling, rightly, that that would be a better consolation.

But when they got back to Holm End the dinner was already cooked. Amy's smart Peugeot was parked in the drive and Amy was in the kitchen wearing a fancy apron and a welcoming smile. The table was set for four, the potatoes were boiling on the stove and she was tossing a green salad.

'There you are!' she said brightly. 'Josh told me where you'd gone and everything. Lunch is served. I bought you a meat pie from Sainsbury's.'

Laura wasn't at all pleased to see her but she

could hardly say so when she'd just cooked them a meal. 'When did you get back?' she asked as they sat up to the table.

'About an hour ago,' Amy said. 'The job in Birmingham's folded. But not to worry. I've got another one back in Worthing. Quite a step up.' She was actually covering for a saleswoman who'd gone to America for six weeks but there was no need to go into details — and especially details like that. 'I was going to write but it all happened so quickly and anyway I thought you'd like a surprise. Neat eh?'

'Where are you staying?' Laura wanted to know.

'Well here, naturally. You don't mind do you?'

'It's not a matter of whether I mind or not,' Laura said. 'There's no room. Jess and Danny are staying here now.'

'Yes. Josh told me. But I could stay with you for a night or two couldn't I? I mean that's a double bed you've got and I wouldn't be any trouble. I sleep like a mouse.' Her face was hard with desperation.

Jessica gave her a scathing look. 'There's no room for you there either,' she said coolly. 'Gran's got a lover.'

Laura was a little taken aback to have the situation stated so boldly but she was impressed too by the easy way her grandchildren accepted it.

To her credit Amy took it with style. 'Ah!' she said. 'Right. Then you hardly want three to a bed, do you? But there's the sofa. I could sleep there, couldn't I? Just for a few days, till I find some-where else.'

But you said that last time, Laura thought, and you were here for months. She was just opening her mouth to say so when the phone rang.

It was Maureen, breathless and decidedly nervous, wanting to know how the children were.

'They're fine,' Laura told her, mouthing the message to them *It's your mother.* 'I was just going to ring you. We've just this minute come back from church.'

'I know,' Maureen said. 'Kitty saw you there. When are they coming home? Have they said?'

'No,' Laura told her. 'We haven't talked about it yet, I'm afraid. We've had rather a lot of other things to do. I'll ask them. Your mother wants to know when you're coming home.'

Going to church might have helped her grand-mother but it hadn't softened Jessica. 'Tell her never,' she said, her chin stubborn.

Laura gave a tactful translation. 'Not yet awhile.'

'But before Wednesday?'

'Oh I expect so.'

'Would they like to talk to me?' Maureen hoped.

Jessica heard that question. 'No they wouldn't,' she said, shouting so that her mother could hear and be in no doubt.

Maureen sighed. 'I was afraid they'd say that. I'll ring again tomorrow. You don't mind do you?'

'Ring whenever you like,' Laura told her. 'I

shall be at work on Monday and Tuesday but I've got the rest of the week off.'

'How come?' Amy asked, when she'd returned to the table. 'Are you taking a long Easter holiday or what?'

'Or what,' Danny said. And proceeded to enlighten her.

She was thrilled. 'But that's wonderful,' she said. 'What a good job I came back. Now I can help you, can't I? Be your runner or something. Get in supplies.'

Laura didn't want her company at all. But the matter seemed to be settled and it would be petty to argue about three nights. 'All right then,' she said. 'You can stay until Wednesday. And if you're offering to help with the work I shall take you up on the offer. I can't say fairer or further than that.'

'Item seven,' the Leader of the council announced that Monday afternoon. 'Roadworks — Laura's Way — Wednesday.' He was annoyed when several of the councillors groaned. 'Yes, yes, I know. We're all heartily sick of it but we have to make a decision.'

It was a sticky afternoon and the council meeting had already overrun.

'Wouldn't you know that damned woman would have a well!' Councillor Dewar complained.

'Many people do, out in the sticks,' Mr Cranbourne pointed out.

'Why did one of them have to be her?' Councillor Dewar said in exasperation. 'That's what I ask myself. She's getting to be a real thorn in my flesh.'

'We should make an example of her,' another councillor said. 'That's my opinion. Stick an injunction on her or something.'

'Unfortunately she hasn't done anything illegal,' the Leader reminded them.

'Have we had a reply from Colonel FitzHenry?' Councillor Mrs Smith wanted to know.

'Not a satisfactory one,' the Leader had to admit, finding the letter in his file. 'He sympathises with our current difficulties — blah blah — however, he wishes to remind us that the land in question was sold to the Ministry of Transport in 1988 — blah blah — the houses currently belong to the occupiers or their mortgagees.'

'There's nothing more to be got from that quarter then,' Councillor Mrs Smith said.

Councillor Dewar snorted. 'I still think we should have the law on the hippies. After all, what are they when all's said and done? A bunch of weirdos. There must be something we could catch them with, if we put our minds to it.'

'I daresay we could,' Mr Cranbourne said, 'but would it be politic? I mean, it wouldn't show us up in a very good light, if we started arresting people for being hippies.' He opened out the centre page of the local paper where there was an article with pictures headlined *'Homes or roads?'* 'We're in bad enough odour locally as it is.'

552

'Mr Cranbourne's right,' Councillor Mrs Smith said. 'Have you seen the *Evening Argus*? That's worse. Maybe we should postpone the start. If we leave them all hanging about in the cold perhaps they'll get tired of it and go home.'

'No, no,' the Leader said. 'Plans are too far advanced to consider postponement. As I told you last week.'

'Then we're committed to it and I suppose we must go through with it,' Councillor Mrs Smith said. 'We're on a hiding to nothing whatever we do. But I would like to remind you that confrontation is costly.'

'If only there were some way of getting them out of those damned trees,' Councillor Dewar said, 'short of pulling them out.' But they'd been looking for a method for over a week and nobody had come up with anything.

'I think we're stumped,' Mr Cranbourne said.

The County Surveyor had been listening to them with great attention for quite a long time. Now he decided the time was ripe for him to make the suggestion he'd been brewing since their last meeting. 'Not quite,' he said quietly. 'There is another alternative. It's a bit complicated and would involve a change of plan but it would be one way of circumventing the demonstration.'

Faces turned towards him, hopefully.

He spread out his ordnance survey map of the area and took up a pointer. 'What we are proposing at the moment,' he said, 'is to cut down these trees here and here, and then bring in the bulldozers and demolish the terrace here and the cottage on the other side of the street. The demonstrators appear to be holding trees here, here, here and here, which means, as we have seen, that they will have to be forcibly removed before work can begin. However if we change our plans and begin by cutting down the trees on the other side of the proposed road, here and here, we could bring the bulldozers in round the back, where the demonstrators aren't expecting them.'

It was a brilliant device but there was a difficulty. A round blue difficulty lying right in the middle of the area.

Councillor Mrs Smith asked the question that was in all their minds. 'But what would we do with the pond?'

'We would drain it,' the County Surveyor said.

'Which would need a pretty powerful pump,' the Leader said. 'Do we have such a thing?'

They did and it could be on the site by eleven o'clock on Wednesday morning.

'Admirable!' Councillor Dewar said.

'What about the cost?' Councillor Mrs Smith wanted to know.

The County Surveyor had some preliminary figures and produced them for scrutiny. It would mean considerable extra expenditure as Councillor Mrs Smith discovered at once.

'It won't be easy on the ecological front either,' Councillor Cranbourne pointed out. 'We'll have to cut down rather more of the trees on that side than were in our original specification.'

Other councillors didn't share his concern. 'What are a few more trees here and there?' one asked. And another said, 'Rather that than a battle in front of the cameras.'

The Leader let them talk it through until they were coming round to the idea. Then he made a decision. 'If there are no more questions, ladies and gentlemen, I propose that we accept the County Surveyor's suggestion. Ostensibly and as far as the media are concerned we leave arrangements as they are, but we order the pump to be in position in case work is held up and we have to change plan. It will all have to be costed by Accounts but I can see no particular difficulty. We could use contingency funds.'

'Admirable!' Councillor Dewar said. 'Then you have my vote.'

'Do we *have* contingency funds?' Councillor Mrs Smith wanted to know.

'Some,' the Leader told her. 'It'll be a pinch but we can just about manage it.'

He looked round the group to test opinion. 'Is that the general view of the committee?' he asked. 'Good. Well I find that very satisfactory. It should be an interesting day!'

Chapter Thirty-Five

The designated Wednesday began with birdsong and a spectacular sunrise. The battle lines were drawn, all four tree-houses fully manned, provisions and water laid in and both newly opened wells camouflaged with tarpaulins and artful bales of hay. Jeff had contrived his day off and baby Jasmine had been evacuated to her grandmother. Molly's dogs were obediently safe in a neighbouring kennels, Laura's cats were in feline high dudgeon in the adjoining cattery. Everything that could be done, had been done. Now it was simply a matter of waiting for the battle to begin.

Kapok and her friends had returned from Winchester in a fury about the impending court case and consequently all the more determined to defend Laura's Way.

'They're really fighting dirty now,' Kapok said, at the end of their Tuesday evening meal. 'We'd better be prepared for anything tomorrow.'

Rad was philosophical. 'OK, they're fighting dirty,' he agreed, 'but that shows they're running scared. This movement is growing by the day. You should have seen the letters they've had at Winchester.'

'Never let the buggers grind you down,' Amy said, cheerfully offering her cigarettes round the table. She'd spent her first two nights on Laura's sofa and had made no fuss about it at all. In fact, apart from filling the saucers with her cigarette ash and the wardrobe in Jessica's room with her clothes, she'd been almost unobtrusive.

Jeff had been none too pleased to come back on Sunday evening and find her in occupation but he hadn't said anything. Now he agreed with her sentiments. Whatever else they were all in this together, holding on until the morning, psyching themselves up to whatever they had to face.

And now the day had arrived and the last-minute preparations were being made — sandwiches and flasks of tea to take up into the trees as though they were off on a picnic. Jeff and Danny were packing the hamper, while Laura and Jessica buttered bread.

John Cooper and Amy were the only ones who were going to work but he had promised he would be home after milking and she said she'd be back as soon as she could.

'I've only got to report in,' she said, stubbing out her cigarette in the saucer of her teacup, 'and then the rest of the day's more or less my own. I'll soon be back. Look after yourselves. Wish you luck.'

The phone rang as soon as she'd gone. It was Maureen, calling to say the same thing and to ask if her children were all right.

'They're looking forward to it,' Laura told her.

'What it is to be young,' Maureen said, adding wistfully, 'I don't suppose they want to talk to me.'

557

Laura looked a question at Jessica who frowned and shook her head, and at Danny who shrugged his shoulders. Had he been on his own he would have come to the phone, for he guessed it was his mother and would have liked to have talked to her before the excitement began, but he couldn't go back on his word now. He had to show solidarity with Jess.

'I'll call you as soon as there's any news,' Laura promised. 'We've got a mobile phone up in the trees.'

'Please do,' Maureen begged. 'I shan't go anywhere.'

'Must get on,' Laura said. 'I've got rather a lot to do. I *will* call you, I promise.' She put the phone down, feeling a bit mean to have cut her off so short. But there wasn't time for sympathy today. There was barely time to breathe.

In Canterbury Gardens, Maureen stood by the phone, her face lopsided with distress and her hand resting on the receiver she'd just replaced, as if physical contact with its dumb white plastic could still maintain some sort of link with her endangered children.

'They won't talk to me,' she said sadly, 'and they won't come home. They're going to stay there for this horrible demonstration. Oh David, this is getting worse and worse. I'm worried sick.'

David was on his way to the Job Centre for an interview and having psyched himself up to it, he felt he couldn't back down.

'Go there yourself,' he told her, 'and I'll follow

on as soon as I can.'

It was what she wanted to do but she was doubtful. 'Do you think I should?'

He opened the door. 'You needn't talk to them,' he said. 'You don't even need to let them see you, if you don't think it would be sensible.' They'd talked this all over so often since the kids left that it was hard to know what *would* be sensible now. 'The thing is you could keep an eye on them, couldn't you. And that's what you want. You go.'

She dithered about it all morning, running the dishwasher, making the bed, tidying the living room, but she knew she was only filling in time. In the end she took his advice and drove to Laura's Way. And was shattered by what she found.

There were far more people there than she expected. The lane was like the approach to a fairground, noisy with crowds and full of excitement. It was a bright spring morning and there was movement everywhere. Pink-tinged cloud scudded across the sky, trees shimmered and swayed in their new fresh green, even the long grass was blown about, now green now silver, as it bowed in the breeze. Only the empty cars were still and there were cars of every description, from H reg to wreck, parked nose to tail all along the lane. Three more arrived after she did and parked close behind her. And the right-hand side of the road was full of people walking up to the demonstration, scarves flying like pennants, skirts and coats bellied like sails. There were kids in jeans and boys in battle dress, young men with beards and young women with beads, respectable matrons in respectable coats and Tory hats, fierce old men with walking sticks, even an old lady in a wheelchair — and a variety of dogs, leaping and barking or trotting and well-behaved. This isn't a crowd, Maureen thought, following them up the lane, it's the world and his wife.

At the top of the lane a mobile TV van had been set at an angle to block entry to the space between the houses. And that was crowded with wild young people. Their faces were painted with tribal signs, their hair tousled or dreadlocked, their clothes indescribably dirty, and they were leaping and dancing to the beat of a hand-held drum and a chorus of empty beer cans. There was no sign of Laura or the children, but there were three well-padded men with cameras on their shoulders and several young women with notebooks in hand who looked like reporters. She saw Toby Fawcett on the other side of the lane talking to Mr Cooper, who was leaning on his garden gate looking suitably rustic. She noticed that the boards had been removed from the empty houses and that the windows looked blank and black and, as she passed Holm End, she could see that it was locked and empty.

On the far side of the lane, in front of Ken Garston's house there were three men in suits. One had a walkie-talkie and was using it discreetly, his head tucked towards it and his face stern. The other two were in serious conversation, their eyes watching the trees. They'll be the contractors, she thought. But where are the machines? Then she noticed the chain-saws. Two of them, partly hidden behind a plain blue van parked at the other end of the terrace and guarded by two men like lumberjacks in check shirts, jeans and boots and tin helmets. So they're going to cut down the trees first. If they can. Which will mean pulling all these people down, pulling Jeff and Danny and Laura down. Probably hurting them. Her heart clenched in alarm at the mere thought of it.

Where are they? she wondered, scanning the trees. She could see three tree-houses, all fully occupied by gangs of grubby young men and women in torn jeans and mud-coloured jerseys. Then she suddenly realised that one of the young men was Danny. He was skimming along a walkway between the trees, holding on lightly to the guide-ropes on either side of him, and he looked completely at home and at ease. There was a lightness about him that she noticed but couldn't place. It took her several seconds to realise that she was watching a boy who looked his age. He'd lost that harassed, old-before-his-time look that had worried her so much and was simply and obviously happy. What an extraordinary thing!

There was a disturbance behind her and she turned to see that the TV van was being moved to make way for an open-topped Peugeot to get through. It was evidently someone important because there was a policeman directing operations. So the police are here too, she thought, and then noticed others waiting about between the crowds and the trees. She watched as the flashy car was inched through the gap and the constable moved the crowd aside so that it could be driven forward and through the gate into Holm End.

Who on earth was it, to be driving so boldly into Laura's garden? Had she given them permission? Then the driver got out, stretching her elegant legs before her, and touched her elegant hair with her finger tips, as she smiled her thanks at her police escort. All was clear. Amy. Of course.

Well you won't be able to get into the house, Maureen thought, because she's locked it all up. But Amy made no attempt to enter. She locked her car, slung her bag over her shoulder and headed off into the crowd. Within seconds she was lost to Maureen's sight.

Now what? Maureen thought. But time passed and nothing happened. The police stood about at the edge of the crowd and watched; the contractors stood together at Ken Garston's gate and watched; the lumberjacks had a picnic lunch, squatting on their haunches, and watched; the crowd milled around and watched; the dance went on and on; and the tree dwellers moved from branch to branch, watching the watchers. Danny had disappeared and there was no sign of Laura or Jessica at all. It was a bit of an anticlimax. In fact, she was beginning to wonder how much longer it was going on when a voice at her elbow said,

'Hello! It's the other Mrs Pendleton, isn't it.'

She turned, wondering who was addressing her, and the person introduced herself. 'Miss Finch, from Tillbury library. I've brought your mother-in-law some posters.'

She looked very neat and purposeful in a long fawn raincoat and a matching fawn sou'wester. The posters were tucked under her arm in a bright green and purple bundle.

'Suffragette's colours,' she said, unfolding the top one so that Maureen could see it. *'Homes not roads'*, it proclaimed, in six-inch white letters shadowed purple on a background of vaguely drawn trees and shrubs.

'Very impressive,' Maureen said.

'I've got a string of them to put on her fence,' Miss Finch said. 'I thought they would look good on the news. If you would be so kind as to hold one end for me we could get them up.' She took a hammer and a packet of nails from the deep pocket of her raincoat and set to work at once, chattering as they worked. 'I think she's so brave. And such an inspiration. We'll put them here, shall we, just below the hedge. They've been eating their lunch right up there in the trees, you know. I've been watching them. Ready for anything, they are. I think it's marvellous. She's going to make a speech in a little while, but I expect you know all about that, don't you, being family. You hardly need me to tell you. They're just rigging up the microphones.'

'Where is she?' Maureen asked. But at that point the microphones coughed into life and answered her question for her.

'Ladies and gentlemen,' Laura's voice said. 'Ladies and gentlemen.' Then she waited for the noise to subside and Maureen saw her. She was sitting in the fork of the horse chestnut outside Ken Garston's house, holding a microphone in her hand, with her hair blown wildly about her face, that lovely shawl draped over her coat and Jessica standing protectively behind her with one hand on her shoulder. To Maureen's admiring eyes they looked like Queen Boudicca and one of her daughters.

'Give them a few more seconds,' Rad advised. He was perched in the tree just above Laura's shoulder.

Laura nodded. Now that the moment had come for her to speak, she was taut with nerves, her heart pounding and her mouth dry. This was much worse than it had been at the meeting in Glendale Memorial Hall, for this time she would be speaking to her opponents as well as her supporters and what she said might provoke a violent response.

The crowd seemed ready for her. The cameras were pointing in her direction. She licked her lips and began. 'I would like to thank you all,' she said, her amplified voice echoing in the space between the houses, 'for coming here this afternoon to support us.'

From her high perch she could see that the

contractors were agitated, walkie-talkie in urgent use, and that the police were watchful, standing in front of the crowd and glancing at their sergeant for instructions.

'When this first began,' she went on, 'we were accused of being nimbys. We were told we were making a fuss because we didn't want our homes destroyed — as if people don't have the right to make a fuss when their homes are threatened. I can tell you now that we don't just have a right to protest, we have a duty.'

'Yes,' her audience said and gave her a cheer, waving Miss Finch's placards.

'If we don't stand and fight,' she said, 'appalling things will be done in our name. That is why we are here this afternoon. We do not want this road. We want to make that quite, quite clear. We do not want this road. Or any other road instead of it. Not just because our homes are under threat to make way for it but because our countryside is under threat, our children's health is under threat, our safety is under threat. And all for what? So that cars can travel at motorway speed from Folkestone to Honiton.'

'Yes. Yes.'

'Why? That's what we want to know. There is already a perfectly adequate rail system between the two towns that could easily be improved to carry freight and passengers with far less pollution and far less danger. Have we allowed the car to become our god? Have we got to sacrifice everything we hold most dear to the needs of a vehicle?

We can't go on building bigger and bigger roads for ever. It's too costly and too destructive. This section of the road is going to cost two hundred and thirty-three million pounds. The total cost of road building nationwide is sixteen billion. Sixteen billion pounds to cover our beautiful countryside with concrete — when we want it left as it is — to fill our children's lungs with polluted air — when we want to keep them healthy. All at a time when we are being told we can't afford to keep hospital beds open or pay nurses a decent wage because we haven't got the money. All at a time when our schools have to sack teachers and sell off their playing fields to pay for the books and equipment they need because we haven't got the money. And yet we've got sixteen billion pounds to squander on roads that nobody wants except the haulage companies and the road builders. Think what good we could do if we'd used that money on our hospitals and schools instead.'

Another cheer.

'A time must come when we have to think about what we are doing. I think that time is now. I think our questions should be answered and I think we have a right and a duty to ask them. I will ask my questions again. Have we got to sacrifice all that we hold most dear to the needs of the motor car? Is the car really our god?'

The doors of the blue van were flung open, blue-clad men were tumbling out, truncheons in hand, their helmets bright in the sun. Laura could see them all quite clearly. This is it, she thought.

This is the beginning of the battle. She looked round at the others to see how they were taking it and noticed, out of the corner of her eye, that there were more security guards running from behind the TV van and that the police had linked arms ready to push the crowd back.

'And this,' she said into her microphone, 'is the only answer the authorities can give. Not argument or even explanation. Just sheer brute force.' She wanted to say more but the microphone had gone dead and the first of the guards had reached the tree and was climbing up towards the treehouse, clinging to the trunk and swinging his truncheon with his free hand.

Hands reached down towards him to push him back. Boots kicked at his gloved hands. Somebody pulled his truncheon away from him and hurled it to the ground. Aysha was being dragged from the tree by her hair, screaming at the top of her voice.

'Get back!' Laura said to Jessica. But her granddaughter was gone and there was no sign of Danny either.

'Grab the old girl!' a voice yelled and gloved hands reached up to catch her legs.

Oh no, she thought, kicking away from them and clinging to the tree. You're not pulling me down. I'll kick your teeth in first. Rad was standing above her with a rope in his hands. 'Tie me to the trunk,' she shouted.

The crowd cheered as she was secured, yelled defiance as the punching and grabbing went on, surrounded the security guards, howled abuse as another girl was pulled to the ground and frog-marched away. Up in the trees, in the heat and stink of battle-sweat, the noise was deafening and the struggle a total confusion.

Suddenly people in the crowd were yelling. 'Look! Look there!' and Laura was afraid that something else and worse was happening. Cling-ing to the tree, she glanced in the direction they were pointing. There was a gross white leg pro-truding from Ken's skylight. It had a dirty shoe on its foot which was waving ineffectually towards the branch of the tree a yard or so below it. Good God, she thought, he's surely not climbing out into the middle of all this. But he was. As she watched, his other leg was pushed through the open window and she could see a pair of filthy underpants looming after it, not quite covering his vast backside.

Then he seemed to be stuck. She could hear him swearing and watched as he man-handled the folds of his belly through the gap, pushing at it as though it were an over-inflated Lilo or the lard-white underbelly of a sea lion or a hippo-potamus.

The security guards had seen him now and paused in their struggle.

'Christ!' one of them said. 'What the hell's that?'

A police sergeant arrived at the foot of the tree. 'Hold on!' he instructed. But Ken was wriggling from side to side and still shoving his surplus fat out into the air. 'Does anyone know who it is?'

It's Ken Garston,' Laura called down to him. 'He lives there.' At that moment the rest of Ken's bulk slid out of the window and he was left hanging by his hands from the window sill, his filthy dressing gown flapping his rank body odour over the watchers below, his gross white legs swinging.

Rad had been sitting on the branch, waiting for him to drop. Now he edged towards him. 'That will never take the weight,' he called to the police sergeant. And he was right. It was splitting already.

By this time, Barney was sitting astride the branch too. 'Come on Sunshine,' he said, taking one swinging leg between his hands and moving it towards the tree. 'This way. We've got you.'

What happened next was like something from a kid's cartoon. Ken let go of the sill and fell face downwards through the air like an evil-smelling blancmange. He landed with a thud, spread-eagled over the branch below, groaning and sweating, his eyes tightly shut and his bulbous arms and legs dangling on either side of the branch. Before anyone could climb up and stop them, Rad and Barney leaned towards him and began to haul him bodily towards the tree-house. Others joined in, panting and pulling, and between them they dragged him into the house and propped him up against the central trunk of the tree.

'Bingo!' Rad said to Laura. 'We've got ourselves a hostage.'

His precipitate arrival had certainly changed the battle. The security guards hesitated, looked up at his panting bulk and retreated to the ground. One took out a mobile and phoned for instructions. More police arrived to join the sergeant. There were several conversations going on but no one in the trees could hear what was being said because the crowd was making such a noise.

Ken was struggling to his feet. His weight was making the entire tree sway. 'I did all this!' he yelled, waving an arm through the air. 'I called all this into being. Me. Ken Garston. You are all in my power.'

'Oh Christ!' the police sergeant said. 'A nutter. That's all we need. Someone get him down.'

Jeff was climbing down the far side of the tree. 'You don't know me,' he mouthed to Laura and the others. Then he was at the foot of the tree, dusting down his clothes. They watched as he walked into Ken's garden and up to the police sergeant.

'Better than Napoleon!' Ken was bragging. 'Oh I know what you all think of me, I'm not daft. I know how you laugh and snigger. Well, you're laughing on the other side of your faces now, aren't you. Eh? Eh? I've done all this. *I* have. Bloody woman. She doesn't feed me. I've run out of chocolate biscuits!'

The contractors had joined the police sergeant. 'I don't care how you do it,' one of them was saying to his security guards. 'Just get him down.'

'You'll need a mechanical hoist,' Jeff said. 'If

you try to move him bodily you could injure him.'

'Who are you?' one of the contractors asked.

'I'm a nurse,' Jeff told him. 'He's my patient.'

'Put me in the picture,' the police sergeant said. And when Jeff had given him a brief account of Ken's mental state and his self-imposed incarceration, 'So what you're saying is he'll need hospitalization. Right. I'll call up an ambulance.'

'And a fire engine,' Jeff said, 'with a hoist.'

'Now look here,' the senior contractor complained, 'is this going to take long? We've got a job to do here.'

'We'll be as quick as we can sir,' the sergeant told him. 'We can't have the gentleman injured, can we?'

But it was fifteen entertaining minutes before the ambulance arrived and by then Joan had been found and brought down from the trees to add her voice to the debate.

'Section him all you like,' she said, when the police sergeant suggested that this might be the outcome. 'He's been round the twist ever since they made him redundant. You've only got to look at him to see that.'

The contractors retreated to confer, the dance started up again while several of the protesters settled to a picnic, the security men smoked and kicked their heels while they waited for instructions, the cameras took happy pictures of the fat man haranguing the multitude, which he did at length and more and more incomprehensibly, Laura was unbound and she and her grandchildren sat in the tree as comfortably as they could and watched.

From time to time there was an odd pulsing sound from the direction of the woods. 'Machines,' Laura said, when Jessica asked her what it was. 'They won't have stopped work at the other end will they. It's only down here they've got to wait.'

And the wait went on even after the emergency services had arrived. First of all, it took a lot of effort to get the fire engine into the lane. Most of the cars had to be driven into a field to make way for it, including Maureen's, and the TV van had to be inched out of the way. Then, when the hoist was in position, it took patience and bribery to coax the fat man into it.

'All to the good,' Kapok said, from her perch above Jessica's head. 'The longer it takes the less time those buggers'll have for hauling us about.'

'I was Napoleon in another life,' Ken declared. 'Leader of men. He talks to me you know. Oh yes. Every night. Wouldn't move without me. He told me so.'

'Well that's nice,' the ambulance man soothed. 'But don't you think that cut ought to be looked at?'

'What cut?'

'The one on your leg that's bleeding.'

'Did Napoleon do that?'

'You caught it on the tree. Napoleon's very upset about it.'

'Is he?'

'Oh yes. He wants you to come down in this hoist and let us attend to it.'

'Did he send it? This hoist?'

'Of course. He's your friend isn't he?'

Napoleon's friend considered this for a very long time.

'Will he come down?' Jessica wondered, as the crowd watched and the cameras whirred.

'There's no telling with him,' Laura had to admit.

But at length Napoleon's friend came to a decision. 'I will do it for him,' he announced and waved his hand when the crowd cheered. His descent was greeted with further cheers which he accepted regally. Once he was on the ground it was easy enough to escort him into the ambulance and drive him away.

His departure left a gap in the afternoon.

'Now what?' Danny asked.

'That depends on the contractors,' Kapok said, looking round for them. 'That's funny. Where are they?'

The word was spread through the trees and down to the ground, where the dancers stopped to look too. There were a couple of security guards loitering by their van and half a dozen policemen still on site but the three contractors seemed to have disappeared and so had the lumberjacks. What was more, they'd taken their chain-saws with them.

'Have we won already?' Laura asked warily. 'Or have they gone for reinforcements?'

Rad said he didn't know. 'It's not like them to back down at the first obstacle,' he said. But the chain-saws were gone. There was no doubt about that and the site was surprisingly peaceful. So peaceful that they could all hear the thump-thump-thump of that distant machinery.

Kapok stood up and turned her head in the direction of the sound. 'Listen!' she commanded. 'Listen will yer! That ain't a JCB. That's a fucking pump. Oh shit! I know what they're doing. They're draining the pond. Come on!' And she was off along the tree walk at once, with Danny and Jessica close behind her.

'Wait,' Rad called. 'Don't all go. It could be a ploy. The rest of you stay on guard.'

Laura left him to organise his troops as she followed the others, keeping her balance as well as she could on the swaying rope-way. They haven't stopped the fight, she thought, they've just moved the battlefield. And wouldn't you know it would be the pond. But she didn't waver. Whatever happened and wherever it was she had to be there and part of it.

Others were on the move too, calling to one another as they climbed and swung. 'It's the pond. Pass it on. They're draining the pond.' By the time Laura reached the clearing a sizeable crowd had already gathered there. She could see the green bulk of the pump and Jessica's blonde hair swinging as she climbed up to stop it.

'Be careful!' she called. But it was much too late for caution. There were security guards all round the pump and battle had been joined. As she ran towards it she could hear yells and screams and the thud of blows. She had a brief glimpse of Kapok and Jessica running into the pond. Then there was a splash and the air was suddenly riven with the most dreadful screams she'd ever heard in her life.

For a few seconds she was so afraid that she had to stand still to get her breath and allow her heart to recover a little, but then she ran full tilt at the pond, knowing by instinct that it was Jessica who was screaming and that it was horror she was screaming at.

The pond was visibly lower and both girls were in the mud at the water's edge, Jessica on her hands and knees and still screaming, Kapok behind her, trying to pull her up. But she seemed to be fixed in position, staring at the mud and screaming endlessly. Two more steps and Laura saw what was the matter. Jessica was kneeling over the grey-brown bones of a full-sized human skeleton, her fingers caught in the eye sockets of its skull.

Chapter Thirty-Six

There was no time for Laura to feel afraid. No time for reaction. No time to think. She was working on instinct and fuelled by adrenalin, with nothing in her mind except the urgent need to protect her young. She hurtled to the edge of the pond, calling as she ran, 'It's all right, Jess. Gran's coming.' She walked into the mud without a qualm, her shoes squelching. 'You're all right, my darling. Give me your hand, there's a good girl.'

Jessica stopped screaming but she was too stunned to know what she was doing. She obeyed her grandmother automatically, lifted her fingers out of the skull, held up her mud-streaked hand to be grasped. But she seemed shell-shocked, her eyes dull.

There were people all around them, helping hands to urge them away from the horror, a kaleidoscope of anxious faces, swimming about them pale as fishes. And one of them was Maureen's.

'Oh my poor darling,' she said, catching her daughter in her arms. 'My poor dear darling.'

And at that Jessica dissolved into tears and began to shake. 'Oh Mum! Mum! Did you *see* what it was?'

'It's all right,' Maureen said, smoothing her

hair. 'They're only bones, that's all. They can't hurt you. You're with me. It's all over.'

'I had my hands right in . . .'

'Yes, my lovey, I know. Come on. Let's get you home shall we. Where's Danny?'

He was behind them, wide-eyed with shock. She put out a hand to him too. 'Are you all right?' And he grabbed it and clung to it, his head against her shoulder.

Laura was suddenly aware that she was achingly tired. She sank on to the nearest fallen branch so that she could rest her head against the tree trunk behind her. The gruesome sight in the pond was a few feet away — pale bones gleaming in the green light — but she couldn't move away from it. Her mind seemed to have lost the capacity to cope with several things at once. Now that Jess was safe, there was only room in it for the brute, bare truth of that terrible skeleton and she had to look at it.

Whoever it was, she thought, he must have been there for years for his bones to be as clean as that. There was rubbish all round him, crushed cans and dirty cigarette boxes, an old shoe, twigs, dead leaves, bits of wood. That chunk just under the water could have been a box of some sort. And he was lying there amongst it as though he were little better than rubbish himself. Now that the first shock was passing she felt sorry for him, whoever he was. But how could a body have been lying there for years, just under the water, without anyone knowing about it? It wasn't possible. It occurred to her that it must have been there on the night of the procession. She must have walked past it hundreds of times on her way to the upper road, especially in the days before she ran a car. She'd used that footpath every day on her way to the bus stop. Once she started work. After Pete left. *After Pete left.* Dear God! It couldn't be!

The police sergeant had arrived and was down at the water's edge, speaking urgently into his walkie-talkie. 'Sergeant Garner here. No. No. Not the demonstration. That's over. We have a skeleton in the pond. Edge of Duran's Wood. Right. Right. We shall need arc lights. Will you notify the police surgeon . . . ?'

She was glad he was in command because she didn't have the energy to do anything except sit and think and there were so many people all around her it was hard to do *that*. She realised — gratefully — that he was deploying his men to disperse the crowd, and 'get those damned security guards out of the way'. It *could* be a box. What if . . . ?

There was somebody crashing through the wood, feet pounding. Somebody running. Jeff, with a blanket over his arm and panting behind him, Amy with a flask of tea.

'Where have they gone?' he said.

'Home,' Laura said. 'Where else?'

One of the policemen was walking towards her. 'If you wouldn't mind moving, madam,' he suggested.

'We're family,' Amy told him. 'This is the lady

who rescued the girl from the pond. She's her grandmother.'

'I think I ought to talk to your sergeant,' Laura said. 'There's something . . .'

'I'll send him over, madam,' the constable promised.

But minutes passed and he didn't arrive. The pump was turned off at last and she was relieved to be freed from its incessant noise. Amy gave her a plastic cup full of tea and insisted that she drink it, which she did obediently. Jeff sat beside her to check that she was recovering and she told him that she was. But she was looking at the dark box-like shape just under the water and thinking.

The crowds were gone. There was nobody left beside the pond except Amy and Jeff and a couple of policemen. No security men, no reporters, no cameras. There were three young men in smart suits and yellow hats standing by the pump talking to the sergeant. But that was all. It was so quiet she could hear a thrush singing.

She could hear what Sergeant Garner was saying too and he was saying it with polite determination. 'Yes sir, I daresay you're right, but you can't proceed until the corpse has been removed.'

The senior of the three men was politely fuming. 'When will that be? Time costs money.'

'Quite!' the sergeant said. 'And, of course, there'll be an inquest. So you'll probably have to wait until after that.'

'It's very inconvenient,' the senior man said.

Sergeant Garner was calm. 'Death always is, sir.' He was being bleeped. 'If you'll excuse me, sir.'

Laura watched as the three yellow hats bobbed away down the path until they were mere gleams in the darkness. Now and at last Sergeant Garner was walking towards her. 'You wanted to see me, ma'am.'

She looked up at him, gathering her strength to face the final horror, if that was what she had to do. 'Yes,' she said. 'I think I might be able to identify the body. I can't be sure, mind. But there's something down there just under the water that might . . .' She stood up. 'Come and look.'

They all walked to the water's edge together. It was very dark now and she could only just make out the shape that had caught her eye. 'There!' she said, pointing at it. 'That box.'

'The arc lights have just arrived,' Sergeant Garner told her. 'We'll wait till they're in position and then we'll get it out for you.'

It took a very long time to haul the lights along the footpath and almost as long to set them up beside the pond. But she waited patiently with Jeff and Amy beside her. None of them said anything. What could they say? At last everything was prepared and the lamps were switched on in a blaze of light so powerful that it hurt her eyes. But it revealed the pond in every detail. Now they could all see the box quite clearly.

One of the constables retrieved it, an oblong

box made of blackened wood, dripping slime. There was a corroded catch on one side and even in that hideous state it was sickeningly familiar.

'I think,' she said, calmly, to the sergeant, 'that if you open it up you will find there is a sextant inside.'

It was opened. The sextant was there, covered in verdigris, but intact in all its parts, still lying in its ancient velvet, just as she'd last seen it twenty-five years ago. She was aware that Jeff was watching her with concern and that Amy was tense as a spring beside her, breathing hard as though she'd been running.

But Sergeant Garner was looking a question at her and she had to answer it. 'It belonged to my husband,' she told him. 'I think that's who we've found. He went missing from Holm End — a long time ago — twenty-five years. He had that sextant with him when he left and this is the path he would have taken.'

She caught a glimpse of Amy's legs running away and then she realised that someone was groaning. 'Oh my God! It can't be!' She turned to see who it was, half knowing it would be David. 'Not Dad! Not after all these years! Oh my dear good God!'

'David?' she asked.

He was staring at the skeleton. 'Maureen told me. I got here as soon as I could. Is it really him? Is it? Oh dear God!'

'I don't think there's much doubt, sir,' the police sergeant said. 'We shall need some details for the police surgeon, but it looks pretty conclusive to me. And you are . . . ?'

'His son.'

'What sort of details do you want?' Laura asked. She was quite calm about it now that she knew.

They were predictable. Name, height, occupation, age when last seen.

'Thirty-two,' she said and she could see him again, walking away from her into the storm, that dark hair catching the light. Oh Pete! I thought you'd left me and you've been lying here all the time.

'Did you report him missing?' the sergeant asked.

She gathered herself to answer him. 'The last time I saw him I thought he was going to join a ship.'

'But he didn't.'

'No,' she said. 'I checked with the shipping lines and the union. All sorts of places. Nobody knew where he was.'

'But you didn't report him missing?'

She told him the truth, even though it hurt her. 'I thought he'd left me,' she admitted. 'We both did, didn't we David.'

'All these years,' David said, speaking slowly because he was still finding it difficult to accept. 'All these years I've been blaming him for running out on us. And all the time he was . . . All these years, I've run myself ragged not to be like him because I thought he'd deserted us and all the time . . . And all the time he wasn't the way we thought he was at all. Poor devil! How did it happen?'

'He must have fallen,' Jeff told him. 'It's very dark in these woods at night.'

'There was a storm,' Laura remembered. 'It was an awful night. Thunder and lightning.'

'All this time . . .' David said. 'It's going to take a lot of getting used to. I've based my entire life on a lie.'

'No,' she said, 'not a lie. Not the truth but not a lie. We just didn't know.'

But his distress was terrible. 'All these years.'

'I don't think I need to trouble either of you any further,' Sergeant Garner said gently. 'If I were you, I'd get back home.' He turned to Jeff. 'If you could just stay with us, sir, until we've removed the remains in case there are any other objects for identification, then we needn't keep Mrs Pendleton, or you Mr Pendleton.'

Jeff would have preferred to go back to the cottage and look after Laura but he agreed to stay and help the sergeant. It had to be done and if he didn't do it, Laura or David would have to. 'He's right,' he said to them. 'I'll stay here. You go home.'

'I must tell Maureen and the kids,' David said but he was anxious about his mother. 'Will you be all right?'

'Yes,' she told him. 'I'm not in shock or anything. You go.' She smiled at him and gave him a gentle push to urge him on his way.

Even so, he went reluctantly and looking back at her from time to time. She watched until he was out of sight. 'Poor David,' she said. But then she noticed that someone was missing and she stood up and looked around her. 'Where's Amy?'

'She ran off,' Jeff told her. 'Just after they opened the box.'

'Oh did she?' Laura said grimly. 'Then if that's the case, I've got some unfinished business to attend to.'

Jeff was alarmed by her expression. Unfinished business sounded a bit too much like a row. 'Won't it wait 'til morning or 'til I get back?' he asked.

But she was already on her way down the path. 'No. It won't,' she said. 'It's waited too long already.'

Chapter Thirty-Seven

The living room was empty but there were footsteps overhead. Surprisingly heavy footsteps for sister-in-law Amy. But that's who it was, upstairs in Jessica's bedroom, frantically throwing clothes into her suitcase. Scarves and underwear lay in piles on the bed, her sweaters were draped over the back of the chair, her suits hung on the wardrobe door. She looked up when Laura strode into the room and there was panic on her face.

'I'm leaving,' she said, tucking a jersey into the case. 'I've got a plane to catch. Tonight. I'm late as it is. I should have told you before but with all this going on it just went clean out of my mind.'

'No,' Laura told her. 'It didn't. You're making it up.'

Amy was breathless with urgency. 'No really. I've got a plane to catch. I'm leaving. Tonight.'

'No,' Laura said again. 'You're not. If you really *have* got a plane to catch it can wait until the morning. You've got some explaining to do.'

'There's nothing to explain,' Amy insisted, folding jerseys as fast as she could. She was so tense her hands were shaking.

Laura sat on the bed, closed the case and held the lid down with both hands. 'There is,' she said, 'and you're going to do it.'

There was a brief unseemly tussle for possession of the case, with Amy trying to prise Laura's hand away and Laura holding on with furious determination. Amy was wild with panic but Laura had the strength of retribution. Eventually Amy gave up and flounced to the window, storm-faced. 'Jeez, Laura! I don't need this!' she said angrily, glaring at her reflection in the black glass.

'But *I* do,' Laura said and plunged straight into the attack while her need and her courage were high. 'You knew he was there.'

Amy went on glaring at her reflection. 'I didn't. How could I have done?'

'You knew he was there. Admit it. You knew. You took one look at that box and you ran.'

Amy turned to make an appeal. 'Why are you being so unkind?' she cried. 'Isn't it bad enough to have seen . . . to have just . . . Look, I didn't know. Believe me.'

But Laura was proof against any appeal. 'Oh come on, Amy,' she rebuked. 'What a bloody silly thing to say. *"Believe me!"* You lie through your teeth. Nobody believes you.'

For a few seconds Amy didn't say anything. She levelled a long look at her adversary across the pile of clothes on the bed. 'All right then,' she said at last. 'I'll tell you. I thought it *might* be him. I didn't know. I thought it might be. Satisfied?'

'No,' Laura said implacably, relinquishing her hold on the case. 'There's a lot more. You can't go on hiding things now. None of us can. *Why* did you think it might be?'

Amy sank into the emptied chair and ran her hands through her hair, lifting it as though she would find truth or strength between the strands. 'You won't like it,' she warned.

'He's been dead twenty-five years,' Laura said. 'Lying there unburied in that awful black water. Nothing you can tell me could possibly be as bad as that.'

Amy gave her another long look, calculating the risk. 'All right then,' she said. 'He was leaving you that night.'

'Yes. I know,' Laura said bluntly. 'He told me.'

There was the most peculiar expression on Amy's face, part defiance, part shame, part distress. She got up, found her bag, rummaged in it for a cigarette, lit up, sat down again. 'He was leaving you,' she said at last, 'to run away with me.'

The news should have been a shock but it wasn't. There was a numbing inevitability about it. Everything fell into place and made sense at last. 'I think I've known that for a long time,' Laura said. 'Ever since you came back. He said there was someone else. I should have guessed it would be you. Molly knew, didn't she?'

'She saw us together. I thought she'd tell you.'

'She hinted, but I didn't know what she was talking about. *Then.*'

'Look,' Amy said, and now her expression was simply shamed, 'I didn't want this to happen. Any of it. I knew it was wrong. I mean someone was bound to get hurt. It was obvious.'

'Then why did you do it?'

'We couldn't help it. We were in love.'

Laura snorted. 'Love!' she mocked. 'You don't know the meaning of the word. You were always in love with someone or other — that boy Ginger, Teddy, Paul with the Dutch name, poor old Joe. You hunted *him* down and you can't say you didn't.'

'Poor Joe,' Amy sighed. 'He was one of life's losers. He never got anything right. But it was different with Pete. I know you won't believe me. Why should you? But it *was* different. I really did love him.'

'So did I and he was *my* husband.'

'I know. I know. That's what made it so awful. I didn't want to love him. Not at first anyway. I just wanted to take him away from you. I'll admit that. Not for always. Just for a little while — to show you I could. But I didn't want to love him. That just happened.' She spoke slowly, taking her time, for she was confessing the most private and shameful emotions. 'It was awful, Laura, truly it was. I've never known anything so painful. And it was worse for him than for me. He was in a bad way. Torn in half, he said. To tell the truth, I thought he'd run out on both of us that night because he couldn't stand it. Joe said he'd gone because he'd warned him off but I never believed it.'

Laura's anger was over, calmed by Amy's confession. It was all such a long time ago it hardly

588

seemed to be her story any more. There was only one thing that concerned her now. David mustn't know about any of this, she thought. He's got enough to come to terms with. Then she realised that Amy was still talking and that she'd said something significant.

'What did you just say?' she asked.

'I said I didn't believe it.'

'Didn't believe what?'

'What Joe said. He said Pete had gone because he'd warned him off.'

Warning bells rang in Laura's brain. 'Warned him off? What do you mean, warned him off?'

'We had a row,' Amy confessed. 'Joe and me, I mean. I told him I was leaving him. I said Pete and me were going away to start a new life together. I tried to explain but he wouldn't listen. He went berserk. He called me all the names under the sun and then he took the car and went. I thought he'd just driven off in a temper. Well you know the way he was. Anyway I waited and waited for Pete to come. We were going to meet at the bus stop at the top of the lane. I was all packed up and everything. But he never turned up. And then there was a storm, with thunder and lightning and everything, and I got soaking wet. In the end I went back home. I didn't know what else to do. I thought he'd changed his mind. Then Joe came back and said he'd warned him off. So that was that. And then two weeks later he got that job in Adelaide and Pete hadn't written or anything so I knew it was all over and I thought we might as well go. I'd lost Pete and he was the only man I'd ever really loved so what did it matter where we lived?'

'My God, Amy!' Laura said. 'Do you realise what you've just told me?'

Amy was still wrapped in her memory. 'About Pete?'

'About Joe. He must have been the last person to see Pete alive. He must have laid in wait for him on the path. He'd have gone that way to catch the bus.'

Now Amy was beginning to see the implication. 'You mean, they could have met by the pond. Jeez, Laura! You don't think he . . .'

'I don't know what to think,' Laura said. 'It's possible. What exactly did he say when he got home?'

'Jeez!' Amy said again. 'I don't know. I can't remember. It was years ago. He warned him off. That's all.'

Laura had remembered something else. 'He had nightmares,' she said. 'When you first got out there, he had nightmares. You told me about them the night you arrived here.'

Amy remembered *that*. 'Yes, he did. He used to scream and yell. Jeez Laura! This is awful.' The possibilities were swirling towards the most dreadful certainty.

'We don't know anything for certain,' Laura warned. 'This is all supposition.'

'But if he pushed him in the pond it would be murder.'

'We don't know he pushed him in the pond,' Laura insisted. 'We don't know *what* happened. How could we? We weren't there. So we're not going to tell anyone. Are we?'

'No,' Amy said earnestly. '*I* shan't, I promise. Leave well alone, that's my motto. I don't want anything else dug up.' Then she realised what a crass thing she'd just said and put her hand to her mouth in dismay.

It was too late. The damage had been done. Laura's face was crumpling into tears. 'Oh God!' she wept. 'To die out there all on his own in the dark. To drown in that awful black water and lie there in the mud all these years with nobody knowing. He didn't deserve that. He was such a good man. And I loved him so much. A good man, a good father. He doted on David. We must never let David know about this. Promise you won't say anything to him. You will promise, won't you? He's got enough to cope with without this sort of suspicion. Oh God. Poor David. Poor Pete. And everybody said what a good navigator he was. Brilliant, they said. That's why I bought him that sextant. And he's been dead all this time, lying in the mud, and I didn't know.'

Amy stumbled across the room and flung her arms round Laura's shoulders, clumsy with anguished affection. She was weeping too. 'Oh don't cry!' she begged. 'Please don't cry! It's all my fault and I can't bear it.'

But now that she'd started Laura couldn't stop until her grief was cried out. She put her hands over her eyes and wept with abandon while Amy cuddled her and rocked her and cried with her.

Up in the woods, Jeff was fidgeting. The long-lost bones had finally been removed from the pond and driven carefully away, the arc lights were gone, the pump was a silent hulk, pale in the darkness. Apart from the low level of the pond, the mud churned at its edge, a few white tatters of discarded litter and two smashed branches lying on the footpath, there was little to show for the evening's drama.

'You don't need me any more now, do you?' he asked Sergeant Garner.

'No,' the sergeant said. 'Thanks for your help, sir. I'll come back in the morning, if that's all right.'

'Quite all right,' Jeff said. Now he could get back to Laura at last.

He ran all the way to the cottage, dark though it was. There was a light in Jessica's bedroom but, to his great relief, no sound of a row. He took off his shoes and tiptoed upstairs. But once he reached the little landing he hesitated.

Laura wasn't in her bedroom and now he could hear murmuring voices coming from Jessica's room. He peered through the half-open door and saw — with a shock of surprise — that Laura was in tears and that Amy was comforting her. How odd! He watched her red-tipped fingers rubbing Laura's back and recognised concern in the tenor of her voice. Whatever might have happened between them earlier on, he thought, they certainly aren't angry with one another now. I shall leave them alone, he decided. He knew instinctively that this was something to do with their past lives and that he had no part in it. The best thing to do was to go to bed quietly and leave them to it — for the time being anyway. If things got violent or unpleasant, which didn't seem likely, he would be on hand to step in. He was aching with fatigue but he was sure he could keep awake to stay on guard.

He was asleep within seconds of his head touching the pillow.

Laura cried until there were no more tears to shed. 'Oh dear,' she said. mopping her eyes. 'I could do with a bit of soap and water.'

'The worst thing,' Amy said. 'It'll bring you up in blotches. Come and sit in the chair and I'll get my cleanser. That'll be much better.'

Laura wasn't sure about having her face cleansed with lotion but Amy was extremely gentle.

'That's better,' she said, as she smoothed Laura's cheeks with cotton wool. 'You're beginning to look more like yourself.'

'What a night this has been,' Laura said, as the lotion eased her stinging skin. 'I never thought I'd end up sitting here with you cleaning my face.'

'Enjoy it,' Amy said. 'You've earned a bit of petting after all you've been through. I thought you were very brave up that tree. I'd have been petrified.'

'I was,' Laura admitted.

'It didn't show. You were marvellous.'

Laura leant her head against the back of the chair. 'Something you said's been puzzling me.'

Amy was working calmly. 'What?'

'It was about Joe. You said he was a loser. One of life's losers.'

'Too right. He was.'

'Then all that stuff about how well you were doing wasn't true?'

'Nope,' Amy admitted easily. 'We failed at every mortal thing. I think that's why he had his coronary. Couldn't make a go of anything.'

'And the big house?'

'A shack.'

'So there isn't any more luggage to follow you over. I *did* wonder what had happened to it.'

'Debts maybe, but no luggage.' She gestured at the suitcase. 'That is the sum total of my worldly goods. I'll unpack it presently. I suppose I can sleep here now that Jessica's gone home.'

Laura nodded vaguely. 'Oh dear, oh dear,' she sighed, 'and I thought you'd done so well too.'

'That's what you were supposed to think.'

'Tell me something. Did you know he was a failure when you married him?'

'No, not really. I had my suspicions.'

'Why *did* you marry him?'

Amy wiped off the last trace of lotion from Laura's forehead, put down the bottle, and looked her sister-in-law straight in the eye. 'To be like you,' she said.

What an extraordinary thing to say! 'Why, for heaven's sake?'

'I was jealous of you,' Amy confessed. 'Always was. Ever since we were kids.'

'Jealous of *me?*'

'Too right. You had everything I wanted.'

'Oh come on Amy, you couldn't have been jealous of me. If anything, I was jealous of *you.* All those pretty clothes and living in a big house and holidays abroad. You were the only family in the village to have holidays abroad. You can't possibly say I had everything you wanted. Compared to you, I barely had anything.'

Amy was sitting at the dressing table, cleaning her own face. 'Yes, you did,' she said. 'You had parents who loved you. Especially your mum. I'd have given my right arm to have a mum like yours. I can remember when you were nearly drowned that time and she put her arms round you and hugged you and said she loved you.'

That seemed such normal behaviour to Laura that she was amazed to have it commented on. 'Well of course she did. I was frightened.'

'I'd have got a wallop if it had been me,' Amy said. 'I had to mind my Ps and Qs all the time.'

'Oh Amy, I didn't know that.'

'Nobody knew,' Amy said. 'We kept it to ourselves.'

Laura was remembering. 'Pete was there, you know,' she said, 'when I nearly drowned.'

'I know. He told me. He tried to pull you out with a stick. He told me when you bought the sextant. He said you were breaking his heart. You'd bought him the most expensive present he'd ever had in his life on the very day he'd decided to leave you. He was choked about it. He kept on and on about how you'd nearly drowned and he hadn't saved you and how much he loved you and how hard it was to choose between us.'

'But he still chose you.'

Amy turned to face her. Now that her make-up was removed her face was vulnerable, just as it had been on that first morning after she'd arrived, her mouth soft and her eyes full of regret. 'I know,' she said. 'It didn't make sense to me either. I told him I'd give him up and go away and leave you both alone and I really thought he'd take me up on it — but he didn't.'

That was truly amazing news. 'You offered to give him up.'

'I loved him,' Amy said simply. 'I couldn't bear seeing him hurt.'

'Oh Amy,' Laura understood. 'You *did* love him.'

'Yes, I did,' Amy said, tears welling into her eyes. 'I told you so. Oh dear! It's a good job I've taken off my mascara.'

The square of sky in the window had grown lighter since the last time Laura looked at it. 'It's dawn,' she said, walking over to the window. 'We've talked all night.'

Amy followed her across the room and they stood side by side in companionable silence, watching the sky grow steadily more and more blue.

'Were your lovers real?' Laura asked. The question was mild, and asked out of tender curiosity, no more.

Amy laughed. 'Oh yes,' she said easily. 'I've never had any trouble getting a new lover. That's easy. It's keeping the buggers that's the hard bit.'

'What about Brooke Curtis?'

'Don't talk to me about him,' Amy said. 'He was the worst of the lot. Dropped me like a hot brick. I haven't had a word out of him since she sent me to Birmingham. And he was a ghastly lover.'

Laura laughed. 'That doesn't surprise me.'

'How did you know?'

'The white Mercedes.'

'Is there a connection?'

'Well you know what they say. Big car, little cock.'

'Spot on!' Amy laughed. 'I sometimes wonder whether any of them are worth it.'

'Some are,' Laura said reflectively. 'But you're right about keeping them. That *is* the hard part.'

Amy's eyebrows shot up in surprise. 'You too?'

'Now and then. It's been twenty-five years, don't forget.'

'You never said.'

'They were private. You have to be private when you've got a kid.'

'Ah!' Amy understood. 'Of course.' She was thoughtful for a moment, then she asked, 'What about him?' and jerked her head in the direction of the main bedroom.

'He could be different,' Laura told her. 'He's unusual.'

'I hope so,' Amy said. 'Truly.'

'You know, it's a silly sort of thing to say, but I don't think I've known you until tonight.'

'When I married poor old Joe,' Amy said, 'I thought we were going to be like sisters. Do you remember those dinner parties we used to have?'

'Don't remind me!' Laura grimaced. 'Weren't they awful.'

'I used to look forward to them,' Amy confessed. 'I'd think, this time it'll be different. This time we'll really talk.'

'And it never was,' Laura said sadly, 'because we never did. I hated those parties.'

Amy sighed. 'We ought to get some sleep or we shall never get up in the morning.'

'Yes.' Laura agreed. 'We should.' But they were loath to part from one another.

'I'll see you in the morning,' Amy promised.

And with that they finally allowed their long night to come to an end.

Jeff's alarm woke them all up at seven. Laura was so heavy with sleep she couldn't open her eyes.

'Stay there,' he said, brushing her cheek with his beard. 'I'll get you some tea.'

'I must get up,' she said, her eyes still tightly shut. 'I've got to go to work.'

'No you haven't,' he said. 'You're on leave. Remember?'

She was too tired to remember anything. The sunlight was so strong it was warming her face. It's going to be a lovely day, she thought, and drifted back to sleep again.

He brought her tea and toast on a tray and when Amy came yawning in to join them he went downstairs and got a cup for her too.

'Thanks Jeff,' she said, in her casual way. 'You're a sweetie.'

The word made Jeff and Laura laugh.

'Oh Amy!' Laura giggled. 'You don't change.'

Amy was genuinely puzzled. 'What have I said?'

'Never mind,' Laura said. 'It's a long story.'

'I'm knackered,' Amy said. 'I shan't go in to work today.'

'Good,' Laura smiled. 'Then we can have a whole day together.'

Jeff was relieved to see them so easy with one another. Whatever had happened between them hadn't harmed either of them. 'That's settled then,' he said. 'I'll leave you to look after one another. You *are* all right, aren't you, Laura?'

It was a pleasant day and an eventful one. Just before eleven Sergeant Garner turned up to tell them that the police doctor had finished his examination and that there hadn't been any problems.

'The details tally,' he said. 'There's no doubt

599

about the identification. There will have to be an inquest, I'm afraid. That can't be avoided. But it will only be a formality.'

Laura said she knew.

'I'm sorry you've had all this to put up with,' the sergeant said. 'It must have been quite a shock.'

'I'm all right,' Laura told him, with perfect truth. 'It isn't like a death for me. Not really. I mourned for my husband years ago. This is just tying up loose ends.'

'There's one good thing about it,' he told her. 'It's put a stop to any further action over the road. They can't proceed until the inquest is over and that could take weeks.'

It was a surprise to realise that they had a police sergeant in sympathy with them. 'Thank you for letting us know,' Laura said. 'We do appreciate it.'

He was looking through the window at the benders. 'Staying long, are they?' he asked, just a little too mildly.

'I shouldn't think so,' Laura told him, anxious to protect her new friends. 'Not now. But they're my guests so they're welcome to stay as long as they like. I wouldn't like to think I had to harass them.'

'No,' he said. 'Of course not. But with the road on hold, so to speak . . .'

'Now what?' Amy asked when he'd gone.

'I think we ought to tell them what he said,' Laura decided. 'If he's keeping an eye on them, they ought to know.'

But they knew already. 'They always watch us,' Rad said. 'That's par for the course. You get used to it. Don't worry. We're off to Winchester for the court case.'

She was disappointed to hear it.

'You've got the look-outs and the walk-ways,' he told her, 'so you'll be all right. You know how to build now and you can keep in touch. If you need us you know where we are.'

They were gone within the hour and the garden seemed empty without them.

'Now what?' Amy asked again.

'Now we've got rather a lot to do. We must go round and tell the neighbours what's been happening but, first, I'm going to ring Maureen and the kids to find out how David is.'

He was a great deal better than she expected.

'We were up till three in the morning,' Maureen said, 'talking and talking, all four of us.'

'And?'

'It's done us all a power of good,' Maureen said. 'It's going to take him a long time to get used to what he's found out about his father but it's all positive. He says he feels better this morning than he's done for years.'

'And Jess?'

'None the worse really. She was wonderful last night. Said all the right things. And so did Danny. I was really proud of them. In a way, they were taking care of us. It was an odd experience.'

'But a good one?'

'A very good one. I'll tell you all about it later. They're just on their way down for breakfast.'

Laura was beaming as she put down the phone. 'Now for the neighbours,' she said to Amy, 'and then I'm going to clean up the lane. Our demonstration left a lot of litter.'

They went from door to door with their news, saying little about the skeleton — apart from explaining whose it was — but a great deal about Sergeant Garner's encouraging opinion.

It took them the rest of the morning, so it wasn't until after lunch that they began to clear up, talking of old times as they worked. After a few minutes Connie came out to join them and, not long after that, Joan arrived to say that she was having a bonfire of Ken's old clothes and some of the junk he'd left behind in the attic and they might as well burn the litter too.

'You'd never believe the rubbish he's left,' she said. 'I shall need a lot of wood to get it going.'

It took them the best part of the afternoon to clean up the lane and to build their bonfire. When it blazed Connie said it was 'as good as Guy Fawkes'.

It was certainly a great deal more smelly. But Laura was glad of it. As the flames leapt and roared and sparks exploded into the darkening air, she felt she was burning away all the bad things in her life — the anguish of loss, the long useless search, the uncertainty she'd carried all these years.

Chapter Thirty-Eight

They buried the mortal remains of Peter Pendleton on a green afternoon in the churchyard of St Mary's where he'd played as a child. It was a simple ceremony at which the rector spoke movingly of the uncertainty that his wife and family had endured during the last twenty-five years.

'Delayed grief is all the more poignant for being delayed,' he said, 'and all the more difficult to contend with. However, that being said, I should also say that, being human, we are blessed with the healing power of memory. You will all have memories of Peter, as husband, as father, as brother-in-law. Enjoy them. Savour them. They will sustain you in the days that lie ahead. Remember that your long sorrow is over, at last. Peter is laid to rest and you can go forward. May God, in His infinite mercy, keep you and protect you and remain with you now and always.'

'Just as well he doesn't know the truth about it all,' Amy grinned. 'But it was a nice service, don't you think so.'

The best thing about it was that it had unlocked their memories and made it possible for David and Laura to share them. They talked about Peter all through their funeral tea, remembering how kind he'd been and how hard-working.

'He used to take me fishing,' David recalled. 'The first thing he did when he got home was to oil the rods.'

'Whatever happened to those rods?' Laura wondered.

'I gave them to Ken Garston when I got married.'

'You didn't!' Laura laughed. 'Then I've just burnt them. On that bonfire we had. You remember Amy. When Joan cleared out the attic.'

'I can remember when you were christened,' Amy said to David. 'He held you at the font. Tiny little thing you were, in a long white shawl against his blues. He was so proud you wouldn't believe it. *My son!* he kept saying. *My son!*'

'He was a good father,' David said. 'I've thought the worst of him all these years and I've been wrong. It's cleared my mind knowing the truth about him.' He paused, as if he had more to say, but at that moment, the phone rang.

It was Toby Fawcett. 'Ah, there you are,' he said, when Laura answered. 'I've been trying to get you all afternoon. I've got a bit of news for you.'

'Yes?'

'Came through midday. It'll be in the paper tomorrow morning but I thought you ought to know first. They've put the road scheme on permanent hold.'

Laura felt quite weak at the knees. 'You mean they're not going to build it, after all?'

'Not for the foreseeable future.'

604

'What about the compulsory purchase order?'

'Rescinded. Letters are being sent, according to the press release.'

'Thank God!'

'They say it's *"in consideration of recent events at the site"*, but between you and me I think it's got more to do with the general election coming and the fact that they're running out of funds. Councillor Mrs Smith's been on the warpath about overspending for weeks. Anyway the long and the short of it is you're off the hook.'

'Thanks for telling me,' Laura said. 'It's very good of you.' She put the phone down and told the others quickly, the words tumbling over one another.

There was a roar of congratulation, a flurry of kisses.

'Brilliant!' Danny said. 'I always knew we'd win.'

'We haven't won,' Laura felt she had to point out. 'They've still got the option of starting it up again. It's only on hold.'

'That'll do to be going on with,' Jeff said, hugging her. 'A lot might happen if they're going to wait until after the election, don't forget.'

'I must tell the others,' Laura said. She was full of happy excitement. 'I won't be long but I must just tell them.'

'Go on then,' Maureen told her. 'I'll make the tea.'

It took her more than half an hour. Naturally. News like that could hardly be dropped on the run. By the time she got back to the cottage, the table was set and the tea made.

'What a wonderful end to the day,' she said, as Maureen poured and the meal began. She looked at David, aware of how much her campaign had cost *him*. If only his problems could be solved too.

He turned to her and squeezed her arm. 'You mustn't worry about me,' he said. 'I'm a big boy now. I shall get another job eventually. I've made my mind up to it.'

'He has too,' Maureen smiled. 'He's got a system. He's listed every single possibility and we're going to write to them all. We're not going to be defeated.'

'And guess what!' Danny said happily. 'Jess has been offered a place at Lampeter.' He was flushed with pride at her achievement.

It was wonderful news and congratulations were loud and heart-felt.

'*And,*' Danny said, when there was a pause, 'we're going to have new carpets. Coloured ones.'

'Actually we're going to redecorate the house,' Jessica said. 'The living room's going to be shades of blue — duck-egg and sky blue — and what was the other one? — indigo and biscuit and hot chocolate.'

'Sound good enough to eat,' Laura laughed.

'The curtains are gorgeous,' Jessica told her.

So many changes, all of a sudden, Laura thought, and all of them healthy. It's changed their appearance too. David looked more relaxed than she'd ever seen him, even in his sober black, the children were more mature and Maureen was blooming.

'I've got a bit of news too,' Amy said. 'If you're interested. I'm going to Edinburgh.'

Laura was surprised. 'When?' she asked.

'The end of the week,' Amy said. 'I've put in for a transfer. New town, new start. I've got to go up this afternoon to finalise everything. And no it's not Mrs Brooke Curtis this time. Really. I know it's hard to believe but I've made this decision on my own.'

Jeff raised his teacup as though it were a glass. 'Here's to new directions,' he said.

Outside in the garden the sky was tinged with rose pink and a blackbird was singing his afternoon song in the branches of the oak, high and sweet and effortless. The forsythia was a yellow cloud beyond the rose garden, the cherry was heavy with white blossom and every flower bed tawny with wallflowers. It's spring, Laura thought, and I've only just noticed.

Amy was on her way out of the house. The tea party was over.

'We must be off,' David said, as he hugged his mother goodbye. 'You are all right, aren't you. I mean we'll stay a bit longer if you'd like us to.'

She assured him that she was quite all right.

'I've got a little job to do in the hall,' she said. 'If Jeff will help me.'

'Does it have to be done now?' he asked when

the cars were all gone.

'Oh yes,' she said. 'Definitely. This is exactly the right time.' She led him into the hall, to the gloomy panelling, the dull carpet runner, the musty light. 'I closed that front door on the night Pete left,' she explained, 'and I've never opened it since. Now's the time.'

'Right!' he understood and took his jacket off.

But the handle wouldn't turn.

'It's overgrown,' Jeff said. There were young fronds of honeysuckle fingering through the hinges. 'We'll have to cut back all the under-growth.'

They took shears and a saw and went outside to see what could be done. The front door was completely obscured, the honeysuckle so thick and so entwined with brambles that it was im-possible to put a hand through it.

It took them over an hour to reveal the door and by then they were hot and sweaty and covered in dust.

'Do you have a key?' Jeff asked.

To her surprise it was still hanging on its hook in the hall. 'You open it up from the outside and give it a push,' he said, 'and I'll heave from in here.'

It took much time and several applications of oil before the key could be eased into the lock but then it gave surprisingly quickly.

'Now!' Jeff called from the other side of the door.

Laura pushed with all her might. But nothing

happened. She pushed again and this time creaked the door open by the merest crack.

'Third time lucky!' Jeff said. 'Now!'

And finally the door groaned open between them, shedding leaves, dust and insects as it moved. White spiders scurried off on haughty legs, woodlice rolled and tumbled, beetles gleamed as they ran, the doorstep was covered in debris.

'Do come in!' Jeff said, grinning at the mess.

She smiled at him and took a step towards the doorway. But her skirt was caught on the bramble. 'Oh look at that!' she said, tugging at it.

'Stay still,' he said, walking out to her. 'It's caught all the way down.'

She stood still while he released her, bramble by bramble, smiling at her all the time, his hands deft. Then having checked that she wasn't attached to anything else, he lifted her away from any other obstacle, over the doorstep and into the hall.

She laughed out loud at him. 'Do you realise what you've just done?'

Of course he knew what he'd done. 'Pruned your honeysuckle and disentangled you without tearing your skirt.'

'No,' she laughed. 'You've carried me over the threshold. I never knew you were so conventional.'

He gave her his wry grin. 'Nor did I,' he said. 'But why not? We're the right age for convention.'

The sunlight was streaming into the hall, making the mirror gleam like water and burnishing the rich brown of the panelling.

'What a difference light makes,' she said.

We hope you have enjoyed this Large Print book. Other Thorndike Press or Chivers Press Large Print books are available at your library or directly from the publishers.

For more information about current and upcoming titles, please call or write, without obligation, to:

Thorndike Press
P.O. Box 159
Thorndike, Maine 04986 USA
Tel. (800) 223-2336

OR

Chivers Press Limited
Windsor Bridge Road
Bath BA2 3AX
England
Tel. (0225) 335336

All our Large Print titles are designed for easy reading, and all our books are made to last.